Praise For
The One

"Flinn does not bite off more than she can chew but takes simple situations and draws out the nuances, the emotions, and the integrity of her characters. In that way, she is like Jane Austen, telling a simple story, with one or two obstacles to the main character's love, but in the end, creating an ending completely satisfying for the reader."

— Tyler R. Tichelaar, Ph.D. and author of the award-winning *Narrow Lives*

"Not since reading Nicholas Sparks have I been this touched by a novel. This book is sure to take you back to the core of what's important in life: true love, family, relationships, and overcoming any and all challenges that come your way."

— Patrick Snow, International Best-Selling Author of *Creating Your Own Destiny*

"Experience a roller-coaster journey of emotional ups and downs. The One portrays a true sensitivity and tenderness of real-life feelings that challenge us all."

— Susan Friedmann, CSP, Author, *Riches in Niches: How to Make it BIG in a small Market*

"Powerful and timeless, The One is a heartwarming story illuminating a love that is, in this age, truly rare. Flinn's depiction of a young woman's ability to remain true to herself in the face of many trials is unrivaled as she powerfully proclaims the importance of faith, family, friendship, and above all, love."

— **Meredith Strandberg, Student, North Carolina State University**

To Susan,

the

ONE

A Novel

Follow your heart!

Mary Flinn

Fiction Worx

Mary Flinn

The One

©2010-2014 by Mary Flinn

All Rights Reserved. No part of this book may be used or reproduced in any manner whatsoever without the expressed written permission of the author. The characters and events portrayed in this book are fictitious. Any similarity to real persons, living or dead, is coincidental and not intended by the author.

Address all inquiries to:
Mary Flinn
mflinn@triad.rr.com
www.TheOneNovel.com

ISBN: 978-0-9907197-2-4

Editor: Jeannine Mallory
Proofreader: Tyler R. Tichelaar, Ph.D.
Author Photo: Mimi Skerrett Williams
Cover Design/Interior Layout: Fusion Creative Works, www.fusioncw.com

Printed in the United States of America

Second Edition 2014

For additional copies, visit: www.TheOneNovel.com

DEDICATION

The One is dedicated to my family. To my parents: Who instilled in me a passion for writing. To my young adult daughters, Jessica and Shelby: I am so proud of you and you largely inspired this story. To my husband Mike: You have been behind me every step of the way. Thank you for your never-ending love. You have always been *The One* for me!

ACKNOWLEDGMENTS

So many people were instrumental in pushing me over the top of the hill to make this book happen. I am grateful for Leslie Murphy, my right hand in this project, and for Denise Ballard and Suzanne Carlson, my first editors and encouragers. I can't thank you enough for encouraging me in this journey towards publishing. Special thanks to Mark Sugg, my football advisor.

Patrick Snow, Jeannine Mallory, Susan Friedmann, Shiloh Schroeder, and Tyler Tichelaar are the dream team who made this book come to life in the lovely pages that follow. I could not have achieved this without all of you.

CONTENTS

Chapter 1: In the Beginning	11
Chapter 2: Lunches	27
Chapter 3: Trouble	43
Chapter 4: Developments	53
Chapter 5: Thick Skin	73
Chapter 6: Surprises	89
Chapter 7: September	101
Chapter 8: The Rug	117
Chapter 9: In the Moment	143
Chapter 10: November	159
Chapter 11: Christmas	169
Chapter 12: Distractions	183
Chapter 13: Pressure	201
Chapter 14: Details	223
Chapter 15: Secrets	235
Chapter 16: Rites of Passage	259
Chapter 17: The Wedding	275
Chapter 18: Six Years Later	287

Chapter 1

IN THE BEGINNING

Was it possible for life to begin at seventeen? Not that there was anything wrong with her life to begin with, she thought. Chelsea Davenport stood in the warm August sun in the backyard of her family's mountain home. It had become difficult to catch her breath, which confused her. An uncomfortable surge of something like adrenaline rushed through her limbs, and she thought she might need to sit down before she fell over. She hadn't felt this way since—When? Maybe her first dance recital en Pointe?

She took a few deep breaths. It was going to be a nice party. She imagined similar parties generations ago—there on the large, rounded stone terrace, now edged with impressive, rich green hostas and thick clumps of pink and white impatiens. Paper lantern lights caught an occasional breeze, strung throughout the leafy Kwanzan cherry trees. They'd add a festive touch after sunset.

More guests arrived, first greeted by the breeze-carried fragrance of heirloom roses from ageless bushes around the expansive green lawn. Chelsea's silver-haired grandmother, Kitty, sat nearby in her wheelchair. Her skin was smooth, its texture that of love letters read and cherished over the years. Even seated in the chair, she retained her regal presence, naturally, since she was the lady of the house. Chelsea's older brother, Jay, lanky and casual in his jeans and white shirt, carefully moved Kitty to the shade of a nearby oak tree. He brushed his tousled blonde hair away from his unexpected brown eyes, and smiled as his grandmother relaxed her squint.

"Better," Kitty managed softly as she took in the afternoon from a better position.

Liz, Chelsea's dark-haired mother, wore an attractive cap-sleeved blue dress, and darted skillfully about the terrace to check the food on the long tables and ice in the large steel buckets placed at each table's end. She poured a glass of iced tea, then carefully leaned down a bit to place it securely in Kitty's hand.

Tom, Chelsea's father, and her Uncle Wayne displayed twin smiles and chuckled as they sampled one of several varieties of beer, ice-cold in the wheelbarrow Liz had draped in black and white toile. Tom picked two bottles from the ice and handed one to Steve Jamieson and the other to Steve's father. Steve's parents had recently arrived from Austin to celebrate their son's engagement to Chelsea's older sister, Charley.

The bride-to-be, glowing with sheer joy, wore a silk lilac-colored dress. The dress ruffles at her neckline fluttered as Charley laughed with the ladies, displayed her ring and shared the story of how she and Steve first met at, of all places, a Halloween party in Greenville. The ladies smiled and admired Charley's diamond ring. Dark-haired Steve sipped his beer from a spot not too far away, smiled, and remembered how their romance had started. He'd gone to the party as a sombreroed Mexican, complete with mustache and serape, and his date had dressed as a border patrol officer. Charley and Steve met as they stood in line for the bathroom. He found Charley and her two roommates, dressed as The Supremes, quite entertaining as they straightened their white gowns. Each clasped a wire whisk wrapped in aluminum foil as a "microphone." He later ditched his date, and after the party, he and Charley went to the Waffle House for a midnight breakfast. "After that, I was as good as gone," Steve chuckled quietly and gazed at his fiancée.

IN THE BEGINNING

One of the ladies held Charley's left hand in hers. "It's such a beautiful ring! Is it an antique? Is it a family piece?"

"Yes, it belonged to Steve's grandmother," Charley replied, beaming.

"Cluster settings were unique then," remarked a guest dressed in a yellow sundress.

"My mother had one almost like it," another said.

Chelsea had regained control of her breathing. She smoothed her hands nervously over her white eyelet dress. What had just happened? Ten minutes ago, Kyle Davis and his mother had walked into her backyard and shared greetings as introductions were made. Shelly Davis had stood willowy and tanned in her silvery green sundress, with chic blonde hair, and a large diamond stud on each earlobe. She had hugged her and said, "Chelsea, you look exquisite!" She held Chelsea away from her and said, "Kyle is here; oh yes, right behind me!"

And there he was, not at all what she remembered. His broad shoulders stretched across his blue button-up Polo shirt, sleeves rolled up—obviously the football player she'd heard so much about. Like his mother, he was also tan, and it seemed as if he'd just come from the beach.

One thing hadn't changed. Kyle's hair was light brown as Chelsea remembered, and streaked with gold from a summer in the sun. It hung over his eyebrows and was mussed, as if he had shaken his head once out of the shower and been done with it. Now with sideburns, his face was strong and square. He had grown manlier in the eight months since that day she'd held his hand at the funeral home. Chelsea tried to appear calm as she studied his face. He looked hard and silent, somehow. His familiar arrogant expression seemed almost emotionless for just a moment. Then his eyes flickered over her and became riveted on her—as if he'd been struck by lightning.

Those eyes…she remembered the intense blue, like swimming pools on a hot summer day. She was somewhat confused to see him in this new light, though. What had happened to the boy she'd grown up with? Was this the friend with whom she had swum in the lake and hiked on mountain trails?

"Hi, Kyle," she had said more softly than she intended. She brushed a strand of her dark auburn hair away from her face. "It's good to see you again." She thought to reach out her hand or even offer him a hug, but he was motionless and the moment was gone. She felt embarrassed.

"Hey, Chels." His voice was quieter than she expected by the looks of him, and strained, almost as if it were all he could say for the moment. Some of the men in the group descended upon them to clap Kyle on the back and shake his hand. They congratulated him on his previous year's prep-school football statistics. Chelsea had learned about his football success. Her Uncle Wayne, who had read about him in the local paper, looked forward to seeing him play for the Wildcats this year. He held great hope that Kyle would help improve the team's success. Soon after Kyle's father had died the previous winter, Chelsea had heard, their family business had gone under. As a result, Kyle would start his senior year at Doughton County High School.

What a total drag to be yanked out of a prestigious prep school—where you were a football star—and come back to this mediocre high school for the best year of school, she thought. So many things explained Kyle's glum face. The men's conversation took him away from her until she only overheard snippets of their comments. "So many pick sixes in one season." And, "You must have magic hands, man." And finally, "You're what this team needs; instill a little confidence!"

She moved on, but she watched him out of the corner of her eye to note how reserved he remained as the men continued with their lavish praise. Then Jay caught up with him. They pumped hands and Kyle looked more relaxed. They moved to the edge of the terrace now, and Jay offered Kyle a beer. Kyle shook his head but followed Jay to an assortment of musical instruments propped against chairs and stools next to Kitty and her shade tree. After everyone ate, there would be music.

Several of Jay's college friends, some of them music majors, the members of his band, "Bangelic," had started to arrive. Jay introduced Kyle to Vanessa, who played the violin. She was beautiful, even goddess-like, with her long wavy black hair and Grecian cheekbones. Emily was there with her flute, and Lauren, Jay's blonde girlfriend, an amazingly talented vocalist, played a little tinkly melody on her hammer dulcimer. Then Sam, with his neatly trimmed beard and crisp T-shirt, nodded at his friends and made his way over to them and propped his guitar next to Jay's. Les, huge, pony-tailed, and bear-like, wasn't there yet with his mandolin, but he was sure to slide in at the last minute, as was his style.

Kyle examined the instruments while Jay explained something to him. Then he noticed Kitty, sitting in her chair a few feet away. Chelsea watched as he approached and extended his hand. Kitty reached out for it and gazed up at him with her clear watery eyes, their color the same as her son and granddaughter's. Kitty looked at Kyle and stroked his hand. He looked back at her kindly, murmuring how nice it was to see her again and that she looked well. Kitty began to cry as she held his gaze. Tears trickled down her cheeks for the loss of his father, and for his sister three years before. It was too much to bear. How could one family endure so much tragedy? Kyle held her hands in his as her tears flowed freely. The two were silent for a few moments. A group nearby watched, not knowing what to say or do. They just let it be. Chelsea knew that Kitty was more prone to emotional episodes after her stroke, but this was more than just a result of her grandmother's stroke. It was shared grief, pure and simple, and no one moved to stop her or make explanations. After a moment, Kyle spoke to her—so softly that Chelsea could only guess what he might be saying. "Thanks, Miss Kitty. We're okay. We're getting there," in his quiet way.

Others wiped the corners of their eyes as Kitty patted Kyle's hand and attempted to speak, but couldn't find the words. All she said was "Love." Kyle nodded and pressed his lips together as he rubbed her hand one more time. She patted his and let it go, then looked up at Tom and Liz. Liz crossed her arm behind Kyle and squeezed his massive shoulders.

Chelsea felt a searing breath tug her body. Suddenly, she wanted to be the one to hug him, take his hand, or just look into his captivating blue eyes again. Breathe, she told herself. Tom squatted beside the chair and hugged his mother as she dried her eyes on the back of her hand. He noticed Chelsea watching and winked at her.

"Well...let's go ahead and eat," Liz said after a moment and people began to move about the buffet tables.

Charley was at Chelsea's elbow, and gently pushed her to the tables, with Steve close behind. "Wow, Chels! He is so hot! You're going to have an interesting senior year," she said breathlessly, as she brushed by on her way to the table.

Chelsea rolled her eyes, no longer hungry, even though the pulled pork smelled wonderful and succulent. She made her way to Kitty's side, knelt beside her, and gave her arm a gentle press. "Are you okay, Kitty?" Kitty nodded. "Are you hungry? May I fix you a plate?"

"Starvin', Marvin," Kitty said, one of the pat phrases she could say automatically. Then she grabbed Chelsea's hand, held it tightly, and pulled her close, conspiratorially. Her excited whisper was warm in Chelsea's ear. "He's...darling!"

"Oh, Kitty, not you, too! What do you want on your plate?" she asked impatiently.

"Oh...," Kitty made a circular gesture with her hand as if Chelsea would know her usual food choices, which would not be much.

"Coming right up," she smiled and made her way to the buffet as the breeze blew the scent of more roses her way.

Chelsea had a well-developed habit of eavesdropping and enjoyed listening to all the conversation. She tried to take in everything as she moved through the crowd. There must be thirty people here, she thought. Uncle Wayne and Aunt Becky were there along with Bri and Brett, her younger cousins. She had greeted an assortment of family friends as they arrived. The band members had all arrived, as had Charley's best friend from school, Emma Lavender, who was to be in the wedding. Of course, cute wiry, dark-haired and dark-eyed Steve was there with his mom and dad, whom Chelsea had just met.

Steve, the dads, and Uncle Wayne were planning a golf outing for the next day. "Oh yes, I brought my clubs," Steve's father said. "Looking forward to playing your course here…not used to mountain courses."

"You'll love it…be hooked after the first round," one of the men answered quickly.

The women buzzed around the table, too. "Lovely party, Liz. Charley looks fantastic, and that Steve is just a doll!"

"He's an intern now? They'll live in Greenville for a while still?"

"Yes, he's going to be an anesthesiologist," her mother explained. Then Liz told someone else, "And Charley has a job at the hospital as a labor and delivery nurse. I think she loves it." Then, ever the hostess, "Would you like a glass of wine, Shelly? I'm having Sauvignon Blanc. How about you, Eleanor?" she asked Steve's mother.

After she spoke with Kitty a bit, Chelsea, still holding her own empty plate, wandered back to the buffet tables. Her towering blonde father slid his arm around her waist. "Hey, sweet pea," he said grinning. "You look absolutely beautiful today." He kissed her cheek and she felt the brushy scrape of his mustache.

"Thanks, Dad," she said. When she idly looked around for Jay and Kyle, she saw they were engaged in conversation again.

"Well, don't think the men here haven't noticed. You've turned some heads today," her father said.

"Aren't you a little biased?" she asked him absently, looking over at the boys again. Kyle looked around too and caught her eye, but before she could react, he had turned to respond to something Sam said.

"Are you having fun?" her dad asked. His wrinkled eyebrows showed he was concerned about her. He was fishing.

"Yeah. Mom's really outdone herself." She took a plate and headed for the buffet. "Are you having fun, too?" Then she deflected. "Do you like the Jamiesons?" referring to Steve's parents.

"They seem nice, in that earth-shoe and granola kind of way," he said, eyes twinkling.

"Oh, Dad! You can be so lame. Especially considering they're both doctors, they seem completely unpretentious. Anyway, I can't wait to hear the music later. The band gets better every time I hear them, and it's good to have Charley home."

"Yep, she can fill up a house," he said, and she knew exactly what he meant. Charley seemed larger than life at times. She thought back to years ago when Charley and Desiree, Kyle's sister and a year younger than Charley, were in high school. They were always running around shopping, being cheerleaders, and going to parties, until Tom and Liz put a stop to Charley's participation in some of those activities.

Desiree, it seemed, went over the top with everything she ever did. She had been the wild and beautiful Desiree Davis, with long, curly blonde hair and an exuberant personality. On a Spring Break trip to Florida during her senior year in high school, she had been walking with friends at night and stepped off a curb. The car that hit her killed her instantly.

Kyle made his way toward her. She froze for a moment and felt heat creep up from her neck to spread across her face. This was ridiculous! She had never been like this about boys. But then, there had never been boys like this in Snowy Ridge before. The piercing blue eyes stared into hers again, and her throat went dry. She tried to swallow. Oh, surely he saw this struggle. The old Kyle would have been smirking by now, enjoying the effect he had on her. But this time, he looked at her inquisitively, picked up a plate, and joined her at the table. The crowded buffet tables had all but emptied, as people sat in twos and threes around the terrace, chatting.

"So, what have you been doing this summer?" he asked earnestly.

"I've...uh, been working for Dad in the nursery mostly. I helped him and Uncle Wayne tag some Christmas trees. And I spent a few weeks at the School of the Arts, in a summer intensive program."

"That's right; you're the dancer. Was it good?"

"Yeah, I liked it a lot...probably more than they liked me."

"Why?"

"I'm not sure I'm what they're looking for," she said, suddenly aware of the amount of food that had found its way onto her plate in her distraction.

"Oh, I've seen some dancers who seem to starve themselves."

She reddened further. This was NOT going well. "Yeah, there was some of that, but I'm *obviously* not like that," she laughed.

"Well, wouldn't you rather look like a woman instead of some kind of...*bird*?"

She looked at him for a moment and laughed again. And then he smiled, which lit up his face. She thought she heard her breath catch. Had he noticed? He looked at the buffet and spooned something onto his plate. "I think you look great," he murmured. And then, "What's this?"

"Oh, it's bleu cheese coleslaw. I made it. It has tomatoes and Vidalia onions in it, if you like that kind of thing."

He made a decadent face. "Mmm," he said and added another spoonful to his plate. They each took a glass of iced tea, walked over to an empty bench, and sat down.

Tom walked by. "Would you like a beer, son?" He shrugged at their questioning faces. "What? It's just one beer, and you're just going a mile down the hill."

"Nice, Dad, just twist his arm."

Kyle glanced over at his mother. "No thanks," he said quietly. "I believe I'm the designated driver this evening."

They looked at Shelly, who was on her second glass of white wine. She laughed with Liz and Eleanor. Tom smiled and replied, "Ah, yes, I believe you may be." He sauntered off with his second plate of pork, cornbread, slaw, and baked beans.

When the breeze blew her hair across her face again, she wrapped her hand around it and tossed it over her shoulder, something he watched carefully. "I haven't seen you around this summer. Have you been away?" she asked.

"Yeah, I was in Duck."

She laughed. "In a duck?"

He snickered, "No, just *Duck*. It's a little town on the Outer Banks. My Aunt Stacie lives there. I washed dishes in her restaurant all summer…and learned how to surf."

"That explains the tan. Was it fun?"

"Washing dishes wasn't…but surfing was."

"You're never really home much are you?" she asked carefully.

He thought a bit before he answered. "No I haven't been. It seems that's been the plan."

She gazed at him but he did not look at her. "What do you mean?"

"Well, it seems I have to change schools every time somebody dies," he said matter-of-factly. "I've only been back here a week and school starts next week. We can't afford for me to go to Christ School anymore, which is okay, really. I don't care where I go to school. It would just be nice to settle somewhere."

"Yeah. But won't you miss your friends there?"

"I guess, but they got kind of distant after my dad…died, so I might as well come back here and hang out with my mom. It's weird, though. We have to get to know each other all over again."

"Why did you go there in the first place?"

He looked out across the yard, past the field, and into the mountains, perhaps hoping to find his answer there. "My parents thought I needed a more structured place, and an all-boys' school sounded good. They were trying to protect me from stuff they thought I'd get into. Desiree was so out of control, and they thought I would be the same way. But I'm nothing like her. Nobody is," he laughed. "They didn't want me around many girls, and they thought I'd like the outdoor program at Christ School. And there was football…"

It was as if he had more to say but left it alone.

"At least we'll be in a new school, with the new campus opening. We'll all start new together." She puzzled over his comment about girls.

He looked at her again and almost smiled. "That's nice of you to say. Have you been over there yet to look at it?"

"No, but we're going for the open house. Have you seen it?"

"Not really, just from football practice. I've seen the locker room in the field house and the football field. Your family's going to the open house?"

"Yeah, you know, my mom taught art there until she quit to take care of Kitty after she had her stroke two years ago."

"That's right. I remember that. Have you lived up here in her house all that time?"

"No, well…we sort of moved in gradually. None of us wanted her to be in a nursing home, so my dad and mom took turns taking care of her and sleeping over. Then it just seemed right to move up here. I'm the last kid at home, so it was easy for us to do it. We're renting out our other house. Some teachers, friends of my mom, live there together. Now I can't imagine not living here. I love it here. It's really our home now."

"It's such a cool house."

"Yeah, I've been learning more stories about the place."

She realized then she wasn't having difficulty breathing. Kyle Davis was so easy to talk to and she was really enjoying herself. The band started up. Then Kyle stood in front of her and offered to take her plate. Her mom watched her from across the way and they smiled at each other. Charley, who had also been watching, assessed the situation and raised her eyebrows, smiling.

Jay picked out a melody on his guitar, a popular song Chelsea recognized when he sang, "more than words." She realized it was the song Charley and Steve had chosen as "their song." She smiled and watched Kyle, who looked at his mother as she chatted with the Jamiesons, Chelsea's parents, and Kitty. It was sure to bring back the same memories for him as the situation conjured for her…their two fathers, friends from college who had forged a business relationship not long after school. Tom had returned to the family farm and tried to salvage it by turning his portion into a landscaping business, now a prosperous nursery.

Apart from Wayne's Christmas tree tracts at the top of the property, Chelsea's grandparents had sold part of their bottomland to a developer who had turned it into a golf course and country club. Stuart Davis was the builder and Tom had gone in with him as the landscaper. That was so many years ago. Things went bad when it became evident that Stuart was price-gouging the project. Tom knew it and wanted to separate himself from the deal, so they shook hands, and after five years together, went their separate ways. Stuart built a large home in the development. The families remained friends and lived in close proximity all those years.

Together, they went to North Carolina State football games, hiked the mountain trails, celebrated birthdays, and later, supported each other in loss and sadness. Stuart and Tom spent many weekends teaching Jay and young Kyle how to fly-fish in the river beyond Stuart's cabin. Charley, Desiree, and their mothers made endless shopping trips together in search of dresses for dances, going to games and cheerleading competitions. Chelsea wondered how anyone could look at this group of people and not think about all the good and bad that had passed between them all.

The song ended and Tom tapped his beer bottle with a fork to get everyone's attention. "Welcome, everyone," he said. "Elizabeth and I, along with Jack and Eleanor Jamieson, are so pleased you've all joined us today as we celebrate the engagement of our children, Charley and Steve. We'd like everyone to grab a glass of champagne and join us as we toast the happy couple!"

"Oh, that's my cue," Chelsea said. She stood and walked to join her Aunt Becky and her cousin Bri, who were already in position at the ends of the tables, to pour and serve champagne to the guests. Soon Kyle was there to help distribute the flutes filled with champagne. After each father said a few special words to Charley and Steve, everyone clinked glasses and toasted them. There was more laughter and conversation as the music resumed. Kyle and Chelsea returned to their seats on the bench. Charley sauntered over to join them there, and Steve went to find a chair to pull up with them.

"So…Kyle," Charley said, as she ruffled his messy hair.

"What up, Charley?" he said good-naturedly, as if they had never been apart.

"How's the team this year?"

"I guess you'll have to come and see for yourself. We have an awesome quarterback and the defensive line, well…hey. Are you guys all still football fans?" He looked specifically at Chelsea.

"Of course; nothing's changed. What position do you play now?" Charley mused casually, chin on her hand, a gold-sandaled foot swinging slowly.

"Cornerback, mostly. They let me play wide receiver in practice sometimes," he said, and rubbed his hands together slowly.

"I'm sure Chelsea will be there to cheer you on. I'll be back in Greenville. But, hey, it's really good to see you. You guys hang onto your hats. Senior year will be a blur if you don't watch out."

They nodded as Steve, holding a lawn chair, joined them. He grinned at Chelsea and shook Kyle's hand. More people joined the little group and talk shifted to plans for the June wedding. Chelsea was to be her sister's Maid of Honor. The reception would take place there in the backyard garden. The couple were to be married in the tiny stone church down the mountain that her family had attended for generations. There was a two-year wait for the picturesque little sanctuary, unless the family were "members in good standing," as they were. The band would probably play and Charley hoped Lauren would sing, and Vanessa, with her string quartet from nearby Appalachian State, would play the violin. Charley and Liz were to leave for Charlotte on Monday to shop for a wedding dress. Secretly, Chelsea was glad to be spared this torture, and anyway, she would be needed to work and stay here with Kitty. They would both see the dress soon enough.

There was a lull in the conversation as everyone enjoyed the music. Eventually, Chelsea got up and helped Liz and Becky clear the food while Wayne and Tom disposed of the trash. The warm afternoon chilled into evening as the cicadas began their own song. Soon, folks said their goodbyes, gave last embraces, and headed home. Liz, arm in arm with Shelly Davis, walked over to meet Kyle before he and his mother went to the car.

"Shelly, it was wonderful to see you both," Liz said. She squeezed Kyle's forearm and gave Shelly a warm smile.

"Oh Liz, it was wonderful to see you, too," said Shelly. "And especially nice to have something to celebrate for a change. It's great to laugh and be with all of you again."

Liz smiled thoughtfully and embraced her friend. "Well, we will definitely do this again soon. It's nice that the kids will be in school together. Will you be at the open house on Wednesday?"

"Yeah," Kyle piped up, surprising them. "I'd like to walk the schedule and get the feel of the place before the first day. I'll look for you," he said. He shot Chelsea a questioning glance.

"We'll be there. Then we can compare schedules," she said, pleased that he seemed eager.

• • •

Later in the evening, Chelsea sprawled on the wood floor of her upstairs bedroom. She pressed her head to the floor and eavesdropped on the talk from downstairs as it rose through a grate in the floor, a necessity in the old days when it was helpful for heat to rise from the wood stove below. One of her grandmother's hooked rugs usually covered the grate, but Chelsea moved it to the side occasionally to catch the news.

"Kyle seems quite taken with Chelsea," she heard her mother say. Then she sighed. "I just hope she won't get her heart broken."

Her dad stuck up for her. "Wait a minute. Don't assume anything like that's gonna happen. Chelsea can hold her own."

As she waited for more, Chelsea gazed at the wallpaper with its faded violets, a remainder of her grandparents' childhood, no doubt, and comforting in its endurance and cheerfulness.

Then Charley entered the bedroom, towel drying her hair. "Oh, God, you scared me! How do you do that?" she asked, referring to Chelsea's position on the floor. Then her eyes narrowed and she said, "Is that my tank top? I've been looking for it everywhere!"

"Uh…maybe. I thought I had one just like it."

"What are you listening to, the parents gossiping again? They're probably talking about you and Kyle," Charley scoffed. Chelsea slid the rug back into place. She held her breath, unwilling to acknowledge her little dream. "Well, he certainly couldn't stop looking at you tonight. It was pretty obvious."

Chelsea attempted her best nonchalant sigh. "It's only because I was the only kid there his age."

"Hmm," Charley mused, not buying it a bit. "I guess the true test will be the first week of school when you see what bait he goes after."

Chelsea's heart sank. A diversion would be nice right about now. She almost wished she'd been included in the bridal shopping trip to Charlotte…almost.

Chapter 2

LUNCHES

Doughton County High School's open house was crowded, as expected, with students and families eager to see the new facility before school opened the following day. Liz Davenport gasped as she and Chelsea entered the main commons area and took in the spectacular mural high on the wall beneath the central skylight. It was a lifelike acrylic painting of a rocky crag, upon which a muscular mountain lion was poised in a hunting stance. "Welcome to Wildcat Country," proclaimed the maroon greeting painted above it. "Oh! This is breathtaking!" she exclaimed and reached for Chelsea's arm. Others also stood in awe as they reacted in much the same manner.

"Just…Wow," said Chelsea, whose neck was getting sore from staring at the spectacular work of art. "Did you know Anthony English painted that?"

"You are kidding! I taught him in my freshman art class three years ago. He was one of my favorite students. I knew he was gifted, but oh…" was all Liz could manage, her hand at her mouth.

"You know he's the starting quarterback this season, right?" Chelsea mentioned.

"Well...I guess he's more well-rounded than I thought. I always liked him. He tried to come across as tough, but he was a gentle soul under all that façade. Just look at that painting! The proportions are perfect."

Cheerleaders, dressed in their maroon and gold uniforms, handed out maps and information to people as they milled about through the bright hallways. Chelsea couldn't help but notice the "new house" smell. Students greeted each other loudly, and parents waved and shook hands with those they hadn't seen in a while. Most of the teachers stood at the doors of their classrooms, chatting with parents and students who stopped by to say hello.

Chelsea saw many of her friends and enjoyed saying hello after the summer's absence, but she was distracted. She didn't want to miss Kyle Davis. Would he show up? Had he been in and out already? Her heart pounded nervously. Girls laughed and formed little circles, admiring each others' clothing, and the boys milled about, joking around and slapping each other's backs. Coach Connelly, the football coach, barreled down the hall with an entourage of boys in tow, talking jovially.

Glen Dunham and Abby Harvey, Chelsea's best friend, appeared behind the football group, saw Chelsea, and greeted her enthusiastically. Abby squeezed her in a hug and did the same to Liz. "Hey," she squealed and produced a small rectangle of paper, "did you bring your schedule?" The three friends studied each other's classes. Chelsea and Glen were in homeroom together, and Chelsea and Abby had honors vocal ensemble together. They all shared lunch. *Finally*, Chelsea caught a glimpse of him in the commons area with his mom, looking at the mural.

"Are you listening to me?" asked Abby impatiently.

Actually, Chelsea hadn't been listening to Abby. Instead, she had paid more attention to other conversations around them. A few girls to her left had noticed Kyle, too. One murmured to the other, "He's the one I told you about. Check it out, girl!" They were cheerleaders, which meant they'd already seen him at summer practice.

The buzz was palpable and gradually other heads turned as Kyle walked toward their group. Chelsea heard someone say, "He's the one who found his father. Remember when we heard about that last year?"

Chelsea felt a wave of uneasiness sweep over her. Surely he would hear these comments, too. How would she feel if it were her? Shelly and Liz greeted each other with hugs. "Did you find a dress?" Shelly asked Liz.

Glen appeared to know Kyle, and they clasped hands in a high five as Kyle approached. "Hey, Chels," Kyle said to her, and his blue eyes looked into hers as if no one else were there. He looked clean and put together in a collared sport shirt and jeans. When he stood beside her, she took in his scent of soap and salt.

She had to break his gaze and decided to introduce Abby. "Kyle, have you met my best friend, Abby? Abby, you remember Kyle Davis, right?"

"Hey," he said to a wide-eyed Abby, who turned abruptly and looked questioningly at her. "I've seen you around with Glen," Kyle said.

"Yes," Abby answered, enjoying the moment. "And you know Chelsea…*how?*"

"Long-time family friends," he said, and gestured to Shelly and Liz.

"Kyle and I are defensive linesmen this year," Glen said before she could ask. "I guess you're in our home room, right? As in Davenport, Davis, Dunham?"

"Uh, yeah, I guess so," Kyle said and pulled his schedule out of his pocket. Moments later Chelsea's head was so close to his that their hair touched. She saw the classes they would share this semester: Calculus, Spanish Four, and lunch. He had no "slide" courses, she noted. He had a drafting class, weight training, and honors English. He was in a different section for that. Neither of them had time to do the AP English reading, they discovered. He had AP psychology, too.

They all agreed to walk around and find their classes as the mothers tagged along and Liz greeted other teachers she knew. Anthony English appeared and walked with them, after giving Liz a hug and telling her how much he missed her. She congratulated him on the mural, and the others did too. He was very tall and impressive with his large shoulders and forearms, and long braids pulled back from his coffee colored skin. His face was angular, almost Egyptian. His huge almond shaped eyes lowered at times when he spoke, causing Chelsea to remember he was shy. He had a warm smile that he was flashing at her now, asking her about her summer as they walked along the fresh-smelling corridor.

Abby flipped her hair over her shoulder and narrowed her eyes as she pulled Chelsea aside. "All right, girl, you've been holding out on me," she whispered. "Where did you *find* this guy? He is so *fine*!"

Chelsea reddened. "It's Kyle, you know?" She tried to sound as though he were just another guy next door. "You remember. Our dads used to work together. He went to middle school with us and then left to go to prep school," she said, her voice low since she didn't want to be overheard in the crowded hallway.

"No girl, that cannot be the same dude." Her brown eyes were wide and sparkling. Then she remembered the sad parts. She stepped closer to Chelsea and slowed their pace. "Was it his dad who…killed himself?"

Chelsea looked at her solemnly for a moment, then nodded. "Not everyone knows it…but yeah, that's what happened."

"I can't even imagine that. And Kyle was the one who found him, right?"

Chelsea nodded. They walked on wordlessly and found the boys, who had discovered the auditorium and were inside, already seated. They sank down in the cushy seats beside them, Glen on Abby's right and Chelsea on the end. "Wow," said Abby. "This is nice! Just think; we'll be singing in here in the fall, and at Christmas. I'll bet the sound system is awesome.

And think about the plays they'll have. Don't you know Elle McClarin will think she owns the place?"

"I'd like to dance on that stage," Chelsea dreamed out loud.

"Talk to Sonya. I bet she'd get you guys up there."

"She and Brad are probably way ahead on that idea." Chelsea imagined her dance teachers on the stage, spacing some new choreography for her and members of the dance company. She pictured Willie Morrison, whirling about like Baryshnikov.

"We have an assembly tomorrow in home room," Glen told Kyle.

"Yeah, they'll tell us stuff like what to wear and what not to wear, the student code of conduct, don't bring no weapons, no nail files, stuff like that. Boring shit," Anthony groaned.

Although stoic, Kyle seemed to be okay. Chelsea was glad he had friends already. She'd forgotten he would have known people from middle school, but as Abby had pointed out, some things had changed.

"Let's check out the cafeteria," said Glen as he hopped up and headed for the door.

Kyle lingered to walk with Chelsea. "So, do you buy it or bag it?"

"Lunch?" she asked. He nodded and she said, "Bag, definitely. I don't eat in the cafeteria. It's too noisy. I like to eat outside as long as the weather's nice. Then I have to bite the bullet and sit in there." She thought about it and realized that football players probably wouldn't exist well on bag lunches and would gravitate to the cheeseburgers and fries. She recalled how Rocky Santoro and the others never seemed to get enough food. Maybe she wouldn't see much of Kyle at lunch. Or maybe she'd have to adjust her noise tolerance.

"Good. Then I'll bring mine, too," he said, to her surprise. "Outside sounds nice. I like the quiet, too."

• • •

After a night of little sleep, Chelsea woke the next morning with a huge—and unexpected—case of first-day jitters. She chalked it up to it being the first day of senior year, but knew better. After a large bowl of Cheerios and a short visit with Kitty and Liz in the kitchen, she showered and dressed in a pair of Capri jeans, her favorite embroidered peasant blouse, with brown leather sandals. As an afterthought, she stuffed her white sweater into her book bag. They weren't used to air conditioning in the mountains, and she thought the new buildings might be cold. She threw the lunch she'd planned the night before into a brown paper bag; then she kissed Liz and Kitty goodbye as she headed out to her car. Fella, their yellow lab, followed her. She patted his head, scratched him behind the ears, and hopped in her car. Her dad would already be at work just down the drive at the nursery.

It took her eighteen minutes to get to the parking lot, with no stops for school buses to slow her down. She checked her watch and planned to leave at the same time the next day. She pulled into the parking lot, found her assigned spot, and hung the red and gold parking permit from her rearview mirror. In her mirror, she recognized the smoke-colored Jeep Wrangler, its convertible top down, as it rolled up into a spot several rows away. She watched as Kyle parked, took off his sunglasses, and tossed them casually onto the dash. Then he jumped down and grabbed a spiral notebook from the passenger seat. He paused, maybe to consider whether to raise the Jeep's top, but then squared his shoulders and walked away. It wasn't supposed to rain today. She tried to read his mood. He seemed… aloof, arrogant, or…miserable?

She got out of her car, a silver Subaru that had been handed down to her after her sister and brother put in some dents and dings. She followed Kyle at length and watched as he headed up the sidewalk, walked past the pear trees and fledgling grass, and blended into the mix of students who seemed in no hurry to go inside. She caught a glimpse of Abby jogging toward her, gold purse slung over her shoulder, hoop earrings glinting in the sunlight. She had forgotten jewelry except the pearl ring Liz and Tom had given her for her seventeenth birthday. Maybe she'd plan better the next day.

The other girls seemed to have dressed for a fashion show. Elle McClarin was clad in a hot pink print sundress that seemed far too short for the dress code. Maybe she was a model for the "what not to wear" assembly, Chelsea thought wryly. Rocky was wrapped around her and looked as if he wanted her to wear him, too. Chelsea rolled her eyes and got past them as quickly as possible. He was the last person she wanted to see today. Too late. He had spotted her. "Hey, Chels," he said, jutting his chin out and scrunching his eyebrows in that serious way that bugged her.

"Hi," she mumbled back. She didn't even look at his lumbering six foot three frame, or the eyes that searched to see her reaction to his posture with Elle. Like she cared.

"Hey, Chels," Abby barked, mimicking the chin-jutting gesture. She had the eyebrows down too. She had been watching. The old drama always made good entertainment for Abby.

Chelsea couldn't help but laugh. "Hey, Abs," she said, doing the same chin-jutting and eyebrow scrunch. They giggled and approached Kyle, who was already walking with Glen.

"Hey, girls! Ready for the big day?" Glen was all smiles and obviously pumped about the start of senior year. Kyle studied Chelsea pensively and smiled at her with his lips together. She smiled back, and wished he would light up the place with his real smile, the smile she'd only seen once since he'd arrived back in town. They walked side by side to homeroom as the bell rang, passed other friends, and said hello. David Greer, tan and green-eyed, spoke, but looked defeated as he passed them in the hall. She'd waited almost all of junior year for him to make his move, but he never asked her out, even though he hung out with her friends most of the time. Abby had lost patience with him early on and complained loudly to Chelsea that she needed to move on and find more date-worthy material. It certainly hadn't been Rocky. He had been a disaster. Chelsea's dance partner, Willie, was hilarious and wildly talented, and he always asked her into the backseat of his car, but she had always managed to escape somehow. She had grown so tired of boys...until now.

Kyle was assigned the seat behind her in homeroom. Glen was in the next row over, making faces at Anthony, who sat in the back of the room with her friend, the lovely and imposing Meredith Everhart, behind him. The first task was to assign lockers, and they went into the hall to open theirs. Chelsea looked at her combination and twirled the dial around a few times with no luck. She was intensely aware of Kyle standing beside her, opening and closing his locker with no difficulty. He smelled like the outdoors, clean clothes, and salt. "Allow me, ma'am," he said softly, then took her combination card, turned the knob a time or two, and opened the door.

"Ta da!" They spoke in unison and laughed, surprised. And there it was, the smile! The bright, white, melt-your-heart smile that astounded her in that instant. "Here, you try it. You just forgot to go all the way around," he said casually. She blushed under the pressure, but somehow managed to get the locker open. He looked at her thoughtfully and said, "I guess you have to hold your mouth just right." His eyes seared into hers and she could not catch her breath; she could only smile at him. Then Miss Rogers ushered them back into the room.

Lunch couldn't come fast enough, and they carried a few books out to a picnic table in front of the gym. "I'm going to bomb calculus," she said worriedly.

"I'll help. Maybe we should study together," Kyle offered. That lightened her mood and she was sure she'd need a lot of tutoring.

"And Spanish Four...I feel like I'm in the middle of freaking *Mexico*! Everyone in there is fluent."

"We'll just talk about calculus *en Espanol*."

"Oh...just...shoot me now," she muttered. They spread their lunches onto the table and opened cold bottles of water.

For lunch, Kyle had two enormous roast beef sandwiches, a bag of almonds, and an orange. "Protein," he commented in response to her expression. "I'll never make it through practice if I don't eat this stuff. What is the dancer eating today?" he asked, with a glance at her carrots and celery and tuna salad. "Not much, I see. How do you get through the day without passing out?"

"I fall asleep in class if I eat too many carbs," she laughed. "It doesn't go over well with teachers."

"Mmm," he said, munching a sandwich.

Then he said, "So which one of these bozos is your boyfriend?"

She tried not to choke on her tuna as she thought of a face-saving response to this startling question. "Uh, no one here," she said and realized that it sounded totally wrong.

"I'm not surprised," he said without hesitation.

Chelsea wondered whether she'd misunderstood him, or whether the bubble had burst and he was just rude.

"No, sorry. I just meant that it's so obvious you're not in their league. They're probably all afraid of you."

She felt flattered and reconsidered. "Why would you think that?"

"Well, because you speak in complete sentences, for one thing. So you don't have a boyfriend?"

"No," she said reluctantly, but not wanting him to see it as that.

"What's your type?" he asked, blue eyes searching.

"Uh, I don't know really. Someone who's easy to talk to. Someone who gets me, you know, without it being hard."

He thought about her answer. "Yeah, it shouldn't be hard."

"What's your type, then?" she asked as Elle breezed by with Rocky in tow. Chelsea tilted her head toward them.

"Who, her? God, no," he grimaced. "She's not my type at all." He looked at his sandwich as he continued. "I like intelligent girls, funny ones, with mad talent…girls who are kind," he said, then looked at her, his eyes smoldering into hers again. "I like girls with wavy dark auburn hair and eyes the color of rain."

Her face burned as his description of *her* became clear. She didn't know what to do or what to say. If he touched her at that moment, surely she would dissolve into a puddle right there on the terrace, she thought.

He studied her a moment. "Pink is a good color on you," he remarked, smiling ever so slightly.

She wanted just to slide off the bench. Then, in a flurry, Abby and Glen descended upon them. "There you are! We've been looking for you," said Abby. "Are you okay, Chels? Oh, sorry, are we interrupting something *private*?" she queried delightedly. She rested her chin on her hand and batted her eyes at Chelsea, who struggled for composure.

"Nah," said Kyle. "You guys are welcome to join us. We were just discussing Chelsea's boyfriend," he said with a glint in his eye meant for Chelsea.

"Ha! You mean Rocky? That is *so* over," said Abby as Chelsea deflated on the bench beside her. Her face was torched.

Kyle cocked his head toward Abby, obviously pleased with his new info source. "Really? What actually happened?"

"Well," Abby seemed to realize she had stepped into his trap. Possibly the daggers Chelsea was shooting in her direction had clued her in. "Um, well, he's just such a *player*. He reels you in to a point, and once he has you hooked, he just cuts you loose, you know?"

Chelsea shrieked inside. "No, no, no! You're making it so much worse," she directed her thoughts to Abby.

Abby floundered. "I hate it when guys do that. You would never do that, would you Glen? You're just the best boyfriend in the whole world," she said. She rubbed Glen's head and squeezed him around the shoulders, in hopes it would defuse the awkward moment. Chelsea concentrated on gathering her trash while Kyle looked down at the orange he was peeling. She wondered whether he regretted setting Abby up.

"So Elle has her claws in him now," Kyle said pointedly and quietly, as he looked up at Chelsea.

It was Glen's turn to chuckle and chime in. "Well, she's just as much a user as he is. Those two are made for each other. She plays the same game he does. Ever since Richard Spencer graduated and went to college, she's been needing a new fix. You watch your back, man," he said directly to Kyle. "She'll go after you, being new and all. You're the kind she goes for."

"Well, Glen, you take care of Kyle, and I'll watch out for Chelsea," said Abby, meeting Kyle's gaze. He nodded at her, his approval tacit.

"Spoken like a true wingman," Kyle said.

Chelsea exhaled.

"Aw, is that what I am, Chelsea, your wingman? I'll be glad to take on the job, not that you need my help." Abby's eyes drifted over to where Elle, Rocky, and a few of their friends stood. Elle thrust her books into Rocky's hands as she worked her blonde hair into a messy bun and fanned herself, which caused her too-short dress to lift a bit higher.

"I cannot believe they didn't send her home in that dress," Abby hissed and Glen chuckled. "You know, she's the kind of girl all of us are taught *not* to be like, but she always gets away with it! It's just disgusting. And don't *even* say I'm just jealous, 'cause I don't *ever* want to be like her," she warned Glen, who held up his hands in defense.

"You go, girl," Kyle said, and his smile diffused the tension. Everyone laughed at his attempt to sound like one of the girls. He put out his hand

and bumped knuckles with Abby. "Okay, I guess we're off to fifth period," he said as the bell rang.

"Wait! What are we doing after the game tomorrow night?" Abby queried. Chelsea had forgotten that their first football game was the next day.

"What do you guys usually do?" Kyle asked as they dumped their trash.

"Depends," said Glen. "Sometimes we go into town and hit The Red Onion or Macado's. Or somebody has a party. We'll give it some thought. The cruise director will get back to you," he said to Kyle and Chelsea, and pointed at his girlfriend. Abby rolled her eyes and slid her arm around his waist, as Kyle and Chelsea headed in the opposite direction.

The next day, talk at lunch was about the game and their required senior graduation projects. That morning, instead of another assembly, they watched a closed circuit TV broadcast in homeroom with Mrs. Darnell, the senior class counselor, featuring a man from a bank in town who represented a program called Cities in Schools. They talked about ways to connect seniors with people who needed assistance in hopes the projects would, in some way, reach the community.

Glen was freaking out. "I haven't even thought about this, man," he said, and raked his fingers around his brown buzz cut. He loosened the tie football players were required to wear on game days. "Have you guys?"

Kyle seemed deep in thought. He was on his second meatloaf sandwich and chewed slowly. His striped tie was already loose around his neck. His shirtsleeves were rolled up, and his hair was back to its normal finger-combed messiness, hanging just over his eyebrows. "Well, I've thought about building something. You know, designing and drawing it out and then doing it from scratch."

Glen nodded sullenly. Abby set down her slice of pizza and piped up, "I've been thinking. And I want to organize a benefit variety show, you know? And maybe I'll have the admission be a canned food donation or money for the food pantry. We can have it in our cool new auditorium.

And Chelsea, you can dance in it. And Willie, too. Want to do the lighting, Glen? Or you can be the DJ for the music. I can get some of the people in vocal ensemble to sing. Some men at my church have a barbershop quartet. I'd have to hold auditions and open it up to the public for the audience."

"Yeah, you could advertise it in the county newspaper," Chelsea said, encouragingly, taking a bite of Triscuits and pepper jack cheese.

"What about you?" Kyle asked Chelsea. "What were you thinking about?"

"I've always wanted to see if I could teach kids to dance. You know—kids who wouldn't normally have the chance to do something like that. If I can figure out how to get a group together and pull it off, we'd need a place to perform. They could be in your show, Abby!"

"Hmm," said Abby. "This all sounds promising. Do you think your brother's band would play?"

"Probably. You can ask him."

"All I know is I've got to get thinking on this one. We have to turn in our proposals by the middle of September," Glen said gloomily. "And find a mentor."

"How about organizing a sports camp?" Kyle suggested. "You could do it here in the new gym. It would be sweet. You could get the underclassmen on the team to help you run it."

"Or maybe I'll learn to cook and have you guys all over for a meal. Hey, Chels, you think your mom would mentor me? She's an awesome cook!"

"How could she possibly turn *you* down, Glen? I'll ask her if that's what you decide to do. She'll be so flattered. You can write a cookbook!"

Glen's eyebrows arched skeptically, imagining this.

They were all silent as the possibilities and the pressure of it all began to sink in.

"I think the thing to do is take it one step at a time, you know?" Chelsea said to Glen. "It's like they say. How do you eat an elephant? One bite at a time," she said. "Make a list and go from there."

"Yep," he sighed. "And hope for the best."

"Exactly! We can do this," she said and saw Kyle's smile. He winked as he took a swig from his water bottle.

"So, what's the plan for tonight?" Abby asked.

"You mean after we kick Wilkes County's *butts*?" Glen said, recharged.

"Of course! Let's go to Macado's for food after the game."

"Good plan," said Glen. Then, with a twinkle in his eye, "You feel a pick six coming on tonight, brother?" he asked Kyle.

"Never know. But it could happen. Anything's possible."

Chelsea remembered "pick six" was their lingo for an interception that was run back for a touchdown, something for which Kyle seemed to have a knack. "How do you do that, exactly?"

"It's just...I don't know exactly. You have to anticipate and pay attention. It's like you're doing a dance with their receiver, but you have to move before he does."

"Sounds kinda like choreography."

"Yeah...I guess it is. Some football players take dance classes to be quick and learn stuff like that."

"That's exactly how Willie Morrison became a dancer. In the eighth grade, his mother made him take a class at Studio One with Sonya. He got hooked on dance and gave up football. He's like a star now."

"I remember him," said Kyle. "We played ball in middle school with him, remember, Glen?"

"Yeah, the dude's built like a *bull*, man. Little and really solid. So, is he gay?"

"*No*," Chelsea said defensively. Willie would like her sticking up for him. He got that a lot. "You're such a redneck! Not every guy who dances is *gay*."

"I wondered why he wasn't on the team. Thought he moved. So you dance with him?" asked Kyle.

"Yeah, he's my partner sometimes. Willie's the only guy in the dance company. He's a phenomenal dancer. He'll go places, and he probably gets more action than some of those meatheads on the football team! 'Cept for you guys, of course."

Glen feigned shock at her comment.

"You will, too…go places, I mean," said Kyle as he bit into an apple.

"Well, I'll have to work a lot harder at it. Willie's a prodigy. I'm not… but I want it more, maybe. It's hard to get the training you need here. My teachers are good, but there aren't many performance opportunities around here. If I don't get into the School of the Arts, I won't have a shot."

"Do you have to audition for that?" he asked, unaware that Abby and Glen were having their own conversation at the end of the table.

"Yeah…and it will have to be damn good, too!"

"When does it happen?"

"I think it's early February, before senior projects are due."

He showed a flash of a smile. "No pressure!"

"Piece of cake, right?"

"Like your sister said, this year could be a blur."

They looked at each other for a moment. It would be hard to do anything outside of school since dance started the next week and football practice was every day for him. Then there would be college applications to turn in, projects to work on, and the audition to rehearse for—not to mention the regular school workload. At least she could talk to him at lunch.

People were walking by on their way to the next class. Out of the corner of her eye, Chelsea saw Rocky and Elle in their game day attire, he in his tie, and she in her cheerleading uniform. Elle eyed her disapprovingly when she saw Chelsea sitting with Kyle, as if noticing her for the first time. She stared and blinked, as if confused. As they approached, Rocky jutted out his chin and said, "Hi Chelsea. 'S up, Kyle?"

"Hi Kyle!" Elle called to him and looked away suddenly as if she saw something fascinating in the opposite direction. Kyle raised his eyebrows as if acknowledging the dis, but ignored them.

"Ready?" he asked Chelsea, then reached for her empty lunch bag and tossed it in the nearest garbage can. He touched her elbow as they walked into the building. "Look," he said quickly. "I'm sorry I said anything yesterday. I wasn't trying to be an ass. I just thought, and was hoping, you had dumped *him*. He's...so...arrogant!"

She was surprised that this had been on his mind and she smiled with relief. "Well, nobody dumped anybody. It never got to that point."

"That's good. I didn't think you'd fall for him, but if he hurt you..."

"Nope. No worries! I'll see you after the game, right? Break a leg!"

He looked puzzled, then laughed. "Oh...right. Thanks."

Chapter 3

TROUBLE

The Wildcats beat Wilkes County, 28 to 20, that night so everyone turned out to celebrate. Chelsea and Abby waited outside the field house for the guys. Anthony joined them and they headed to Macado's, where they commandeered a large booth and ordered burgers and sandwiches. Anthony had thrown two touchdown passes, Glen and Kyle had done their jobs covering Wilkes' receivers, and Kyle had fulfilled the prophecy of picking off a pass and running it in for the last touchdown. They were pumped and everyone was loud with excitement. There were fist pumps and back slaps as players congratulated each other. Kyle slid into the booth beside Chelsea. Anthony sat across from them, with Abby and Glen beside him.

"Scoot on over here, baby. I ain't gonna bite you," Anthony said to Abby. He was clearly buzzed with the win. They heard a noisy discussion at another table with some cheerleaders convincing the waiter that everyone at the table was eating, and the waiter reminding them that if they weren't eating, then they'd have to leave. "Happens all the time, man!" Anthony complained about the hassle.

"All right, man, we're gonna start counting for your record tonight," Glen said to Kyle about the pick six. "How many did you get last season?"

"Uh...three last season, I guess, and some other interceptions. It's just luck, man," said Kyle. "What's the record for Doughton?"

"I don't know, but we're gonna find out."

Chelsea took a sip of her Diet Coke as a maroon uniform and blonde hair swirled into the seat beside Kyle. "Here's my hero," cried Elle McClarin as she draped her arm across Kyle's shoulders and squeezed him. She was smiling at Kyle and narrowing her eyes at Chelsea simultaneously. How was that done? "Did you get my goodie bag today? I made yours. You did great tonight," she said to Kyle.

"No way," mouthed Abby in Chelsea's direction. Elle didn't notice, as she grabbed Kyle's chin and kissed him squarely on the mouth. Anthony grimaced openly.

"Here, Glen," she said, shoving her digital camera in his direction. "Take a picture," she commanded as she snuggled next to Kyle and grinned. He snapped it obediently as Abby scowled at him. "Thanks! That's going on my Facebook tomorrow."

"Here, let me get one of Kyle and Chelsea for you," said Abby, then quickly took the camera out of Glen's hands. "That will look good on your Facebook, too! Smile, Chels." Kyle lifted his arm and draped it snugly around her and pulled her close. And man, did she ever smile! Abby viewed the picture she had taken, and said, "Aw, that is so *presh*! Kyle, will you take one of me and Glen? And don't forget this *awesome* quarterback right here!" Kyle snapped away and Anthony cheesed it up for the game.

Elle took the camera, reviewed the photos, and clicked a button a couple of times. "Thanks, guys! Oh, my food is here. See ya later, *babe*," she said, ruffling Kyle's hair and swirling out of the booth.

"*Dude*!" Anthony laughed and continued, "You got pink shit...all over your mouth, man!" He laughed again, and gestured to his own mouth.

Kyle turned to Chelsea, rubbing his mouth. "Please, get it *off*," he said to her earnestly. She had to laugh, and wiped Elle's lip-gloss off his lips with her napkin. It was kind of pleasant, considering how livid she'd been just seconds ago. His arm was still around her. She was almost dizzy and her heart pounded so hard she was sure everyone could hear.

"You've been *slimed*," Glen said in a playfully sinister voice.

"Maybe you should get an S.T.D. test," Abby giggled, and then they all laughed.

"She deleted those pictures of you guys, didn't she?" Abby winked at Chelsea. "I'm definitely checking out her Facebook in the morning."

"Dang, girl…you're all about some Facebook stalking," Chelsea complimented her.

"I told you I'd be your wingman, right?"

Kyle removed his arm when the food arrived, but the heat from it stayed on Chelsea's shoulder while she ate. The good feeling she had from that touch was frazzled when she thought about Elle's mouth on his. She knew it wasn't his doing, but she couldn't help the ire she felt. He looked at her as the others chatted boisterously. He rubbed her free hand under the table as if he knew what she was thinking.

"Want to go?" he asked, surprising her. Half of her sandwich had filled her up, but she was sure he was still hungry.

"Where? What have you got in mind?"

"I have an idea," he said. Then he wiped his mouth and told the others they were taking off. He dropped a ten and a five-dollar bill on the table and they slid out of the booth.

Abby's eyebrows shot up and she looked at Chelsea pointedly. "Okay. Call me, right?"

"Sure. See you guys. Thanks for the *pass interference*," said Chelsea, winking at them all. Anthony nodded and smiled, and Glen laughed and bumped knuckles with her across the table.

The top was still down on Kyle's Jeep and the night air remained surprisingly warm. As he pulled into the street, he asked, "Is this too cold? I can put up the top…"

"No, don't" she said. "It's nice, actually," then twisted her hair into a knot for the ride. "So, where are we going?"

He looked pleased. "What time do you have to be in?"

"Twelve-thirty."

"Well, that gives us about an hour. Did you know there's a meteor shower tonight? We can watch for a while if you want to."

She smiled. "Yeah, we used to do that when we were kids. We'd take blankets and go out to the field behind Kitty's house to watch them."

"It's a clear night and it's late enough. We should see some. I was going to take you on the parkway, but I don't think we'll have time."

"Let's go to the golf course. Or, we could just go to my house."

They drove along and the warm air was soothing. He had music on, "The Pretenders." They rode along wordlessly, glancing at each other from time to time. The song changed. She knew that one, too—"Foreigner?" she asked.

He glanced at her. "Yeah, I put it on my ipod today."

"You like the old music. So do I." The song played on, a slow, pulsing melody, and the title "Waiting for a Girl Like You." She saw him glance at her again out of the corner of her eye. Busted.

When they arrived in front of the elegant old farmhouse, Kyle took in a deep breath. "Wow, this place must have been something in its day, you know? It *still* is." As he pulled into the drive and stopped, she took in the semi-circular drive, as if seeing it for the first time. It was ringed by tall, manicured boxwoods. The large front porch, draped with hanging ferns, was inviting, even in the dark. The side portico had once been used for carriages and wagons dispatching passengers. Now it had a convenient ramp for dispatching Kitty in her wheelchair. Fella rose from the porch and loped out to greet them.

Kyle hopped out of the Jeep. She said, "I think everyone's asleep. I can tiptoe in and get us a blanket." She reached down to pet her dog. "Hey, Fella…are you on guard tonight?" Fella yawned comically.

"Hold on. I think I may have one…right here," he said, and produced a dark green blanket from the backseat.

"You carry that with you regularly?" she asked suspiciously.

"Yeah," he said matter-of-factly. "You know, for when you might get stuck in bad weather, or for star-gazing, or makin' out, or whatever…" he grinned at her with a twinkle in his eyes.

"Is it safe to sit on that thing?"

"Believe me; this blanket hasn't had much action."

She took him across the front yard and into the field at the side of the house. Her hair fell loose as he spread the blanket on the knoll where they would have a clear view of the sky. "I saw one!" he said suddenly. Fella sidled up to Kyle and sniffed and licked at the bottoms of his jeans.

"I missed it," she said as they stretched out comfortably, side-by-side on the cool, cushiony ground.

He sighed loudly. "God, it feels good to lie down. It's been a long day!"

"A good day."

"A very good day. Best I've had in a long time. Look! There's another one!"

"I saw it!" They watched in wonder at the galaxy above them, surreal in its clarity. It was as if the show were just for them. Streaks of white darted here in the black sky, then there, and over there. Millions of stars were just overhead. Chelsea felt herself smiling. "Careful, he'll start spooning with you if you encourage him," she warned as Kyle scratched Fella's weakness, the spot right behind his ears.

Kyle chuckled as Fella settled himself happily beside his legs. "Man, this is incredible! How many times do you get to see something like this in your life?" He took her small hand in his, warm and large. His fingers entwined with hers and he stroked her hand with his thumb. They were quiet for a while, each contemplating the feeling and watching the star show.

"You knew about my dad," he said suddenly.

"What? About how he died?"

"Yeah. At first my mom didn't want anyone to know it was a suicide, but then it kind of got out and people knew."

She thought back to the conversation she'd overheard through the grate in the floor the night her family learned the news. Tom and Liz had talked about Shelly's wish to tell everyone that Stuart Davis had died of a heart attack, instead of by drinking himself into a deadly stupor, on top of prescription pain pills he no longer needed. She'd heard that Kyle, who was home from school as a surprise, had found his father, cold and unresponsive, on the floor of his cabin. Her parents disagreed with what Shelly was doing. They thought it put too much pressure on Kyle to deal with it that way. She remembered they had been angry about it. They also understood that Shelly was having her own difficulty dealing with it as well.

His grip on her hand was tighter. She rolled her head to the side. He was still looking at the sky. "I knew," she said softly. "I heard my parents talking about it."

He dropped her hand, then rolled to his side and propped his head on his hand. "Really? Tell me...."

"I just remember they felt so bad for you because no one was going to talk to you about what really happened."

His face held a far-away look. "Yeah, that's kind of what happened. No one really did. And if they knew, they didn't know what to say. What *do* you say, you know?"

"I know. You just need people to be there…and bring food," she said, trying to keep it light. She wasn't sure she wanted him to know how much she really knew.

"Your mom came over with food once or twice a week. It was great. She knew we didn't have church folks to do it."

They were quiet and then she said, "So how did it happen…you know, when you found him?"

He stared into the sky, still rubbing the back of her hand with his thumb—as if it calmed him. "Well, I came home on a Saturday morning. I was supposed to go to a dance that night, but my date got sick, so I called my mom on the way and told her I was coming home. She was taking a class in town and told me she'd see me in the afternoon. Said my dad hadn't been home the night before. Sometimes he would go to the cabin and not come home. I thought it was kind of weird, but it didn't seem to faze her. Anyway, I got there at about eleven o'clock in the morning, and his truck was there. The door was locked, but I had my key and went in… and he was…there. Just lying on the couch like he was sleeping. I called the EMS and they came…and the detectives. That yellow crime scene tape was across the drive when my mom drove up." He grew quiet.

"Is this hard for you? You don't have to tell me," she said. A chill ran through her, and she felt her face pull inward, the opposite of the smile she'd had just moments before.

"I know. I've never talked about it with anyone, except my mom." He paused, then finished. "And, well, the cops that day, and a little bit with the headmaster at school when I got back."

"Not in all this time?" She rolled over and faced him the same way.

"No. He left a note. It was on the coffee table. It had been folded up, like he'd been carrying it around for a while, or maybe tried it before."

"What did it say?"

"Just that he couldn't live with himself after all the things he'd done in his business. How he'd been dishonest for so long. And he was sorry, and that my mom had tried to help him, and your dad had tried to tell him. He didn't want me to be like him. He wanted to stop hurting her…stuff like that."

She was shocked. "What brought it all on?"

"My mom said they got audited by the IRS and the company owed a ton of money in discrepancies they found from way back. Invoices from the subs didn't match up with the bills he had sent out. After he died, my mom had to get Frank Maynard, another builder we know, and Patty, her attorney, to help her sort through it all. But she had to liquidate the business in the end."

"I'm so sorry…"

"Her real estate business isn't going so well either, you know, with the economy and all, so it's kind of bad right now. She doesn't have much income. She's renting the cabin. She spent so much time going through the whole process and trying to deal with it. She sent me to live with Stacie for the summer so I'd have something to do while she still works on it. The hardest thing was calling her that day to tell her what happened. That, and the memory of seeing him that way. It plays out every day…the first thing I think about in the morning and the last thing I think about at night… and a million times in between." He was shaking his head, looking down.

"I'm so sorry…I can't imagine what you and your mom must have gone through." She thought about how he had brought this up. "How did you know I knew about it?"

"It was the way you held my hand that day at the funeral home. You just sat there with me and held my hand and looked at me. Somehow, I knew you knew it all—and I wanted to scream. But you were just…there, holding my hand and keeping me from jumping out of my skin. Like an angel. I've thought about that for so long." His voice was barely a whisper.

She pulled her hand away, placed it on the side of his face and stroked her fingers through his hair. Even in the dark, his eyes were like deep water, clear and piercing. His handsome face looked so vulnerable. He reached for her face and ran his fingers down her cheek. He pulled her closer to him, slowly, and then touched his lips to hers, softly at first, and then with more feeling. She tasted him and breathed in his familiar scent as she pulled his face closer.

He broke away and fell onto his back. "How do you do this?" he asked incredulously.

"What?"

"You can just look at me, or touch me, and I'm just…laid open… completely. It's like you see all the way through me."

"Uh…I don't know."

"Like last week at the party; I felt so *drawn* to you. I don't want to be away from you. It's like I just *need* to be with you. Like…I know I should go right now, but I just can't make myself leave."

She couldn't believe what she was hearing. Her arm was getting numb, so she pushed herself up and sat beside him, Indian style. She combed her hair off her face. He slid close to her and rested his head in her lap, hugging her knee, as she stroked his hair. He sighed softly. Sometimes you just didn't need to talk, she thought. They sat like that for a while and watched a few more stars shoot across the sky. She would remember this forever. A creaking noise came from the front door and Kyle sat up as they turned to look.

"That you, Chels?" her father's voice, hoarse with sleep, called.

"Yeah, Dad."

"It's late…come on in."

"Okay, sorry." Fella sat up and shook himself.

The door shut and they stood up, picked up the blanket, and shook it out. Kyle folded it and put it under his arm as they walked back to his Jeep. "What are you doing tomorrow?" he asked.

"I have to work until two. Do you want to come up…around three?"

"Yeah, I can do that. What do you want to do?"

Kiss you some more, she thought, smiling. "Anything. We could ride the horses…or go for a swim in the lake…or both."

"You still have Fred and Dot?"

"Yeah…" She stepped in closer as he opened the door and pulled her into him, and pressed his lips hard against hers, then one more time with such tenderness. He kissed the top of her forehead and then climbed in the Jeep and cranked it up. She watched as he backed into the road and drove down the hill.

As she floated up to the front porch, she laughed as she gathered her hair in her hands and thought how silly it was to have been mad at Elle. How ridiculous!

Chapter 4

DEVELOPMENTS

Liz and Kitty were in the kitchen when Chelsea made it downstairs, dressed in her green shirt and khaki shorts, the White Horse Farms Nursery uniform. She had tied her hair into a loose bun in anticipation of the hot day ahead. It would be slow, which would be good, allowing her time to think.

"Well, good morning, sweetheart," said Liz, kissing her on the cheek as she came in to fix her lunch. Kitty sat at the long farm table and sipped her usual cup of tea, with a pile of green beans in front of her for snapping. Chelsea greeted them and went to the fridge, pulled out bread and ham to make a sandwich, and grabbed a plum to pack in her lunchbox. She saw her mother's tray of ceramic figures on the table.

"You two look busy already," Chelsea remarked.

Kitty nodded. "Therapy!"

"You were out late last night," her mom commented as she shifted scrambled eggs onto a plate of bacon. Her eyes left the question hanging in the air. Chelsea forked some of the eggs and a piece of bacon onto a small plate, and took a sip of orange juice.

"I was home before curfew, actually. Kyle drove me home from Macado's after the game, and we sat outside and watched the meteor shower. But we were *well* chaperoned," she said, glancing at Fella, who thumped his tail hard on the floor beside Kitty.

Her mother smiled and exchanged knowing glances with Kitty. "That's nice. And we heard you won the game. He seems like a changed young man," she said, more a question than an observation.

"I know," said Chelsea. "He was so cocky when we were younger."

"Well, I think he's very sophisticated and well-mannered. He was just lovely at the party. All the ladies were talking about him, weren't they, Kitty?"

Kitty smiled and nodded.

"Well, you'll see him again today. He's coming over about three. We're going to take the horses down to the lake and go swimming."

Liz looked surprised. Chelsea took a bite of eggs as she stood at the kitchen island. After rinsing her plate and placing it in the dishwasher, she grabbed a piece of bacon and headed toward the door. "I'll send Dad up for lunch. I'll eat at the store. Oh, and I need to ask you something, Mom. Would you consider being Glen's mentor for his senior project? He wants to learn to cook and he thought you would be a great teacher since you *are* such a good cook and all." Her mother looked uncertain. "Maybe you could teach him how to fix guy food, you know like tailgate stuff and chili. What do you think?"

"Well, there's a wedding to plan on top of everything else. But if we're cooking for us, he might as well tag along. Sure, why not?"

"Thanks, Mom! I'll tell him," she said on her way out the door. Fella accompanied her down the road, past the barn and to the nursery in the curve, where another road connected from the main road, bringing customers up to the nursery. There was a large area to the right where the Christmas tree lot transformed the place from Thanksgiving until Christmas Eve every year. Now, in late August, it stood empty, bordered by a split rail fence.

After tossing her lunch and a water bottle into the little refrigerator in the office, Chelsea grabbed a hose and began watering the perennials outside. She'd save the potted impatiens and geraniums under the canopy for later when the sun was higher. She spotted her father carrying invoices to the back, where Jay and the landscape crews would be waiting for their daily job assignments. She heard them talking over their coffee, then they started up the trucks. Tom waved and signaled that he would be back soon. No one else was about. It would be that way most of the day, she figured.

As she thought back over the evening before, a familiar heat crept up her neck to her face. It seemed to happen every time she thought about Kyle Davis. It was embarrassing, she thought, and she hoped she'd hidden it from her family members, who were beginning to notice the two of them were spending time together. Certainly, none of this had been lost on Abby Harvey, who quizzed her at every private opportunity. And then, speaking of Abby, Chelsea's cell phone buzzed in her pocket, signaling a message from her friend. She flipped it open and looked at the text message: "U need 2 c FB! OMG! When r u off?"

Chelsea's heart plummeted. She clicked back a quick text message of her own: "2 but Kyle's coming here at 3."

"B at ur house at 2:10!"

Oh, this can't be good, she thought dismally. She wasn't into Facebook and didn't even have a camera. Abby seemed to be friends with everybody and could retrieve the latest scoop with a few clicks of the mouse.

Chelsea looked up. Her father was standing in front of her. She tried not to appear as rattled as she felt. "Hey, Bushman," she quipped. She and Jay had given Tom the nickname when Tom had bought the canvas hat with a large brim and sharp leather band. To them, the hat made him look like he had come in from the Australian Outback. It did the trick for keeping the sun off his face and neck, and it was actually attractive on him, but it was their duty to give their old man a hard time.

"Hey, sweet pea! Fun night last night?"

"Yeah, it was," she smiled.

"Heard they had a great win. I saw the highlights on TV. Kyle played a good game. An interception and a touchdown, right?"

"Yeah, he was pretty stoked."

"Was that him with you out in the yard last night?"

"Yes, sir."

"Cozy, was it?"

"Dad, it wasn't like that. You know I'm not like that. I was home early and we were watching the meteor shower."

Tom nodded quizzically, as if he wished he'd thought of something like that when he was young, and getting the same third degree he was dealing out. He picked up another hose and watered the perennials across the aisle from hers.

"Kyle talked a lot about his dad last night," she began.

Her dad wrinkled his eyebrows and his mouth pursed as if a question were forming. "I can imagine he's still having a hard time dealing with Stu's suicide."

"Yeah, I think he is, and his mom, too."

He stared into the coreopsis as he spoke. "Shelly talked to your mother about it some at the party. She feels bad about having sent him away, especially after he'd just come home from school for the summer. But really, she's had a lot to deal with—getting that company off her shoulders and squaring things up with the IRS. It's been eight months, and she's almost done with it. It's a crying shame what he left her with."

"Dad, I don't understand. I thought they had a lot of money. How could it be so bad?"

"Well, it was partly the economy. His business wasn't making money. No one is right now. And when the auditors came up with the figure he owed, he didn't have it. He was going to face charges on top of the money the company owed. So he just…checked out…and left her with it."

She was silent in disbelief. "How could he do that, Dad?"

"Honey, I don't know. He was doing it when we were in business together."

"Can you imagine how Kyle feels about it?"

"I know, baby; they were really close. He probably had no idea. He must feel quite disillusioned about his father."

"Well, he's coming over here today and we're going swimming. Don't say anything to him, okay?"

"Not a word," he said solemnly.

They went about their business. Chelsea checked her watch every few minutes in anticipation of seeing Abby's discovery—not to mention her next encounter with Kyle. At two o'clock, feeling hot and sticky, she waved to her dad and bolted out of the store and up the road. She *had* to have a shower. Abby was pulling her silver Honda Civic into the driveway as Chelsea rounded the corner to the front door and met her on the porch. "Come on in. I gotta get a shower."

"I'll log on while you do that. Where's your laptop?"

"In my room on the desk," she said, peeling off her shirt as they tromped up the stairs. She threw her clothes on the white iron twin bed in her violet bedroom and grabbed her robe before dashing to the bathroom. She showered quickly and washed her hair, glad she'd shaved her legs the day before. When she returned to her room, Abby was seated at her desk, already scrolling through the pictures on Elle McClarin's profile.

"You are *not* gonna believe this," she said. She stood up so Chelsea could sit in front of the screen as she toweled her hair dry. There were lots of shots of Elle's face here and there, smiling and smooching for the camera, Elle in her orange bikini at the beach, Elle in her cheerleading uniform and with various friends: Kendra, her cheer buddy and usual sidekick, and Rocky Santoro, pleased to be entwined with her in most of the shots. Elle's current profile photo took Chelsea's breath. There was Elle, grinning, eyes sparkling, beside Kyle, who looked aloof beside her, pressed involuntarily into the letter D of her uniform at Macado's the night before. As she scrolled down, there were more pictures of him, taken at football practice and grainy-looking, as if *someone* had zoomed in to make the images appear closer. There was another shot from school. It looked as if he had been aware of the photo, but he looked wary and didn't display the desired smile. And then, the one that sent her reeling was a headshot of him, head inclined to the right with his large smile meant for the camera. "That's the one Glen took of him with *you* last night," Abby said ominously. "She cropped you out of it, obviously. This makes me sick! She's stalking him," she said the words slowly as if Chelsea were slow on the uptake. But Chelsea was already there, and a knot formed in her stomach where she had felt punched a moment before.

Abby watched her—empathizing with her best friend's feelings. "But Chelsea, we know that picture was with you. And look how happy he looks. I've never seen him smile like that, you know?" She let that sink in for a moment and then moved on to a better topic. "Forget her. She's such a sicko. What happened after you two left last night? I know it was good..."

Chelsea was still reeling. "We came back here and sat out in the yard watching the stars. There was a meteor shower..." Abby looked unimpressed. "And he talked about his family some. I don't want to get into it, you know?"

"I'm sorry; I guess it's personal. I know you're private about your guys."

"Well, it's like I don't want to jinx it, you know?"

"Okay, my cue to leave. I know he'll be here in a few, so I'm outta here. Have fun!"

She was down the stairs and out the door as Chelsea logged out of the Facebook page, after taking a last look at the profile. Abby had made a comment on the good picture of Kyle. It said, "Hey, wasn't that Chelsea Davenport being squeezed by Kyle Davis? Don't crop her out next time." Chelsea laughed and murmured under her breath, "That's my wingman!"

• • •

She panicked when she realized she had five minutes to throw herself together. She pulled on her favorite swimsuit—black with tiny silver peace signs all over it—then slipped on jean shorts and a T-shirt. She raked a comb through her hair, stuck her feet into leather flip-flops, and slicked on lip-gloss just as she heard a knock at the front door.

Liz greeted Kyle as Chelsea grabbed two beach towels out of the linen closet, took a deep breath, and forced herself calmly down the stairs. He smiled up at her as she came into view and they headed out the back door after he said hello to Kitty. Kyle seemed fresh from a shower, too, with his clean smell and wet hair raked back. He wore a long-sleeved navy T-shirt and faded orange swim trunks.

"What did you do today?" she asked as they approached the white barn.

With Fella hot on his heels, Kyle smiled and reached down to ruffle his head. "I went for a run and then mowed a couple of yards for my mom."

"Not yours?"

"Yeah, I did ours, too. And I helped her out with a couple of properties that are for sale. None of them are much to mow, really."

"So you ran and did three yards while I watered flowers all day?"

"Hmm. Must have been slow at the nursery."

"Yeah, it will be until mid-September and then people start planting their pansies and all the fall stuff. But today was my last day…until Christmastime. I'll be in the dance studio this time next Saturday." They were at the barn. Fred and Dot nickered and tossed their heads as company arrived.

"Do you guys still do the Christmas celebration in the barn?"

"Yeah, it was a lot of fun last year. Jay's band played and we served hot cider, cocoa, and gingerbread. The little kids get their pictures taken with Fred and Dot, and Dad sells a million of Wayne's Christmas trees. My mom sells those ceramic angels she makes. She was going to work on some this morning, I guess. I saw them out on the table ready to be fired."

"My mom has one of those," he said quietly and, of course, she remembered. It was the one with the long and curly blonde hair she'd given to Shelly and Stu when Desiree died. She looked up at him tentatively.

"So how long's it been since you've ridden a horse?"

"Uh, a couple of years…never in swim trunks, though."

"Well, we won't go far, unless you'd rather ride than swim," she offered and he shrugged. "Okay, well, you put on their blankets and I'll get the saddles."

As he flipped a blanket onto Fred's back, she noticed Fred had laid his ears back and blown loudly through his nose. "Knock it off, Fred," she said. In a few minutes, both horses were ready to go and they walked them out to the yard to mount. Kyle went up on Fred first and then she swung easily up onto Dot's back. As they started for the road, Fred balked for a moment and flattened his ears again. "Oh, come on Fred," she cooed, and clucked to him. Kyle nudged him forward with his heels and tapped the reins a bit more on the horse's neck. Fred stepped forward and followed Dot and Chelsea out into the road.

Behind her, Chelsea heard Kyle clicking to Fred and saying to him, "Atta boy, Fred, keep up. They're leaving us in the dust." She held the beach towels and turned around to check on them. Fred stopped and snorted, then laid his ears flat against his head and looked at her over flared nostrils. Kyle nudged him again and clicked to him.

"Come on, Fred; let's go," Kyle said, tapping the reins again. Fred stepped forward again, this time making a circle around to the left, and headed straight back to the barn. "Uh...Fred, no, boy, wrong way!" Kyle said, shakily.

Chelsea turned Dot around and followed them back to the barn. She jumped off Dot's back, and ran over to Fred, who was walking determinedly back into his stall with Kyle aboard. He turned and looked at her sheepishly. "Uh...any help here?" She covered her mouth with the back of her hand to hide the smile she could not contain. "How do you say 'back up' to a horse?"

She laughed. "I don't know; how about, 'back up, dammit'?" She walked over to Fred, took hold of his bridle, and spoke to him evenly. "Back up, dammit!" Fred laid his ears back and did not budge. He did not respond to her tugs. Kyle began to laugh and she laughed, too.

"Well, this is embarrassing," he said, laughing, as he slid off Fred's back.

She was nearly doubled over with laughter, and he shook his head and wiped his eyes. As they composed themselves, he looked serious. "Hey, you're not gonna tell anybody about this are you? I can already hear it in the locker room."

"No, no," she laughed. "Your secret is safe with me. Okay, plan B. Let's get the saddle off this old coot and we'll take Dot to the lake."

"Can we both get on her?"

"Sure. She's a lot younger than Fred." She had the saddle and bridle off Fred in moments and Kyle helped her put them into place in the tack room. She folded his blanket and then hoisted herself up on Dot. She held out her hand for Kyle, who managed to swing up behind her, and, after some wiggling around, got adjusted. When he slid his arms around her waist, she felt her back arch instinctively, and the familiar heat started to race up her back. She felt him breathing behind her. They walked Dot down the road and past the nursery. Tom approached and waved at them, a curious look on his face. "Fred was being obstinate," she called to him, and he nodded, chuckling.

"So did you set me up for that, or what?" Kyle asked slyly, after waving to Tom.

"Absolutely *not*," she said. "You never know with Fred, though. He's getting old and set in his ways."

It was a nice ride down to the lake. They listened to the cicadas buzzing and the breeze picked up, which made a cool break in the day. Some clouds were rolling in and Chelsea thought it might rain later, which is typical in the mountains. Around the next bend, the lake came into view. It wasn't large by any stretch, but there was a dock, and plenty of room for a little boating and fishing. It was spring-fed, and the cool water would feel good.

They dismounted and let Dot wander to the shady trees near the dock. "She won't get a wild hair and run off, will she?" Kyle asked.

"No. Dot is very predictable, unlike our *other* friend."

They strolled to the dock and he helped her spread out the beach towels at the end, away from where the skiff was moored to one side. He peeled off his shirt and was in the water before she had kicked off her flip-flops. He surfaced and whooped with the shock of the cold water.

"Wow! It's colder than I thought it would be," he said, flicking his head hard to the side, producing the hairstyle she saw every day.

She laughed, and peeled off her own clothes as he watched intently. She dove in and came up next to him, wiping water off her face. "Damn, girl, you're ripped," he said, admiringly. "You don't have a thing to be worried about."

They swam about for a while, then floated on their backs, which was amazingly relaxing. He helped her dive off his hands by forming a stirrup for her to step into and then tossing her forward. They laughed at their first few clumsy attempts. Then she jumped higher every time.

They climbed out and dried themselves before sitting on the towels on the hot wood. She counted eight sections, upon discreet inspection of his stomach, as he sat beside her on his towel. She reached for his shirt and held it up to read the back of it. "The Sound Side?"

"Yeah. That's Stacie's restaurant. Breakfast, lunch, and dinner six days a week; and on Friday and Saturday nights in the summer, bands play. It's a hot spot of sorts."

"What kind of music?"

"Lots of different stuff. I told Jay he should take his band down there. They'd fit right in. My favorite was a soul band called South Street. They played there a few times. Played all the classic stuff, Wilson Pickett, Sam

Cooke. They had a black girl who sang. She was phenomenal."

"So that's why the restaurant is called The *Sound* Side?"

"That, and it's also on the Sound. It's in an old marina. It's a cool place and the food is great. Sure kept me busy. I was supposed to be staying out of trouble, you know," he said. He inched toward her and touched her arm with his as they sat with arms wrapped around their knees, the sun drying their skin and hair.

"How did Stacie keep you out of trouble?"

"Oh, she kept me washing those dishes all day. And she'd scream 'He's jailbait' at any girls who had eyes for me," he squawked. "Most of the people who worked there were in college, looking for something fun to do over the summer, make money, and party. But she didn't let me do any of that."

"But she let you go and hurl yourself into the sea on a surfboard?" she laughed.

"Yep, every Sunday when we were closed. But I had a babysitter for that, too. Tyson, an older guy who worked in the kitchen, used to go with me. He lived down in South Nags Head, and I'd drive down and meet him early on Sunday mornings. We'd go to Frisco or Buxton. That's where the best swells were."

"No pot-smoking or drinking?"

"Nope, that wasn't part of the deal! I was there to wash dishes and lift weights in Stacie's spare room and behave myself or else I had to come home. So I pretty much behaved myself."

"Did your mom make that deal with her?"

"Yeah, and you don't mess with Stacie. She's tough as nails. Plus, it's a nice place and I really didn't want to leave."

"Sounds like rehab."

"Yeah, it was—sort of." He was quiet, and she knew more would spill out in a minute. He looked out at the lake, and then down between his feet. "I kind of went off the deep end after my dad died. I was like...so angry about it all, you know? I was away at school and my mom didn't want to talk to me about it and tell me what was going on, so I sort of lost it. I drank a lot and ended up getting a D.W.I. one night. Not good for a football player, you know, but luckily the season was over. My mom got it expunged from my record, but you can only do that once before you turn eighteen, so I've had my shot. Now, if I want any kind of scholarship, I've got to keep my nose clean."

"Are you looking at football offers?"

"Well, a few schools have contacted me. If that doesn't work out, I'll need to go for an academic scholarship."

"That's why you're working so hard," she murmured.

"Well, I want to be an architect, you know, and become a builder like my dad...but not *like* my dad. I can't do the things he did, the drinking and all that. I'd never run a business the way he did. I don't want to be like him. There's a lot to be said for restraint," he said, then turned toward her.

"So tell me; why are you working so hard in school if you want to be a dancer?" he asked, deflecting the attention.

She laughed, "Gotta have a back-up plan if dancing doesn't work out. Even if it does, dancers don't quit their day jobs."

His cell phone played a Journey song on the towel behind him. He answered it and talked for a moment until she figured out Glen was on the line. It sounded like there was a problem. "Wow, man...Yeah, are you okay? Are you going there now? Yeah, I know where it is. I can come get you. I can be there in maybe...thirty minutes. Sure, man, no problem.

Okay, see ya."

"What happened?"

"Glen wrecked his mom's car. He's okay, but the car is probably totaled and he needs me to go get him. His mom's stuck at home and pretty pissed off, I would guess. I'd better get going," he said, then pulled his shirt over his head, and stood up.

"Well, if he needs cheering up, tell him my mom will be his cooking mentor," she said.

Kyle folded up their towels as Chelsea got dressed. They found Dot and headed back to the barn. After putting away her tack, they walked to his Jeep in the driveway.

"Hey, I need to ask you something," she said awkwardly. He raised his eyebrows, leaned against the car, and folded his arms. She rearranged the pile of wet towels she held. "Do you know you're being stalked? Abby showed me on Facebook."

He ran his hand over his chin and his eyebrows went up again. "Oh yeah, I forgot she was gonna check that out this morning. I didn't look at it. What's there?"

"Elle McClarin has lots of pictures of you on her profile. You might not even have known she was taking your picture in some of them."

"Hmmm…you know what? I'm not worried about her, and you shouldn't be either. If it gets out of hand, then we'll deal with it." He smiled at her, but it was not the full smile she needed. "Really, don't think about it. I'm not."

He opened the door, but before he got into the Jeep, he pulled her into him and murmured into her hair. "I had a great time with you, even though it got cut short." He kissed her on her temple and she lifted her face to kiss him softly on his lips. He drew her closer and returned the kiss.

"See you at school? And remember our little secret!"

∙ ∙ ∙

That night after dinner, she and Liz dried the last of the dishes and placed them in the cabinet. When her cell phone rang, it was Kyle. "Hey," he said, "Glen is still over here. My mom convinced his mom to let him stay for dinner, and we thought maybe you and Abby would like to come and hang out with us a while. If you can come, we'll call her. Please say you can. It might be his last night out for a while, you know?"

"Hang on, I'll ask," she shot a glance at her mom, who apparently had overheard every word. Liz nodded, and gestured her to go on. "Thanks, Mom. I won't be out late." And then to Kyle she said, "Yeah, I'll come down. I'll be just a few minutes."

As she pulled into the driveway of the Davises' sprawling home, Chelsea's heart sank. There was a "For Sale" sign in the front yard. Shelly's name was listed as the realtor. When had this happened? It shouldn't have surprised her, with what she had learned last night and today, but the thought of them being swept away from here, *now*, was more than she could understand. Why would this happen at the beginning of his senior year? Abby pulled in behind her, and then they walked quickly up the driveway to the house.

"Man, this is some crib," Abby said breathlessly. They walked by pink and purple flowers lit with landscape lighting, then came to the large, curved walnut doors within the stone entryway. Chelsea rang the bell.

Shelly Davis greeted them warmly, dressed in a sleek pair of white Capri pants and a silver top with matching silver sandals. Her stylishly choppy blonde hair framed her face elegantly. The diamond earrings gleamed like miniature ice cubes. She likes squares, Chelsea thought when she noticed her large ring. Familiar swimming pool blue eyes twinkled when she saw

Chelsea, and she ushered the girls graciously into the foyer. "Hi ladies," she said. "The boys are in the kitchen finishing up the dishes," she said, gesturing to the left. "Go on in."

They went in through the foyer, past the dining room, and through the family room, where a movie played in surround sound, most likely something Shelly was going to watch. She curled up on a comfy brown sofa as the girls went into the kitchen.

"Hola, chicas!" Kyle greeted them, folding a towel before draping it over a ceramic hook beside the sink. Chelsea hadn't been into this house in several years, and it appeared they had remodeled. She had never seen such a kitchen—rich golden wood cabinets, topped with dark speckled granite counters. The appliances were stainless steel and a copper hood topped the large gas range. Copper pots hung just below, next to a deep farm sink flanked by double ovens. To the left, a backlit bar revealed a wine cooler with glassware in leaded glass cabinets above it. A green glass bowl of pears, lemons, and limes sat artfully on the countertop. The stucco walls had an old world look to them. Chelsea felt it had a European feel, not that she had ever been to Europe. Kyle looked perfectly at home in his navy Sound Side shirt and baggy shorts, wiping the countertops with a sponge. Abby, like Chelsea, was sucking in a large breath.

"Did you know Kyle can cook?" Glen asked delightedly. "His mom made spaghetti, and he did the meatballs."

That must have been the source of the delicious aroma in the house.

"It smells fabulous," Abby swooned and Chelsea nodded.

Kyle grinned at her and she felt her heart swell. "You may have more than one mentor for your project, then," she said.

"Yeah, I'd say that seals the deal," said Glen. "So your mom said yes?"

"Yes, she did. Y'all will have lots of fun. And I want to sample everything you cook."

"Okay, I guess I've found myself a project, then!"

"Hey, I'm sorry about your wreck," Chelsea said as Abby went to him and circled her arm around his waist. He reciprocated the motion and they swayed together by the island in the kitchen. He smoothed her veil of silky black hair as she squeezed him and kissed him on the shoulder.

"Well, thanks. I guess we'd better make the most of this night, 'cause it looks like I'm grounded for, like…*ever!*"

"Maybe not," Kyle said encouragingly. "Would you ladies like to head down to the *man cave* and shoot some pool or something?"

Chelsea and Abby exchanged apprehensive glances. "Oh, I'm *so* good at pool!" Chelsea said.

"As good as I am at horseback riding?" he grinned again, with a wink at Chelsea. He led them through a mudroom and down the stairs. His phone played in his back pocket. He reached for it, frowned at the caller ID, and hit the ignore button.

"Who was it?" asked Glen.

He shrugged. "Prank call."

The "man cave" was as spectacular as the rest of the house. A large bar hugged one side of the imposing room, and across from that, a dark green pool table stood below a stained-glass billiards light. Another area held a pair of black leather couches and matching chairs draped with red blankets. Red and white accents and N.C. State memorabilia were everywhere. A large plasma TV was mounted on the wall across from the couches. Trophies adorned a case against the far wall.

Kyle opened French doors and stepped outside. Chelsea followed. "Does it feel stuffy in there to you?" he asked.

She breathed in the fresh air and murmured, "No, but it feels really good out here," as she looked out onto the stone terrace, with its outdoor kitchen and comfortable rattan furniture. "Wow, Kyle. This place is amazing." She suddenly felt embarrassed about her home, something she had never felt, but then, he had admired it and called it special just the night before. "I didn't know your mom was selling it." She looked at him hesitantly. "What are her plans if it sells? You won't move away, will you? It's your senior year."

"It won't sell. Not in this market. If it does, we can live in the cabin until I graduate. Then I'll be off to college and my mom can do whatever she wants. She wants to downsize. It'll just be her when I'm gone. The cabin is for sale, too. It's not likely both places will sell at the same time."

She pondered this for a moment. "Does it make you sad?"

"Not really. It's just what we have to do."

"Hey, you want me to rack 'em?" Glen called from inside.

"Go ahead," he replied, then slid his arm around Chelsea's waist and pulled her back before they went in. "Do you want to do something tomorrow, just the two of us? Like go on a hike or something?"

She laughed. "You need a boyfriend, not me."

He lowered his eyes and then looked down at her. "No way. How else am I supposed to get you alone…so I can have my way with you?" he said softly and shyly. It was so endearing she had to look away. She knew he was being funny, but it touched her just the same.

"Well, we have a load of calculus to do…"

"I can come down to your house and we can work on it first, and then go find a trail somewhere," he said, kissing her behind her ear. "We'll figure it out. There won't be much time…when things get rolling, you know?"

She nodded, "No, I totally get that."

A hint of thunder rumbled in the distance. He took her back inside and went over to the rack on the wall to select his cue. Glen was rubbing chalk on the end of his. Abby was behind the bar, pouring Diet Dr. Pepper into State cups. She winked at Chelsea.

"You break," said Glen. Kyle bent expertly over the table and smacked the cue into the triangle of balls, which sent them skittering across the table. Two striped balls went into pockets.

"Will you help me?" he asked Chelsea.

"I'm sure you don't need my help, but I'll be glad to watch," she said. She got two of the drinks and carried them back to the table. His phone went off again as he made the next shot, undistracted. He looked at it again and hit the ignore button, as he had done previously.

"Tell her to stop calling you, man," Glen complained. Kyle did not react, but turned the phone off and returned it to his pocket before he turned to his next shot. Abby raised her eyebrows at Chelsea, and suddenly, she wondered whether Elle was the person calling him. Abby looked sharply at Glen, who shrugged and said, "I was just kidding. I don't know who it is."

Chelsea swallowed a sick feeling. Kyle seemed to be doing everything he could to show her that she was the one he wanted to be with. He wasn't making a show of the situation with Elle, if that was really what was going on. Most guys she knew would have enjoyed the extra attention and rubbed it in, but clearly, that wasn't his style. This should have reassured her, but still she felt uneasy. She didn't want to know and didn't plan to ask. His concentration seemed unbroken since he had knocked in all the stripes and was lining up the eight ball.

"Well, that was nicely done," Glen said, wiping his hands together as the black ball thudded into a pocket. "I should've known you could run your own table. I'm breaking next game."

Chapter 5

THICK SKIN

It rained during the night and was muggy going to church the next day. Daisy Frazier, Kitty's long-time friend, had taken her from there to lunch and then to spend the afternoon together as they did every Sunday. It was a nice way to spend the day, and Kitty always looked forward to it. It also gave Liz and Tom a well-deserved respite. After a lunch of chicken salad and sliced homegrown tomatoes with mozzarella and fresh basil, Liz went to take a nap, and Chelsea changed into jean shorts, a tank top, and tennis shoes for the hike. She hoped Kyle wasn't planning on anything more hardcore than that. She pulled her long auburn hair into a ponytail and stuffed a bandana into her back pocket. She was helping Tom load the dishwasher when Kyle's knock came at the door. She let him in and they got to work on their calculus homework at the kitchen table with Fella at their feet. Tom reached for a Molson from the fridge. "So, where y'all off to after this?" he said.

When Kyle looked at Chelsea, she shrugged. "I was thinking about the waterfall trail behind your church," Kyle said. She was relieved it wouldn't be too strenuous.

"That's where Charley used to take y'all hiking after she got her driver's license, isn't it?" Tom said, remembering.

"Oh yeah, those were the white-knuckle days!" Chelsea said and Kyle laughed. "Do you remember that? Swinging around those curves going up there and hanging on for dear life?"

"Yeah, she was *not* the best driver," Kyle remarked.

"Oh, she still drives like that," Tom commented. "Will it bother you if I watch the game while you work?" he asked, as he sauntered into the living room and turned on the TV. Like there was any chance in hell he would allow them to go to her room, Chelsea thought.

"No, Dad," she said. She rolled her eyes at Kyle, who was flipping pages in the textbook, and ready to work, as if in a hurry.

"It might rain later, so we'd best get started." They worked together for thirty or forty minutes, and she asked lots of questions about how he worked the problems. One had stumped him, too, and they would ask about it in class the next day. Finally, Kyle shut the book and they filled water bottles before saying goodbye to Tom and taking off.

They drove to the little Episcopal church and parked behind the mission center. Chelsea imagined Charley's wedding that would be held there in the late spring. "Do you remember how to get to the trail?" she asked.

"I think so…it's been a while, though."

They found the trail sign and headed into the cool fragrant woods, dim from the canopy of trees overhead. They were climbing within minutes. Ferns and wildflowers grew abundantly on the forest floor, and she breathed in the musty smell of wet leaves and fallen trees. Sticks snapped as she listened to the soft thudding of their footsteps and followed his lead. He held branches back for her here and there as they tromped along the brushy trail. The rush of the waterfall was audible in the distance. Soon, they were climbing up and over rocks and grabbing onto large roots to hoist themselves to the next levels. They climbed higher and breathed harder as they gained elevation. The waterfall roared nearby and came into view after the next few sets of rocks and roots. They stood for a moment and caught their breath as they watched the white water cascading over the boulders, crashing and pooling down below. Rhododendrons and mountain laurel were thick around them and pale green lichen and rich moss covered the bark of sticks and the lower sections of trees.

The air moved coolly around them, and Chelsea felt a few wisps of hair that had escaped her ponytail blowing slightly in the breeze. He smiled her favorite smile, took her hand, and led her to a platform of flat boulders at the top of the fall. They sat together, arms wrapped around their knees, still out of breath from the climb. She felt the heat waving off him and his skin was wet as his shoulder touched hers. She felt the moisture on her own skin and felt a drip of sweat trickle down her chest. She turned to him and breathed in his musky, salty smell. He smiled again, then dropped the small pack from his back and pulled out their water bottles, from which they gulped thirstily. She pulled the bandana from her back pocket and soaked it with water. She offered it to him first. He said, "No, you use it; I brought one, too," and produced his own. After wiping her face, she laid the wet cloth on the back of her neck, pulling it around to rest on her throat, and gazed out over the white water, peaceful and contented.

He watched her. He reached over to push a stray strand of her hair away from her face and tuck it behind her ear. She leaned against him, and noticed that their skin had cooled down considerably. He stretched his arm behind her and pulled her closer. "This is the best, isn't it?" he murmured. The roiling water over the rocks was mesmerizing. She closed her eyes and rocked into him. She didn't want to talk for fear of breaking the spell. How long could she will this moment to last?

His arm tightened around her, and she felt him breathing into her hair. Every cell of her body lit up in response to the feel of his skin on hers. He kissed her cheek softly, and then her ear, and her neck behind her ear. She raised her face to his and his lips brushed hers, and then took hers, hard, and she tasted salt. His hand moved down her throat and rested on her collarbone. A small moan escaped his lips; then he stopped, pressed his forehead against hers, and held her face in his hands.

"Don't you like this?" she whispered breathlessly.

"Oh yeah, I like this just fine," he breathed. "I don't think your dad would like this too much, though," he laughed quietly. "He'd be after my head…and maybe a few other body parts, too."

She didn't doubt it. "What's happening here?" she asked, looking up into his unbelievably blue eyes, which were locked with hers.

"What's happening here is…I'm putting on the brakes. And I guess I need your help with this. I'm trying not to be stupid, you know?"

She did know, and if things had gone further, neither of them would have liked the consequences. "I know…sometimes being responsible sucks."

"Yeah, it does," he said. He rested his chin on top of her head and looked out over the majestic view in front of them. "Restraint is much harder than I thought it would be…with you…literally," he chuckled. He held her lightly now, and as she sank back against him, she felt him exhale long and slow.

Just sitting like this was okay with her. *If this is all I ever get, it was worth it,* she thought. She closed her eyes again to the rushing of water and felt his thumb making small slow circles on the back of her hand.

"So, what do you dream about?" she heard him say softly.

She laughed and thought, *besides you?* But she did not say it aloud, still concerned with maintaining the magic. "I guess…traveling, seeing the world, dancing in a place that challenges me, but where I can hold my own. Just, you know, being happy…kind of like this," she said and the words she ventured made her tremble.

He tightened his arm around her. "I know," he whispered into her neck. "It seems…so easy, doesn't it?"

"So *you're* happy, too, right now?" she asked him tentatively.

"I am. I never expected to feel this way…after everything that's happened. I've just been kind of…dead, and confused, for a long time."

"Well, I won't let you feel that way again…if you'll let me," she said, pressing the back of his hand to her lips. Thunder rumbled long and low. A breeze blew in and she felt her skin, cooler now, prickle with the chill. The thunder came again, and this time it rumbled in a circle around them and rolled around the mountain, bringing gray clouds with it. He rubbed her arm and the back of her neck before giving her a quick kiss.

"We'd better make tracks," he said, and reloaded the pack. The trip down was far faster than the trip up, and they made it back to the Jeep as the first raindrops pelted down on them. The wind gusted and the wipers beat steadily as Kyle wound his way carefully around the curves down the mountain, toward the road that would lead them back to Snowy Ridge. She was quiet so he could concentrate, as the rain was coming sideways in sheets across the windshield. As the farm road came into view, the rain subsided a bit, but he drove underneath the portico to let her out without getting wet.

"Today was great," she said, smiling shyly at him.

He held her hand and leaned over in the seat to kiss her. "Si," he murmured, laughing into her ear. "Gracias. A manana, chica."

• • •

School seemed less overwhelming and took on the feel of a pleasantly settling routine. Lunches were full of easy banter between the four of them, and occasionally with friends who stopped by to chat. When she and Kyle weren't together, Chelsea found herself daydreaming about the time they had spent together—watching the stars, swimming, sitting by the waterfall, kissing, and just talking. She couldn't believe the intimacies he had shared with her in such a short time. Who would have thought he would have opened up to her this way? She would've never thought he'd like the same things she liked, instead of the frantic text-messaging, non-stop video games, and partying that went on with the other guys she knew.

She was particularly excited about starting back to her dance classes that day. After taking a quick inventory of her dance clothing, and Pointe shoes, she got dressed and drove to the musty old stone building in town that was Studio One, her second home for the past twelve years. She was early as usual when she pulled into the parking lot and trudged uphill to the doorway.

Music pounded and tires screeched behind her. She laughed, knowing it was Willie. He would be mad that he hadn't gotten there first. He slammed the door of his ancient green Maxima and slung his bag across his shoulder. He shook out a multitude of short tiny braids all over his head, and his gap-toothed smile impishly charged his dark face. "Girl! Wait up! You're lookin' *good!*" He started up the hill in a pair of footless black tights, red Crocs, and a white T-shirt. Sonya would surely scold him about not wearing street clothes over his dance attire.

"Hey! I was wondering when you were finally going to speak to me. You've been so busy chatting up Tia Thompson in vocal ensemble. You've got it bad, don't cha?"

"You got that right…cheerleading captain and all. I got it goin' *on!* You jealous, baby?"

He held the door for her, and they went to the last studio and dropped their gear on the floor, then sat down so she could put on her Pointe shoes. They heard Sonya and Brad in the office, talking and laughing.

"So, I guess it's over between us then," she said, an impressive pout on her lips.

"Oh, you'll always be my number one, you know that," he said. Then he swung his legs out into a one-hundred and eighty-degree straddle and leaned across the floor to grab his feet as he watched her tie her satiny pink shoes. "And speaking of cheerleaders, what's that psycho-blonde got on you?"

"What do you mean?" She frowned, knowing he was referring to Elle, who was also in their vocal ensemble class.

"She's always shooting daggers at Tia. You know, she's still pissed because Tia made captain and she didn't. But *you*! OMG, girl, if looks could *kill*! What'd you go and do to her?" he cried, animatedly.

"I'm not sure. She didn't even know who I was until now, you know?"

"Ohhh…you don't still have that thing going for Rocky, do you? Now, she's all about some *Rocky*," he said. He stood up and stretched a foot across the barre, looking at himself in the mirror.

"Don't remind me," she said miserably. "I was such a dumbass last year. What was I ever thinking?"

"Trust me, you weren't! But you better watch out for her. She's bad news. She's in our drama class, too, and lemme tell you, she is a drama *queen*," he said. "So, did you like it at N.C.S.A. this summer?" he asked, changing the subject.

"I did. I'm going to apply for next year. Auditions are in February."

"You'll knock 'em dead, baby," he said. "Lemme tell you about Richmond! I stayed up there at my grandma's for six weeks and took class every day. They like me, I can tell," he said, puffing out his muscular chest, and she had no doubt this was indeed true. Who wouldn't be awed by the number of pirouettes he could turn, or the height and breadth of his leaps across a stage. They'd be begging him to come and dance with the Richmond Ballet. It must be wonderful to have that confidence. "They told me to come back and audition for them after I graduate. I'll be up there the next *day*, baby!"

"That is, if somebody else doesn't snatch you up first," she murmured.

"Like, who else gonna see me up here, huh? We're *hill*billies, honey!"

She had to laugh, but he was right. He was more frustrated than she was by their limitations. At that moment, other dancers began to arrive. Sonya, tiny and sparrow-like in her black tights and tunic, entered carrying a handful of CDs. She squealed and grinned, then went over to her two favorite dancers and gave them a group hug. Tall and handsome Brad, the contemporary and modern dance teacher, glided in behind her and greeted them enthusiastically. It felt good to be back in her element again and she felt her own confidence surge as the class progressed and the music and movement overtook her.

When she returned home that evening, she was surprised to see a white Range Rover in the driveway. Shelly Davis must have had dinner with her folks. Her heart thumped at the thought and she ran up the front porch steps, then slowed herself, not wanting to appear anxious. As she closed the door, she heard her parents and Shelly talking on the sun porch. She peeked around the corner and saw them seated casually on the flowered sofas and ottoman, with Kitty in the mix. Shelly and her parents were having a glass of red wine.

"Hi, sweetie!" Liz greeted her, and everyone stood to hug her. Shelly gave her hand a squeeze. "I made a plate for you out in the kitchen," said Liz. "I know you're starving. How was dance?"

"It's *so* good to be back! I'll probably be sore tomorrow, but it is *so* worth it." She excused herself and went to the kitchen in search of sustenance. After microwaving the plate and filling a glass with ice water, she nestled herself into the island on her stool, forking bites of savory chicken pie into her mouth, chewing gratefully. She listened to the conversation that floated in from the other room.

Shelly was speaking. "Oh, I know. Kyle seems to be so happy since school started. I think it was the right decision to have him finish high school here. You don't know how relieved I am. I know I haven't made the best calls with him. His friends are so cute. That little Glen from the football team is a sweetheart! And it's nice that he and Chelsea are doing things together."

"Well, he always looks content when I've seen him," Tom chimed in as Chelsea held her breath.

"He's carrying a heavy load this year, and I don't want him to be too distracted. He really buckled down at Christ School and his grades were excellent, even with everything that's happened. Hopefully, he can find the right balance here."

"Right," Liz agreed. "They don't want to blow it now. Chelsea has worked hard, too. With all the dancing she does, she can't afford to veer off course. Hopefully, they won't get 'senioritis' too badly. I remember how it was with Charley and Jay. It'll be time for them to graduate and go off to college before we know it. I can't believe that this time next year, we'll be empty-nesters!" They all laughed.

Chelsea stopped chewing. Suddenly, she didn't want the year to fly by as they'd predicted. She closed her eyes and wished time would stand still so she could get a grip on the new and amazing dream she was floating in. She felt like she'd just seemed to find her way, and it could be pulled out from under her before she knew it. "But that's life at seventeen," she sighed. "Change."

• • •

Thursday morning, she and Abby waited outside for the guys to show up in the normal place, but neither arrived before the first bell. Glen had been mortified to have to ride the bus since the car wreck and tended to squeal in at the beginning of homeroom. Kyle had been helping him out, giving him rides home after football practice every day. It turned out the car had not been totaled after all, but it needed to stay in the shop for a couple of weeks. Glen was grounded and his savings account was to be depleted to help pay the damages. Abby felt bad for him and commiserated with Chelsea as they walked to their lockers. "Yes, he'll be working at Wendy's every waking moment until he leaves for college…if they don't fire him for not being able to get rides in. Kyle and I are trying to take care of that, though." She looked at Chelsea thoughtfully. "He really is a nice guy. I'm glad you two are together."

"Is that what we're calling it?" Chelsea asked dubiously.

"Yep, and here he comes now. Have a nice day," she said, then slipped past Chelsea's locker and on to her own.

Kyle sauntered up beside her, one hand in a pocket, book bag slung over his shoulder. He wore a white T-shirt, stretched beyond belief across his ever-expanding shoulders, and a threadbare pair of jeans, complete with holes at each knee. "Hey," he said sleepily. His eyes looked bleary and even though he was clean-shaven and smelled fresh from his shower, his hair was even more out of place than usual. She wondered whether she should fix it for him. He looked at her, noticing the extra time she'd taken with her own appearance, and said, "Your hair's straight. It's different. I like it."

She smiled. "Thanks. I can't say the same for yours today!" She gave up and laughed as she reached up to smooth the stray piece down on top of his head. His blue eyes widened for a moment as he met her look. "Do you own a mirror?" she asked, smiling at him indulgently.

"Thanks. I was in a hurry this morning," he said softly. Then, "You're beautiful." They were walking in the hall now. He never touched her at school. Not the way other couples went around, seemingly joined at the hip. Even Abby and Glen held hands most of the time they were together. It was probably best. His eyes alone were enough to accelerate her pulse.

They slid into their seats as Glen glided into the room, giving them the Rocky-like chin-jutting and eyebrow-scrunching gesture that had become their private joke. They laughed and looked around, then waved at Anthony and Meredith, who were chatting in the back of the room.

At lunch, Kyle and Chelsea stopped at the vending machine for bottled water before they sat down at their table. A figure lay on the far bench, knees raised, and feet on the bench with an arm slung across a forehead. They stopped short, thinking it was an emergency of some sort. Chelsea approached first. "Are you okay?" she asked.

The arm moved to the side and Elle McClarin stared up at her irritably. She sat up and spun around to sit at the table across from where they would sit. "Yeah, I'll be fine in a minute." She had been eating an apple. "It's this blood sugar thing I have," she said, fanning herself. She looked at Kyle as she spoke and ignored Chelsea as they both sat down on their bench. "When I used to dance a lot, I'd pass out sometimes."

"There are cupcakes in Miss Rogers' room if you need sugar," offered Kyle, unimpressed.

"It's her birthday," Chelsea said, and Elle rolled her eyes.

"I know that. It's just Tia kissing up to her for making her captain of the squad," she said with an acid tone. Then she leaned forward and folded her arms across the table to accentuate her already noticeable cleavage. She changed the subject. "So Kyle, I'm having a party at my house on Friday after the game. Do you want to be my date?"

He raised his eyebrows nonchalantly as Chelsea began a slow boil. "What, trouble in paradise, Elle?"

"Not yet," she smiled beguilingly at him, then leaned forward some more.

Chelsea struggled for composure and decided to study other parts of Elle. She really was a beautiful girl, if you could get past her toxic nature.

Her eye shadow was interesting—coppery, with silver around the lashes, and little sparkly white corners on the inside. Her medallion earrings set off her blonde hair nicely and she tossed it skillfully as she waited for Kyle's response.

"Well, I don't date girlfriends of friends…and Chelsea and I are already on for Friday. Right?" he said, looking to her for help.

"Yeah…cookout at my house after the game. I guess if you're having a party, you wouldn't be able to come," she said with an attempt to look disappointed, and amazed at how quickly she had manufactured the lie. But when you're fighting a battle like this, why not?

Elle shot her a look that screamed, "As if!" Then she turned to Kyle again, tossing her hair as a way of dismissing Chelsea. "Well, if your little soirée falls apart, just call me," she said. Then she rose from the bench and sashayed away with her half-eaten apple.

Kyle chuckled and shook his head as Chelsea debated whether she had an appetite for her lunch. He yawned as he dumped the contents of his bag on the table. Chelsea decided to ignore the obvious and glanced at him sideways.

"You look so tired today. Were you up late studying for the calculus test?"

"I should have been. My mom had a bad night," he said.

"What happened?"

"She went to 'Wine Wednesday' with some of her realtor buds and they got hammered," he smiled.

"What's that?"

"They have half-price bottles of wine at Canyons on Wednesdays. I don't know how many they drank, but she was pretty plowed when they dropped her off."

Chelsea groaned. "Did she get sick?"

"Oh, yeah. She spent part of the night wrapped around the john. And then she wanted to *talk*."

"About what?"

"Oh…all the stuff. You can imagine. She hasn't said anything to me in almost nine months and she decides to spill it all the night before our first math test."

"Why now?"

"I don't know. I guess since I'm home, she feels more comfortable venting. I don't think she was very happy…even before all the bad stuff started happening…Wow, it's…embarrassing telling you all this about my family," he sighed, looking out across the parking lot.

"Don't be embarrassed. It's just families."

"Yours is so…*normal*."

"Oh, we have our moments. It was hard at first when we took over caring for Kitty and moved in there. Everybody was on edge."

"I watch the way your parents are with each other. I wanna be like that someday."

"So, you didn't sleep?"

"Not much. We're cooking out at your house tomorrow night?" he chuckled.

"I guess we are," she said sheepishly.

"I'm proud of you. You came up with that one pretty quickly," he said.

She sighed. "I'll have to check it out with my mom. But it should be fine if I do the shopping and fix the burgers before the game. Do you think Glen's mom will let him come?"

"Maybe so, if he tells her he has to do the grilling as part of his project. You think your mom would go along with that, being his mentor and all?"

"Sure," she said absently.

"You know, we don't have to do this. Screw Elle."

"Oh, that's exactly what she wants," she chortled as Glen and Abby showed up at the table and they explained the plan.

• • •

On Friday, Chelsea had to pass up lunch for an appointment with Terry Riley, the representative from Cities in Schools, to talk about finding a resource for her senior dance project. She sat on a bench outside the counseling center, eating a pear, and looking over her English notes. The maroon uniform appeared beside her before she could react. Elle was sitting on the bench with her hair pulled into a ponytail as Chelsea looked up, surprised. "So…you think you can date a guy like Kyle Davis," she said pointedly.

Chelsea was shocked speechless by the attack. "What?"

"You're going to have to share, you know. He's the one all the girls want. You won't be able to hold his attention for long. Even if you did what you had to do to keep him, it wouldn't last," Elle said frankly, as if giving advice to a friend.

"Leave him alone, Elle. You don't know him," Chelsea said boldly, finding her voice.

"Oh, yes I do. I know all about guys like him and what they need. Anyway, you don't want to get serious about a guy your senior year. He has money being thrown at him from colleges all over the place—West Virginia, Clemson, Virginia Tech, State. He'll be so far away you'd never see him even if you tried to make it work. You should just give it up before you get hurt."

Chelsea blinked and her eyes gave her away. How did Elle know this and she didn't? Rocky Santoro was surely her source.

"You didn't have a clue, did you? You shouldn't get too attached. I usually get what I want."

"What about Rocky?" Chelsea shot back.

"What about him? He knows the score. Just think about it," she said, and pressed Chelsea's arm as she got up from the bench when Terry Riley came to the door.

"Who's next?" he said excitedly, clapping his hands together.

• • •

Kyle was waiting for her on the bench when she came out, floating uncomfortably, as if she were having an out-of-body experience. "How'd it go?" he asked, puzzled at her expression.

"Uh…good, I guess. He gave me a grant application. He suggested I write a grant to get an activity bus to bring some girls to an elementary school on Saturday mornings for dance classes," she said, barely able to concentrate. He looked at her questioningly, trying to assess her mood. She needed to divert this conversation. "Did you know he played offense for ASU? He came back here to live after college and wanted to give back to the community so he's doing this."

"Hmm…Yeah, that was his story during the broadcast the other day," he said. "Did you get a chance to eat lunch?" he asked.

"No, I wasn't hungry," she said as they started to walk toward their next class. As she tossed her bag into the trash, she noticed he carried a similar bag, decorated with little football stickers and stars and red and gold letters. He tossed it in the can as well. "What was that?" she asked.

"Elle's goodie bag. Same crap as last time."

Chelsea swallowed dryly and felt the nauseating knot forming again in the pit of her stomach. She would need to develop a thick skin if she were going to make it through this year.

Chapter 6

SURPRISES

Chelsea wiped a tear from under her eye as she wandered the grocery store aisles that afternoon, distracted. She checked the items on her list, but was mostly still stinging from her encounter with Elle earlier in the day. As much as she hated to admit it, Elle was probably right. There was no point in starting a relationship with anyone now, much less a guy like Kyle Davis. He would most likely get tired of their lame little walks in the woods, and then the restraint on his part, and probably hers, too, would get old and he'd lose interest in her. She could even imagine him pursuing Elle, the two of them strolling down the hall, her hand in his back pocket, laughing together at some provocative line she'd whispered in his ear. And they would look good together.

She shook her head at the image and forced herself to look intelligent for the cashier as she paid for the ground beef, buns, and chips that would be a late dinner after the game. It had started already, anyway, the distancing. The Labor Day weekend was beginning, and NC State's coaching staff had invited Kyle and his mom to be guests at State's season opener. They planned to drive to Stacie's on the Outer Banks after the game for the long weekend. It was a brutal drive, and he might not even come back until Tuesday. She imagined him surfing with his older friends again, or sprawled on the beach with the local girls chatting him up, or sitting around a beach bonfire at night. This was insane, she thought. What was she thinking?

Her own plans were much less exciting. She, Liz, and Kitty were going to Winston-Salem to meet Charley and go shopping for bridesmaid dresses on Saturday. Jay would be around on Sunday and there would be a family picnic up at Wayne and Becky's with the cousins. She'd probably hang out with Abby on Labor Day and go swimming or to the movies. It would be their last day to vegetate for a while.

The football game was another exciting win at home for the Wildcats. Chelsea sat in the stands with Abby on one side, Willie on the other, Meredith Everhart in front and David Greer to Abby's left. Abby had made a face at Chelsea when Dave grabbed his spot on the bleachers. He didn't say much, which was usual for him, but it was still awkward at first when he joined the chatty bunch. He threw Chelsea several sidelong glances but did not speak, and after a time, she forgot he was there. The three girls cheered wildly for Glen, Kyle, and Anthony, while Willie divided his attention equally between the game and the cheerleaders, giving Chelsea a running critique of Tia Thompson's excellent flying, tumbling, and dancing skills. Chelsea watched every move Kyle made and deliberately avoided watching a certain section of the cheerleaders.

The score was lopsided, due to Anthony's two passes for touchdowns, one to tight end Rocky Santoro, and Kyle's and Glen's excellent blocking. Glen recovered a fumble, which later led to another touchdown, and the fans were clearly stoked about what looked to be a promising season. The atmosphere in the new stadium was electric, with loud drum rhythms and horns from the marching band and the colorful uniforms. She loved to watch people at games, and she noticed Shelly Davis in the stands with Glen's parents.

After the game, they chatted with friends a bit before it was time to meet Kyle and Glen at the field house. Chelsea invited Willie and Tia to her house for hamburgers, but he declined.

"Thanks, but we got some plans already. *Private* plans, if you know what I mean," he laughed, handsome in his designer jeans and tight shirt.

"Oh!" she pretended surprise. It was so much fun messing with him. "You're not going to Elle's party?"

"Are you kidding?" he shrieked. "Are you looking at this?" he said, pointing to his cheek and then at the back of his hand. "I'm the wrong color to go to her house! Besides, today in drama she was talking up going to Joe's tonight for pizza after the game."

"No talk about a party at her house?" Big surprise.

"Not that I heard. There's Tia now…gotta fly! See you Tuesday, girl! Y'all have fun," he laughed and was off after Tia.

When the four of them walked through the Davenport's front door, a succulent aroma wafted from the kitchen and Chelsea knew her mom had helped. She must have sensed something wasn't quite right earlier. "Baked beans," Chelsea cried and led her friends to the kitchen where Tom and Liz sat cozily, sipping wine at the butcher block island. Tom motioned them to be quiet, and Chelsea knew that Kitty would already be asleep in the downstairs bedroom. She was glad she'd forewarned her friends about it. Liz and Tom had been watching sports highlights on the small TV Liz kept on the kitchen counter. Tom greeted Kyle with a handshake and a back slap. Abby gave Liz a hug and asked what she could do to help.

As they walked through the connecting hallway from the living room to the kitchen, Glen sucked in a breath. "Wow! I've never seen a stone floor in a kitchen before!" he said to Chelsea, taking in the surroundings.

"It's *really* old. A long time ago, this kitchen was detached from the rest of the house, for fire safety reasons, and because it was hot in here in the summer with wood stoves going," Chelsea explained. "This hall was a breezeway, but over the years it changed a bit. This is the gentlemen's room," she said, and indicated a small room on the right of the kitchen, which now served as her dad's office.

"For like...strippers and stuff?" asked Glen, as the others had gone in to talk with Tom and Liz.

"*No*, goofball," she said, swatting him with some papers he'd carried in. "It was a place for them to come with their dogs after hunting, then sit around smoking stinky cigars and drinking their bourbon...or moonshine, or whatever!"

"Oh, the *man cave*!"

"Yeah, I guess."

As they joined the others in the kitchen, Chelsea introduced Glen to her father. Liz greeted him warmly. "Hi, Glen! So they sprung you for the night?" she asked, remembering the grounding arrangement Chelsea mentioned.

"Yes, ma'am! I am here on official business. I brought the mentor contract for you to sign. I really appreciate your agreeing to take me on."

"Oh, it's my pleasure! I know we'll have lots of fun," she said, taking the papers.

"The first thing I want to cook is whatever it is you've got in that oven!"

"Those are Chelsea's favorite baked beans." She winked at Chelsea, who murmured, "Thank you" to her mom and hugged her around the neck. Liz had set paper plates, condiments, and a basket of potato chips on the island. Chelsea went to the refrigerator and retrieved the plate of burger patties she had made before she left.

"I turned on the grill when we heard y'all drive up," Tom said in his mountain twang. "We thought you might want to eat on the sun porch, you know, to give Mama some quiet."

"Oh, sure, Dad. Good idea." She pulled a spatula out of a crockery pitcher beside the stove and motioned Kyle outside with her while the others looked over the papers and discussed the cooking project.

"May I help?" he asked, taking over the platter of burgers and opening the lid to the grill. He slid the patties onto the grill as she watched, hands on hips.

"You played great tonight!" she said, then gave him a squeeze around the waist and he set down the platter.

"Thanks! Everybody had a good game. Anthony was hot."

"You're so cool about it. What's it like when you lose? What should I do in a case like that?" she asked tentatively.

"Hmm," he said, thinking about it. "I think it's about the same, but you could hold my hand. I always like it when you do that," he added, returning the hug. He looked down at her and studied her a moment. "You're in a good mood. I was worried about you earlier today," he said. "Was something bothering you?"

Her face flushed and she remembered the burning conversation with Elle. She hesitated before she could think of how to answer. He waited, watching her eyes. She might as well come clean. She mustered her most courageous voice and shook her head. "It was just something Elle said to me at lunch. But I'm over it."

"Whatever it was, you shouldn't pay any attention to it. Everything she says is so...twisted."

"I know. But...well, she kind of warned me that she likes you and that I shouldn't get my hopes up about you." Suddenly her strong voice was gone.

He looked down at her and snorted. "See...that's just what I mean." He looked into the dark trees, considering his response. "Chelsea, that's why I like you. You are *not* like her. Remember, I told you she's not my type, right? And remember I told you that you're my type. I know about girls like her. You're the one I want to be with, not her...not anyone else."

As he spoke, he slid his hand into the back pocket of her jeans and pulled her close to him. As she remembered her daydream from the grocery store, she gave a little gasp and opened her eyes wide.

He pulled his hand away. "I'm sorry. I guess I'm getting ahead of myself," he said, and a concerned look crossed his brow.

"No! No, not at all; you just surprised me," she laughed.

"Well, in that case," he half-smiled, then looked down at her and returned his hand to her pocket.

"Maybe we'd better scoot around so my Dad doesn't get the wrong idea if he's spying on us through the kitchen window."

"Oh, I'm sure he'd be right on target," he chuckled, but obliged her by pulling her around to his right so they stood at the end of the grill. Just then, Glen appeared with a small plate.

"Hey, this is supposed to be my job! Ready for the cheese? Everybody wants cheese, right? Okay, I guess I'm interrupting," he said, then handed Chelsea the plate and headed back inside.

She laughed. "No, come on out! Where's Abby?"

"Bartending. She's pouring Cokes. I'm going to help her." He was back through the kitchen door in the next instant.

They stood, arms around each other, for a few moments, and she watched him flip the burgers.

"Are you excited about going back to the beach and seeing your friends?"

"Well, actually, I'm trying to talk my mom out of going out there."

"Why? I thought you had plans."

"It's a really long drive for such a short time. It's friggin' *seven* hours on a normal day, but on Labor Day weekend, forget it. We're thinking about spending the night in Raleigh. Take a tour of the campus and eat at Magiano's; maybe she'll want to do some shopping or whatever. But it's *three days.* I don't want to be gone three days," he said and his eyes seared into hers. She could not breathe as his fingers gently touched her cheek and pulled her face into his muscular shoulder. She felt him kiss the top of her head.

"Oh, God, they're still at it," Abby muttered to Glen as they came out the back door with drinks. "Your parents said to tell you goodnight and that they're going to bed…and to keep it down."

"Did you put the cheese on yet?" asked Glen as he handed a cup to Kyle.

"Waiting on you, man," Kyle said. He accepted the drink, but he kept his arm around Chelsea.

"So, what's up with you guys? Are you like, a *couple* now?" asked Glen.

"Oh, Glen, just come on out and say what you mean," said Abby, rolling her eyes at Chelsea.

Kyle laughed. "I like her," he said to Chelsea. "She's so feisty. And he's so *blunt.*"

"Well, you'll always know where you stand with my friends," she said, grinning at them.

"So, are your intentions honorable?" Glen asked seriously, in his most fatherly voice.

"I have to say they are, sir," said Kyle, just as seriously. "Do I need to get you guys' permission to date this young lady?"

Glen wrapped an arm around Abby and asked, "What do you think, sweetheart?"

"Oh, I think Chelsea can speak for herself. She doesn't need my permission. And Glen, put the cheese on the burgers, and let's go check on those *baked beans,*" she said, and smacked him softly on the chest. He coughed, tossed a piece of cheese on each burger, and they went back inside, snickering.

Kyle's hand was still in her back pocket. They were quiet for a moment. He pulled her into him again and looked down at her. "So…now you know."

"What is it I know?"

"That…I'm really into you, and I need you to be my girlfriend. That is, if you want to be," he whispered, closing his eyes and pressing his mouth against her forehead.

"*Need?*"

"Definitely," he whispered and his eyes remained closed. He kissed her then, tentatively at first, and then long and slow. She kissed him back the same way. "Are you saying yes?"

"Definitely." She leaned into his strong chest and felt his arms fold around her. They swayed slowly from side to side as he caressed the side of her forehead with his lips.

"Oh, crap!" He opened his eyes and grabbed the spatula, turning to the burgers that were about to burn on the grill.

•••

The shopping trip had been much more fun than Chelsea had anticipated. Kitty had the best time of all since it was rare for her to be out doing things most people took for granted, and being with the girls seemed to be just what she needed. Charley and her friend Emma Lavender met them at the Village Tavern for a lunch on the terrace, and then they hit the bridal boutique. Thanks to Emma and Charley's research on the Internet of what must have been every bridesmaid dress in existence, they'd narrowed the search for the perfect dress to a handful of prearranged choices already in the fitting room. Charley had chosen lavender as her color, with Emma's influence, no doubt, and they decided upon the best dress in a relatively painless amount of time. Liz was delighted with lavender, especially with the rhododendrons that would be in bloom in June around the church and in their backyard. She and Kitty agreed that lavender and white petunias would go in the ground around the terrace as soon as the last frost was past.

With that task taken care of, Charley, who still had the shopping bug, asked lots of questions about Kyle and Chelsea. When it appeared that Chelsea might indeed have a date for the homecoming dance, Charley urged Liz to buy Chelsea a beautiful strapless, knee-length dress of a deep crimson. She assured Chelsea it would be perfect for their dance. She tried it on and the saleslady gushed that it was "mesmerizing" on her figure, and just her color. Chelsea turned back and forth in front of the three-way mirror. Other ladies in the shop agreed and Liz bought the dress. After paying at the jewelry counter, they parted ways. Since Charley was low man on the totem pole at the hospital, she was slated to work over the holiday. She and Emma headed back to Greenville.

Chelsea spent Sunday helping her dad clean the barn and gave Fred and Dot baths. After her own bath, she cleaned her room and made potato salad for the picnic. Liz shucked corn and put together another pot of the famous baked beans. At mid-afternoon, Jay swung in from his campus apartment and helped load the Tahoe. Kitty rode in the backseat with Chelsea and Jay for the short ride up the steep hill to Wayne and Becky's house. It was relaxing and entertaining to be with her family, and after dinner they sat on the large deck overlooking a rolling patchwork quilt of Christmas trees that dotted the landscape beyond the backyard.

Wayne and Tom told stories and had them laughing and sighing. So many memories. As she leaned against the railing, she watched her parents, sharing a lounge chair. Tom stretched out with his long legs to one side. Liz, perched comfortably beside him, pressed her hand against his knee and laughed, as he and Jay remembered the rat snake that visited their pantry. Tom rubbed the back of his wife's neck and rested his hand on her shoulder, and laughed about the way Jay, who was then fourteen years old, had tried heroically to poke the snake into a pillowcase with a stick so he could keep it as a pet. Becky and Kitty wiped their eyes and laughed. In the end, Jay caught the snake, and they eventually convinced him to release it into their grandparents' barn where it could serve its life purpose. Liz and Tom looked at each other, smiled and shook their heads.

Chelsea had always taken this kind of gathering and the closeness of her family for granted, but now she realized what Kyle had been talking about. What her parents had was special, and her family truly enjoyed being together. What other daughter-in-law would have graciously given up her career to take on the care of her husband's mother, as Liz had done with Kitty? It had been hard at first, when Kitty could be so uncooperative, but Chelsea knew that her mother and Kitty had an extra-special bond, and Kitty was a person like no other. Liz probably enjoyed Kitty's company even more than her own mother's. So unusual, so comforting. The helpfulness, the connectedness they shared wasn't like most families she knew. Kyle's family probably had not been like this, even though they'd spent time together, traveling, and doing things she had never done, much less imagined. Kyle wanted to be like her parents, she remembered. It was the ultimate compliment.

Jay stood beside her, bumped her affectionately, and leaned on the railing, too. He sipped from his beer bottle and crossed his arms. "Whatcha thinkin' about?"

She caught herself. It was what she always thought about these days. Was it so obvious to everyone else? She cast about in her head, trying to come up with a sensible answer. "Just…everyone…and how nice it is to be here with everybody, you know? Except, I'm sorry Charley can't be here. I don't think many families get along this well, do you?"

"Yeah, you're right. That's why all of our friends like to spend time at our house. Since I've been out of the house, I think I appreciate it more. Home's good. Like Mom says, there's nothing more important than family. And there's nothing like my own bed, which I'm really looking forward to sleeping in tonight!" he said, yawning and stretching his arms above his

SURPRISES

head. The conversation came to a lull and it was getting dark. A chill had crept into the night air, and Kitty rubbed her arms. Bri and Brett helped Wayne collect glasses and beer bottles from the deck and carry them inside, as Becky blew out the candles.

On Labor Day, Chelsea slept in until the midmorning sun woke her after ten o'clock. Jay was making pancakes in the kitchen when she padded downstairs, following the enticing aroma. In the afternoon, Kyle and Abby came over and the four of them went swimming in the lake. Fella followed them and decided to swim as well. He seemed to take extra pleasure in trotting up onto the dock and shaking himself all over them before stretching out in the sun to dry off. Kyle said he and his mom enjoyed the football game and their stay in Raleigh. The talk turned to college choices, football, and recruiting. Kyle explained that he'd always wanted to attend NC State, but if Virginia Tech offset the out-of-state tuition, he would jump at it. Both schools were talking money, and his mom urged him to entertain all the options. Clemson was in the mix as well, and he had the grades and SAT scores to eliminate the out-of-state tuition, so far. Each school offered architecture degrees, which was what he wanted.

Lying on her stomach and absorbing the warmth from the sun, Chelsea calculated the distances from each school to Winston-Salem, where she hoped to end up, at the School of the Arts. The boys talked on and on about football, the team, the coach, and how App State was expected to do this year after winning three straight national titles. Abby needed to leave to visit Glen, who was still under house arrest, and Jay planned to do some laundry at the house before he returned to his apartment. They packed up and wandered slowly back to the house, Fella at their heels. No one wanted the holiday weekend to end, but it was inevitable.

Kyle lingered at his Jeep until the others left. He sat in the driver's seat sideways and pulled her in to give her a hug. He breathed in the scent of her, and groaned into her ear, "I missed you! I told you I couldn't do three days without seeing you."

"At least there's school," she murmured into his neck. "What are you doing tonight?"

"I'm going to talk with Frank Maynard, my mom's builder friend. I want him to mentor me for my project. I figure if I want to build something, I'd better get started so it can be finished before the bad weather gets here."

"What do you plan on doing?"

"He told my mom about this organization that brings groups in during the summer and fall to do building projects and home repairs for people who can't do them themselves. He knows of a project they might let me do, and they'd supervise me. It's building a deck on this lady's house…or mobile home, maybe."

"That sounds like just what you wanted to do."

"Yeah, I'm hoping I can be done with it by Thanksgiving, and then if there are delays for some reason, I'll have time to get it done before the snow comes."

"Wow, you boys are really on the ball! I'm going to work on my grant tonight. Meredith's helping me with it; she's a good writer. And Miss Rogers is my advisor, so she can help. It will be a while before I can get my group together. Abby and I have been looking at the calendar, shooting dates around…with my UNCSA audition and other things going on, her show will probably be either late January…or after Valentine's Day. And I need to meet with Sonya McIntire to see if she'll mentor me. Or maybe Brad will do it."

He saw she was getting worked up. "Hey, take a deep breath! It'll be okay. We have until March," he said, wrapping his arms around her and stroking her face. "Remember, we can *do* this…one bite at a time."

Chapter 7

SEPTEMBER

Chelsea overslept Tuesday after a fitful night's sleep and was the last to arrive outside the commons. Abby and Glen stood with Kyle in a large group. From what she heard as she approached, the previous Friday's football game was the topic of conversation. Anthony, Rocky, Elle, and Kendra were in the circle as well, and Elle was talking loudly.

"Well, Kyle, you can always be a cheerleader if you want to give up the football team. Maybe then I could get somebody competent to hold me up without *dropping* me!" she said. Kendra looked chagrined, obviously being one of the stunt group that had dropped her. It seemed Chelsea had missed that scene on Friday night. Elle spotted Chelsea out of the corner of her eye and stepped in toward Kyle, saying, "By the way, I've wanted to see this for myself. Are your abs really as hard as they look?" She reached forward, pressed her palm flat onto his stomach, and held it there, massaging him, as he took a step backward in surprise. So many things happened in the split second as Chelsea approached. Her breath caught sharply in her chest and she had a fleeting thought to turn and head in the opposite direction. Somehow, her feet kept moving forward, and then she was right beside Kyle, just feet away from Elle. Kyle was reaching for Elle's hand and removing it from his body. She saw Rocky's jaw muscle tense, the way it did when something bugged him. She felt her face flame. Suddenly a parade of hot expletives flashed, cartoon-like before her eyes, and she wondered how no one else heard them. Abby was making large eyes in her direction and mouthing one of the expletives Chelsea was thinking.

And then Abby spoke while everyone else gawked, speechless. "Uh, Elle, I don't think those are *yours!*" she said, referring to Kyle's abdominal muscles.

Elle's usually raised eyebrows went up another notch. "Oh, are you *married* now, Kyle?" she said and looked pointedly at Chelsea, whom Kyle had just noticed as he turned his head at Elle's glance.

"I don't see how that would concern you," he said casually, and the other guys crowed and guffawed appreciatively. He turned and extended his hand to Chelsea and steered her backward, away from the group. "Hey," he said oddly as he walked her down the sidewalk, rolling his eyes.

"Do you need a bodyguard?" she asked incredulously, her face cooling.

"No, see, I have a *beautiful* guardian angel and she just got here," he said, low in her ear, stretching his arm around her shoulders and giving her a squeeze. People had witnessed the little scene and looked at them. By then they'd arrived at their lockers, and she realized she was shaking. He noticed and looked at her poignantly. "Don't let her get to you. It's what she wants," he said, and then he took her elbow and pulled her close to him.

She met his blue eyes and shook her head. "I know…I can't help it. It's just…I can't stand her *touching* you!" She realized her hand was flapping ridiculously and looked away. "I don't even do that," she murmured.

"She's just pulling your chain," he said. He kissed her cheek before they turned and went to homeroom. She thought of more expletives as the bell rang.

The weeks moved quickly. Dance classes were exciting, with the company learning new pieces they would soon perform. Chelsea craved the new choreography, and felt her self-expression take on a deeper form than she was used to. She met with Sonya and Brad, and Sonya gladly agreed to take on Chelsea's project as her mentor. Chelsea spent every evening after class and a late supper sitting Indian style on her bed, studying. She was too focused to get tired, but she knew it would hit her at some point.

Meredith, Anthony, and Chelsea formed a support group of sorts in their English class and sat together in the library, where they researched and planned for their projects. Miss Rogers critiqued Chelsea's grant and they submitted it for approval. Anthony wasn't yet satisfied with his own ideas related to painting.

Chelsea was the one to have the epiphany. "I heard Brad and Sonya talking about trying to find someone to create some scenery for the studio. They want to do the second act from *Giselle* in the spring, and Sonya has been saying they don't have the money to pay anybody. Willie's been thinking about building the sets for his project. Maybe you could paint it. Would they let you guys collaborate?"

Anthony's almond eyes narrowed for a moment and then lit up; the smile that followed lit up his entire face. "Maybe. That's brilliant! I'm going to ask Miss Rogers right now."

"So tell me about your project," she said to Meredith.

Meredith smiled her serene, slow, Cheshire Cat smile and rested her chin on her hand. "I've actually been working on mine for a while, but I didn't really know it until just a couple of weeks ago. You know my mom had breast cancer, right? Well, I decided to do a photojournalism project about survivors. You know, people who have survived bad things? I'm doing a book on my mom's case, and I'd like to get a couple more. I have lots of pictures of her before and after she was diagnosed, during her chemo, and when she lost her hair…and all the people who helped. I want to tell her story. Then I just talked to Keely Streeter."

"She has leukemia, right? I heard she made homecoming court."

"Yeah, she did. She's been at home getting special tutoring. Her brother wasn't a match to be her bone marrow donor, but they found someone from a donor bank who *is* a match. It's a girl from App, actually. They've met, and they're going to do the bone marrow transplant in about a month. I've been taking pictures of them, and interviewing them, and right now, I'm researching leukemia. It's been really emotional."

Chelsea was impressed. "Wow! That will be priceless for you and your mom. You said three. Have you found the third person?"

Meredith's warm green eyes opened wider, and she ran her fingers through her short brown hair, cut in a fashionable bob with one side a little longer than the other around her chin. "Actually, I told Kyle about this the other day in psychology class. I didn't think he was really paying attention to me…and then he said, 'You should talk to my mom.' What do you think he meant?"

Chelsea took a deep breath and exhaled slowly. "Well, she's grieving. His mom has been through a lot, you know, when his sister died her senior year in high school, and then last year when his dad committed suicide."

"Oh, I didn't know…I remember hearing about his dad dying, and I knew about his sister."

"Yeah. I'm a little surprised he thought she'd talk about it. But maybe it's what she needs to do."

"I'm sure it would be painful for her. I hope I'll be able to handle it, you know, gracefully?"

"I'm sure if anyone can, it will be you."

"Thanks. He said he would talk to her about it. I might need your moral support if I get the nod," she said.

By the second week in September, all the projects were on "Go" and everyone seemed to breathe a little easier. March seemed a tolerable distance away. Chelsea worked on her college applications and asked Meredith to take some pictures of her in the dance studio for the required portfolio for U.N.C.S.A. It was chilly in the mornings and sometimes foggy, and the days felt crisp. Fall was in the air. Football was all the buzz around school; the Wildcats had won three games and lost one. Kyle was getting to play wide receiver, and he and Anthony had connected for three touchdown passes so far. Kyle mentioned to her proudly that ASU was talking to Anthony about the following year. He explained that Anthony's family didn't have much money and that Anthony always thought he would join the service after high school. Playing for ASU would be a dream come true for him, especially with App's recent string of championships.

After lunch on Friday, Kyle and Chelsea held hands as they walked to her locker. She had forgotten her copy of *Ethan Frome* for English class. Anthony and Meredith waited to walk with her to class. As she stood with Kyle and opened her locker, they were aware of a commotion just down the hall...a book being slammed on the floor...loud, angry girls' voices.

"I just don't get it!" Elle's voice was harsh from several feet away. "What the hell does Kyle see in her? She's so *ordinary!*" She was practically yelling. Chelsea felt cold, and she stared at the book in her hand.

"There's *nothing* ordinary about Chelsea Davenport. You should just get over it," Kendra Williams muttered. "You're really starting to piss Rocky off."

Chelsea felt Kyle close beside her. He closed her locker quietly, but she would not look at him. She knew the blood was draining from her face, making her pale. "Come on," he said softly, and walked her toward Anthony and Meredith. He had circled his arm around her waist, and as they reached Anthony, Kyle handed him his books and said, "Hold this a minute?" He looked at Chelsea with a half-smile on his face and she felt his arm slide competently up her back. His other hand cradled her face as she felt herself being pushed back into a graceful dip. He closed his eyes and kissed her passionately—right there in the middle of the hallway! Someone was clapping and she heard a catcall or two. She realized then what he was doing, and she dissolved into laughter under the press of his mouth on hers. He pulled her up and kissed her again. "Will you be my date for the homecoming dance?" he asked earnestly.

"Yes," she breathed.

"Good," he smiled. "I really hoped you would. Well, have a nice day. I'll see you later," he said, then took his books from Anthony.

Coach Connelly walked by at that moment and said brusquely, "Hey! No PDA in the hall. Let's show a little restraint there, Mr. Davis!"

"Oh, you have no idea!" Kyle laughed in the cocky way Chelsea remembered from the eighth grade. His eyes sparkled as he strutted away, flicking his hair as he passed Kendra and Elle, who stared wide-eyed.

"Mmm-mmm!" Anthony said. "That was *hot*, man!"

• • •

The last Saturday in September was set to be "Chili Night." Glen planned to make his debut as a chef under Liz's supervision at the Davenport's backyard fire pit. They'd have a bonfire, and serve the debut batch of "Tom's Thunder Chili" in Styrofoam bowls at the fireside. Everybody who was anybody would be there. It was the only way Glen could escape from being grounded, and they'd make the most of the event. Liz had invited Glen's parents with his permission, and he had agreed, knowing it could only improve his image.

Kyle stopped by to help stack firewood and put together the bonfire after Chelsea arrived home from dance class. They went back to the kitchen, where Liz and Glen were huddled over the sink. Kyle called, "Hi, honey, what's for dinner?"

Glen turned around sheepishly and said, "Uh…maybe filet of finger?"

Liz followed him with a large band-aid, which she was attempting to fasten around his left index finger. "I was chopping slaw and wasn't paying attention," he said, chagrined.

"Oh, no!" Chelsea cried.

"I think this bandage will do the trick," Liz frowned. "It wouldn't do for me to have to take you to the hospital for stitches on your first day as chef. Your parents would never allow you to come back," she giggled.

"You'd better listen to your mentor," Kyle scolded him, then popped his friend on the rear.

"What else can we do, Mom?" Chelsea asked.

"Nothing. I think we're all set; don't you, Glen?"

"Yeah. This will simmer a few more hours and everybody's coming at seven. I'll be back here at six-thirty to throw the cornbread in the oven."

"Do you mind if I take Chelsea for a little drive up on the parkway?" Kyle asked Liz.

Liz smiled, somewhat used to this now. She knew they hadn't had a chance lately to do much of anything together. "Sure, but be back here about 5:30, okay?" Chelsea knew that was mom-code for six o'clock at the latest.

The three friends left the house together and Kyle held the door of the Jeep for Chelsea. She pulled her jacket around her against the chill. A bonfire will be perfect tonight, she thought. After they dropped Glen off at his house, Kyle headed toward the parkway.

"So, who's coming tonight?" Kyle asked.

"Abby, of course. She's going to pick up Glen, or maybe his parents will just bring him over. Meredith and Anthony, and Willie and Tia…"

"Not Dave Greer?" he said with a twinkle in his eye.

"I don't think so," she said, not amused that Kyle thought he had more on her.

"So, Anthony and Mer have kind of a thing going on?"

She smiled. "Yeah, I think so. They seem really cool together. I want to be Meredith when I grow up."

"That's high praise," he said, grinning. She grinned back. She loved it when he smiled. He was doing it more and more these days.

They drove on the parkway for a while. The leaves had just started to change colors and soon the parkway would be one huge traffic jam. She was glad they had come now. As the amber light of afternoon glanced across the windshield, she squinted, having forgotten sunglasses. She breathed deeply and thought of apple butter and raking leaves. As U2 played on the radio, she hummed along to "Beautiful Day." He had just pulled off onto one of the scenic overlooks when his phone played from his pocket. As he answered, she heard most of the conversation on the other end.

"Hi, Mom, what's up?" he said and then listened. Shelly explained something about being tied up with clients and needing him to do something. "Yeah…uh, I'm with Chelsea right now. We're about fifteen minutes from there, why? Yeah, hold on," he said, and covered the mouthpiece. To Chelsea, he asked, "Do you mind taking a little detour? It might take about half an hour or so."

She looked at her watch and thought there would be plenty of time to get back. "Sure."

"Okay, we'll go on over there now. If you're not there when I'm done, I'll just lock it back up." He disconnected and a frustrated sigh popped from his lips as he looked over at her. "Would you mind running over to the cabin with me?" She shook her head. "My mom's with clients and she wants to take them over there to show it. She wants me to go over and crank up the heat, and turn on some lights. You know, make it cozy. It shouldn't take too long."

"No, that's fine. I've never been there."

He seemed distracted and drove in silence for a few miles. They wound down the mountain, turned a couple of times, and ended up on a road she had never seen. He made a sharp turn and drove up a short driveway. A midsized rough-hewn cabin with a wide wraparound front porch and a red tin roof sat nestled quaintly in a clearing amidst rhododendrons and trees full of green and orange leaves. She breathed in sharply. "This is beautiful!"

"And for sale…" he said absently, sitting for a moment, unmoving.

It dawned on her then. "You haven't been here since that day, have you?" she said in a small voice. He shook his head and looked at the front door, then sorted through his keys. "Is this going to be hard for you?" she asked and then instantly regretted having posed such a stupid question.

"Maybe not," he said, glancing down at her hand. She reached over and squeezed his, and then he sighed and opened the door of the Jeep.

After he unlocked the front door, she followed him into a large room that included the kitchen and family room, surrounded by picture windows. The river was just visible through the windows, down through the trees. A rock fireplace at one end of the room opened onto a sunroom on the other side. A fishing creel hung above the mantle and two antique rods crossed over it. Candles of varied sizes adorned the mantle, accompanied by a collection of bear figures, some dressed in fishing vests. Chelsea thought the fresh smell of the wood walls and floors was heavenly. Kyle went to the wall, flipped on indirect track lights, and adjusted the thermostat as she took in the surroundings. She peeked inside a doorway, which revealed a bedroom with a dark metal bed covered in a multicolored earth tone quilt, with photographs of the river and waterfalls on the walls. He took it all in as well, and she saw his eyes stop and linger momentarily on the brown leather couch in the main room. He looked out the window at the large wraparound deck and then said to her, "I think I'll go out there and blow off some of those leaves."

"Okay. Do you want me to do anything? Maybe dust a little?"

He looked relieved somehow, and said, "Yeah, sure. There should be a cloth and some stuff in here." He opened the cabinet under the sink and she found what she needed. "Thanks, that's a good idea," he said, with an almost-smile, and went out a side door. As she sprayed the cloth with furniture polish and wiped it across the smooth rich wood of the kitchen table, she heard the blower crank to life. She watched him out the window, in his gray plaid flannel shirt, concentrating on sweeping the air back and forth across the deck, blowing leaves off and over the side. He finished and looked out toward the river, then seemed to remember that she was inside. She heard him bumping around outside, putting away the blower and shutting the door as she folded the cloth and returned it to its place under the sink.

He sniffed. "Smells good," he said. He looked around and leaned against the kitchen counter next to the sink where she stood. He crossed his arms the way she had done. "My dad built this place."

"I heard that. It's fantastic."

"So, this is where my old man used to hang out."

"Nice. Did your mom come here with him?"

"I guess not, at least, not toward the end. Not when he was up here to figure it all out and needing his space. I did the same thing I guess."

"What? Figured it out?"

He sighed and laughed, "Yeah, up at school, by myself when I wanted to be, which was easy to make happen."

"And did you figure it out?" she asked, searching for his eyes.

"Yeah, I thought I did. But maybe I had it all wrong," he said. He met her gaze with a vulnerable expression.

"So, what did you come up with?"

"I just…thought that in the end, we're all really alone, you know? You just have to cope with whatever you're dealt all by yourself…and you just…move on. It's really not that hard."

It was the saddest thing she had ever heard. Her heart ached to hear it coming from his mouth.

"But…what about love?" she asked softly.

"What about it?" he said just above a whisper and looking at her dead on.

"You don't think anybody loves you?" She felt a desperate warmth flood her face. He looked ashamed, somehow.

"What difference does it make? You're still alone."

"I love you, Kyle," she said with certainty in her voice and her eyes locked on his. "And no, you're *not* alone." After a moment, he reached for her arm tentatively and she moved in to embrace him, pulling him closer to her.

He gathered her into him and held her, rocked her, breathed in the smell of her and sighed. "Chelsea, I love you, too," he murmured against her face. He buried his face into her neck and she felt his warm breath against her skin. "Oh, God," he whispered. She felt wet tears, hot on her neck, and pulled him closer, knotting her fingers in his hair. When she kissed the back of his neck, he took a deep breath and exhaled roughly. "This changes everything for me," he said softly and held her face in both hands. "You're doing it again, cracking open my soul."

"Is that bad?" she whispered, and unable to let go of him, she pressed herself into him.

"No, I'm getting used to it. And I think I like it. It's just so...unexpected!" he closed his eyes again and sniffed. "I never know what's going to happen with you. It's good, though." He kissed her, just as unable to release her, and they stood there, rocking together in the kitchen. The sound of tires on gravel shook them out of the moment. He let her go and wiped his face with his hands. She combed her fingers through her hair and straightened her clothes as they heard car doors closing and enthusiastic remarks from the people in the driveway. She checked her watch and knew it was time to go.

He pulled open the door and greeted his mother and the fiftyish couple with her. As they climbed the stairs and crossed the porch, Chelsea appeared beside him and smiled at Shelly. A worried look clouded Shelly's face, but she greeted her cheerily, taking her hand and giving it a squeeze. Shelly introduced them, and then Kyle told her they'd be heading on out. The couple was enthralled with the place and immediately began asking Shelly questions. "Oh, just *smell* the *wood*, Jim," the woman said.

"This is how a mountain cabin should be," Jim remarked and followed his wife into the main room. Kyle's eyes fell on the couch one last time, and then he closed the door behind them.

•••

They decided "Chili Night" was to be an annual event, and Glen would do the cooking from here on out. When they all came back next year from college for homecoming weekend, they would converge on the Davenport's bonfire pit and catch up over chili and S'mores. The Davenports stood by the fire, chatting amiably with Glen's parents, who seemed to be enjoying themselves. Kitty was there for the occasion as well, tucked under a plaid wool blanket. She listened eagerly to Willie, who entertained everyone with his mile-a-minute commentary on anything anyone wanted to talk about. They sat around the fire in chairs or on the large logs surrounding the fire.

SEPTEMBER

"Why do they call this 'Tom's Thunder Chili'?" asked Anthony, stirring his bowlful and tasting it.

"You'll find out soon enough…so I'm told," joked Glen. Everyone laughed.

"It's a good thing we're outside then," laughed Willie. "Just everybody, turn your butt away from the fire!"

Tia rolled her eyes. "And to think this guy is going to be my escort for homecoming!"

Liz took interest. "Oh, that's right. Congratulations, Tia! Chelsea told us you'll be on the court next week. Who else is representing the senior class?"

"Keely Streeter and Elle McClarin," she said.

"What are you wearing?" asked Abby and Meredith at the same time; then they giggled.

"Oh, girl, you should see it," Willie cried, scrunching his face in ecstasy.

"It's a gold beaded gown with a one-sided thing here," Tia said, indicating her right shoulder.

"Well, it sounds beautiful. I hope the weather will be mild and you don't freeze," Liz said.

"Oh, my job is to keep her warm," Willie chimed in.

"I'm going to wear my coat until we start to drive up to the float," Tia said.

Chelsea looked at Kyle; she remembered he had asked his mother whether Tia's father could use his dad's convertible for the ceremony, and Willie and Tia had been thrilled. He was turned toward Chelsea, one knee bent in across the log they shared, and she mirrored his position. There was cheese on the side of his mouth from the chili, and she reached up to wipe it off. He grinned and held her hand there for a moment, kissing her palm. She felt his face, rubbed her thumb over the scratchiness of his jaw and chin, and looked contentedly back at him. When a flash of light caught her eye, she realized Meredith had just taken their picture.

"Busted," she said to them and smiled her contagious smile.

"Now that's Facebook material for you, Kyle," Abby said and winked at Chelsea.

"I'll tag you guys and send it to you," said Meredith. "You need to get hooked up, Chelsea. I want to be your friend."

"I guess I need to get a camera," mused Chelsea. "I'll need it for the project for sure." She was watching Meredith snap photos of the food and everyone eating for Glen's presentation.

A boom box was playing in the background, and Glen was singing along comically to "Walk This Way." The chili, slaw, and cornbread were soon cleaned out, and they moved on to roasting marshmallows for S'mores. Tom had taken on the job of loading marshmallows onto people's skewers, and Glen was placing the chocolate bars on top of graham crackers when Michael Jackson's "Thriller" began to play.

Willie jumped up, beside himself with fun. "Come on, baby girl; this is what we *do*!" He pulled Chelsea up by the hand. They had learned the dance together and performed it at a Halloween festival last year. They took on the ghoulish persona, which was even more effective next to the fire, and the guys howled at Willie's facial expressions as he and Chelsea danced the rigid, lurching moves. Abby and Tia joined them, and everyone laughed at their attempts to look dour and garish. Meredith pulled Anthony, Glen, and Kyle into the act, and soon they were all stepping it out in the yard. She snapped several pictures, some through the flames of the bonfire for effect. Kitty laughed so hard she had to wipe her eyes.

When it was over, Abby cried, "Oh, this is *so* going in my show! Will you two do it, and you guys too?"

Chelsea and Willie agreed, but Kyle and Anthony looked skeptically at each other. "I'm wearing a *disguise*," Anthony declared, but then laughed and gave in. "It *was* fun!"

"I'll do it if you do it, Glen," said Kyle, laughing and shaking his head.

"I'm in," said Glen, clapping his hands and rubbing them together. "You should turn out most of the lights and get some dry ice going. Then we could slink in through the audience and be like…*touchin'* people and creeping them out! We could smear dirt on us and have *leaves* sticking out of our hair and wear raggedy clothes…" He was on a roll.

Act one of Abby's variety show was solidified, and they sat around the fire for a while longer before the group dispersed for the night. Kyle was collecting trash and shoving it into a garbage bag as Willie slid onto his spot beside Chelsea on the log.

"So, *now* I know what psycho-blondie has on you," he said wickedly, eyeing Kyle across the fire pit. "I guess I was wrong about her and Rocky. She likes *him*," he said. "How come you didn't say anything? Afraid of hurting my feelings?" he laughed at her gently.

"I don't know," she said, shaking her head. "I'm so afraid it's going to fall apart if I acknowledge it, you know?"

"Oh, big word, girlfriend. But I know where you're comin' from. So he's the real deal for you?"

She hugged her knees and stared into the fire, her chin propped on her arms. "Just stop it, okay?" she laughed and rolled her eyes.

"Nah, I'm trying to be supportive here. I got your back on this one. Y'all got it going on. *I* should know, right?" He grinned at her, showing off his gap, and then winking at Tia.

She laughed and grabbed the back of his neck and rocked him back and forth. "All right, buddy. Thanks. I'm gonna help clean up now," she said, standing up and helping to carry things inside.

Chapter 8

THE RUG

Doughton County High School's homecoming game against Ashe County packed the stands of the new stadium and the band was bumping. The temperature was forecast to dip into the upper forties during the evening, which wasn't too bad, unless you were wearing a strapless evening gown at the halftime homecoming court presentation. Chelsea was glad she was not among the contestants, but the excitement was palpable, more for the long-standing football rivalry than for the court. It was rumored that recruiting scouts from a couple of colleges would be there, and the usual news media planned special coverage for the game. During lunch that day, Anthony, Kyle, and Glen discussed who might be watching them that evening. Anthony hoped to have a scout from Appalachian State and Kyle was banking on NC State's people being present.

Abby insisted on driving that night. Chelsea was puzzled at her resolve.

"I thought Glen's house arrest was over," Chelsea said at lunch.

"It is, but Kyle promised to drive him tonight so that if *I* drove, we'd each get to have *alone* time later. You get it, right?"

"Sure, I guess. We're all still going to the Mellow Mushroom afterwards, aren't we?"

"Yeah, I think everyone is still on for that," Abby said distractedly.

They wedged their way into the stands with Meredith, in their red and gold attire. It was different not having Willie and even David Greer to sit with during the game. Willie was escorting Tia and Dave was Keely Streeter's escort, which Chelsea thought was sweet. Meredith planned to meet Keely's mom and Keely's bone marrow donor at the track just before halftime. She would need to get in place to take pictures, partly for the yearbook, and partly to document Keely's story of surviving leukemia. They all hoped it would be a self-fulfilling prophecy.

The score went back and forth during the first half, with Ashe County ending on top fourteen to seven at the break. Anthony had connected with Kyle for the only touchdown, and Kyle was expected to play defense in the second half. The cheerleaders were out in full force, having combined the JV and Varsity squads for more effect, since girls from each squad were in the court. At the half, the presentation float was driven to the fifty yard line, and the procession of convertible sports cars drove slowly down the track, displaying each young lady, the announcer naming her, her escort, and who drove her car.

Abby and Chelsea stood on the bleachers on tiptoe to catch glimpses of the beautiful gowns and hairstyles being displayed from the backseats of the cars. The girls, on the arms of their well-dressed young escorts, were barely recognizable in their finery. Chelsea pulled her coat around her and hopped up and down for warmth, her red scarf pulled up over her chin, again glad she was not among the girls on the court. When the seniors were announced, she and Abby paid particular attention. Keely Streeter rode elegantly atop the back seat of a black Mercedes convertible, the only contestant to wear her coat for the ride. Her usual short blonde hair was long tonight, due to extensions her friends had attached to the wig she usually wore, and it suited her well. As the car slowed to a stop and Dave got out and reached up to assist her, she removed the coat, which revealed

THE RUG

a warm strawberry pink gown cut high around the neck and low in the back. Meredith had explained that it was the perfect style for covering her port-o-cath, and the color made her radiant. Dave took her hand and escorted her to the float, his hand at her back constantly.

To oohs and aahs, Tia came next, glamorous in her enormous smile and gold beaded dress, hair swept up to the side and curled, in keeping with the one-strap theme of the dress. Chelsea and Abby whistled and whooped for them as they were announced over the loudspeakers. Willie looked equally dashing in his black suit and proud smile. He took her hand and made a flourish as he helped her out of Kyle's father's silver Audi. They were perfectly matched as two of the shorter people on the court, but definitely two of the most stylish.

Last, Elle McClarin made her entrance on the back of a classic red Stingray, wearing a black sequined dress with a scandalous neckline, with her shoulder length blonde hair straight and sleek. Since Rocky was on the football team and could not escort her, she had asked her last year's heartthrob, Richard Spencer, who had returned from college for the homecoming occasion. There was plenty of talk about how that was likely to go over. With Elle, there was always drama.

Chelsea and Abby could not pick out Meredith in the crowd with all the people—parents, students, and alumni—as the announcement of the runners up and the queen began. Chelsea watched the faces of the three seniors as the queen was announced. "Keely Streeter!" rang out over the loudspeakers and the crowd cheered and applauded their agreement. Elle's smile remained glued in place without even a flinch, and Tia jumped up and down, smiling and squeezing Willie's arm, as a somewhat shell-shocked Keely accepted her bouquet of red roses and the silver tiara.

Later when Tia and Willie joined them in the stands, Chelsea saw Tia hand something to Abby, who subtly slipped it in her pocket. David joined them later, and mentioned that Keely had gotten cold and had gone home with her parents. Meredith was still on the sidelines, taking pictures for the yearbook.

The second half got underway and Willie was back with his usual running commentary of the game, not so much about the cheerleaders. Tia was changing clothes and would meet up with them later. "There are all kinds of scouts here tonight!" Willie said excitedly to Chelsea and Abby. "What you bet App gives Anthony a serious nod tonight—and those State boys are all over your man, Kyle!" he said approvingly. "With Kyle back in there on defense, they're not scoring any time soon!"

Ashe County lost possession and Rocky Santoro ran one in for a touchdown as the crowd went wild. It went back and forth a while with Anthony unable to pass to his double-teamed wide receivers because of Kyle's performance in the first half. The handoffs to the running backs weren't getting anywhere either and the third quarter was over. As the fourth quarter began, Ashe County started a drive, and made three first-down runs in a row. The Doughton band cranked up to give the crowd and the team a boost. Chelsea watched Kyle running down the field. He eyed his receiver, shifted to the right when he shifted, and watched the quarterback. Then, explosively, he picked off the pass in midair at the thirty-three yard line and took off the other way. The crowd exploded. Glen blocked for him as he gained ground, dodging one more tackle and passed the forty, the thirty, the twenty, and then he streaked into the end zone. The stadium erupted and the band played the school fight song.

"Oh, man! Did you see that? Now, *that's* opening up a can of *whoop-ass!* That's your man's second pick six of the season, baby! One more and he has a record. Look at him," he said laughing. Chelsea screamed and pumped her arms in the air and they all high-fived each other. The players chest-bumped each other and Kyle talked animatedly, helmet in hand, and appreciatively slapped Glen on the back. The extra point was good and the score was twenty-one to fourteen. With less than five minutes

THE RUG

remaining on the clock, the special teams got back in position, ready for the kick. As Chelsea watched, Kyle picked out his man and shadowed him in front again. The handoff was nowhere near them, nor was it on the next play. Then on the third down, the lob came at Kyle's receiver and they lined up again, doing the same dance as before. The receiver caught the ball in midair and came down ready to turn and run down the field. Kyle was right on him as he landed and made the tackle upon his contact with the ground. They smacked hard on the ground to the groans from the crowd. Kyle popped back up, and extended his hand to pull his man up. The player was down, and Kyle waited a minute to let him catch his breath. He stepped to the side and then back, extending his hand again. The player did not move.

"Wide receiver number 51 for Ashe County is down, tackled by number 78, Kyle Davis, for the Wildcats," the announcer reported. There was a lull in the stadium as the crowd waited for the player to move and get to his feet. Kyle watched and then bent over him, taking off his helmet and looking for the trainers to come out onto the field. He raked his hand through his hair and paced back and forth, as the trainers knelt beside the motionless receiver, identified as Eric Bennington. Kyle paced some more and one of the officials placed a hand on his back and spoke to him. He nodded and ran back to the sideline to stand with Coach Connelly, who had his arms crossed over his chest. They spoke a moment, heads together, Connelly's hand on Kyle's shoulder. Chelsea held her breath, her hand covering her mouth, as Willie muttered, "He's not moving. This can't be good."

Kendra Williams went down on one knee, and the other cheerleaders followed her lead. Kyle stood with Coach Connelly and one of the news cameramen on the sideline, reviewing the play on the camera screen. Willie showed this to Chelsea, and as Coach Connelly placed his hand on Kyle's back and nodded, Willie said, "It was a clean hit." David Greer agreed. Eric Bennington remained motionless on the field, and Kyle continued to pace the sidelines, with Glen and Anthony talking to him. EMTs carried a stretcher onto the field and attended the player. Kyle went down on both knees and pushed his hair back, held it with his hands, and bowed his head. His Wildcats teammates knelt down around him. It was eerily quiet in the stands as they all watched Eric being taken to the ambulance.

Willie hugged Chelsea with one arm. "Say a prayer, baby," he said in a low voice.

"God, I hope he's okay," Chelsea murmured. Abby held Chelsea's hand and they looked at each other helplessly. Chelsea's heart was racing and she heard comments in the crowd. "Man, wouldn't you hate to be the kid that hit him?" There was a lot of head shaking and she saw many grim faces.

Eventually, the game resumed, and the last minutes played out fruitlessly as Kyle sat on the bench with his head in his hands. The taste of the win that had been so thrilling just moments before felt surreal and inconsequential. Students and parents drifted solemnly out of the stands, met up with friends, and made plans without the revelry they had all anticipated. Tia had returned in warmer clothes and found Willie and the group. They waited a while and talked about what to do next. Chelsea knew Kyle would not want to hang out and eat pizza somewhere, even though that had been the plan. She figured he had skipped his shower and would want to find out Eric's condition as soon as possible. They made their way through the crowd to the field house, and as she had predicted, Kyle was at the door in jeans and a light blue sweater listening to Coach Connelly talking on his cell phone. Glen appeared behind him, pulled his own sweater down over a T-shirt, and listened as well. The coach snapped the phone shut, talked to them briefly, and then went back into the field house as Kyle spotted her and walked over. He took her hands and pulled her into a hug.

"Hey! I'm so sorry," she said. "What have you heard?"

"We don't know much yet. He's still unconscious. They just got him

THE RUG

into the ER, and they're going to do a CAT scan. I'd kinda like to go over there."

"Sure, of course. I'll go with you."

Abby handed him a set of keys and gave him a sideways hug. "I'm sorry, too. The guys say it was a clean hit."

"I know…I thought it was. I don't know what happened. He was just out cold, just like that," he said, wiping his hand across his jaw and shaking his head. "We looked at it on the sports cam and it didn't seem that hard, either…no flag or anything." Kyle looked at the keys in his hand and looked at Chelsea. "I'm sorry. This was supposed to be a surprise. My mom gave me the Audi for the weekend. I guess it won't seem so special right now. Would you rather go with everybody else and maybe I can call you later?" he asked, looking concerned.

"No. No, I want to be with you right now," she said, hanging onto his other hand and snuggling next to him. He squeezed her hand in return.

"I think we've all decided to go over to the hospital," said Glen, looking up from his conversation with David, Willie, and Anthony, who had just appeared from the field house.

"Hey, y'all," said Anthony. "Coach said he'll be there when everybody clears out. Their coach just left to go on over."

They walked to their separate cars. Kyle opened the door of the sleek Audi and tucked Chelsea inside, then put up the top before it growled to life. Chelsea had never touched a car like this, much less ridden in one, but at the moment, the effect was lost on her. The smell of rich leather was pungent, and it still had its new car smell. He turned down the music, which sounded amazing on the sound system, and backed carefully around the people still milling about.

"Are you okay?" she said, cautiously, not knowing what to do.

"Actually, I'm a little shaky, but I think I can get us where we need to go."

It didn't take long to get to the hospital. They looked for the appropriate signs, and Chelsea pointed him to the visitor parking lot near the emergency room. Other cars' lights peeled in behind them. They walked hand in hand through the automatic doors and asked at the desk about Eric. The attending nurse told them to have a seat in the waiting room. A familiar woman with salt-and-pepper hair came out of the back, holding her coat over her arm, trying to get Kyle's attention.

"Oh, hey, Mrs. Connelly," Kyle said to her.

She hugged him around the neck. "Hi, Kyle! I came in the ambulance with Eric and the assistant coach. His mother wasn't at the game, and Dean is trying to get hold of her to give her directions. It may be a while before she can get here. His coach just got here. They just took him back for the scan. He's still out. Honey, why don't you sit down? You don't look so good." She took his arm firmly and steered him to a chair in the waiting room. Chelsea felt so relieved. Thank God someone was in control! They sat in chairs and watched others they knew from school come in and mill around. No one knew what to say or do.

Shelly Davis appeared at the door. She looked frantic. "Why didn't you answer your cell phone?" she cried as Kyle stood up to accept her hug.

"I didn't hear it. Sorry, maybe it's dead."

"You could have called me. I was so worried."

He shook his head. "I'm sorry, Mom. I just drove directly here. I'm not really thinking straight, I guess." Chelsea found a vending machine and deposited coins for a cup of coffee for him, as Coach Connelly arrived and got an update. The nurse's assistant called Mrs. Connelly back inside. Coach made Kyle sit again. The little throng of people who had surrounded him had abated a bit. When Chelsea handed him the coffee

THE RUG

cup, he looked up at her gratefully. His hands were shaking, and he tried to hold it steady without success.

"Here, I'll hold it until you need it," she said and Coach relinquished his seat to her. He stood next to Kyle and talked to him in a soothing voice. "Look, Kyle, you made a clean hit. I've talked to their coach. We don't know what happened here, but it's not your responsibility. I know you feel bad, but you were just doing your job out there tonight. No one's holding this against you." She noticed he did not say, "He'll be okay," or, "Everything will be all right." The grim look on his face told her to prepare for bad news. It was not lost on Kyle either, and he looked down at the floor and sniffed. She put her hand on his back and rubbed his shoulder. His mother sat on his other side and patted his leg.

Chelsea looked up at their friends; some of them were standing in a circle talking, and some of them were sitting in the chairs, waiting and watching the other happenings in the waiting room. A mother with her two children sat across from them; the younger child was whimpering on her lap, holding his ear. Two big men sat in the corner, talking on their cell phones and chewing gum. Another man was being directed to go outside to smoke a cigarette. Abby raised her eyebrows and tried a small smile in Chelsea's direction. Players from the other team began to arrive, looking around for their coach who was still in the ER with Eric.

Coach Connelly's cell phone rang. He stepped aside to take the call. It was Eric's mother, and Coach updated her and gave her directions to the hospital. "Can I call you right back? I see my wife coming out right now…sure."

Mrs. Connelly looked competent and serene, even in this situation. She saw Shelly and waved a greeting as she went to speak to her husband. They talked a moment, and then he called Mrs. Bennington back. After Coach Connelly had a brief conversation with her and nodded to his wife, Mrs. Connelly went back into the ER with his cell phone. Coach returned to Kyle's group and told them that the doctors were prepping Eric for surgery and that his parents would be there within the next twenty minutes.

Shelly put her arm around Kyle, who held his head in his hands. He seemed to be dissolving in front of them. "It's okay, sweetheart," she said to him soothingly. Chelsea held his knee; as she pulled it close to her own, she could feel him shaking.

The conversation among the teenagers began to pick up. Some of it was noticeably louder and some was not about the situation at hand. Coach Connelly corralled them all to tell them that he and the team appreciated them all showing up, and that it looked like it was going to be a long night for Eric and his family. He suggested they all go on home, and he said he would pass along more information as it became available. Most of the kids took off; a few from Doughton came over to speak to Kyle and press his hand before they left. Chelsea stood up and went to talk to Abby and their group. She still held Kyle's coffee. They wanted to stay and support Kyle, but they didn't want to get in the way, either.

"Will you call me when you know anything?" Abby said into Chelsea's hair as they hugged each other. The boys stood close by.

"Yeah, I'll let you guys know. It could go on for a while."

Before they left, Shelly walked over and said to Chelsea, "Honey, why don't you go on with them? We'll be fine here, and Kyle will call you when we know something." Chelsea's heart sank.

"No, Mom, let her stay…if she wants," Kyle stood beside her and held her around the waist, to Shelly's surprised look. "If you want," he said considerately, and she nodded immediately.

"Kyle, it could be a very long time. I think you should go on with your friends, Chelsea," she said, taking command of the coffee cup.

"Oh my God," he muttered, rolling his eyes. "At least let me walk her

THE RUG

out," he said and walked to the door with them. The rest of the group went a few steps to the parking lot and held up to wait for her as he gathered her up in his arms and buried his face in her hair. "I don't know what her deal is. I'm so sorry. This is turning out so…awful. I just want to be with you right now. It's probably for the best, though. It might be a really long night, and you have dance tomorrow."

"I don't care," she said, clinging to him and holding his head. "Will you call me? Anytime, okay? I don't care if you wake me up; just please let me know."

He looked at her with anguished eyes, nodded, and pressed his lips together. "I will."

"I love you," she said, her voice breaking as he kissed her powerfully and held her one last time before turning back to the automatic doors of the ER.

The surgery did not go well, and Kyle and his mother went home around three in the morning with no real news of any improvement. Chelsea had not slept well after telling her parents what had happened and getting in bed after midnight, herself. Saturday afternoon, she came back into the house after her dance class and hung the beautiful crimson dress on the coat hook by the front door. The night before, she had packed a bag with her shoes for the homecoming dance and other things she would need over at Abby's house, where they would get ready. The house was empty, except for Fella, who licked her toes. Tom and Liz were tailgating with Jay and his friends before the Appalachian game. Wayne and Becky had picked up Kitty, since the plan was for Chelsea to be at the dance all evening. She sighed and wondered how much any of them would really enjoy the dinner and the dance, even if it were in a nice hotel this time. She had just set Fella's food bowl outside the back door with him when she heard a knock on the front door.

Kyle stood at the door, freshly showered, and wearing her favorite gray plaid flannel shirt, but his face was anything but composed. She looked questioningly at him and opened the door, but he did not step forward.

"Eric died this morning," he said and caught his breath, putting his hand over his face.

She gasped and her hand went to her mouth; then she reached out for him and touched his arm. "No! Oh...*no*," she gasped again, her heart pounding.

He turned away, covered his face with both hands, and bent over, walking toward the front porch steps. She was right behind him, trying to steady him as he collapsed onto the top step and fell into her as she sat down beside him. He was sobbing and holding his face. She rocked him back and forth, held his shoulders, and tried to soothe him. It was freezing so she hugged him closer, pressing the palm of her hand to the side of his face as if, somehow, she could hold him together.

They sat there for a moment, and she was about to suggest they go inside when he spoke. "I killed him, Chelsea," he said just above a whisper, his voice thick with anguish.

She shook her head firmly. "No! *No* you didn't, Kyle. You played *football*, and you knocked him down, and for some reason he died, but you did *not kill him*." She pulled his face around to make him look at her. "You weren't responsible for this," she repeated the words Coach Connelly said to him the night before. "Come inside. It's freezing out here," she said, taking his hand and pulling him through the door. The old wooden floor creaked as she led him over to the couch and tossed a couple of soft pillows out of the way. They sank down into it together. He sprawled beside her and she held his head to her heart as one would do with a small child.

"Tell me what happened."

He shivered as he geared himself up for the conversation. "Coach Connelly called the house this morning about eleven o'clock and told my mom that Eric had been on life support and that the family took him off as soon as they were all together…but he died before they could take out the tube."

She stroked his hair and kissed his head. "What do they think happened?"

"They don't know. 'It never happens like this,' they said. Something could've been there that they didn't know about and when he took the hit, it started a hemorrhage."

"Like an aneurysm or something?"

"I guess…they really don't know." He was quiet a moment.

"You never slept, did you?" she said, stroking his face.

"No, not really. Eric's dad called me about an hour after we talked to Coach Connelly. That was the toughest conversation I've ever had," his voice drifted off.

"What did he say?"

"That it wasn't my fault, that I shouldn't feel the way I feel right now…"

"I'm so, *so sorry!*" she murmured into his forehead.

He sighed. "God, this *sucks!* If there was ever a time to get drunk…" He sat up a little and saw her dress hanging across the room. He looked up at her anxiously and said, "Chelsea, about the dance…"

"Oh, I totally understand. We can't go…"

He shook his head. "You'd be a knockout in that dress. Where's everybody?"

When she explained, he smiled. "Your dad is like…the tailgating king, isn't he?"

She laughed, "Yeah, he is. He has all the spirit wear in all the colors:

red for State…purple for ECU where Charley went and, of course, black and gold for App."

He thought a moment. "Hmm…What is he gonna do when you're at the School of the Arts?"

"I guess he'll just have to grow a goatee and learn how to drink *chardonnay*," she laughed.

A laugh bubbled up from him too. "I knew there was a reason I had to come here today. You keep me sane," he said, placing his hand on her heart. "I had to see you today."

She kissed him and snuggled his head against her again. She reached for the phone beside the sofa and called Abby to explain the situation. Abby was with Glen, and they understood completely. She mentioned that she wasn't sure she and Glen felt much like going to the dance either, after hearing this sad news. Chelsea set the phone on the sofa beside her, felt Kyle breathe deep and heavy, and realized he had fallen asleep on her shoulder. Smiling, she settled herself comfortably and stroked his hand, which still rested over her heart. He would need all the sleep he could get, and she was willing to stay like that as long as they could. She put her head back on the sofa, realizing that she, too, was exhausted, and dozed off.

Awakening, she heard the familiar song play from his back pocket. He did not budge, and she could not fathom how to reach his phone in their current position. By the time she thought about how to shift him over to reach his pocket, the phone was silent and she relaxed again. In another minute, the house phone rang and she answered it quietly, "Hello?"

"Chelsea? Hi, it's Shelly Davis. Is Kyle there?"

"Yes, ma'am…he's asleep right now," she said quietly and she felt a stiff silence from the other end.

"What? Where is he?" she said, sounding confused, or irritated. It was

THE RUG

hard to read her tone. Kyle stirred and sat up, wiping his mouth with the back of his hand, slightly disoriented.

"It's your mom," Chelsea said under her breath, and then to his mother, "He fell asleep while we were sitting here on the couch…talking." Did that sound bad?

"Could you have him come on home? Coach Connelly is coming over here, and people have been calling him. I think the man from NC State wants to come by, too. He's still in Boone."

"Sure, I'll tell him. Bye," she said and Shelly thanked her as they disconnected. It was an odd kind of conversation, she thought, and she'd started to glean the difficulty Kyle must have had in the past trying to be open with her.

"Okay," he said sleepily, the gloom returning to his handsome face. "I guess I've been summoned." He kissed the back of her hand and started to stand up.

"Wait just a minute before you leave," she said, getting up and going to the kitchen. She returned a moment later with a glass of water, a bottle of Tylenol, a wet cloth, and a stick of mint gum. "Survival kit," she explained to his questioning look. "I always have a headache after I cry," she said, holding up the Tylenol and giving him the glass of water. He took two of the pills with a long swig of water, and she held the cold wet cloth over his eyes. He groped around like a blind person and comically grabbed her shoulders and hugged her.

"God, you're an angel," he whispered, and she handed him the stick of gum.

"*That's* for your recruiter," she said, smiling at him, and pulling him off the sofa.

• • •

He called her late Saturday night and asked her to imagine the two of them dancing a slow dance together, since they hadn't gone to the dance. He told her he imagined her in the red dress and it was driving him crazy. He sounded subdued, but better than she expected. He wanted to come back up to her house, but his mom was keeping a close watch on him. Earlier, he'd met with the recruiter and Coach Connelly, who had tried to convince him nothing had changed and encouraged him to put one foot in front of the other. They said goodnight as she lay snuggled in her bed, looking through her window up at the stars.

The next day she tried to call him and text him without success and she wondered whether his phone had died or he had lost it. It was nerve-wracking not to talk to him. She needed to hear his voice and know he was okay. She felt the loss, too, and called Abby for consolation. She spent the day listening to classical music, trying to select something to which she could choreograph her audition piece. Later, after dinner, she went to her room and sat on her bed. She was reading her current novel assignment from English class when she heard the doorbell ring. Tom answered it and she heard him greeting Shelly Davis. Liz had been expecting her, apparently, from an earlier call she had made to Shelly, checking on her and Kyle. Why hadn't she thought to call Kyle's home phone? Tom excused himself to his office, and Liz opened a bottle of wine. Chelsea listened for a moment, but the conversation was muffled, so she guiltily slid the rug away from the grate to get better reception. They had been talking about the injury, the funeral arrangements, and the recruiter who had paid them a visit.

Liz was talking. "How's Kyle doing after all this?"

"Oh, Liz, he is *just devastated*. He was making such good progress from everything else, but this has just pulled the rug right out from under him again. I made him take a sleeping pill so he could rest, so I thought it would be okay to come up here and visit. I felt like I just needed to *vent* to someone..."

"I'm sure it's been a hard couple of days for both of you," Liz commented.

"So many people called him. Every time he would drift off, that damn cell phone would ring again, so I just took it. He tried to do some homework, but I can tell he can't concentrate. I turned the ringer off our phone at one point."

She heard Liz setting down her glass. "Well, I know Chelsea is very concerned about him," she said. "She mentioned that she hadn't been able to get in touch with him today."

"Mmm," said Shelly. "You know, they really seem to be getting serious. It concerns me a little."

"Why, sweetie?"

"Well, you should have seen the way they were together the other night at the hospital. They seem so...intimate with each other. Nothing against Chelsea, but I think they're way too young to be this involved, don't you?"

Chelsea held her breath and felt her eyebrows crank upward as she sat alone on her bed in the lamplight.

Liz laughed gently. "I do think she likes him, but I don't think it's quite like that."

She imagined Shelly shaking her head. "I don't know...the way he *looks* at her...and the way she looks at him."

Liz sounded urgent then. "Was Chelsea doing something *inappropriate?*"

"No, not really. It's just this *connection* they obviously have. I was just surprised. I hope it doesn't get out of hand, you know?"

"Oh, Shelly, I think you're overreacting a little."

"Can you blame me, Liz?"

Liz was quiet and then she said, "I guess not, Shelly…but I don't think you should worry about it. Chelsea is very level-headed." She was quiet again for a moment. "You must have really worried about Kyle in that department when he was away at school."

Shelly chuckled. "Oh yes, I certainly did. We knew that even at the boys' school, we were giving up a lot of control. But now that he's back, I think I worry about him even more because I can see him every day. He grew up and I missed it."

"Oh, but it's a good thing, isn't it?"

"Sure. I *cook* a lot more. That boy can eat! We talk more, too. He seems mature, focused. I think he's trying to *reinvent* himself to be nothing like Stu. He seems really *together* in a way, but you never know. I just don't want him to make the same mistakes…"

"Have faith in him, Shelly. He's been through so much. He might be stronger than you think."

They chatted some more about her business and the settling of Stuart's estate, and then Shelly mentioned that the cabin had been sold. Chelsea's heart pounded and she thought of Jim and his wife who had loved the cabin the same day she saw it. She was sure it was a relief for Kyle's mother to have that settled, but sad for them, too. She panicked, and wondered what would happen if the house also sold. Shelly explained to Liz that she was going to pull the house off the market until after the holidays, and soon Chelsea lost interest in the conversation.

At school the next day, banners were posted here and there in the commons and in the halls. *We love our Wildcats*! A smaller red and gold sign with a big red heart was taped to Kyle's locker, *DHS Loves # 78*, made by Kendra and Tia, she had heard. He met her at their lockers before the bell, looking miserable. She hugged him wordlessly and he sighed heavily.

THE RUG

"This is going to be some kind of day. Everybody'll be talking," he said vacantly.

"I wasn't sure you'd be here. I tried to call you yesterday…"

"I know…my mom's had me under quarantine, like I'm some kind of *freak*. It's really starting to piss me off. Do you know she drugged me last night so I could sleep?"

"Well, you probably needed it," she said as they walked to class. People looked at them and showed Kyle sympathetic glances. "She was at our house last night, so I heard her telling my mom about it."

"Yeah, well I feel like a freakin' zombie right now."

"Are you going to practice today?" she asked carefully.

"Yep, putting one foot in front of the other. Might as well get on with it."

At lunch, he was not waiting for her as he usually did. She figured he was already in the cafeteria where they had been eating now that the weather was cooler. She passed the door to the terrace on her way to buy a bottle of water from the vending machine and she saw him, sitting outside on the end of their bench, probably freezing, and staring straight ahead. He did not see her, so she turned back to get her drink. When she turned around, she froze. Elle was sitting on his lap in a white pea coat, with her arm around him, rubbing his shoulders, and kissing him on the side of his face. When he stared ahead as if she weren't there, Elle looked perplexed, then looked up and saw Chelsea. He said something to Elle and patted her back dismissively. She stood up and Chelsea passed her on her way into the building.

"Just stay away from him," she said in a harsh voice and Elle's eyes cut to the ground, without her usual smirk.

Kyle saw Chelsea and walked her way. He hugged her and muttered,

"Jeez!" into her hair as they went back inside.

Glen and Abby were waiting for them. Abby was incredulous. "A ho is a ho is a ho," she said. Chelsea had to laugh.

"Some things never change," said Glen, chuckling. "She's been putting condoms in his goodie bags every week…with a banana," as if it were a great joke. Kyle shot him an unappreciative glance and they headed into the cafeteria. It was like making an entrance with a rock star, what with all the glances, tight-lipped smiles of encouragement and nods they got, and people pressed his hand as they went by. Chelsea felt her own face redden, although she was far from the object of attention.

Chelsea and Kyle sat at a table while Abby and Glen went through the line for pizza.

"So my mom was there last night?" he queried. He emptied his lunch bag onto the table, seemingly oblivious to the attention. She assumed it was because it was probably a replay for him.

Chelsea looked around, peeled an orange, and offered him a section. "Yeah. I didn't see her, but I heard her tell my mom that the cabin sold."

"Yeah. I can't believe it's gone. I just wonder if some day she'll regret it. I know she didn't want it any more…" he drifted off. She thought that even though it was a harbor of sad memories for Kyle, maybe one day he would have wanted to go back and have it for his own family. It was, apparently, what he was thinking too. "Maybe one day I can build another one like it. At least there's money for college now," he said.

"Less pressure for you," she nodded, agreeing. "And she's pulled your house off the market?"

"Yep, nowhere to go now if the place sells. That and it's just a lot of change right now." He was quiet for a while and then said, "Eric Bennington's funeral is tomorrow. I'm planning to go. Coach Connelly's going

THE RUG

to take me and some of the guys. I still can't *believe* this." He ran a hand through his hair and sighed as Glen slid into the seat beside him and Abby settled herself beside Chelsea, trying to make eye contact with her to assess the situation. "You going tomorrow?" Kyle asked sideways to Glen.

"Yeah, man. I'm there. Anthony, Rocky, Aiden, and Nick Caffey are going too. How ya doin' today?" Glen asked a little uneasily.

"A little stoned I guess. I still haven't woken up from that sleeping pill my mom gave me last night. I have to go by and see Ms. Darnell after I eat…you know, for some counseling."

Chelsea tried to encourage him. "You'll like her. She's really nice. She and my mom are good friends. She won't make you feel awkward."

He sighed again and they ate in silence. When it was time for him to go, Chelsea offered to walk with him. "You don't have to babysit me, you know," he said, almost smiling.

"Oh, I know. I just thought I could run interference for you…you know, in case of another *attack*," she tried for humor. He chuckled, stood, and they collected their trash, then said goodbye to Glen and Abby.

He circled his arm around her. As they passed Kendra on the way out, she smiled and greeted them the way everyone else had. "Nice sign, Kendra," Chelsea said to her, smiling, and Kendra looked appreciative. She squeezed his shoulders as they passed Rocky and Elle at their lockers and Kyle hugged her a little tighter, which Elle noticed, chagrined.

After that day was over, each day got a little better, although Kyle was quiet mostly and rarely laughed or smiled. When he did smile, it was usually at Chelsea. She brought him homemade cookies and slipped him notes through the vents in his locker door. He stayed busy with practice and meetings with his mentor on the project that was to get under way over the weekend. They had plenty of schoolwork to do and she looked forward to Sunday when they could work on calculus together by themselves. Never had she thought she would look forward to anything remotely related to math!

The athletic department had arranged an activity bus to take students to the away game that week. It seemed the school was doing what it could to rally around the team, and especially Kyle. Abby showed Chelsea a Facebook site on which people from DHS, Ashe County, and all over the state had posted well wishes to him, and let him know he was in their prayers; that he was *not alone*. It made her heart swell to read it all, and her eyes had brimmed with tears to know that so many people cared enough to take time to encourage and support him.

On Friday night, every parent of every player on the team showed up in Hickory for the game. No one wanted to be that mother, getting a call from out of town, requesting that she meet her son in the ER of a strange hospital. Kyle had described the reception he had gotten from Eric's parents as one of the most emotional experiences of his life, and she knew he'd had a few.

Even Chelsea's parents decided to go to the game as a show of solidarity toward Kyle and Shelly. They drove Shelly, Abby, and Chelsea to and from the game. It was actually a fun night, even though Chelsea felt as if Shelly watched her carefully and listened more than intently to everything she said. It turned out to be the second loss of the season for the Wildcats, but it had not been a blowout. Anthony had run in a touchdown himself, Kyle had caught a pass for a sixty-yard touchdown, and Aiden Caffey had scored on a handoff from Anthony. The Cats went home feeling satisfied with themselves, even though not on top.

Saturday night, Glen and Abby put together a four-couple date at the movies. Anthony and Meredith, and Willie and Tia met them for a Denzel Washington suspense flick they had all wanted to see. Enough action and enough people were involved to create a good diversion for Kyle, and Chelsea was grateful to her cruise director friend, once again. Kyle was tired from working on his deck project that day, as well as the toll of getting through the week, so it wasn't a late night.

That night, she looked at herself in her bathroom mirror after washing her face. She tried to imagine what he saw when he looked at her. Her eyes *were* unusual, not gray, not green or blue, and so light there was hardly a color at all…the color of rain, he had said. She touched her lips, full and curvy, like her mother's, and quick to smile. She brushed her dark auburn hair that reached just below her shoulders, and pulled it to one side absently, the way she did often during the day. He always watched when she did that, and she noticed his eyes would come to rest on her collarbone and flash momentarily.

She returned to her room, pulled the window curtain back, slipped under the white bedspread, and pulled up the lilac blanket, huddling underneath to get warm. She liked going to sleep looking at the stars and listening to the owls hoot in the woods by the barn.

After church and lunch on Sunday, Kyle called and asked her to come over to study. As she drove up the driveway, she noticed with relief that the "For Sale" sign was no longer there. Kyle met her at the door in a long-sleeved gray thermal shirt and jeans as she walked up, and he held the door for her. He did not kiss her like he sometimes did.

Shelly was curled up on the brown sofa with a book; a mug of tea sat on the lamp table beside her. "Hi, sweetie," she greeted Chelsea. They spoke briefly, and Chelsea took in the framed pictures on the tables and walls. Pictures of the family in front of the Eiffel Tower; Desiree and Kyle in skiwear in a snowy place, Utah maybe; Kyle and Stuart holding up a large fish and grinning. He pulled her into a room near the front door, his dad's office.

"Here's what I'm working on," he said, showing her a plan set on a large drafting table. "This is the deck I'm building." Beside it was a photo of an old, faded mobile home in the woods, with a small front stoop and a ramp leading down from it.

"That's the house?" she asked.

"Yeah. The deck will cover three-fourths of the front of the house, so they'll have a place to sit when the weather is nice. Another group will be coming in the summer to build a roof over it."

"Wow," she said, inspecting the plan he had drawn. "Nice ramp. This looks professional."

"Thanks. I had help from Frank. And a younger guy from the building group is my foreman, but he's giving me lots of rein."

"Who lives there?"

"It's a lady and her three little grandkids that she's raising. She has emphysema and she's not in good health. It's important for her to get outside and get fresh air. It's sad. *I'll* never smoke," he said.

"Want to work in the kitchen?" he asked.

"Sure, I prefer a kitchen table," she said, smiling. He seemed tired and melancholy, which she could understand.

He offered her something to drink, but she declined and they got down to work. She was keenly aware of his mom, turning pages and shifting her position on the couch in the other room. It was going to be a quiet session, she figured, so she concentrated on what they were doing, even though it was extremely difficult with him so close. She smelled the faint coconut scent of his hair when he raked his fingers through it, and she searched for the turquoise blue of his eyes when he spoke. He was almost bored, she thought. After a while, she heard Shelly leave the den, walk upstairs, and lift the lid of the washing machine.

"Are you okay?" she asked tentatively.

He sighed. "Yeah. I'm sorry, I guess I'm kind of a buzz-kill today…"

"It's not a problem. I just like being here," she said, touching his hand.

He was silent a moment and then said, "What are you doing with me?"

"What?" she said, astonished, feeling her heart sink like a stone.

"Aren't you just sick of all this *shit*?" He looked at her with imploring blue eyes.

"What do you mean? I thought you *knew* the way I feel about you," she said uneasily, trying to read his mood.

"I mean, I feel like such a *wreck* right now. I can't get anything going. You don't need somebody like me…"

She covered his lips with the tips of her fingers. "Stop, stop, *stop*," she whispered. "Don't even say this to me. You're way off," she said firmly. She stroked his face, feeling the scratchiness where he shaved and the warmth of his skin under her hand. He did not respond and looked at her with eyes full of angst. She said slowly, "I told you I love you…and I meant it. Nothing has changed for me. Things *will* get better. I know you feel horrible. I see it in your eyes…the way you carry yourself. I *totally* get it. But let me help. You're not in this alone."

"I know," he whispered, closing his eyes. "It's just so unfair, dragging you through all this, too. You don't need this."

She pulled her chair closer around the corner of the table. "I don't care. Come here," she said and pulled his head into hers and held him. "I'm not….going anywhere. I love you so much." She kissed his temple and then his cheek, and then his mouth pressed into hers. He pulled her out of her chair and into his lap, wrapped his arms around her, and caressed her neck with his fingers. His hand rested on her throat as he kissed her desperately.

"I just can't believe you love me. There's no good reason…" He shook his head and she kissed him again.

"I don't want to hear this again, young man," she scolded. "I'm *in* this. You'd better just get used to it." She was lost in his kisses when she heard Shelly coming down the stairs. She shot up, went into the kitchen, and found the cabinet she remembered, then asked him whether he wanted a Coke.

Shelly walked into the kitchen and asked cheerily, "How's the studying going?"

Kyle's hands were covering his face; he raked them through his hair and said, "Just great, Mom."

Chapter 9

IN THE MOMENT

As Halloween approached, Glen became a fixture in the Davenport's kitchen and was now able to prepare a meal without letting blood. Abby needed something to do while everyone else worked and danced, so she became an employee of White Horse Farms Nursery. Willie and Chelsea had started rehearsals for Studio One's annual Christmas extravaganza. Brad Helmsley had choreographed a modern, edgy, and aerobic ballet to "Carol of the Bells," the version by the "Trans-Siberian Orchestra," in which the two of them and three other dancers twirled and hurled themselves maniacally across the stage. It was exhausting but absolutely brilliant and sure to steal the show. Chelsea was also learning the "Mirliton" dance from *The Nutcracker* and hoped to use it for her ballet audition in February. Sonya had danced the part herself as a student at the School of the Arts.

As she and Willie left rehearsal on the third Saturday in October, he mopped his face with a towel and shook out all his little braids. "Woo! 'Bells' is gonna kill me," he said, catching his breath.

"I know. I'd like to go soak in a hot bathtub right about now," Chelsea said.

"What's stoppin' you, baby?"

"Glen and my dad are smoking a butt today. I can probably say hey and disappear, though."

Willie made a disgusted face, as if he had smelled something foul. "Say what?"

"You know, a Boston butt…*barbeque*? It's for his cooking project. Mom thought it was a *manly* thing for him to learn how to do."

"Sounds kinda per*verted* if you ask me."

"Well, you should come over tonight and have some. We'll make a perv out of you, too. Bring Tia. There'll be enough food for an army. Abby and Kyle will be there too, so come!"

"Y'all just a partying buncha folks. I'll talk to her. How's the man doing after all the bad luck?"

She thought a moment, "You know, it's just hard. He still feels so bad for Eric's family. He and his mom have been through similar circumstances, so he's taking it pretty hard. But he's getting better. Football is getting easier, even though they lost again last night. He isn't planning to give it up, although it would be fine with his mom if he did."

"Tell me about *that!* My mama's so glad I'm a dancer now. So much safer…now if I can just make a living at it."

Chelsea laughed. "How good of a waiter are you?"

He looked miffed. "I ain't gonna be waitin' no tables!"

"No, you won't be, but if *I* were trying to dance for a living, *I'd* have to wait tables!"

"Nah, girl, you'll be all right. What time tonight?" he asked, swinging into the seat of his beat-up Maxima.

"Seven?"

She met everyone in the backyard after a long soak. She wore jeans and a new teal shirt she had bought shopping with Abby the day before. She had taken time to put on a little make-up and glass earrings. Her dad whistled at her as she walked outside. Liz and Tom stood arm in arm, laughing and talking with Glen around the smoker, from which a savory aroma drifted.

"Where's Kitty?" Chelsea asked.

"She was tired from shopping today. She's taking a little nap. I'll wake her up before long," Liz said, smiling at her.

Tom checked his watch. "Abby should be getting off about now. I may walk down to see if they need any help closing up. Jay's staying to eat, too."

Glen handed Chelsea his camera. "Will you take our picture?" he asked as Liz stood beside him and he removed the top of the smoker proudly. She snapped a couple and zoomed in on the meat.

"It looks fantastic and smells out of this world," she complimented Glen. "Are you putting this all in a cookbook?"

He looked at Liz and they grinned. "Actually, I decided to make it a calendar with a different dinner or theme for each month we're in school. There's tailgating food, burgers for the fall. I'm actually going to cook a turkey at my house for Thanksgiving…and you're in for some surprises."

"Wow! Chef Glen!"

"Too bad I'm not twenty-one. Your mom knows some *bangin'* drink recipes."

"Oh yes, she does."

"Yeah, I'll be eighteen in two weeks. I can go get shot at in Iraq but I can't drink a beer. Go figure."

Chelsea heard a crunching sound and turned to see Kyle coming around the corner of the house with Fella at his side.

"Hey, everybody! You look great, chica," he said to Chelsea, his large smile spreading across his face. He hugged her and then said to Glen, "When's dinner, sweetheart? I could smell this a football field away. It's awesome."

"Soon...a *butt*...just for you, hon. Time to take it off and let it rest." Kyle held the large pan for him that he indicated.

Abby and Tom returned and Liz asked for Chelsea's help in the kitchen. They set out paper plates and the baked beans and potato salad Glen had made earlier. Liz took a pan of rolls out of the oven and Chelsea arranged soft drinks and a bucket of ice on the kitchen counter.

"I'm going to wake up Kitty. Don't you need your jacket outside, honey? It's getting chilly."

"Nope. I've got a good-lookin' man to keep me warm tonight," Chelsea said, winking at her mother.

Liz sighed and played along, "Ah, yes, I remember young love! And he seems like a happy man tonight." She disappeared down the hall.

Glen led the way inside with the roast in hand, followed by Abby in her green nursery shirt, then Kyle and Tom, who were discussing the previous night's game. Jay popped in next, also wearing a green shirt, and greeted everyone, glad to see Kyle. Chelsea's cell phone buzzed in her pocket. She checked the message and announced that Willie and Tia couldn't make it. Kyle's arm went around her shoulders as they all stood around the kitchen, chatting.

"Did you work on the deck today?" she asked him.

"Yes, and I'll be *hurting* tomorrow. We poured the footings and set the posts all around; hung the joists. It was tricky getting it all level and plumb. It's a good thing they have a back door. This is going to be a slow process for them with me just working on the weekends. The kids are cute. They like to watch. How was dance?"

"Brutal...I'll be sore, too. It's going to be amazing, though. Everybody's pretty excited."

"Can't wait to see."

They waited around for the pork to cool before it could be pulled for serving. They spilled out into the living room and Abby began talking about Kendra's Halloween party the next week and the costumes they should wear. Glen rolled his eyes. She ignored him. "Okay, it's all about the props, right? I'm going to be Captain Hook and have a foil hook taped to my hand, the coat, the mustache and the hat…and Glen is going to be the *crocodile*!" They laughed.

"She's making me wear a dang *alarm clock* around my neck…the kind that ticks real loud."

"You guys should be Peter Pan and Wendy," she said, struck with her new idea.

"Ain't no way in hell I'm Peter Pan," Kyle said firmly, shaking his head.

"Oh, come *on*!" Abby cried.

"That's right…gotta put your foot down. I picked the croc over Peter Pan, myself," said Glen.

"You could be Smee," offered Chelsea. "He's kind of cool. I can be Tiger Lily…or Tinkerbell?"

"*Tink*!" Both boys spoke in unison, then laughed. It was good to hang out and have fun, like normal again.

After a delectable dinner, photo ops, and clean-up, everyone left, and Kitty settled in with Tom and Liz on the sun porch, for a game of Bananagrams. Kyle hung around and helped take out the trash. Chelsea found a wool blanket, and they cuddled together on the front porch swing in their jackets with Fella, who was licking Kyle's shoes.

"He won't leave you alone," she noticed. "He must smell Bono."

"Nah, he just knows I like him. Bono lives with Frank and Faith now," he said, referring to their chocolate lab.

"Why?" Chelsea asked, disbelieving.

"Well, after my dad died, my mom let Frank take him. Frank loves to duck hunt and so does Bono, so they kinda found each other. I saw him today, actually. Frank brought him to the worksite. The kids love him."

Chelsea couldn't believe it. *She gave away his dog?* She could not bring herself to say it aloud.

He laughed quietly. "He was my dad's dog. I'm not around so much anyway. And I won't be hunting much, now."

She wondered how he always seemed to know what she was thinking. And usually she knew what was on his mind as well. She thought about what his mother had said to Liz that night about their *connection*. Maybe there was really something to it. She snuggled into him. Fella circled a couple of times, then settled at their feet.

"Don't you get angry about things like that?" she asked softly.

He thought about it. "Yeah, I get really angry. I just save it for the big stuff. You're thinking about the stuff my mom does?"

"I guess. You're way more forgiving than I could ever be."

"Well, she's just…I don't know, trying to be in control. She's always been like that, and it's been hard for her lately."

"She can't control you when you go off to college." The thought made her sad. She saw what Shelly might be feeling.

"Exactly, so she has to cash it all in now. I'm all she has left, you know? I can deal with it a few more months. She better not think she's moving into my dorm with me, though!"

"Now *that* would be downsizing!"

He made a face in the dark and squeezed her. "Wait till *we* have kids.

I try to remind myself it can't be easy." It's surely the rhetorical "we," she thought. Still, it sent a little shiver through her.

"Do you think about college much?" she asked.

"Yeah, I do sometimes, but I don't want to right now."

She felt the same way but kept silent. The uncertainty was too much to think about. If this could just last forever, this place, these arms around her, this feeling. His mother said they were too young to be this involved and it scared her.

"You're really good at living in the moment," she murmured.

"Not really. It's usually kind of hard for me, but when the moments are *this* good, it feels easy," he said, kissing the top of her head.

"I wish I was more like that," she said.

"Usually you are. Usually you're the one who brings me back. I need that."

"What changed with you this week? You seem so much more at peace with yourself."

"You made me realize that I'm really not alone. So many people have been nice to me, not that I deserve it, but I mean, people I don't even know are *praying* for me. That's pretty humbling. And then I think about how bad the Benningtons must feel; my deal is *nothing* compared to what they're living with. It's a lot easier for me to pick myself up than it will be for them. I still feel bad, but it's not so much about me," she felt him sigh. "*And*, this love thing you've got goin' on with me is working," he said and held her tighter inside the blanket.

"Hmm…you are *not* like the other seventeen-year-olds I know."

"You're not like the other girls I know, either. I'm glad we're not into all the drama, worrying about what to wear, what movie to go see, who's pissed off at who, you know?" She laughed, thinking he didn't believe they were involved in any drama. "I'm so over high school. That's when I think about college. But I wish you'd be there with me," he said quietly.

She decided to live in the moment. So she reached into his collar and pulled him closer, then kissed him.

• • •

It was a busy week, with the chorus concert on Tuesday and late rehearsals at the studio. To Chelsea's relief, there wasn't any more noise from Elle, and she wondered whether Elle had finally given up her annoying pursuit of Kyle. Elle still studied her in vocal ensemble and continued to walk right by her and look the other way abruptly when they passed in the hallway.

With the hectic week, Chelsea found herself dozing in English class and Meredith bumped her elbow more than once to save her embarrassment. Toward the end of class, Miss Rogers gave them time to work on research for their projects. Meredith asked Chelsea to sit with her at a table in the back. She took out a brown envelope and looked up at Chelsea tentatively. "I have something I think you should see," she said seriously. "Do you remember when I told you what Kyle said about me talking to his mother for my journalism project?"

"Yeah," Chelsea said, starting to get the drift. "I guess with what happened to Kyle, you might be rethinking the timing?"

"Well," Meredith began uncertainly, "I want to show you these pictures and get your opinion. No one else has seen these. You know that we switch off taking pictures of different things for the yearbook, right? When I was down on the sidelines taking pictures at homecoming, I stuck around and took some of the game." She pulled a sheaf of five-by-sevens from the envelope and handed them to Chelsea. There were pictures of Anthony backing up for a pass, Kyle running in for a touchdown, Kyle and Glen chest-bumping each other, Kyle standing on the sidelines with Coach Connelly's hand on his shoulder, Kyle with his helmet in his hand, holding his hair, Kyle on his knees with his head in his hands, and then sitting on the bench staring, stricken, between his feet. As Chelsea thumbed through the pictures, her heart sank a little further with each one.

"Mer, these are…powerful shots." She looked questioningly at her friend's large, serious green eyes.

"I almost felt *bad* when I saw them. It's probably hard for you to look at them."

Chelsea nodded. "But that's what makes them so good. It tells the whole story."

"I know. So, I guess what I want to ask you is: do you think *Kyle* is the one I should be talking to? Not his mother?"

Chelsea's eyes widened. "You want to do the story on *Kyle*?"

"Only if he could talk about it…everything. It's a lot, I know. And it might be too soon; I don't know. I thought you could tell me. I think I know how you feel about him," she said, smiling.

"If you had asked me last week, I would have said no. Now, though, you should ask him."

"Will you tell him about it first? I don't want to catch him totally off guard. If he's having a bad day, that would be the last thing he'd want to hear about in the middle of school."

"Yeah, I'll talk to him. That's really considerate of you."

"I think I'm beginning to see how hard it might be to be a journalist. You know, when you're talking about real people and the things they suffer through…"

"You picked a heavy-duty topic, that's for sure."

• • •

Kendra's Halloween party packed the Snowy Ridge Clubhouse with an assortment of vampires, ghouls, and other recognizable characters. Kyle picked up Chelsea and they met Abby and Glen to form the Peter Pan ensemble, minus Peter and Wendy. Glen was hilarious as a crocodile. Abby had made him a papier-mache croc head and a long green tail to wear with his green clothes. The clock hung around his neck on a large chain and tick-tocked audibly as they stood outside the clubhouse. Abby had drawn on her mustache and curled her hair in ringlets for the part of Captain Hook, and she'd attached an aluminum foil hook to her hand. Her black hat was made of foam board, and she'd found a crushed velvet jacket that looked like a relic from someone's prom back in the seventies. Her ruffled shirt, black pants, and tall black boots made the costume complete. Chelsea snapped pictures of them with Abby's camera.

Her pale green dance dress with little gossamer wings attached had her freezing in the fall chill. She had found little silver flats at Walmart and attached glow-in-the-dark ping-pong balls on the toes with hot glue. She wondered how long they would last. Her prop was a little jar of sparkly white glitter that she dusted on people in need of some magic. Kyle looked dirty and roguish as Smee, wearing little wire-rimmed glasses and a striped shirt with suspenders, and his head tied with a red bandana. His mom had found a clip-on hoop earring for one of his lobes, and he was unshaven. Abby took their pictures, then got Anthony to take a group shot of them. He and Meredith were dressed as Jack Sparrow and Elizabeth Swann from *Pirates of the Caribbean.* "Of course," Chelsea said. "He has perfect hair for the role!"

Kyle looked her up and down, appreciatively. "Just how is this made?" he asked, referring to the little dress she wore.

"It's just a leotard with a skirt attached."

"Nice," he smiled. "Cold?" She nodded vigorously. He wrapped an arm around her to keep her warm as they entered the clubhouse where music was bumping and bodies were grinding away under a disco ball. They presented their invitations at the door and said hello to Kendra's parents, who escorted girls with purses to a closet so the purses would be locked up safely for the evening. Kendra looked like Hermione Grainger in her Hogwarts robe and maroon and gold tie. She grinned at them all, and Glen quipped, "Hey, you stole my tie!"

"Wrong school, hon," she laughed and took them back to where refreshments had been set up on a table decorated in black and orange and strung with spiderwebs. "You guys look *great*!" She pulled out her little red camera and took some pictures of them as they hammed up the opportunity. Chelsea spotted Harry Potter behind Kendra in a similar robe and asked her, "Is that Aiden Caffey?"

"Yes! Would you take our picture?" Kendra said, jumping up and down and pulling Aiden over to their group. Anthony stuck his chin in between them and grinned, exposing his little teeth in a large pirate smile. Meredith appeared beside Aiden and they cheesed it up some more. As she laughed and snapped away, Chelsea was aware that others had found them. They were talking above the music but it was still hard to hear the conversation.

Kyle said, "Thanks! You look very…pink!" When she turned around to see whom he was talking to, she noticed a Playboy bunny dressed in cuffs and ears swaying beside him. Elle, it appeared, had sampled some alternative refreshments prior to arriving. Kyle looked at Chelsea with raised brows. Elle ignored her and said to Kyle, "I've got some different entertainment for *you* out on the golf course for later if you're up for it." She pretended to hold something to her lips, then inhaled.

"Thanks, but I'll pass," he said as she swayed a bit more.

"I am *so drunk*! Hey, what do you think of us as cheerleaders so far?" Elle asked, changing the subject as Kendra came to help steady her.

"Y'all seem okay. I never had cheerleaders, so I can't really compare," Kyle said, attempting to keep the conversation neutral.

"You've never *had* a cheerleader?" She laughed and looked at Kendra, who joined in the joke. "*Well*—we'll just have to take care of that! You should be well prepared," she said boldly, a not-so-subtle reference to the goodie bags she'd given him. Kyle cast his eyes about to see how to extricate himself from the encounter. "We'd hate for you to miss out on any extracurriculars," she said, having trouble with the last word and laughing at her attempt. Rocky watched them through narrowed eyes from across the room.

Kendra looked abashed and gave Chelsea an apologetic glance. "She and Rocky did a *bunch* of tequila shots in the parking lot," she explained. Glen and Anthony also heard.

Chelsea watched with interest and then reached for Kyle's hand. "Wanna dance?" she asked him. He took her hand and they walked a few steps away, where they were joined by Captain Hook and the crocodile.

"It's so weird how Kendra is the only girl Elle ever talks to," said Abby. It had gotten to the point where instead of being angry about Elle and her unwanted advances, they spent time trying to analyze her unusual behavior.

"Well, she talked to *me* once this year, although I have to say it wasn't worth listening to," Chelsea replied, trying for coolness. Kyle chuckled and hugged her shoulder as they watched the other costumed guests walk by. "How about a little fairy dust?" she asked, then shook her jar of glitter and gave them all a sparkly dusting. "I'll put a spell on you" blared in Bette Midler's unmistakable voice from the DJ stand and they laughed.

"Want something to drink?" Kyle asked.

"Sure, just not from *her* punch bowl," she said and he chuckled. When he and Glen went back to the table, Elle was at Chelsea's shoulder instantly.

"Are you supposed to be *Tinkerbell*?" Elle asked, fluidly in her condition.

Chelsea nodded. Abby looked surprised that she could be wrong—maybe Elle would talk to other girls after all.

"I have a bra you should wear that would, you know, help out up there," Elle said, gesturing to Chelsea's chest. Chelsea's eyes narrowed with disdain. "But actually, it probably wouldn't fit you...really. Maybe you should shake some more fairy dust on yourself. It couldn't hurt," she said and spun around to talk to someone else.

"What a stinking *bitch*! Oh my God, Chelsea! You should just go drop-kick her butt," said a disgusted Abby.

Chelsea pursed her lips. She felt blown away by it all. "I have no idea what to say to that, you know?"

"How about this?" Abby said and gestured a backhanded slap with her hook across two feet of air.

"Don't think I wasn't dying to do it. And your hook there makes it *way* more impressive!" She even managed to laugh.

"Whoa, whoa! What's going on?" asked Glen. The guys had returned, and they handed each girl a plastic cup.

Abby was still fuming. "Elle was just a total bitch to Chelsea."

"It's not that big of a deal," said Chelsea, rolling her eyes.

Then Abby turned to Chelsea. "She's trying to get to you because Kyle likes you and not her."

"That's right," Kyle said. He shrugged his shoulders and hugged Chelsea again. "If you'll notice, Kendra's parents are watching, and I think Miss Playboy Bunny is gonna be history in a bit. Either that, or she'll be off somewhere hurling." They looked over and saw Kendra's parents talking with the other two chaperones. They all watched Elle and Kendra, who looked a bit nervous. Rocky, in Hugh Hefner silk pajamas, walked over to the two of them.

A slow song started. It was "Unchained Melody," a fifties classic and the theme song from the movie *Ghost*. Kyle pulled Chelsea out to the edge of the dance floor, setting their drinks on a nearby tray. He wrapped his arm around her waist and held her hand close to his chest. He sighed into her hair and said, "This is so much better!" A short guy in a lab coat and little braids was dancing beside them with an even shorter nurse in scrubs. Chelsea winked at Willie. He bumped her comically and flashed his nametag in their direction. "Dr. Love," it said, and she and Kyle laughed.

"Thriller" came on next and the whole group practiced their dance in the center of the floor to enthusiastic attention, and several others joined the fun. Chelsea noticed Rocky and Elle arguing at the back of the snack table. Aiden was trying to calm them down. Kendra was deeply involved in a somber conversation with her parents.

Kyle and Chelsea found a table and sat down for a while by themselves. She told him a little bit about Meredith's idea for his story as part of her project and he listened quietly. He took off his bandana and twirled it absently on his index finger, thinking. She couldn't assess his mood and was afraid she had upset him.

"I'm sorry. Did that upset you?" she asked, putting her hand on his arm.

He looked across the room, pursed his lips, and then turned to her. "No, it didn't. I just think it's sweet that she asked *you* about it first. I'm glad our friends think that much of us, you know? And I don't think I'd mind talking to her about it. What do you think? Should I do it?"

"You really are *surviving* a lot right now," Chelsea answered. "And that's what her whole thing is about. If she goes through the process with you, it could only help."

"Things change every day. Sometimes I'm up and sometimes I'm not. If I hear something that reminds me of my sister or my father, it can kind of shatter the day, you know? And now, football is…it's really difficult. I can't...I can't really play defense right now. I sit there and watch guys get hit, and I can only think about what happened with Eric. When I get hit, I think my mom is up there wringing her hands." He shook his head. "But I just deal with it."

She rubbed his shoulder and hugged him.

"I don't know what I'd do without you," he said softly, meeting her eyes. Then he looked away. "I'll talk to her. But not tonight."

Rocky walked over and asked whether he could sit down. Kyle excused himself to go to the restroom and Rocky sat. Chelsea looked at him, wide-eyed. "What? You're *talking* to me now? Where's Elle?"

"Aiden took her home. He was our DD tonight. She was out of hand."

"She's always out of hand," Chelsea muttered. From the look on his face, she thought Rocky seemed to agree. "What are you doing with her, Rock? Even for you, this is a stretch."

He winced. "Ouch! That was harsh, Chels. But you're right. I don't know what I'm doing. She's just using me."

"And *you're* not using *her*?" she asked archly.

"Yeah, I guess I deserved that," he admitted. "I know I blew it with you, Chels, and I'm sorry. That was the dumbest move of my life. I watch what she does to you and Davis, and I'm sorry about that too. I'm about done."

"With her, or with this conversation?"

"Damn, would you lighten up? I really am sorry. I'll say something to her if it will help."

Kyle was back. "Nice PJs, dude. Are you hitting on my woman?" he said arrogantly, but she knew he was being funny. She liked it. He and Rocky seemed to get along, but Kyle definitely maintained the upper hand, and she was impressed.

"Nah, man, I know the score. Just chatting."

"I think we're leaving now," Kyle said. When he threw a questioning glance her way, she nodded immediately. He held out his hand to her and said to Rocky, "Later, man." She let him sweep her along in what was no longer her fantasy, but her life. She looked down at her shoes. Even the glow-in-the-dark ping-pong balls had survived the night.

Chapter 10

NOVEMBER

Rocky must have made good on his promise to talk to Elle. They were apparently still on, and she kept a low profile after the Halloween spectacle. Her greatest offense continued to be abruptly looking the other way as she passed Chelsea in the halls at school. She kept a watchful eye on Kyle but refrained from anything inappropriate or unsolicited. School became a pleasant place to be most of the time.

Kyle was becoming his old self again, and the lunchtime conversations were again boisterous, as their group expanded in the cafeteria. Chelsea continued her research on choreography alongside Meredith and Anthony on the computers in the media center, and her dance rehearsals had a new and powerful energy each evening.

The next football game was away. Chelsea, Abby, and Meredith drove together to cheer the guys on. The Wildcats won, 48 to 14, and rolled back home on a cloud. They celebrated Glen's eighteenth birthday the following night. His family invited Abby, Chelsea, and Kyle to surprise him at Makoto's for the occasion. Chelsea discovered Kyle liked sushi as much as she did, and he promised they'd return to the restaurant for a special occasion. He had been working hard on the deck and another weekend would almost finish the project.

They had had to wait until Sunday night for their calculus rendezvous, and they decided to hole up in the quiet sun porch as Liz, Tom, and Kitty watched a favorite TV show in the living room. Kyle seemed restless, and as they finished up, he snapped his book shut, stretched his arms above his head, and extended his legs out in front of him. He pushed the sleeves of his light blue V-neck sweater up and scratched his arm, yawning. She pulled him up and led him to the flowered sofa, where they collapsed against each other. She ran her fingers through his hair and kissed the side of his mouth.

"What's up?" she asked, looking up into his blue eyes.

He closed them, smiled, and said, "Just really tired. I'm thinking about school. What's your average in calculus?"

"I think I have a high B. What's yours?"

"Ninety-seven last time I checked."

"Holy cow! You're bucking for that scholarship, aren't you?"

"Hmm. Did I tell you I sent in an application to the University of Virginia?"

Her heart pounded. That would be far away. "U.V.A.? When did this come about? Are they recruiting you?"

"They invited me up to a game in two weeks." He looked at the puzzled expression on her face. "U.V.A. has a top-notch architecture school. Have you ever been to Charlottesville?"

"Once, when we were little. My parents took us to see Monticello. I remember it being really pretty."

"Monticello's beautiful. Thomas Jefferson was an amazing architect. Charlottesville's a neat town, too. I think I'd like to be in a place like that. Got to have some hills, you know. And it's not far from D.C. That would be cool. You could come up and visit."

"But the football team?" she queried apprehensively.

"It's okay…but I can't let it be the driving force in my decision. I could get injured and not even play. I need to be in the best place, academically, for what I want to do. And you never know. They could change coaches and the whole picture could be different."

She brooded over the distance but was afraid to bring it up. She was quiet.

"You could come to some games. They would play Wake Forest in Winston," he said, reading her mind. "And after the season is over, we could meet back here on weekends."

She closed her eyes and took a deep breath. "I know…I'm just not ready to go there yet. I'm trying to live in the moment."

He put his arm around her, pulled her closer to him, and touched her forehead with his own.

"It's not going to change anything…for me at least." He held her face in his hands and kissed her gently. "I might not even get in. I'm just talking," he said, kissing her again.

"I don't know that I'll get in to N.C.S.A. either. Maybe we can just stay here and go to Appalachian and be together."

"Like Abby and Glen."

"Exactly."

"Lucy and Ethel, Fred and Ricky," he said, and she laughed while she kissed him again. "So what is your back-up plan? You've never said."

"I've applied to E.C.U. They have a physical therapy program, and I could go all the way through for my Master's. I know enough from helping with Kitty that I think I would like it, or even occupational therapy. They have dance there, too. And I've applied to U.N.C.-G. for dance."

He held her hand. "How's the audition coming?"

"I'm working on the ballet. It's the "Mirliton" dance from *The Nutcracker*. It's hard, but it's coming along. Sonya thinks they'll like it because it's their choreography. I haven't found the right music for the contemporary one. It has to be classical, and it's not really what I had in mind. I'm trying to figure out what I want to portray, and the music will be everything."

They were quiet for a moment. Then he said, "When football is over, I'm going to need to get a job. I've got to start putting some money away."

"When will you be finished?"

"Probably around Thanksgiving. If we make the playoffs, we won't last long."

"You could work the Christmas tree lot from then until Christmas. Dad always hires a bunch of high school guys to help him out. It's just for a month, but it's something. He pays better than minimum wage, if I remember right."

"If I get to see you more that way, sign me up!"

She was thinking again, and it was his turn to ask her, "What are you thinking?"

"Well...I don't know if I want to know this," she said, shaking her head.

"What?"

"You know the very few minute details of my past, but I know nothing about your old girlfriends."

He froze for just an instant and then said, "Ah, I thought we were living in the moment. Why do you want to do this?"

"I'm curious about you. The more I get to know you, the more I want to know everything about you. Is it bad?"

He laughed and stroked her face, "No. It's not bad. There's not much to tell, really."

"I somehow doubt that."

"I guess, I mean, I've dated girls here and there, but there's been no one like *you*. You're the ultimate cool, sexy girl I've been waiting for. What more do you need to know?" Her face flushed and he took her hand and threaded his fingers through hers. "You worry too much."

"So there's not gonna be a day where we run into someone and it becomes weird?"

"No way. I can promise you that."

She snuggled against him, forgetting for the moment that her family was just on the other side of the opposite wall. "How is this happening? This isn't real," she murmured, feeling the softness of his sweater on her cheek.

"Oh, yes it is," he said and kissed her again.

• • •

Autumn's pleasant crispness and palate of colors rapidly swirled into the dramatic gales of November, and along with the weather, the pace of everything else had taken off in a tear. Schoolwork continued to weigh heavily on Chelsea, and Kyle's trip to U.V.A. the following weekend left her hanging, strangely. She and Abby filled the time, with Abby sleeping over at Chelsea's house, planning the variety show, and Chelsea's dance classes. Her grant had been approved and she met with the school counselor at Snowy Ridge Elementary School about pitching her project to the students. She chose third- and fourth-grade girls, as Sonya had suggested, picked a song for her choreography, and developed a timeline compatible with Abby's show and her own audition. The Christmas extravaganza was just weeks away.

Thanksgiving came quickly and Shelly took Kyle to visit her parents in Charlotte for the holiday. The Christmas tree lot was to open the Friday after, so he was expected back to start working there with Glen and

Anthony on weekends, and as the football practice schedule allowed. The Wildcats would play at least once in the playoffs. No one would even see Wayne and Becky until Christmas Day, with their "choose and cut" tree business in full swing.

Glen was around most of the time, getting tips from Liz on how to prepare a turkey in a baking bag in the oven. Liz shared her recipes for dressing, sweet potato soufflé, their favorite green beans with almonds, and pumpkin pie. On Thanksgiving Day, delicious aromas from the feast filled the house, as well as the congregation of relatives that arrived at both the farmhouse and Becky and Wayne's house. Aside from Liz's parents, Charley was home, solo for the last Thanksgiving before her marriage, and Jay was back in his own beloved bed for the long weekend.

As they recovered from the lavish feast, Chelsea, Charley, and Jay had to forego the traditional after-dinner walk, due to a soaking rain that began earlier in the day. They sat in candlelight in the violet bedroom, piled companionably on Chelsea's twin bed, and chatted in their sweatpants, munching Tums.

Jay was talking from the foot of the bed. "This time next year you'll be an old married lady," he said, eyes twinkling at Charley.

"You say it like it's a curse," she retorted, mildly offended.

"Isn't it?" he snickered. He flipped his blonde curls, so unlike their mahogany hair, out of his eyes.

"Well, I'm sure Lauren wouldn't like to hear you talking like that!" Charley scolded him, swatting his leg.

"Whatever…I don't think the ball and chain's for me."

"And have you told her this?" Charley asked as Chelsea listened intently.

"I don't know…I need to say something soon. She won't be expecting it. We've been together so long I think she just kind of assumes it will never be over. It's like an old habit you can't seem to bring yourself to break, you know?"

"That's awful!" Chelsea said, hoping she would never become someone's tired old habit he couldn't wait to break.

"Really," Charley agreed. "If you really feel that way, then you need to cut her loose now. Don't lead her on. On the other hand, if you're really committed to her, that's what it's all about."

"No, that's your gig, Mrs. Jamieson. I'm not there yet."

"Why not?"

"I can't stand the thought that she's the last girl I'll ever *sleep* with. I'm *way* too young for that."

Chelsea felt oddly disturbed. No one would have guessed that was how Jay thought when he and Lauren were together. They did act a lot like brother and sister, but she figured they ran a little deeper than that.

"Well, if you dump her, it better not mess up my plans for the band to play at my wedding," Charley threatened him. "Can't you wait until the middle of June?" she said, halfway teasing.

"Y'all are terrible," Chelsea complained, hugging her pillow absently.

"I hear you're the latest to be bitten by the love bug," Charley said, calling her out. They were both watching her and she hoped the dark room camouflaged the burn rising in her cheeks.

"So it's you and Kyle? Even *I've* figured this out," laughed Jay. "He's the kind of guy who could get *any girl he wants* and he's all about *you*! What's up with *that*? What, are you putting out?"

"You're such a *jerk*," Chelsea said, smacking him with her pillow.

Charley rolled her eyes, seeing Chelsea's expression. "Leave her alone. Chelsea doesn't have time to go to the bathroom, much less *put out*."

Jay held up his hands and extricated himself from the twisted mass on the bed. "Okay, enough of this conversation," he said and bid them goodnight. They heard him brushing his teeth and then closing his bedroom door quietly.

Charley stayed on the bed and wrapped the lilac thermal blanket around her as they got into Indian-style positions on the bed. "I remember those days, when you can't find a minute to be alone with your boyfriend," she said, uncharacteristically sympathetic. "What's it like for you two? I've missed a lot, apparently. Do you really like him?"

"Yeah," said Chelsea. "More than just *like* at this point." It felt strange to talk about him; it was as if she were betraying a trust, which she was not prone to do.

"Tell me more. You're not…?"

"No. God, no. I mean, I *wish*, but it's not happening. It's like you said, for one thing, we don't have any privacy. Mom and Dad and Kitty are always here, and his mother watches us like a hawk when we're over there. I can't decide if she likes me or not. She's *way* overprotective of him, which is weird, considering she shipped him off to boarding school for three years and then to the beach last summer."

Charley looked at her somberly and was quiet for a few moments. Then she said, "I'm sure she likes you." She looked out the window and they listened to the rain.

"Then what did I do to make her so distrustful?"

Charley sighed. "It's not you…and it's not Kyle either."

"How do you know?" Chelsea asked, suspiciously.

Charley turned to her in the dim candlelight. "It's because of what happened with Desiree."

Chelsea shook her head. "I guess losing a child would be incredibly difficult, but Kyle is the only one she has left. She should be enjoying him and making every minute with him count."

"That's only part of it. *Desiree had an abortion...* about three weeks before she died."

Chelsea was too shocked to speak. "What?"

"That's what started Shelly's denial about everything. She didn't want anybody to know. Mom and Dad knew. I knew about it because Desiree told me. And then after she died, of course, they weren't going to talk about it. Kyle didn't even know."

"They never told him?"

"Not unless it was a lot later. He was in the eighth grade. What good would it have been for him to know something like that? He's never mentioned it to you?"

"No. He's told me a lot of things, but not that."

"He might not know *still*."

Chelsea sighed deeply. "Ohhh...I wish you hadn't told me. It's not my place to know this."

"This is coming from you, the eavesdropping queen!"

"Things are different now. That would really hurt him. He's been through so much already."

"Yep, you've grown up and fallen in love. That probably explains why Shelly is all over your case. She doesn't want a repeat of any of that. I'm sure she worries about Kyle."

Chelsea nodded, remembering Shelly's worried comments to Liz. That's what she meant when she said, "Can you blame me, Liz?"

"He's really responsible about it, though. He's put zero pressure on me. What was it like, going through that with Desiree?"

Charley thought a minute, remembered, and laughed somberly. "Actually it was harder on me than it was on her. I thought she would be so devastated. *I would have been.* She'd only been with this guy twice. Then he dumped her and she found out she was pregnant. She never told him. You would've never known it bothered her. She and Shelly just took care of it. And then three weeks later, she got hit by a car." She looked meaningfully at Chelsea.

Chelsea's eyes widened. "Are you saying she walked out in front of that car on *purpose?*"

"There's no way to know, but it makes you wonder, doesn't it? It drove Shelly and Stu crazy. All the kids she was with in Florida were bombed, so they didn't know what happened. She was walking with them one minute and the next minute she was in the street. They said they'd been partying and everybody was having fun…and then it just happened. Stu and Shelly really beat themselves up for letting her go down there."

Chelsea shook her head and put her hands over her face. "I really wish I didn't know this."

Charley smiled at her. "You really are in love, aren't you? Don't worry about it. Things will happen when you're both ready. You shouldn't rush into it at this stage of the game."

"I know that. That's not it at all. I just don't want any secrets between us. He doesn't deserve it."

"Wow, Chels. You're a mile ahead of Jay Davenport on the maturity scale!"

Chapter 11

CHRISTMAS

Despite the craziness of it all, Christmastime was Chelsea's favorite time of the year. She and Abby worked in the nursery in Christmas tree sales over the Thanksgiving weekend. The boys looked so competent and friendly as they hoisted trees off the lot, sent them through the bagger, and then tethered them into place atop their customers' cars. Their work was exhausting, but they decided it was more fun and just as effective as the weight training they were missing. They were covered in sap at the end of each night.

The little shed they used for a store was filled with mistletoe and sweet-smelling garlands and wreaths, tied with red, gold, and silver ribbons. Holiday music played merrily in the background. Tom kept a barrel of firewood lit to warm everyone's hands and to provide a spot for camaraderie, or to steal a quick kiss when there was a lull in business. Chelsea loved the smell of the greenery and couldn't wait until they set up their own tree in the house. Everyone they knew made it a tradition to stop in and buy their trees there, or up at Wayne's, where they saw many of their friends. Fred and Dot were a popular draw, and children stood on a bench in front of their garland-draped stalls for pictures. Chelsea would not get to help much after the weekend due to her intense rehearsals and the performances coming up in two weeks. Even though she'd miss the first DHS playoff game on Friday, she looked forward to the next Friday and Saturday night when the annual Christmas celebration would take place.

The Wildcats lost the first playoff game by an overtime field goal to a school from Greensboro. It had been a much better season than they'd had in recent years, so they were proud in spite of the defeat. The local paper gave them a decent write-up as well. Kyle made one more pick six and set the record for Doughton, which put him in the limelight even more. The following Saturday was the "Christmas in the Manger" celebration. The band was set up in the barn with some sheep statues and an actual manger for effect. Jay and Lauren appeared to be on track as usual and Chelsea wondered whether he'd said anything to her after his little revelation over Thanksgiving. Fella enjoyed the event as much as anyone and wagged his entire body in excitement when anyone paid attention to him. Liz and the girls sold gingerbread and hot cider in addition to their wreaths and Liz's ceramic angels, and Tom helped children onto Fred and Dot's backs to pose for their parents' Christmas card pictures.

On Saturday night, Kyle, Glen, and Anthony were back after their last high school football game. Chelsea was in the barn, cleaning up after Fred, and Kyle slipped away to meet her in the familiar stall. He wrapped his arms around her waist and pulled her close, kissing her with cold lips and pressing his red cheek to hers. "I'm sorry," he said, realizing he was covered in Frazier Fir sap. "I forgot I was so sticky. I hope I didn't get this on you."

She pulled him back to her and kissed him again as her response. "How does it feel to be a former high school football player?"

"It's surreal, I guess. We just keep checking off things we'll never do again, don't we? My mom cries every time I do something for the last time."

She nodded and smiled at the thought of that. They leaned against the rough wood of Fred's stall. Jay, seated on a bench with Emily, began picking out a slow, sweet melody on the guitar, and she joined him on her flute. The song was a different arrangement of "Away in a Manger." As a long-standing tradition, Kitty had picked a little girl to go and lay a baby doll into the manger.

Chelsea felt tears prick her eyes. Music always got to her, especially at Christmas. She turned to watch them and pulled Kyle closer from behind her. "This is so *perfect*," she breathed and she felt him laughing quietly in her ear. It took so little to make her happy, she imagined he was thinking, but with him there it was really no small thing. There would never be another Christmas like this. They listened to the song and then went back to work selling trees and greenery.

The following week was Studio One's Christmas Extravaganza, performed by the Studio One dance company and guest artists Sonya had invited from the university. The weather was good and both shows were well-attended. Chelsea's "Mirliton" dance was flawless, and she and Willie threw themselves full out into the finale with "Carol of the Bells," which got a standing ovation both nights. Kyle, her friends, and all of her family members took turns working at the tree lot on different nights so they could all come to watch, and Chelsea had quite a collection of flowers by Saturday night. Kyle took her to Makoto's for sushi after Saturday night's performance.

"I knew you would be awesome, but this was *amazing*!" he said, holding her hand on his knee beside her at the sushi bar. "I didn't want it to end," he said with admiring blue eyes. "When is the next thing you do?"

"After the audition, then I guess at Abby's show, and then not until the Spring concert in May. Sonya has the company dancing the second act from *Giselle*, and Willie and I have the leads as our senior dances."

"Count me in for every show."

"I saw Willie and Anthony's plans for the stage set and they look incredible. Sonya is so excited. She got permission to perform it in the school auditorium, and the school will let her store the scenery there as long as they have room, which is a huge help. I'll miss her so much when I'm gone from here. She's been great to Willie and me."

"Did you find the music for your audition?" he asked.

She smiled. "I finally did. I really think it will be what I wanted. It's kind of different. It's very…*emotional*. There's lots of bass and cello in it, and it's happy and sad in different parts, and just short enough for what they want." She didn't tell him he inspired the piece. He would see it for himself at the Spring concert. The happy parts were easy to express. The sad part was how she felt watching him go through the hard times, and how she would feel in the fall when they would go their separate ways.

He was watching her and asked, "What's wrong?"

"Nothing in the world right now. Things couldn't be more right. I just feel blessed…like I'm floating at the moment," she murmured, feeling him tracing circles on the back of her hand with his thumb.

The following week was easier, with only dance class and no rehearsals. Football was over and the banquet was Friday night. Kyle came to the Christmas tree lot the next evening wearing his maroon and gold football jacket, finally able to display his varsity letter. She had heard from Glen and Anthony that Kyle had received the most valuable player award as well. He changed into his other jacket and they worked all evening at the lot. Sales were slightly slower than the previous weeks, so there was more time for the boys to goof around. It started to snow, and by about eight o'clock, the ground was covered enough for them to make snowballs to throw at each other clandestinely when they didn't have customers. Liz asked Chelsea to take Kitty up to the house, and Kyle volunteered to go with her. It was hard to get her wheelchair across the crunchy snow, but thankfully, they didn't have far to go.

CHRISTMAS

As Chelsea started to take Kitty back to her room, she asked Kyle to build a fire. A few minutes later, she emerged from the hallway and heard the snapping and crackling of dry logs catching in the fireplace. She found Kyle standing at the window, rubbing sap off his hands with sanitizing gel, and watching the snow come down in fat, wet flakes.

"What's this?" he asked her as she came to stand beside him and watch the snow. He pointed to a capital "*A*" at the bottom corner of one of the old windowpanes. She laughed.

"That is my great, great, great Aunt Annette Davenport's initial. She scratched it on the glass after she became engaged in the early 1900s. The story goes that she wanted to make sure the diamond was real, so as soon as her fiancé left, she cut her initial in the window pane."

"Wow," he whispered.

"I guess you didn't see this one," she said, and pointed to the opposite corner, where a small "*C*" was etched in the glass.

"Charley?" he asked, a slow smile spreading across his face.

"Oh yeah," she said, and he wrapped an arm around her.

"Hey, before everyone else comes in, I want to give you your Christmas present," he said, his blue eyes sparkling. "We're leaving Christmas Eve for Charlotte, so I want to give it to you tonight."

"I have yours, too," she said, taking his hand and leading him to the tree. She breathed in the scent of the fir tree and found his gift. The twinkling colored lights and the firelight were the only lights in the room and they sat on the hearth with presents in hand.

"Open mine first," he said, handing her a long box wrapped in silver paper and tied with a shiny red ribbon. She untied the ribbon carefully and slipped her fingernail under the tape. He laughed impatiently and said, "I knew you'd do it like that!"

"It's too pretty to mess up. I love Christmas," she giggled, and opened the box. She gave a little gasp. It was a delicate silver necklace with a small freeform hammered silver star, set with the tiniest sparkling clear stones. She looked up at him, speechless.

"*They* won't cut glass. They're CZs. But I always think of you when I see a star."

"I love it," she managed to whisper. She held it in her hand and felt the smoothness of the silver and the bumpy little stones under her fingers.

"See, I think God sent you to me that night when we watched the stars falling, the meteor shower. I fell in love with you that night. Every time a star streaked across the sky, I made a wish that you could be for me. I was wishing like crazy."

Her eyes were wet and she felt a chill as he took her face in his hand and kissed her tenderly. "This makes me so happy. I love you," she whispered. She turned around and he moved her hair to fasten the chain around her neck. The little star fell just inside the hollow of her collarbone, and he touched it, gazed at her, and then kissed her again.

"Okay, open mine," she said and they laughed as he ripped the red and white snowflake paper and white bow off his box. He opened the box and lifted out a creamy ceramic angel that fit the length of his palm. He held it carefully, taking in the long, curling mahogany hair and the light green-gray eyes and then looked up at her.

"This is you?" he asked softly.

She nodded, and looked at the heart the angel held in her hands. "I asked my mother to make it so I could give it to you. Merry Christmas!"

"My angel. It's *perfect*," he said. He pulled her closer to him and kissed her again. Then they heard the back door bump open and shut as Tom and Liz came in, knocking snow off their boots, and coming in by the fire.

"Oh, good, you built a fire," Tom said, rubbing his hands together. Then he realized they were having a moment. Liz entered the room and sighed happily.

"You opened your present?" she asked Kyle.

"Yes, ma'am, and I love it," he said, smiling.

Chelsea rose and went to her parents. "Look what Kyle gave me," she said, fingering the necklace at her throat.

"It's just beautiful," said Liz. "Merry Christmas, you two," she said, her brown eyes shining. "I'm going to make us some hot chocolate." She left to join Tom in the kitchen. It sounded like he had beat her to it, running water from the sink.

Chelsea was clinging to Kyle again, when her phone "Jingle-Belled." She looked at the caller ID and looked questioningly at him. "It's *Sonya*," she said, puzzled, and flipped open the phone.

"Chelsea? It's Sonya. I'm at the Stevens Center and just finished watching *The Nutcracker*. You'll never guess what happened," she said loudly.

"What?"

"One of the Mirlitons was messing around before the show today and twisted her ankle. She couldn't dance tonight and the understudy is out sick with the flu. Well, they hated having just one of them up there. You know, what really makes it so good is when there's a duet and they are so beautifully synchronized. So I was talking to John...." She was going a mile a minute and Chelsea had to hold the phone away from her ear. Kyle heard it all. "We were talking about you, and I suggested he put you in the show for the matinee tomorrow, and of course, he said yes!"

Chelsea laughed incredulously, "*Of course?*"

"Well, it's the *same choreography you just did.* You're definitely the bomb at this dance and I told him that. Of course he believes me. He and I have known each other for years. *He* respects my judgment—even if you don't. Look, if you want to do it, get down here in the morning and do a couple of run-throughs and we'll all see. I'll stay here tonight and take you through it. I really think you should do this."

By then, her parents had come back into the room, carrying steaming mugs of hot chocolate. She was too dumbfounded to take hers, so Kyle accepted both mugs and gave Tom and Liz a meaningful look. It grabbed their attention immediately, and they waited to listen to the rest of the conversation. Chelsea didn't respond. She looked helplessly at Kyle, who nodded at her vigorously.

"Chelsea, you can do this! This is an opportunity you can't afford to pass up. This could be your *audition*! I *know* you can pull this off," said Sonya. Tom and Liz raised their eyebrows.

"Okay…I'll come. Can I call you right back? I need to talk to my parents."

"Sure! I know you'll be great!"

Chelsea flipped the phone shut and looked at her parents, who were waiting for an explanation. When she told them what Sonya had proposed, they said in unison, "Absolutely!" Kyle, grinning, nodded his agreement with her parent's response.

"This is your shot, chica," he said softly, handing her a mug of chocolate. She sank back to the hearth and held the cup shakily to her lips. Kyle sat beside her.

"I just worry about this weather. How much snow are we supposed to get?" Liz asked, looking out the window.

"No more than three or four inches was what I heard," Tom replied, looking a little wary. "I still don't know if I want you driving down there by yourself. Unfortunately, you know we can't come," he said. She thought about the tree sales and her mom needing to be there with Kitty. Normally, Wayne and Becky could have helped out, and on a weekend other than the one before Christmas, it wouldn't have been an issue. Tom and Liz exchanged apprehensive glances.

"I can take her down there in the Jeep," Kyle spoke up.

"Well, that's a thought," Tom said, stroking his mustache that had become more silver than blonde. He looked at Liz, who looked relieved.

"I'd be so much more comfortable with that," she said. "Would your mother be okay with it?"

"I can call her," he said and pulled out his own phone.

Liz looked from Kyle to Tom and then to Chelsea. "Maybe I should talk to her."

"That would probably be better," Kyle said, looking relieved.

They called Shelly and cajoled her into approving the trip. Then Chelsea was back on the phone with Sonya, working out the details. "She said if they like me, I'll have to color my Pointe shoes red," she said, smiling tentatively. Kyle hugged her, laughing.

Liz looked sad. "I hate that I'm going to miss it. My baby hits the big time," she said, and wrapped her arms around her daughter.

Tom joined them in the hug. "You'll be *fabulous!*" he said, kissing the top of her head.

Although the snow ceased during the night, powder covered Davenport Farm Road. Nonetheless, Kyle drove carefully down the mountain and found the main roads had been plowed at daybreak when they left. She looked at him approvingly, noticing he had dressed up for the occasion, wearing black jeans, and a black shirt with tiny silver stripes under a gray V-neck sweater. The Jeep was warm inside and she turned off the music. "Is it okay for now?" she asked and he nodded, understanding.

"Did you sleep?" he asked, watching her sip her coffee.

"Not a wink," she said thickly.

He smiled reassuringly. "You'll be fine," he said.

"I just hope I don't throw up in your car," she said, taking a deep breath and closing her eyes. It was going to be a long drive.

Sonya and her friend John Jacobs met them at the stage door and ushered them inside. Chelsea introduced Kyle and they all shook hands. "Here's a ticket for you," said John, handing Kyle a ticket for a balcony seat. "We should have a full house today, considering we only got a dusting of snow. It will be gone by this afternoon." Chelsea's stomach flip-flopped when she heard that. She walked onto the stage and looked out at the cavernous house, dark and musty like old theaters she'd been in before.

"Chelsea, let's get you warmed up. Angele will be getting here to go over the dance with you in about forty-five minutes. Let's try on the costume first, though. Have you eaten?"

Chelsea shook her head quickly and swallowed audibly. "Couldn't. But I brought a bagel with me and an orange for later."

Sonya smiled, "Okay. Kyle, there's a place backstage where you can wait while this goes on, or you can just sit down here, if it's okay with Chelsea," she said, gesturing to the house seats.

He looked at her and said, "Maybe in the back?" and Chelsea nodded. He'd brought his laptop and a book for something to do, so he went down the stairs and up the dark aisle.

After the warm-up and the run-through with Angele, Chelsea felt a little more like herself. John was enthusiastic about the performance, and suggested she get to work coloring her shoes with a large red Sharpie and sew on the red ribbons he held. She needed to try on the costume again for the costumer in case she thought any alterations were needed. They would go through the finale next, but so far, it looked like a piece of cake, he said, reassuring her.

When they broke for lunch, Angele invited them to walk down to Foothills Brewery with her. Chelsea was able to manage part of a BLT on sourdough bread, as Angele and Kyle chatted about the School of the Arts. Angele mentioned more than once how the performance that day would be important in securing a place for Chelsea next year. "I can't believe you've never danced with a full-blown ballet before," she said. Then, after seeing Kyle's face, "You're just so good, I mean. I doubt this will be a whole lot different than what you've done before with Sonya. I can tell she's taught you well. You have excellent technique."

Kyle told her about the snow they'd had in the mountains and got her talking about other topics as they walked back to the theater. He kissed Chelsea and said, "Break a leg" with a wink. He found a spot in the lobby to work on his project paper while the cast warmed up onstage. Later, when the curtain went up, Chelsea watched the first act backstage, and she and Angele dressed in their red-and-white-striped tutus at intermission. After putting on her lace cap, choker, and lace gloves, she took several deep breaths, and on their cue, she and Angele took the stage for their introduction by the Dew Drop Fairy. A few minutes later, the real thing began. "Eleven piqué turns," Chelsea said over and over to herself. "Don't forget to count." She watched Angele out of the corner of her eye. When they moved into each other's sight, they smiled and Chelsea began to feel the chemistry and the charm of her own character and let herself be transformed into the role. Suddenly, it was comfortable and she felt the familiar sense of power and shimmer she loved when she performed. The stage lights felt warm, charging her body. The turns were just steps away—*one, two, three, four, five, six, seven, eight, nine, ten, eleven*—and then they were each down on one knee with arms stretched into the air.

It was over! The applause was thunderous, and the crowd cheered and whistled. She heard "Bravo!" amidst the applause. She and Angele smiled even more at each other again and curtsied before they darted off the stage. She ran into Sonya's arms. "I knew it would be exquisite," Sonya exclaimed, clapping her hands, and beaming at Chelsea. "You were seamless, both of you!" They took their places to get ready for the finale. John watched her from across the stage and gave her a wink and a thumbs-up. The finale went off well, and she was glad she and Angele were in the back for the remaining steps that were not familiar to her.

Sonya snapped their picture as they exited the stage after the curtain call. They were expected to change clothes immediately. "That will be for your parents," Sonya said, handing them each a red rose. When Chelsea emerged from the dressing room, she found Kyle backstage with the throng of families and friends waiting for their dancers. The Sugar Plum Fairy posed for pictures with aspiring little ballerinas in their festive Christmas dresses.

Kyle grinned and presented her with a bouquet of red and white flowers wrapped in cellophane and tied with a red ribbon. "That was beyond words," he said gathering her up in a huge embrace. He kissed her and she laughed, wiping her red lipstick off his lips. "This is a good look for you," he said commenting on her makeup. "You look so much older. It's really hot!" he growled in her ear, noticing Sonya and John behind them. They congratulated and thanked Chelsea, and Sonya made sure they were okay to drive back up to Boone. John shook her hand and told her he looked forward to seeing her in February at the auditions. She thanked him for letting her dance. Sonya wished them both a Merry Christmas and took them in a group hug before they parted ways.

"I'm *starving*," Chelsea said as they floated arm in arm to the Jeep. They stopped at the Mellow Mushroom to celebrate before hitting the road for home. During the drive, they talked about everything, listened to music, and held hands.

"Wow, you're really fired up," he said. "I guess it's like me after a big win," he said, grinning at her.

"*Nothing* could be better than this," she said, feeling the smile that been on her face since she'd first taken the stage that afternoon.

"I can only think of *one* thing," he said, surprising her with his intense eyes on hers for a safe moment. Then he returned to concentrating on the road.

"Hmmm," she said. "Well, I guess that's out..."

He looked rueful. "Yeah, I guess you're right...for now. It's better like this, you know? This way I know I really love you and that I'm not just addicted to sex with you."

She blushed with the intimacy of his feelings. Still, she was curious. "Why are you so sure about this?" she asked. "I don't think I have the same resolve."

He chuckled. "Don't even tell me that! It's because every time I kiss you and think it's going anywhere, I see my dad in my head, telling me he's gonna disinherit me and chop off my *wang* if I get someone pregnant!"

She made a face. "What?"

"Yeah, imagine having *that* thought every time we make out."

She looked confused. "Why would he say that to you? I'm sure he was just kidding around."

"Oh, no, I think he was pretty serious. When I was in the eighth grade, he and my mom sat me down and let me have it. I didn't even have a girlfriend. I don't know *what* brought it on, but it definitely stuck with me. That, and the fact that I see *your dad* in my head with him. It's enough to *really* creep me out," he said, shuddering, and did not notice that she was doing the same thing.

She had to change the subject. "Well, I'd like to scare them *both* out of your head...for selfish reasons, obviously." She saw him smile slightly. "Anyway, thanks for being with me today. I had the time of my life. You're really good for me."

Chapter 12

DISTRACTIONS

The Davenports invited the Davises for dinner on New Year's Eve. There was a lot to celebrate in addition to the New Year. Chelsea had received letters of acceptance from E.C.U. and U.N.C.-G., and Kyle had heard good news from State, Virginia Tech, and Clemson. Shelly was impressed by Chelsea's opportunity to dance in *The Nutcracker*, and Kyle's deck project was almost finished, thanks to a surprising mild spell in the weather just after Christmas. He and Chelsea sequestered themselves in her father's office, where he showed her pictures of the project he'd emailed to her. He showed her how to download her own pictures from the camera she got for Christmas, and he helped her set up a Facebook account. They snapped one of themselves and put it on her wall with a "Happy New Year!" caption.

School started back up and senioritis was the hot topic among most of her friends. Chelsea was too wound-up to think about schoolwork, and thought about her upcoming dance class of elementary school girls. Classes were to start on Saturday morning before her dance company rehearsal. Sonya was pushing her to learn something new for the U.N.C.S.A. audition, since the director and doubtless other people on the panel had already seen her "Mirliton" performance. Brad was supervising her choreography for her contemporary dance and was moved by the emotion she put into it. February and March were speeding toward her like a train, and she hoped for no other distractions before it was all over.

But it was hard to avoid distractions at this point in the year. Everyone she knew had turned, or was turning eighteen, and there would be lots of parties. She would be seventeen until July, so it didn't seem fair. She felt like such a kid. Kyle and Glen talked incessantly about snowboarding and planned to try out their Christmas snowboards as soon as they had a chance and could afford lift tickets. Abby was planning their Spring Break trip. She and Meredith had been online, checking out rental houses in Myrtle Beach for the last week in March. Meredith was spending time with Kyle, interviewing him and taking pictures at his house, his worksite, and with permission from the new owners, at the cabin.

Saturday night was supposed to be a boys' night on the ski slopes, so the girls planned to go to a party at Rocky Santoro's house. Aiden Caffey was turning eighteen, and the word was that Rocky's parents were out of town, so a big throw-down was in the making. When Kyle and Glen heard about that, they said they didn't want the girls to go without them, so they postponed their snowboarding. Chelsea was worried about Elle being there, but Abby said Rocky had broken up with her over Christmas.

By the time they got there, cars were already parked on the side of the road in front of Rocky's house. It was raining, so Glen wasn't quite as bummed about not getting to snowboard. Music blared from the house, and two guys were rolling a keg around to the basement door as they went in. All the football players and most of the cheerleaders were there, along with everyone else Chelsea knew. Huge football players enjoyed themselves and let themselves go after having abstained from drinking during the season.

The party was in full swing downstairs in the dimly lit basement where snacks, soft drinks, and several bottles of liquor were out on the bar. Aiden and Rocky were playing "Guitar Hero" while lots of people stood around watching and drinking. Glen and Kyle were delighted to find Rocky's pool table. Anthony and Nick were sitting at the bar and Meredith poured drinks. They said hello and talked about their Christmas vacations while Kyle and Chelsea leaned against the bar. Meredith wanted to see Chelsea's necklace. Abby mixed rum and Diet Pepsi for Glen and herself, and she gestured to Kyle and Chelsea. Kyle said over the music, "Just Pepsi," and Chelsea did the same.

"Do you seriously not ever drink?" Chelsea asked, close in his ear so he'd hear her over the music.

He laughed, "Not at this kind of party, and especially not since I'm driving tonight. You?"

"I guess I'm more of a wino," she said. "Pepsi is fine for tonight. We'd better watch those two," she said, smiling at Glen and Abby as they toasted each other. They found Anthony and Nick and chatted as Kyle and Glen waited for the pool table to open up. Chelsea was in the midst of telling Abby about her new dance students when Kendra came down the stairs followed by Elle, both wearing rain jackets and wrapped in colorful scarves. They went directly to Aiden and gave him birthday hugs. Rocky seemed glad to see Kendra, but gave Elle a stiff greeting. He answered the phone someone handed him, talked briefly, and then hung up. He told Aiden they'd have to turn down the music. "Noise complaint," Chelsea heard him say. The girls sidled up to the bar and helped themselves to chips and dip.

"Hey, guys," said Kendra, smiling and tossing her hair, cut in a stylish C-shaped bob that hung just below her chin.

Elle flipped her own blonde hair to the side, munched a chip, and reached for the rum and a Coke. "Oh my God, I don't believe you guys are here! Y'all never come out," she said furrowing her brows at Chelsea and Abby. She squeezed a lime into her drink. Then she smiled at Kyle. "How was *your* Christmas?" she cooed, then turned her back on the girls and propped her elbow on the bar beside him. "I saw you got a snowboard from Santa." He nodded and looked around.

"She's been on his Facebook page," Abby said in Chelsea's ear. "Surely she's seen your pictures all over it, too."

She was saying things into Kyle's ear that Chelsea couldn't hear, and he was trying to decipher it and answer her. He said something about Charlotte and then something else about the deck. Aiden came up and struck up a conversation with the two of them. She whispered something into Aiden's ear, and then she squeezed Kyle's arm, picked up her purse, and walked past the pool table with Aiden. The table came open and Glen went to pick out a cue. Kyle spoke into Chelsea's ear, "We don't have to stay here long if you don't want to. Want to leave after this game?"

"It's fine...whatever you guys want to do," she said to Abby and him. He chose a cue, then set his drink down on a small table near the pool table. Glen racked up the balls and Meredith came back over to talk about Spring Break.

"So, who all is going?" asked Chelsea.

"Abby and Glen, Anthony, and hopefully, you and Kyle," Meredith said.

"Hmm," said Chelsea. "I'd really like to go. Somewhere warm sounds really good at the moment, and I'll be so ready to have a break from school. I can't speak for Kyle, though. There's probably no way his mother will let him go."

Abby's eyebrows shot up. "Why not?"

"Because of what happened to his sister on her Spring Break," Chelsea answered glumly.

"I thought about that, too," said Meredith. "But it won't be the same without him, especially not for you." They got a whiff of something sweet and musky in the cold air, blowing in through the door someone had left open.

Chelsea looked at Glen and Kyle, who were shooting pool. Kyle was bent over the table, aiming for a solid ball when Glen hooted. "Dude, who brought the *weed*?"

"It won't be *any* fun if you don't go," Abby said to Chelsea. "My mother is going down to be around in case we need her. But she agrees we need to do a trip on our own, since we'll all be going away to college in just a few months." She spoke louder since someone had cranked the music up again.

Elle walked up to the pool table and put her drink down on the little table. She looked in the mirror, rummaged through her red purse, put on lip-gloss, and rearranged her hair. Kyle was moving around her with his cue, trying not to bump into her. She was laughing and telling him something in his ear again. He laughed and shook his head. Chelsea watched as he lined up another solid ball. Glen waited impatiently, hoping to get in another shot. Kendra and Aiden, who'd been standing around with Rocky and Nick, giggled and made their way over to the food table just as Elle went upstairs, beckoning to Kendra.

Kyle sipped his drink after beating Glen yet again, and Glen demanded a rematch. Since no one was waiting, Kyle racked the balls and Glen broke. Other guys stood around, drinking cups from the keg of beer and reaching across the bar for chips and crackers. Some watched the game of pool and others tried their hand at "Guitar Hero." It was getting more crowded with the sheer size of some of the guys, and louder as the music ratcheted up another notch.

Abby looked at Chelsea, and they eased out of their position near the bar as other people replaced them to mix more drinks. Rocky laughed and placed another fifth of vodka on the bar. "Do you think we should leave? This party might get out of hand soon," Abby said into Chelsea's ear.

"Yeah, maybe after their game is over," Chelsea said. She made eye contact with Kyle, who sipped his drink and watched Glen's next shot. He nodded at her. He rolled his eyes as Glen walked around the table again and took another look at his shot. When he smiled at Chelsea, they raised their glasses to each other and sipped their drinks. Glen missed his shot and it was Kyle's turn again. Kyle shook his head, as if clearing his vision, and leaned across the table at the shot he wanted. He missed, and Glen crowed, taking his next turn. Glen made two in a row, and Kyle shot again and missed.

"What's wrong with you, man? You never miss! Not that I'm complaining," Glen said, making his next shot and then lining up the eight ball. Kyle wiped his face with his hand and blinked his eyes at Glen's victory.

"Damn…" was all he said, and then Chelsea rounded them up to leave. She took Kyle's hand and he blinked his eyes hard at her, shaking his head strangely. They took their cups and Kyle went upstairs first, followed by Glen, and then Chelsea and Abby. Kyle staggered on the stairs and reeled backward suddenly. His cup fell from his hand, spilling what was left of his drink on the wood stairs.

"Whoa, now," Glen said, reaching out a hand to Kyle's back and steadying him on the stairs. "I got him. What have you been drinking, man?"

Chelsea and Abby backed down the stairs. Chelsea went to the bar for some paper towels to wipe up the spill while Abby tossed the cup into a wastebasket. Upstairs, they looked around for Kyle and Glen as some people watched Aiden unwrap some of his presents. Glen came out of the bathroom as Abby was starting down the hall to look for him. "There you are," she said. "Where's Kyle?"

DISTRACTIONS

Glen looked sheepish. "He went in there with Elle," he said, indicating a closed door.

"What?" Chelsea screeched.

"I don't know. I had to *pee*," he said defensively.

She went to the door and knocked, calling his name.

"Go *away*," came Elle's laughing voice from the other side. Chelsea tried the knob but it was locked.

"Great," she said, rolling her eyes at Glen, who shrugged.

"Sorry. She said something about something *special* she had for him, and he just followed her right in there like the *children of the corn*, or something…"

"Oh God, remind me never to leave you alone with our children!" Abby said, then pushed him aside and pounded on the door. "Kyle! Come on, we're leaving," she shouted through the door, but all they heard was a giggle from the other side.

More people had come up from downstairs and Rocky was among them. Abby went to him. "Can you get Elle out of there?" she asked. "Or just open the door so we can get Kyle and go?"

Rocky looked confused and then angry. "Jeez, that's my parents' bedroom." He shook his head and said disgustedly, "She likes playing with my mom's lingerie." He pounded on the door himself. "How long have they been in there?"

"Fifteen minutes?" Glen shrugged. "How did he get so drunk?"

"He was drinking *Diet Pepsi*," said Chelsea. They looked at each other and then noticed that people were leaving in a hurry.

Nick Caffey appeared at Rocky's side. "Dude, there's a cop in your driveway."

Rocky's face contorted and he groaned. "No friggin' *way!*"

"Uh, *way*, dude," said Nick, and then he clapped a hand on Rocky's large shoulder. "Great party, man, but we're outta here."

"Go out through the basement," said Rocky as he pounded on the door again. "Elle, get out! The cops are here!"

Anthony had been watching, and he and Meredith headed toward the stairs. "Sorry, y'all," he said to the group. "We're going. Appalachian don't need to hear about this, you know? Good luck."

"Hey, get that liquor in the cabinets downstairs on your way out," Rocky ordered.

"What about the keg?" Anthony asked.

Rocky shrugged. "I don't know…can you get it outside?"

"I'll try, man," said Anthony.

"Come on, we'll help," said Chelsea, and she, Abby, and Glen followed Anthony downstairs.

Anthony rolled the keg out the door while the girls put away the liquor and threw away the cups. They heard a loud knock on the door and skittering footsteps coming down the stairs. Kendra ran out the back door, throwing things in her purse and digging for her car keys. She looked sheepishly at Chelsea as she said goodbye. Elle was right behind her, laughing raucously, and throwing on her rain jacket. "Have fun with the po-po, y'all," she called on her way out the door.

"Shit, what are we gonna do?" asked Abby. Chelsea had a bad feeling.

"Well, seeing as how Kyle drove, nobody's leaving yet. Anyway, we can't leave him here. Where the heck is he anyway?" Glen asked, and they tromped back upstairs. The sheriff was talking somberly to Rocky at the front door. Glen dashed into the bedroom with the girls behind him, but he stopped and pushed them back. "Give me one second, ladies," he said, shutting the door.

Hearing cars pull away from the road, Chelsea went into the living room. She looked out the window and saw several cars remained, so she wondered where the rest of the people were. She saw Kendra pull out into the road and drive away. Chelsea raked her fingers through her hair and looked helplessly at Abby. Her heart was pounding. Having written down Rocky's name and his parents' names, the sheriff turned to Abby. Chelsea heard the bedroom door open and ran to see what was going on with Kyle.

Glen emerged from the room. "He's out like a light," he said with an odd expression. "Did you say he hadn't been drinking?" he whispered to Chelsea.

She nodded, "Just Pepsi."

"It's like he's been drugged," he said, dragging his hand across the back of his neck. "I can't move him!"

"Why didn't you let us in there before?"

"He was, uh, decorated."

"What?" she said as the sheriff approached to get her name and information. He peeked around the door and they both looked in at Kyle, lying on the bed, dead to the world.

"Can you get him up?" he said to Glen.

"Uh, no sir," said Glen.

"Anyone know his parents? We'll need to call them."

Chelsea and Glen exchanged worried looks. This wasn't going to be good. A deputy came through the door with a breathalyzer. The sheriff told him to start with Rocky, then told the rest of them to have a seat. He was calling Rocky's parents, who, until that moment, had been enjoying themselves at a pharmaceutical conference at the Grove Park Inn in Asheville.

Glen was getting text messages as they sat on the couch, waiting. He laughed silently.

"What the hell is so funny?" Abby muttered, seeing no humor in the situation.

"Half these guys are out in the woods waiting for the cops to leave. They're probably freezing their asses off and soaking wet by now!"

Chelsea rolled her eyes. "Okay, I'm going to call Kyle's mom. Better me than *them*, right?" She sighed, referring to the sheriff and his deputy, who was now motioning for Abby to blow into the breathalyzer.

She made the call and explained the situation as tactfully as she could—that Kyle was not able to get up and they weren't sure why. In a crisp voice, Shelly said she'd be right over and requested Rocky's address, which Chelsea had to get from him. Abby was back from her breath test, so it was Glen's turn. "That call did *not* go well," Chelsea told Abby. "I'm sure she hates me now. How did he get like that? Do you think someone drugged him?"

"Oh, you mean someone like Elle McClarin? Yeah, my money's on her. Jeez, I can't believe I had to blow," said Abby glumly.

Chelsea blew a zero and then the sheriff addressed all of them to see whether they had called Kyle's mother. Chelsea said she was on her way and the sheriff looked hard at all of them. "Your parents are on their way home," he said to Rocky. "You'll be getting a citation. You two might slide," he said to Abby and Glen. The deputy, who stood nearby, was definitely the good cop of the two of them. He smiled and shook his head as he wiped the breathalyzer with a disinfectant wipe, and recorded more information on the pink papers he was preparing. "As for sleeping beauty in there," bad cop said, leaning his head toward the bedroom, "who wants to tell me what happened to him?"

Chelsea spoke up immediately. "He wasn't drinking at all. We think someone might have drugged him."

"What?" Just as Chelsea said they thought he'd been drugged, Shelly Davis walked through the front door, car keys in hand. "Where's my son?" she asked. The deputy took her to the room where Kyle still lay flat on his back, legs hanging off the bed, as if he had fallen back while sitting up, the same position as earlier.

Chelsea turned to Glen and whispered harshly, "What do you mean, he was *decorated*?"

Glen looked uneasy as Abby and Chelsea's eyes bored into his. "Uh, he was slightly *undressed*, and there was a real cute pair of polka dot and lace panties covering him up. I just zipped him up before the po-po got a peek. There were panties all over the bed, so I cleaned up a little," he said lamely. Chelsea groaned, imagining what had gone on. "Don't worry though; nothing could have happened."

"And just how do you figure that?" Abby countered, irritation in her voice.

"There was nothing there, you know? I would know this," he said, rolling his eyes. "She was only in there like twenty minutes with him and he was, like, in a *coma*! Come on, he won't even *remember*!"

Shelly sat on the side of the bed and had a conversation with the officer. "They think he was drugged?"

The sheriff gestured them over. "This young lady says he didn't drink all evening."

Chelsea shook her head. "Just Diet Pepsi. He drove. He would never drink and drive. And then it was like he just got all messed up. He was blinking and shaking his head. When we were going up the stairs to leave, he fell and dropped his drink."

"Yeah, and he was missing shots at pool," Glen said incredulously. "I've *never* beat him at pool before!"

"Who poured his drink? Did you see anyone do anything to his drink?" the dark-haired sheriff asked.

They looked at each other and shook their heads. "I poured his drink myself," said Abby.

"Can you think of anybody who *might* have tried something like this?" he pressed.

"Well," said Abby, "we have our suspicions, but we can't prove it…"

"Who roofies a *guy*?" asked Glen, laughing. Everyone shot him a look, indicating there was no humor in it.

"Really," said the younger deputy. "It's kind of counterproductive."

"Isn't this illegal?" asked Shelly. "I could press charges if I knew who it was, right?"

"Yes, and yes," the sheriff told her. "Where is the cup he was drinking out of? We could run it for prints. I'm going to need the names of everybody who was here, and who you think did this."

"I threw it in the waste basket downstairs," offered Abby and the younger officer followed her downstairs.

"Ma'am, you'd have to get a urine test from him to see what the substance was. It's going to be a long shot to try to pin this on somebody here tonight, but you could take him to the hospital and have him checked out," advised the sheriff.

Shelly shook her head. "I just hate this! My son has been through so much! He doesn't need this," she said intensely and glared at Chelsea and the others. "Come on, guys, think! Did you see something? *Who do you think did this?"*

They exchanged nervous looks. Abby raised her eyebrows, urging Chelsea to say it.

"We think it was Elle McClarin. She's kind of been after him all year," she said, lowering her eyes.

"Why didn't I know about this?" asked Shelly.

"He tried to play it down. He didn't want it to upset Chelsea," Abby said. She looked compassionately at her friend.

"That's so like him," Shelly mumbled. "Okay, let's get him up and in the car. Can I go ahead and take him?"

"Sure," said the sheriff. "But I don't think you're going to be able to manage him, actually. He's out cold at this point. I think we should call EMS to transport him."

Shelly put her head in her hands and seemed to crumble. Chelsea put her arm around her awkwardly, but then Shelly reached up and took her hand. "I just can't believe this is happening," she said breathlessly. She looked at the sheriff. "What about the rest of them...and his car?"

"Are any of these kids okay to drive?" he asked the deputy.

"Her," he said. He pointed at Chelsea while sealing Kyle's cup in a plastic bag.

"Can you drive Kyle's Jeep to your house?" Shelly asked. Chelsea nodded. "You come with me," she said to Glen. "I'll call your mother and tell her I need your help."

"You can spend the night at my house, like we planned," Chelsea said to Abby, who nodded wordlessly. Abby texted a message to her mother, much safer than talking at this point.

It took only a few minutes for the EMTs to arrive. They took Kyle's pulse and blood pressure before lifting him onto the gurney and sliding it inside the truck. Shelly carried his football jacket, and handed Chelsea the keys to the Jeep. Chelsea knew there was no way his mother would allow her to accompany them to the E.R. She wiped tears from the side of her face as Glen gave her shoulders a squeeze. They agreed to meet in the morning. Abby and Chelsea would bring the Jeep over when Shelly called. Glen looked at the formidable Shelly and turned to Chelsea again, whispering, "Pray for me!" She and Abby did not laugh, but took Kyle's keys, got into the Jeep, and drove away.

Over pancakes the next morning, Chelsea told her parents what had happened the night before, and although they were not happy, they listened to the story, which Abby corroborated by nodding at appropriate times. Indignant, Chelsea said, "I wasn't even drinking, and I had to blow into that damn breathalyzer!" Abby's role was not highlighted.

Tom shook his head, stroking his mustache, "Well, sugar, you did the right thing. You know that. That was a party you probably could have skipped."

Liz nodded, ruefully. "I think you girls did the right thing. Who would do something like this?"

"We think it was Elle…" Chelsea's voice trailed off.

"She's the one who's caused all the problems with Kyle this year, right?" Liz sighed. "There's always a girl like that," she said meaningfully to Tom, who immediately looked defensive.

"After all these years, you still remember that stuff…," he said, rolling his eyes.

"Back in college, Julie Carmichael used to drive me *crazy* trying to get with your dad," Liz exclaimed. Tom threw up his hands. "And I have to say, at first, you didn't do anything to discourage her! You ate up the attention! I had to *beg* you to put a stop to it."

Chelsea and Abby exchanged amused glances. Liz had only had one cup of coffee. Kitty was laughing, saying, "Slut! I remember," and they all laughed.

"I'm just glad you all are so responsible," Liz said. "I worry about you because of what other people do, but this helps me. Now I know you're making good decisions."

"Yep, I'm about as boring as they come," Chelsea said to her mother's wistful smile. The phone rang, and it was Shelly asking whether Chelsea and Abby could come over and bring Kyle's Jeep. The sheriff was on his way, and he wanted to talk to them again. Tom told her they would be right down.

They exchanged nervous glances as the girls left the house, Chelsea driving Kyle's Jeep and Abby following in Chelsea's Subaru.

Shelly Davis was drinking coffee from a large blue cup that read: *I Don't Do Perky.* She welcomed them, and the girls responded with appropriate pallor as they entered the large stone foyer. The sheriff hadn't arrived yet, and they smelled bacon and eggs coming from the kitchen. Glen greeted them as if they were twin Messiahs and hugged Abby with unnecessary vigor. "Long night, babe!" he murmured into her ear, and she nodded, understanding. Shelly escorted them into the great room where they sat on the sofa while she went to get Kyle. They sat like children on the principal's "time-out" bench and didn't say much. Glen broke the awkward silence. "It was roofies. Prepare to get *fingerprinted.*"

Chelsea and Abby shot each other astonished looks as Kyle was being marched stiffly down the stairs in his pale, destroyed jeans and a white Henley T-shirt that almost matched the color of his face. He smiled vaguely at her, acknowledged Abby and Glen, and sat on the brown couch beside Chelsea, then dropped his head into his hands. "Ouch," he said, trying for humor, and they laughed to help him out.

Chelsea attempted to be brave. "What time did you get home last night?"

"Not till after two," Shelly said in a sleep-deprived voice. "I want to say thank you for watching over Kyle," she said, surprising them all. "Glen told me *much* more than I ever wanted to know about what happened, or what we *think* happened last night. I'm glad Kyle has friends like you," she said, her voice softer than before, and her look was directed at Chelsea. Kyle looked confused and his mother said to him, "It's okay, honey, you'll find out all the details soon. I have to tell you that Sheriff Conrad is going to be here in a few minutes. He wants to get fingerprints from the four of you, and then he'll get Elle's as well to match up what they found on the cup from the party. If none of them match, he'll probably look into checking out everyone else from the party."

Kyle sighed heavily and his head sank lower into his hands. When Chelsea rubbed his leg, he looked at her out of the corner of his eye. Shelly watched them and Chelsea moved her hand away, reflexively.

"I'm going to clean up the kitchen. I'm sure Kyle has questions for you before the sheriff gets here, and I certainly don't want to hear any more of it," said Shelly, taking her coffee cup out of the room.

He wiped both hands over his face and sighed. "Okay, what happened?"

They looked at each other and Glen asked, "What do you remember?"

He sighed again and leaned back into the brown sofa, reaching for Chelsea's hand. "We went to Rocky's house and everybody was drinking, but us," he said, glancing at Chelsea. "I remember Elle showed up, and you and I were shooting pool. And that's about it," he said, looking befuddled.

Glen continued, "We think she might have slipped a roofie in your drink. We were trying to leave, and you almost took us all out when we were going up the steps. I had to go pee, and you followed Elle into Rocky's parents' bedroom…" Kyle's eyebrows raised and he placed his hand over his eyes as if it hurt. Glen continued. "She had pulled your pants down, and when I found you, there was a pair of panties over you and more like them all over the bed. You were in a coma at that point, so I zipped you up and tried to get you presentable for the police."

Kyle groaned and tried to hide behind both hands. Chelsea rubbed his leg again.

"Nothing happened, bro. You were, uh, clean; know what I mean?"

"God," Kyle mumbled. "And my *mom* knows this?" He groaned again. He looked at Chelsea and shook his head slightly. "This is so bad. I'm so sorry. Damn, my head hurts!"

"So now the sheriff is coming over here to fingerprint us all so he can check it with what's on the cup. Abby, you, and I all touched the cup. You didn't, did you, Chels?" Glen asked. She shook her head.

"Do you want some water?" she asked Kyle.

"That'd be great, thanks. I feel like I've swallowed a desert."

Chelsea rose and courageously walked into the kitchen, filling a glass with tap water from the sink. Shelly was next to her, filling the dishwasher with the breakfast dishes. She gave Chelsea a small smile and said, "I really do appreciate you guys sticking by Kyle last night. I just worry about him so much…" she said, her voice trailing off.

"I know," said Chelsea. "He really does try to do the right thing. I hope you know I'm trying not to make it any harder for him."

Shelly looked questioningly at her and then seemed relieved. "I'm glad you're in his life," she said gently and gave Chelsea's arm a squeeze. The doorbell rang and they went into the foyer to welcome the sheriff.

Chapter 13

PRESSURE

It was a weird week at school, to say the least. Starting Saturday afternoon, Elle called Kyle and screamed at him about sicking the cops on her and having her fingerprinted like a common criminal. Disgusted by the whole thing, he told her that's what happens when you're a suspect in a drug case. She was not happy. When he questioned her about the encounter in the bedroom, she told him he had been a willing participant and it was too bad he did not remember. She did not admit to slipping anything into anyone's drink. School was intense all week, with Chelsea trying to ignore Elle, while wanting to rip her limb from limb. To top it all off, Abby and the deputy had apparently fished the wrong plastic cup out of the wastebasket so none of their fingerprints were on it. Even if it had matched up, the sheriff explained, there was no real evidence that any of them had doctored the drink. They needed an eyewitness or a confession, and Elle was not talking. So much for escaping the drama, Chelsea told Kyle, to his chagrin. Life moved on.

Chelsea's dance students were a sweet little group of nine girls; all were students at Snowy Ridge Elementary School. They met early on Saturday mornings at the school via the activity bus Chelsea had arranged through Cities in Schools and her grant. Classes were scheduled for six weeks, excluding Chelsea's audition the first Saturday of February, and they were to end with a performance at Abby's variety show the third weekend in February. Abby allowed them to bypass the audition, and Chelsea had looked over the stage to see where they would enter and exit, and where they could dress. The girls were eight and nine years old, and about as different from each other as nine girls could possibly be. Payton, with her dark ringlet curls and contagious laugh, was the standout. Even though she'd never danced before, she picked up the first steps easily. Little Lily, pale and freckle-faced, with shoes untied and wondering why she was there, was at the other end of the spectrum. Chelsea spent the first class on creative movement and taught the girls a few basic steps. She wasn't too worried about the dance. It would be more like acting than dancing anyway. The girls were hungry, so the second week's class started with sausage biscuits Chelsea brought from home.

"Where's Lily?" Chelsea asked the other girls the second Saturday. They munched biscuits in the lunchroom that served double duty as the auditorium, on the steps of the stage.

"She wasn't on the bus," said Molly and the other girls nodded. Payton's eyes got wide and she cried, "There she is!"

Chelsea turned to see Lily walking into the room in her dirty pink coat and uncombed blonde hair, with Kyle Davis, in his sap-stained jacket, toboggan in his hand. She smiled in surprise to see the two of them together and asked, "What's this? How do you two know each other?" Lily ran to Chelsea and hugged her.

"She missed the bus. Did you know she's Mrs. Jennings' granddaughter? The lady whose deck I built. She had a medical emergency this morning and Lily didn't go out for the bus. I was over there waiting for the building inspector to come for the last inspection when all this happened. But she didn't want to miss your class."

"Is everything okay now?" asked Chelsea.

"I think so. Lily's aunt came over and took her grandma to the doctor's. Her big sister will be home so Lily can go home on the bus," he said and then lowered his voice. "She seems kind of fragile, you know?"

"Yeah...thanks for bringing her. I'm glad you were there and could help her out. Small world, isn't it?" He nodded. "Want one?" Chelsea asked, offering Lily and him a biscuit.

"Sure, thanks," he said and Lily took hers quickly. "You made these? What time did *you* get up this morning?"

"I can't have hungry dancers on my hands, now can I?" she said, grinning at Lily and grabbing her up in a hug. Lily giggled as she munched on her biscuit and Chelsea handed her a juice box.

"So, are we still on for practicing 'Thriller' tomorrow?" Kyle asked.

"We are...my house at one-thirty. Did you know Kyle could dance, Lily? He's going to be in the show like you guys."

Lily looked at Kyle skeptically and laughed.

Kyle laughed, too. "You'll never know it's me, Lily. I'll be wearing a disguise! I gotta go. I left Frank up at the house waiting for the inspector. Thanks for breakfast," he said. He reached toward Chelsea but then thought better of it with the young audience eagerly watching every move.

"Thanks for bringing me, Mr. Kyle," said Lily, smiling shyly at him.

He winked at her. "See ya," he said to them, waving, and left the lunchroom.

"Wow, Lily, I can't believe you know him."

"He's nice. He has a really cute dog, and he brings us food when he comes, too."

"Yeah, he is nice."

That night it snowed again, but this time, the forecast was for at least twelve inches. Chelsea was exhausted from the week. She and her parents were watching a movie on TV and eating popcorn. She peeked out the front window at the large, fat flakes swirling down in the porch light. A moment later, there was a knock at the door; she went and peeked through the peephole, but saw no one. She opened the door and stepped outside onto the porch, wrapping her arms around herself against the cold, pulling the nubby ice-blue turtleneck higher up around her neck for warmth. She looked to the right and then to the left, wondering whether she had imagined the knock. Just then, a cold, hard object hit her in the right side. She gasped and jumped, then looked back around to the right, where she saw Kyle standing in the snow in her front yard, grinning devilishly at her, with Fella at his side, wiggling his entire body frantically.

"Oh! You are *so dead*," she yelled and ran down the stairs, glad she was wearing her tall suede boots. She quickly balled up a handful of the cold wet snow and let it fly, just grazing the back of his leg before he was on her, grabbing her and swinging her around in the snow. "You'd better be glad it was me and not my mom who answered the door," she said, laughing, feeling his frozen, scratchy face burying into her neck.

"I was watching! I saw you look out the window and figured you'd be at the door first. I'm proud of my boy Fella, here. He kept quiet so I could surprise you," he said, patting Fella on the head. Fella was still wagging himself all over and panting happily. Kyle cocked his head and said with a twinkle in his eyes, "I thought we could use a diversion. Do you want to go sledding? I'll wait while you change."

She loved to sled. "I don't know. After reading *Ethan Frome*, I don't want to end up wrapped around a tree, unable to walk for the rest of my life like his lover."

"See, the difference between me and Ethan is that I'm smart enough to stay away from *trees,"* he said and laughed in her ear. "I was going to take you to the golf course. It's much safer there!"

"Okay. You can come inside. We have a fire going."

"Wait. I need to tell you something first. I got my letter from U.V.A. today. I'm in!"

Her heart skipped a beat. She was happy for him, but sad for herself. It was so far away. She blinked hard and then smiled at him. "Wow... congratulations! Now all the pressure is off. All you have to do is sign," she said wistfully, referring to "Signing Day," when he would sign a letter of intent to play for the college of his choice.

"Yeah, I just need to keep my grades up. Like I said, we can meet back here on weekends, and you can come for visits on the longer breaks. We'll make it work," he said, grinning. He was soaring, and after the last few days, it was good to see. She invited him in and he visited with her family while she changed into ski pants and her down jacket.

The snow continued to swirl around them ethereally as they made run after run down the slopes of the golf course, with Fella running alongside the sled, trying to keep pace. He trotted back up with them each time and they laughed at his enthusiasm. "He won't budge when we get home," Chelsea said as they loaded the sled and her happy yellow dog into the back of the Jeep and made for home. Everyone was asleep when they returned. They kicked snow off their boots, shed their coats, hats, and gloves. The fire was down to embers, so Kyle tossed another log on, poking it to flames with the andiron, as she heated water for hot chocolate. As she had predicted, Fella crashed by the hearth and did not move. They sat together on the hearth and Kyle chuckled gently, looking at Fella, "He looks like an alligator!" Then, looking at her, he stretched his arm around behind her waist and kissed the side of her mouth. She sighed contentedly and snuggled sleepily against him, feeling the fire warm her back.

"Will your mother let you go on our Spring Break trip?" she asked, knowing the answer.

"Nope," he said matter-of-factly. "She wants me to go to the Outer Banks with her and visit Stacie. I guess that would be the next best thing. I hope you don't mind, but I asked if you could come with us."

"Why would I mind?" she asked, surprised.

"I know you'd like to go to Myrtle with everybody else. You should. It would be really fun," he said absently. "She said 'No' anyway."

Chelsea's heart sank. "Why? I thought she liked me now."

"She does. She loves you, actually. But she knows *I* love you, too. She thinks we'll mess around," he laughed in her ear.

"Yeah, well, we might!"

"Ah, that's a good way not to get invited back. Remember, I'm trying to *humor* her," he said, his chin on top of her head.

As she thought of the story Charley had told her over Thanksgiving, a wave of uneasiness swept over her. She held him tighter around his waist and sighed. "Will you ask her again? You can always try wearing her down," she said hopefully.

He chortled. "Is that how you work Tom and Liz?"

"Well, I don't really have to do much with them."

"That's because they *trust* you," he said simply.

"Well, Shelly should trust you, too, and our fathers should just get out of your head!"

He laughed and kissed her tenderly. They basked in the warmth of the fire and Chelsea cradled her head against his shoulder.

• • •

The boys spent all their extra time snowboarding, which gave Chelsea and Abby time to go maniacally about their business. Abby worked furiously through the details of planning her show, while Chelsea combed consignment stores shopping for men's shirts and short skirts as costumes for the girls' dance to Shania Twain's "Feel Like a Woman." She had looked everywhere for jazz oxford shoes and wrote a letter to all Sonya's students' parents asking for cast-offs in specific sizes. Charley offered to search the different shops and studios in Greenville and Chelsea was down to the last two pairs. Maxine, of Maxine's Dancewear, agreed to donate both pairs for the cause. "Honey, you've been buying shoes from me for the last ten years. This is the least I can do for you and those little girls," she had said. The girls were starting to get excited and their dance was coming along.

Sonya taught her new ballet choreography as part of Act Two of *Giselle*, and Chelsea was frantically memorizing it for her audition that was rapidly approaching. The contemporary piece was perfect. Brad was extremely pleased with her efforts, giving her only minor corrections. Sonya had also approved Meredith's photos of Chelsea in the specified positions required for the audition.

The Thursday before the audition Chelsea panicked, having lost her math book one day before the calculus test. It wasn't like her to lose things, and how could she misplace her textbook? Kyle came over after her last rehearsal of the week so they could put their heads together over his book to study for the test. She had a bad case of nerves due to the upcoming audition. He wished he could go with her, but he and Anthony would be involved in signing their football letters of intent at the school on Saturday. He rubbed her hand before leaving that evening and reassured her, "It will turn up. You'll do fine on the test."

As they walked up to their lockers the next morning, Chelsea was surprised to see her calculus book on the floor in front of her locker. "Someone probably just picked it up by accident, thinking it was theirs," Kyle said. They went into class and took their seats. As Mr. Halberg told them to clear their desks, she flipped through the book, looking for Wednesday night's homework she hadn't turned in. A small rectangle fell out into her lap and she held it up, doing a double take at the image she saw. It was a photograph of Elle, wearing only a black polka dot bra, sitting on top of Kyle, who was lying on the bed, eyes closed. She batted her eyes, looked again, heart pounding, and couldn't believe it. He was looking at her now, smiling, glad she had found her book and could stop worrying. She was sure her face was flaming red, and she felt the strange expression Kyle was seeing. He looked bemused and was about to ask her what was wrong when she heard Mr. Halberg speaking directly to her.

"Is something wrong, Chelsea?" he asked, eyeing her oddly over his glasses. She shook her head instantly and then shot a look again at Kyle, who looked more confused. He had his test paper in front of him, and she returned the picture to her book and placed it carefully under her desk. The student in front of her was waiting for her to take the test papers and pass them back. Her throat was strangely dry and she had difficulty swallowing. Kyle was watching her, but she could not look at him. She'd always imagined what had happened that night in the Santoro's bedroom, but seeing that image was more than real to her. Elle's hand in her hair and that *expression* on her face was more than she ever wanted to see, much less remember, for the rest of her life. A nauseous knot turned in her stomach, and the words and problems on the test swam in front of her. It took everything she had to get through the test; she felt as if she were suspended above the room most of the time as she concentrated on each problem.

As they walked out of class, Kyle caught her arm and demanded, "What is *wrong*? What happened? Are you sick?"

"Yes, I am, actually," she said and cast her eyes about. She held her math book close to her and pulled out the picture, then looked around to make sure no one else would see. Nothing she could say could prepare him for what she was about to show him. She shrugged and held up the picture.

He took it, looked at it, and blinked, his mouth forming an "O," as if a gasp were coming but was frozen. He looked at her and then at the picture again, blinking hard. "Where the hell did this come from? Who took this? Who else was in that room?" He shook his head as if trying to dispel the image. "This makes me *sick*. Who would *do* this?" he said. He tried to return the picture to her, but she made no move to take it.

"I don't want it," she said vaguely. "I don't ever want to see it again. As if I could control what's burned into my head right now."

He was holding the picture by the corner as if it were someone's used tissue. "Uh…okay. I don't want it either, but I think we should keep it." He looked helpless.

"Do you remember when this first started with her, you said that if it got out of hand we'd deal with it? Well, I think it just got out of hand. I think you need to do something. I just can't handle it anymore," she said and walked toward the door to the parking lot.

"Where are you going?"

"Home, I guess. I can't stay here," she said as she walked further away from him.

"The audition…" he began.

"Yeah, it's tomorrow. Nice timing, right?"

She drove home, feeling suspended above the road. Her mother was out, probably at Kitty's physical therapy, so she went into her room and curled up on her bed under the soft lilac blanket. She lay there for what seemed like hours. Eventually, her mother was sitting on the side of her bed, waking her up.

"Hi, honey. Are you sick?" asked Liz, stroking the hair off her face with a chilly hand.

Chelsea sighed. "Dancers never get sick. I just had a really bad morning."

"Do you want to talk about it? Kitty and I had lunch out, and now she's resting if you want to talk."

Chelsea sighed again and sat up. "There's a picture of Elle and Kyle from that night. I found it in my calculus book. I guess someone took my book and put it in there so I would find it."

Liz shook her head, "Why would someone do that?"

"Someone is really twisted, Mom," she said, shaking her head. "It means that Kyle and Elle weren't in the room by themselves, which is sicker than I ever thought. He doesn't remember anything. I've just had enough, you know?"

Liz pressed her arm and rubbed it. "I'm so sorry, honey, and now of all times…"

"I know. I think I'm just going to go over to the studio and go through my dances again. Sonya will be there, and I should be able to use the Company studio. I can't think of what else to do to calm myself down."

"What about Kyle?" she asked, concerned.

"Mom, I just can't talk to him right now. He's been calling. I don't know what to do."

"Oh, honey. Okay, let me fix you some lunch and you go to the studio."

• • •

Chelsea left the lights off in the studio. After a long warm-up, she went over the ballet first. The contemporary piece would definitely be harder today, considering it was all about Kyle, and she wasn't courageous enough to do it yet. Sonya and Brad had figured something was up, other than pre-audition nerves, and had prudently left her alone. She stretched her arms over her head and rolled her head around, starting the music. The joyous notes of the cello called her to stretch her body into the open moves, reach high into the air, make the turns, leaps, and pirouettes that mirrored her own joy and happiness. When the bass section began, the moves pulled inward. She pulled her arms in, as if comforting and cradling someone in her arms, rocking back and forth, rolling on the floor, and jumping into the air, turning and pulling in again, feeling the angst. She realized tears were streaming down her face and the moves were more intense than they had ever been. She finished in a crouch on the floor, hand pressed to her cheek.

She opened her eyes, vaguely aware of a dark figure in the doorway. Willie was frozen there, his eyes glued to her, and a tear glistened on his face as well. His hands went to his face and he took a step forward as she got to her feet. He took her in his arms and breathed deeply. "That was beautiful, baby," he whispered. "If they don't let you in over there tomorrow, they're nuts!"

She sniffed and smiled at him. "How did you know I was here?"

"It wasn't hard to figure out. I saw your man at school and he told me what happened…said you weren't answering your phone. Don't beat him up over this. He's sorry, baby," he said, rocking her.

"I know. I just can't think about it right now."

"I understand. Will you do it again for me?" She nodded and he went to sit in front of the mirrors while she prepared; then he hit the music on her cue. Out of the corner of her eye, she saw him moving slightly with her, smiling and looking anguished at all the right times. When she was through, they decided to go for coffee as the sun was beginning to set. They sat at a table at Char, and pretended they were rich and famous, laughing and sipping their lattes.

Willie's chin rested on his hand and he stroked the dark blue and purple print scarf around his neck. "You know, your dance wouldn't be nearly that fierce if all this shit hadn't happened today. You just gotta use it tomorrow. I don't think you should talk to him until after the audition if it makes you dance like that!"

She laughed, knowing he was right. "It seems mean, though. I want to talk to him...now."

"Do what you want. He's just miserable. You shoulda seen him at school. We thought he was gonna *kill* Elle! And then he had Kendra outside the gym before cheer practice. He was really grilling her. She probably took that picture. And she probably knows what happened. But I still don't think you should talk to him until you get back from your deal tomorrow," he said, smiling wickedly. "Then you two can have some kinda *hot* reunion!"

"You're so bad," she said, embarrassed.

• • •

When Chelsea and Liz pulled into the driveway around six o'clock Saturday evening, Tom had pizza waiting. He and Kitty were eager to hear the details of the audition. Although she was exhausted, Chelsea felt contented, knowing she had done her best. Liz talked positively. She had not seen the audition, but she had a feeling it went well. Chelsea's phone buzzed on the table beside her, signaling a text message. Liz squelched Tom's rolled eyes, mouthing, "It's Kyle."

He was at the door in ten minutes. Chelsea took him to the sun porch where they sat stiffly beside each other on the sofa.

He took her hand tentatively, and they said, "I'm sorry" in unison, and laughed nervously.

Kyle searched her eyes, not knowing where to start. "I know you were hurt, looking at that stupid picture…but you've got to know that wasn't me."

"I know. I wasn't mad at you. I just couldn't be there at school and see her face again. I had to get out."

"No, I totally get it. I don't know how you sat through that test. I talked to her and tried to get her to admit what she did. She's not giving an inch. She's really pissed at Kendra. Kendra's the one who took the picture and put it in your book."

"What? She was in there with you?"

"Yeah, and I talked to her about it. She never thought it would get like that. She hates Elle and wanted to get back at her. She thought if she showed you that picture, then you'd show it to the principal. Then Elle would get some type of discipline, since she's not cheerleading anymore, maybe get thrown out of the play, or something."

"That's not a bad idea. I don't know why I didn't think about it. But it didn't happen at school, so there's probably nothing they can do…Did Kendra say she knew about the roofies?"

"She wouldn't say. She and Elle will probably never speak to each other again. We made such a scene that Miss Rogers kicked me out of the gym and I left. This isn't over. I'm so sorry, Chels. I never wanted anything like this."

"I know. We'll just put it behind us. I'm sorry you were upset with me."

"Not upset *with* you. I was worried about you and the audition. So, how did it go?"

She smiled and looked at his earnest blue eyes. "Way better than I thought. I went to the studio to dance yesterday and Willie was there, watching, and all the emotions kind of came to a head. He advised me to use it today. It was so…*raw*…the contemporary one. I think they really liked it. The ballet was okay. They asked me about the choreography and what I was doing with the girls in my dance project. I guess they looked at the pictures. John Jacobs was on the panel and he was pleasant, but noncommittal. I guess I'll hear something in a couple of weeks. I felt good about it."

Then she asked him, "Did you sign?"

"Yeah," he smiled. "I signed with Virginia. It's a done deal now."

"Congratulations. I guess I'll read about it in the paper tomorrow."

"And on the ten o'clock news tonight," he smiled. "My mom was standing behind me wearing blue and orange, of course," he laughed.

"Of course," she laughed, and he took her hands in his again, running his thumb along the back of hers.

"Listen, I just want you to know how much you mean to me," he said, his blue eyes smoldering into hers. "You pulled me out of a deep, dark hole and I owe you everything. No one has done what you've done for me. I'd never screw that up. I didn't mean to hurt you."

She couldn't breathe for an instant, and her eyes were suddenly wet with tears. "No, you didn't hurt me. It's always been her. But I'm sorry if I hurt *you*. I just wish it were over."

"I know. It's such a hard thing to deal with. We'll get through it." He smiled at her and touched her lips with his, gently, tentatively. She returned his kiss with purpose and pressed hard against his mouth for a moment. His hand slid around her neck and pulled her closer into it. She tasted the sweetness, as her tears became part of the kiss. He held her face away then, and wiped her tears with his thumb. "Does this mean I'm forgiven?" he asked with the beginnings of a slow smile.

"You are, of course. Am I?"

"You've done nothing wrong. What do you think?"

"I think I like this," she breathed into the side of his neck. He laughed softly and gathered her into his arms and she sank into the warmth of him. "I don't ever want to go there again."

"You got it," he whispered.

• • •

On Monday, Kendra was the model of contrition; she stopped to speak with Chelsea and Kyle at the lunch table. Elle was like a volcano, just waiting to erupt, all day, and it had Kendra pretty rattled. She apologized for her part in the fiasco and seemed clearly distraught.

"I know why you did what you did, but I think the only person who needs to see that picture is Sheriff Conrad," said Chelsea and Kendra's eyebrows shot up. This was not the response she wanted.

"Did you know my mom is dying to press charges against whoever drugged me?" Kyle asked her. "I know she did it. The sheriff has been investigating, but they don't have anything to go on. Kendra, if you know something, you should talk to him," Kyle said, boldly, watching her carefully. "Did you see her do anything?"

She shook her head, looking nervous.

"Well, what is it?" he said impatiently, searching her face. "I *know* there's more to it than this."

"I know. I've thought about it all weekend and I can't sleep, I've been so upset about it," she said.

He shrugged, "So…what is it?"

"You know I took the picture, right? Well, there's a video, too," she said. Chelsea couldn't help making a face, but Kyle cautioned her with his eyes to let Kendra finish.

"What's on the video?" he pressed her.

"She's sitting on you and talking about you, and how she shouldn't have given you so much, because you were passed out and that it wasn't fun."

Kyle and Chelsea exchanged surprised looks. "That's exactly what he needs. Do you have it on your camera still?" Kyle was talking fast. She nodded. "And do you have your camera with you right now?" She closed her eyes and nodded again. "You should take it to Sheriff Conrad. Let's go now. I'll drive you over there and talk to him with you." Chelsea raised her eyebrows, afraid he was scaring her.

"I can't just leave school, now," said Kendra, balking at the idea.

"Sure you can," Chelsea said. "I walked right out of here on Friday. This is *important*."

Kyle leaned forward, elbows propped on his knees, and fidgeted with his fingers. He looked up at Kendra and gave her that familiar, penetrating blue stare that never failed to mesmerize Chelsea. "I'd really like to put an end to all of this. I can't stand what it's done to Chelsea. It's the right thing to do," he said quietly, and seriously.

Chelsea knew Kendra had practically stopped breathing. She reached for Kendra's hands, which were in her lap. "If you want, I'll go with y'all," she said, equally as serious. Kendra appeared to be wavering.

"I wouldn't mind missing drama class, actually. Elle is going to glare at me all the time, anyway," she mumbled.

"Might as well make it worth it," Kyle said softly. His slow smile spread across his face, and he winked at her. She smiled, blushing slightly and lowered her eyes, biting her lip. Chelsea shook her head ever so slightly at him and he gave the slightest shrug back. He placed his hand on top of theirs and said, "All for one?"

Kendra sat up and took a deep breath, "All right, let's go, before I talk myself out of this," she said in a low voice and they sprang off the bench and headed for the parking lot.

• • •

Elle did not come to school the rest of the week. The buzz was that she had withdrawn from school after being removed from the cast of *High School Musical*. She'd texted Abby that she was pulling her song out of the variety show. Willie, Tia, and Kendra were sure they'd heard Elle had gotten a job at Mallone's as a hostess, so they all vowed never to eat there again. Shelly Davis said nothing, but they knew she had pressed charges. Still, with Elle out of the picture, Chelsea felt bad for her in an unsettling way.

"I thought you'd be thrilled," Abby said, curled up on Chelsea's bed. She and Chelsea were going over the list of performances for the show, getting ready to email everyone the order of the program and deleting Elle's name from the list.

"I know…so did I. But I feel sorry for her in a way. I can't help wondering what makes a person become so toxic? She needed attention in the worst possible way. What made her turn out like that?"

Abby cleared her throat, "Well, her father left her and her mom in the lurch when she was little. She's always felt a need to have attention from men, and if she couldn't get it the right way, she'd just invent something she thought would do the trick."

"Thank you, Dr. Abby," Chelsea said with raised brows, laughing.

"You *know* that's *why*," Abby said impatiently. "Just wish her good riddance and pray for her *freaking soul*."

"You are the *queen* of compassion, and I'm so glad you're my best friend. You keep it real, girlfriend."

"You got that right. Now, let's talk about Saturday night! Isn't Kyle's mom cute, wanting to host Glen's Valentine's Day dinner?"

Chelsea smiled wistfully. "Yeah, I have to admit I was shocked! It's really sweet of her to have us over and suggest we wear our homecoming clothes since we never made the dance that time."

"My mother would never think of that in a million years," exclaimed Abby. "Kyle's mother can't be as bad as you think."

"Oh, I'm sure she's not, she's just a *tad* overprotective," she said, thinking she had inherited her father's gift for understatement. She knew her mother had played a large part in the arrangement, being Glen's mentor. "So, what's on the menu?"

"It's a surprise," Abby grinned. "Did you know they've invited Anthony and Meredith and Willie and Tia?"

"Willie told me. He's hoping it's not another barbequed *butt*!"

Abby threw her head back and laughed. "He cracks me up! Tell him I think he's safe!" She giggled again and then said, "I have a surprise for Glen myself! I'm glad Mer will be there so he will get decent pictures for his calendar."

"So, it's something we can all see?"

"Yes. Your mom is absolutely gonna love it!"

Abby and Chelsea arrived at the Davises' house Saturday evening for the Valentine's Day dinner party. Liz had arrived earlier to help Shelly get set up and help Glen with his dinner preparations. Kyle met the girls at the door and took their coats. His eyes flickered over Chelsea, and seeing her in the red strapless dress, he gave an involuntary shiver, which sent a quick flush to her cheeks. He was so handsome himself, she thought, in a pair of black pants and a dark gray shirt with a black and silver striped tie. They clung to each other for a moment. Then he kissed her, touched the star necklace at her throat, and wished her a Happy Valentine's Day.

"Thank you for the red roses," she whispered in his ear. "They're beautiful."

"I have another surprise," he said, blue eyes twinkling. "Mom said you can go to the Outer Banks for Spring Break with us…if you still want to. It might be kind of lame, but…" It was all she could do not to tackle him there in the foyer. She wrapped her arms around his huge shoulders and beamed.

Everyone was decked out for the occasion, feeling and looking grown up and sophisticated. There was lots of chatter and joking about the man chef that had been created out of this project, but with Liz's help, no one had ever complained about his food so far. Succulent aromas wafted in from the kitchen. They went in to greet everyone and have a glass of sparkling grape juice.

Shelly gave Chelsea a hug and winked at her. "You look *gorgeous* in that dress," she said. Liz also winked at her. Shelly was taking pictures of the couples with Liz and Glen in the kitchen. She, Liz, and Glen's mother were dressed to match in white tuxedo shirts and black pants as the "wait staff." Abby brought in a large box wrapped in red paper with a silver bow and set it on the coffee table. Meredith and Tia looked at Meredith's book, the result of the photojournalism project she'd just finished that day. Meredith smiled at Chelsea and Kyle, and then asked them to sit down so they could take a look.

"I wanted to see you both look at it together. It's kind of a Valentine's present for y'all tonight," she said. Then she smiled, handed Kyle the book, and moved toward the fireplace. "You don't need to read it all right now, except for the part about you, of course," she said to Kyle.

They sat on the sofa, next to the fireplace, and Kyle placed the attractively bound book across their laps. He flipped through the first pages, the story of Meredith's mother's fight with breast cancer, and they looked at all of the pictures. Then came the pictures and story of Keely Streeter's victory over leukemia, her homecoming shots, the girl from Appalachian who had been her bone marrow donor, arm in arm with her before and after the procedure, and pictures of Keely back at school with her funky-chic short blonde hair and wide smile. Chelsea's arm went around Kyle as he turned the page, and they saw a picture of him, smiling, with an arm draped loosely around his mother's shoulders, standing on the porch of the cabin. Chelsea felt her heart skip a beat, and she heard his breath catch almost imperceptibly. He looked up at Meredith. "Has she seen this?"

Meredith shook her head. "I wanted you to see it first."

There were the photographs of the game where Kyle stood on the sidelines, hand in his hair, then on his knees with the other players, and on the bench, staring at the ground. Chelsea smiled at the photo of the two of them sitting on the log at the bonfire, Kyle holding her palm to his face and smiling at her. He pointed to a quotation on the page: "I don't know if I could have gotten through this without her." She tightened her arm around him and he hugged her. There were other photos—Stuart Davis at the river casting a fly rod, Desiree in her cheerleading uniform—and photos Chelsea had seen before: the Davis family in front of the Eiffel Tower, Stuart, and Kyle holding up the large fish, and Kyle and Desiree on the ski slope. There was also a shot of Kyle, Lily, and her family on the deck he had built for them, with Bono at his feet. The last picture was one she didn't realize had been made, of "Smee" and "Tinkerbell," holding each other in a slow dance at the Halloween party.

They looked at each other and closed the book. Kyle went to give Meredith a hug. "This is awesome. This has really helped me, that's for sure," he said with certainty.

Meredith grinned with eyes shining. "I'm glad my stories all have happy endings! I made copies of your pages for you and your mom."

They were being called in to dinner. Abby carried her package into the kitchen where the whole group was circled around the island. Glen, with his white shirtsleeves rolled up and red paisley tie loosened around his neck, set a platter of twice-baked potatoes on the island. There was a delicious looking cheesecake on the bar, surrounded by chocolate-covered strawberries. Liz watched him proudly, letting him have his moment. There were *oohs* and *aahs* as he unveiled the main dish, chicken breasts stuffed with Canadian bacon, goat cheese, and rosemary. He set it beside a bowl of green beans almandine.

Shelly clasped her hands together and said, "Now I understand what all the talk was about. Glen, this is *amazing*!"

He shook his head incredulously. "I know! I amaze myself sometimes!" Everyone laughed. "I owe my success to Mrs. D here," he said and put an arm around Liz. "Not bad for a grand finale, is it?"

Abby handed him the large gift. "I'm *not* doing this for you every Valentine's Day, but this is a little something special for tonight," she said, winking at Glen and giving Meredith a nod to have the camera ready. In typical guy fashion, he ripped the paper from the package and opened the box. Everyone gasped as he pulled out a white chef's jacket. Black embroidery across the breast pocket read *Chef Glen*, and he laughed out loud with pleasure.

"Wow! This is *so cool*!" He laughed again and looked at her with a huge grin. "You're the butter to my bread, baby," he said and gave her a hug, then slipped the jacket on over his shirt as Meredith snapped photos. They posed behind the island with the dinner on display. Then he hammed it up with Liz, brandishing a carving knife in the air, which she swapped out for a wire whisk.

"I have unpleasant memories of you with knives," said Liz.

Chapter 14

DETAILS

On Monday, Elle was back at school and rumors were wild, but she maintained a low profile, looking generally aloof and bored. She didn't speak to anyone, although she ate lunch with Aiden Caffey in the cafeteria. It was intense at first, trying to ignore her, and Kendra seemed to have the hardest time with it. She'd joined Chelsea's group at lunch, which was fortunate since it was a hotbed of chatter and plans for the upcoming variety show. Chelsea shared the butterflies Abby was having. She was anxiously wrapping up the details and making lists of everything to head off any possible disaster. All Kendra had to do was listen and chew, for which she seemed grateful.

Abby ran her hands through her hair and spoke animatedly. "Can you believe it? The donated coffee was *whole beans*? I had to take it back into the store and have it *ground*. Good thing I checked before Saturday night!"

Chelsea went over Abby's checklist of personnel for the show. She had arranged check-in people to check in the performers and canned food donations and cash. For intermission, she had organized coffee and drink servers as well as dessert servers. There was an emcee for the show, a D.J. to run the music, a lighting person, and even a dressing room attendant. She'd assigned times for the set-up and clean-up crews to show up, and, thanks to Miss Rogers, she had a slew of volunteers. Miss Rogers had offered extra English credit to anyone who signed up and showed up to help. Another section of her notebook was dedicated to signed photo permission forms for anyone under eighteen, and receipts of donations, required with the school's tax ID number. Chelsea brought her a small stack of forms from her little dance troupe and had arranged an extra run for the bus the evening of the show to transport the dancers and their families to and from the show.

They were all a bit nervous. This was their "Thriller" debut, as well as Willie and Chelsea's "Carol of the Bells" performance, and the little girls' "Feel Like a Woman" dance. Kendra listened with rapt attention to all the details and heard Chelsea talking about the Saturday morning run-through with her dancers and Willie, who was going to work the sound and lights as a dress rehearsal, since there wasn't one scheduled. The little girls were nervous, having never performed before. They would be the second act in the first portion of the show, and a row of seats in the auditorium was reserved for them and their families so they could enjoy the rest of the show. Fliers had gone around the school and announcements had been made there, as well as at Abby's church, and a large crowd was expected.

"There could be two-hundred people here," Abby cried nervously. Chelsea grinned at her. Abby, like the rest of them, was unused to dealing with large numbers of people and the anxiety of the situation was getting to her.

"You'll be fine," Chelsea reassured her. "You were smart to have an emcee since you'll be occupied with running the show. It's going to be great!"

Kendra volunteered to be Abby's assistant for the evening. Abby grinned, saying, "That would be awesome! I'd love the help!" They both appeared to relax.

Early Saturday morning, the activity bus dropped off the young dancers at the high school auditorium. Chelsea met them with chicken biscuits and orange juice, a "dress rehearsal" splurge from Bojangles. They ate in the commons on benches and waited for Willie to arrive. He showed up in a black parka, black sweatpants, snow boots, and with a bag slung over his shoulder, while sipping from a large coffee cup. He looked like a sleepy SWAT team member and the little girls' eyes widened with interest.

Chelsea grinned at him and he squinted at her. "You owe me big for this, baby," he said, unsmiling. They cleaned up their breakfast remains as he opened up the sound and lighting booth and began turning on panels. Chelsea was glad he was in drama class and knew his way around the theater.

They walked to the stage with their bags and began to warm up. Willie removed his parka and sweat pants and the girls openly gawked as he pirouetted in his tights and black T-shirt that said in purple writing, *Dancers Do It With Attitude*.

"Girl, these kids look scared to death!" he said low in Chelsea's ear.

"Of *you*," she reminded him, giving him a little shove, and he laughed.

"They never seen a black person before?" he asked and she shrugged.

"I'm sure it's just the *tights*," she said. Then she got her group together to walk around the stage, showed them the dressing room, where they would enter and exit the stage, and where they would sit with their families after they performed.

"Willie and I will be dancing in the second act, and Mr. Kyle, too," she said, winking at Lily, who grinned. "You'll really like being on stage, once you get used to it. Now, let's get dressed, and Willie will fix the lights and start your music. I'll be standing down there," she said, gesturing below the stage. After changing into their costumes, they ran through the dance the first time. The girls were a little shaky, unfamiliar with the new surroundings. "Let's try it again from the top," Chelsea said, and they got into their starting positions and did it again. Willie clapped and whistled and the girls began to relax and smile. They did it one more time and it was one-hundred percent better.

"That was great! Do you like dancing up here?" asked Chelsea, truly excited for them. "Y'all look so cute. The audience is going to eat you up. What do you think, Willie?"

"Y'all are sassy! I thought it was *fierce*," he exclaimed, and they laughed at his compliment.

"Do you want to see *our* dance?" Chelsea asked the girls, and they nodded.

Willie ran through a couple of jumps and pirouettes as the girls got seated in the auditorium. Chelsea took her place as he went back to the booth to start the music, then raced down to be ready for his cue. Chelsea took the stage first and then Willie joined her. They had changed the choreography to adjust the dance for the two of them, and when they finished, they were both out of breath and panting. The girls stood up, clapping and whooping, eyes bright with excitement.

When Chelsea asked whether they wanted to practice one more time, they nodded, saying "Yes! Yes!" and jumping up and down. Chelsea took them backstage again so they could practice their entrance. The last go-round was by far the best, and they seemed inspired for the evening's performance.

As they changed clothes, Willie closed up the booth, then got into his street clothes, too. "Wow, this is gonna be a long day, girl," he said, referring to the class and rehearsal they had before the show that night.

"I know, we're gonna sleep in tomorrow! I guess this is what it's like for professional dancers."

He smiled at her. "You did a good job with them. They'll rock the house tonight...and so will *we!*"

DETAILS

Chelsea arrived at the auditorium as soon as she could return and met Abby, who was scurrying around with her clipboard and cell phone, with Kendra in tow, carrying CDs and red plastic tablecloths. "You look like quite the event planner," Chelsea told her friend.

Other people had arrived for set-up and were placing signs around on the walls. Other volunteers erected tables near the auditorium doors for check-in and canned food collection—jobs that had been assigned to Kyle and Glen. Some girls brought in boxes and paper bags for the donated food. Chelsea made her way to the dressing rooms, her assignment for the night, with her troupe's costumes in paper shopping bags, their names printed in red marker. Abby handed her a program and reminded her to have her cell phone on vibrate and on her at all times so they could communicate from any point in the theater. "Wow, you're super efficient! I'm impressed," said Chelsea.

"This was Kendra's idea. She's been really helpful."

"How are you holding up?"

"So far, so good. Just really excited. The performers are all starting to arrive. I just saw Jay, Lauren, and Sam come in. My mentor's here and we've been taking some pictures. Meredith is awesome, and Anthony and Dave are up in the lighting booth getting set up. People have already brought in food. Glen's keeping a tally so we can tell the audience the grand total at the end of the show. I hope I have enough boxes. Are you all set for backstage?"

"Yeah, I'll check on my little girls. Send them on back when they get here, and I'll show their parents where they can sit. The only other people who need to change are the 'Thriller' dancers and Willie and me."

Performers were arriving and milling around with family members in the auditorium. Children had started to play on the stage, but Chelsea tactfully directed them off, trying to make eye contact with their parents. The stage crew closed the curtain and began arranging chairs for the first performance. Her girls arrived and made their way down the aisles with their families, who looked around in awe at the beautiful auditorium. Chelsea went out to greet them and show them where to sit. Lily walked in with no one else, looking sad. "Isn't your grandmother coming?" Chelsea asked, putting her arm around Lily's bird-like shoulders.

"My aunt's bringing her and my brother and sister. They couldn't get her on the bus with the wheelchair," she said. Then her face suddenly lit up into a smile and she pointed to the back of the theater. "There they are!" Her aunt was pushing her grandmother down the aisle in her wheelchair, accompanied by the siblings and some cousins. Kyle followed, with Chelsea's parents and Kitty. He introduced Chelsea to Lily's grandmother, who shook Chelsea's hand and said, "I'm glad to finally meet you. I've been hearing about you from both of these folks," she said, indicating Lily and Kyle. They'd already met Chelsea's family, so they took their seats in the handicapped section. Kyle went back to his station, and Chelsea took the excited crew of girls backstage.

Things started to happen fast, and suddenly it was show time! Sonya popped in backstage and saw the girls, gave them hugs and told them to break a leg. "You too, chickadee," she said to Chelsea. "Brad is out there, too, saving my seat." She blew them a kiss and they heard Abby's voice on the microphone, welcoming everyone to the show.

When it was time for the girls to take the stage, they listened excitedly as the emcee described how the group was formed and that the presentation was choreographed as Chelsea's senior project. Her heart pounded, but she managed to look confident for the girls' sake. Then the emcee left the stage and the girls were on. Chelsea slipped down the side steps and knelt in front of the stage, near Meredith, who was photographing all the acts. The music started and the audience laughed as the girls struck their first pose, hips jutted out, and pretending to sling purses over their shoulders as Shania Twain sang out, "Let's go, girls!" They definitely portrayed the attitude they had discussed, especially little Lily, who seemed instantly transformed. Chelsea's jaw dropped and she laughed as they came down their line, pretending to polish a nail, apply lipstick, or tease a strand of hair. They sparkled like little stars in their make-up, men's shirts, and short skirts, hair combed and styled. They definitely put on the show that they had in them. Chelsea grinned proudly at them as they peeked at her from time to time. And then it was over as Shania sang, *"I feel like a woman!"* When they hit the last note, the audience rewarded them with loud applause, cheers, and hollers, and Chelsea heard the special whistle her dad always did when she danced. As she looked back at him, he smiled broadly at her. Her eyes prickled with hot tears, knowing her girls had really nailed it. The girls beamed and took their bows, held hands and ran off the stage as tears streamed down her cheeks. She felt a huge wave of relief wash over her as she ran back to meet them backstage, where they hugged each other and celebrated.

"You guys were great! You were *perfect!*" she cried, her heart bursting with exhilaration. She was so proud of them. Then, before the next act went on, the little troupe slipped through the doors and sat with their families, who were all smiles and hugs at their daughters' achievements.

At intermission, families and friends crowded around the girls, exclaiming over their performance. The girls seemed amazed but thrilled with the praise. Kyle grinned at Lily and grabbed her up, spinning her around. "You *rock*, little girl! You were the best one up there! That was *awesome*."

Willie was right behind him, saying, "Y'all were *smokin'!*"

"My *face* hurts from smiling," Lily giggled.

Tom, Liz, and Kitty, and Sonya and Brad congratulated Chelsea and the girls. For the project board display, Meredith took shots of Chelsea and Sonya and then all the girls in their "woman" personas. Willie and Chelsea took the girls back to the dressing room where they changed quickly and went back to their seats. Then Willie and Chelsea changed into their "Carol of the Bells" costumes and waited for their cue. They got a nice ovation from the audience, and then the Bangelic players got in place for the three songs they would perform. As they played, Abby and Kendra escorted the "Thriller" dancers back to the dressing room where they dressed and got made up for the final act. They scattered and took their places at different entrances to the auditorium. The plan was for them to have no introduction, to create more suspense. When the lights in the theater went out abruptly, the audience gasped. Smoke curled up from dry ice near the stage and eerie purple lights lit the stage. "Thriller" began as each participant slunk in, glided stealthily down the aisles, touching a shoulder here, someone's hair there, startling people and creating a stir.

Chelsea stifled her laughter to maintain her role and glanced at Kyle, Anthony, Tia, Willie, Glen, and Abby as they played their parts onto the stage. The dance began and the audience got into it, laughing with rapt attention. Some of the children were up in the aisles, imitating the moves on their own. Glen and Anthony seemed to compete for the most ferocious face, but no one could top Willie's expressions as he held his place front and center, looking like Michael Jackson himself. Kyle's eyes were evil slits; Chelsea felt a rush of appreciation that he had gotten into this and seemed to be enjoying himself. She saw Lily pointing at him from the audience. Abby and Tia were hilarious, and she found herself laughing at one point, despite her best efforts to maintain herself. At the end of the number, Vincent Price laughed wickedly and the audience was on its feet, wild with applause and cheering.

After everyone had bowed and left the stage, laughing and feeling the rush of the performance, Abby went back out with Devon, the emcee, who handed her the final tally for the cans of food collected. Abby again thanked everyone for coming out to support her project. When she asked the crowd whether it had had fun, there was another enthusiastic roar. She announced that they had collected nine hundred and fourteen cans of food, and raised three-hundred and forty-five dollars in cash for the food bank. More thunderous applause erupted from the audience of more than three-hundred people.

People rose and left, but it seemed like more than half of them stuck around to congratulate the performers and tell Abby what a great job she'd done and how much fun the night had been. All generations were represented and everyone had had a good time. Chelsea got lots of accolades, too. Her little cluster of dancers and their families all embraced her, and she walked out into the cold night with them to see them off on their bus. Kyle went to help load Mrs. Jennings into her daughter's car with Lily, the two siblings, and her cousins, all packed like sardines in the old Dodge Caravan. He met Chelsea on the sidewalk as the bus pulled away from the curb and swung her up in his arms. "You guys did fantastic!"

"Thanks," she murmured, smiling into his jacket.

"You accomplished a lot with those girls, you know. The sky's the limit for them, now. They never thought they could do anything like this. You just gave them their first ticket out of this place."

She held him close with both arms. "Who would ever want to leave this place? Not me. Not now."

• • •

Two weeks later, Chelsea was in her room, dressing in a black pencil skirt, dark red blouse, and a fitted black jacket, all borrowed from Charley for the occasion. She slipped her feet into black patent-leather pumps and wondered how she could possibly walk down the stairs in the ensemble. Then her mother appeared in her doorway.

"You look really good," said Liz, eyes sparkling. "Very professional."

"Thanks," Chelsea mumbled. "I think I'll put these on downstairs," she said, toeing off the pumps and checking her watch. The senior project presentation judging was in an hour, and she was almost ready to go.

"Good idea. Dad's warming up the Tahoe. Do you have the video of the dance on your laptop?"

"Yeah, I think I'm all set," Chelsea said, confused by her mother's odd look.

"You didn't check the mailbox today, did you?" said Liz, looking a little irritated.

"No," she said. Then, seeing her mother break into a smile, she yelled, "My letter came?"

Liz laughed and handed Chelsea a small, fat envelope, the size of a wedding invitation. "Rejection letters aren't usually this fat," she said.

Chelsea saw U.N.C. School of the Arts printed at the top of the envelope. She ripped it open and read the first line aloud, "Dear Chelsea, We are pleased to inform you of your acceptance into our dance major program..." She saw John Jacobs' signature. "*Oh my God!* Mom, I'm in! I'm in!" She threw her arms around her mother and heard her father's heavy footsteps tromping up the stairs. "Dad, I'm in! I'm in! I can't believe it! I'm the last one to hear! Oh, I'm *so* relieved!"

Tom embraced her and picked her up a good foot off the floor. "Never had a doubt in my mind, sweet pea! Now you can relax and cruise the rest of the year."

"Well, and keep your grades up, of course," Liz threw in.

"Oh, of course," said Chelsea. "But it's like a huge weight is gone. Even with tonight, I'll just be able to look at the panel of judges and say 'I'll be attending the U.N.C.S.A. in the fall as a dance major!' I love the sound of that. I have to tell *Kyle!*" she exclaimed, picking up her phone from her bed and pressing his speed dial button.

"Is *his* button number *one?*" Tom asked Liz, a hurt expression on his face. Liz giggled and gave him a hug around his waist.

After a brief conversation with Kyle, she picked up the pumps and headed down the stairs. She'd assembled all of her materials for the presentation in the assigned classroom. She loved the project board, decorated with the smallest shirt and a skirt, a small purse, a bottle of nail polish, and a lipstick. There were photographs of the girls in different stages of their rehearsals, getting off the bus, Chelsea shopping for the costumes and shoes, she and Sonya in the studio, pictures from the performance, and the whole group and Sonya. She'd loaded the video from the show onto her laptop and the judges would get to see the performance for themselves.

"I have to show this to you before you leave," Liz said. She brought out a large calendar with a picture of Glen, holding a hamburger and shrugging, on the front. The title was *A Guy's Gotta Eat*. Chelsea laughed and flipped through each month, which featured a picture of one of his dinners and the corresponding recipes. There were burgers and baked beans in September, barbequed Boston butt and slaw for October, the Thanksgiving turkey and fixings for November, pork tenderloin, green bean casserole, and chocolate cake for December, Tom's Thunder Chili and cornbread with S'mores for January, the Valentine's Day "dinner for a date" for February, corned beef sandwiches and home style potato chips for March, a Mountain Man's hearty breakfast for April, and barbequed baby back ribs for May. "Glen brought this over for me today. Aren't the pictures great? He's going to serve chocolate-covered strawberries to the judges tonight."

Chelsea laughed. "And wearing his chef jacket, I hope. Mom, this is priceless. It's just…*so* Glen. I know you're proud of him. Thank God; now we know Abby won't starve. She can't cook a lick."

"Okay, time to head on out," Tom said. He slung her computer bag over his shoulder. "Grab your snow boots. It's snowing again. You'll never make it home in those shoes!"

Chapter 15

SECRETS

Chelsea sat on the tile floor of the bathroom, wiping the dusty baseboards with a bleach-soaked cloth, listening to the wind outside. The trees outside the bathroom window made the sound she liked when their branches rubbed and creaked together, and sometimes snapped and popped. She stared vacantly at the afternoon light that played on the old, claw-footed tub in front of her. Clouds blew across and faded the light. The weather would be getting warmer now, teasing them that Spring was near. She had promised her mother she would help with spring cleaning before she left in the morning with Kyle for Spring Break. Liz's laughter threaded up the stairs, and Kitty's voice joined hers as they finished dusting downstairs. Kitty's job had been to wipe down picture frames Liz brought to her as she cleaned the downstairs baseboards herself.

Chelsea peeled the rubber gloves from her hands and poured the bleach solution down the drain. She wandered into her room to check her luggage one more time. Her parents had given her a small rolling case and matching overnight tote for Christmas, and this was her first opportunity to use it. Kyle was going to pick her up at seven in the morning. She had not packed as many shorts and bathing suits as her friends had. Even for early April, Kyle said Duck was likely to be cold and windy most of the time. She didn't care. Just being with him away from school would be wonderful, even with Shelly observing their every move.

He arrived on time in the morning, grinning, and alone in his Jeep. Shelly had left earlier in the Audi. She'd promised he could drive it from time to time while they were down there. The seven-hour drive was filled with conversation, tunes from Aerosmith on the iPod, then Journey and John Mayer. They stopped at lunchtime for burgers in Raleigh. The roads for the rest of the trip were strangely flat, and the world around them became more remote as they approached the coast. Then came the last bridge they crossed before actually hitting the beach—Kyle's favorite part of the trip.

His face broke into a smile as he said, "This is where you leave it all behind you and start to relax! It's a different world here." He put down his window and breathed in the salty air. She did the same, wanting to feel what he felt. She looked forward to taking in everything he knew there. He pulled over into the parking lot of Kitty Hawk Elementary School so they could put the top down. She wound her hair into a knot for the remainder of the ride. The sun was warm and there was a slight breeze. She smelled the salt and something else vaguely primitive, like fish, or old shells—not unpleasant, but different.

They drove a few more miles in traffic that she hadn't expected. She thought of the Outer Banks as being desolate and isolated, but an unending stream of cars headed for the first warmth since the coldest, snowiest winter in a long time. Kyle seemed to read her thoughts. "It's like this at Easter and other holidays. We'll get there soon," he said, reaching for her hand. And soon, they pulled into a small development. She saw the ocean, just past the silvered, wood-sided houses, and the boardwalk leading to the beach across the dunes. She breathed in again, hearing the uneven swell of the ocean just beyond them.

"That's it," he said, inclining his head to a large house on the right. It was the same silvery wood as the others and sat high above a stilted base, with porches around the top. The Audi was parked underneath, beside a white Volkswagen Cabrio, and they pulled in behind the cars, extracted their bags from the back, and tromped up the stairs.

A slim, blonde woman in a long skirt and long-sleeved shirt appeared from the door. Her hair was tied into a similar bun as Chelsea's, and she was tanned, fit, and beautiful, and smiling the same blue-eyed smile as Kyle and Shelly. It was impossible to guess her age, anywhere from late twenties to maybe forty. Laughter bubbled up from her as she reached out for Kyle, barely waiting for him to get to the top of the stairs.

"Hey, Stace! How've ya been?" he laughed as he dropped his bags and she wrapped herself around him. He picked her up and twirled her around. "You look *awesome*!"

"And look at you, Kylie! You look…so *big*! My God, you've grown a foot this way and that! You need sun, honey," she exclaimed, holding his shoulders and taking him in. Then, seeing Chelsea, she broke into another smile. "And you're Chelsea. Welcome! I've heard *tons* about you and it's *all* good, trust me," she said, winking at her and giving her a warm hug. "You're even more gorgeous than I heard. But I'd expect nothing less for this guy. He's choosy, to say the least. He's never brought a girl here before."

"Thanks, Stacie," Kyle said, rolling his eyes. "I guess I have *zero* mystique with her *now*! Where's Mom?"

"Right here," Shelly called, appearing at the doorway with two pink drinks in martini glasses, and handing one to Stacie.

"I put her to work immediately," Stacie said, winking at them. "Bikini martinis. Want one, Chelsea? Shut up, Shelly. The girl's on vacation and we're not going anywhere for a while."

"Can I show Chelsea her room, first?" Kyle said, laughing incredulously, picking up her bags and gesturing for her to follow him down the hall. "And *that's* my mom's baby sister!" he whispered discreetly, taking her into a small, cheerful room with a pastel bedspread and matching curtains.

"I like her," murmured Chelsea. Just then, he swept her up into his arms and kissed her passionately, pushing her down on the bed. She moaned and pushed herself against his hard chest, kissing him in return.

"We're going to have so much fun," he said and propped himself up on his elbow, stroking her face and neck.

"So, where do you stay?" she asked, pulling him back in for another sweet kiss.

"Usually right here. But this time, I'll be on the futon in the work-out room."

"And your mom?"

"Probably bunking in with Stacie on her big king-sized bed. Usually Tyson stays there, but she's probably put him on hold for a few days."

"I thought he was…younger?"

"He's thirty. She's thirty-nine or something. To them it doesn't matter. You'll meet him later, I'm sure."

"Here you go, Chelsea," sang out Stacie, coming into the room with a glass for her and a beer for Kyle. He shook his head, unbelieving. "Just to celebrate your homecoming," she grinned at him as he took the Corona Light and stuffed the lime down into the bottle. "I've reminded your mom you're going to college soon. Might as well get a little practice in, you know," she laughed a throaty, infectious laugh that Chelsea instantly liked. "I'm so glad you guys are finally here. I have to go back to work at four-thirty, but you should come for dinner and stay for the music afterward. Tyson will be there. Hey Kyle, I have a surprise for you. Your *favorite band* is here for the weekend."

"*South Street*? No way! That's awesome."

"Yeah, and we're getting your mother out tonight too. I have some real estate friends I want her to meet. If she ever gets up the nerve to come down here, I hope I can help her get set up. She's doing better, right?"

Kyle looked somber for a moment and nodded. "Yeah, it's been over a year now since Dad died. She's done with all the estate and the tax people. If things would slow down with me, I think she'd relax more. Maybe this week will be good for her."

"Yeah, I heard you've had a rough time this year," she said, stroking his arm. "I'm sorry things have been so hard."

"It's fine. I've had great support from this angel beside me," he said and pulled Chelsea's hand into his lap.

Stacie's face went soft and she crooned, "I'm so thrilled that you're in love. Oh, you two are adorable together!" They laughed and she wiped the corner of her eye. "You're going to make me cry. Now go say hello to the beach!"

They poured their drinks into plastic cups and traipsed down the stairs in shirtsleeves, feeling the warm breeze ruffle their hair and clothes. They held hands and walked over the boardwalk across the dunes to the beach. They kicked off their shoes at the end of the boardwalk. Chelsea took a deep breath of the ocean air and was immediately enamored with this place Kyle loved. She sipped her drink and he took a pull off his beer, and she thought how adult she felt. She wondered whether Shelly would continue to be this calm. She sure hoped so. The sun sparkled over the water as if millions of shiny silver dimes floated there, wafting about on the waves. They walked to the edge of the tide, and Kyle put his arm around her and pulled her close, breathing in the scent of her hair. "I've wanted you to be my beach girl," he said in her ear. She snuggled into him, finished her drink, and felt warmth radiate all over her body. They sat down on a knoll of sand carved out by earlier waves and watched as gulls circled overhead, at times diving into the sparkling water. The sound of the waves was mesmerizing, and they leaned against each other, feeling relaxed and lazy. Chelsea closed her eyes and let the sun warm her against the slight cool of the breeze. Kyle tightened his arm around her.

"I can see why you love it here so much," she said.

"I'm glad you're here with me. It means a lot that you came."

"I would go to Tibet with you and think it's great," she said, laughing gently. "But seriously, this is amazing. I thought it would be colder, though."

"So did I. Maybe things are looking up for us," he said, kissing the side of her cheek and stroking her hair away from her face. "I'm going to take you everywhere. There's so much to do."

"Yeah, besides celebrating your birthday on Tuesday. Wow, eighteen… I'll be going out with an *adult*. That's *so* hot!" she said, reaching for his neck and pulling him in for a kiss. "Will you take me surfing?"

He laughed. "I think we'd need wetsuits for that. This water is pretty cold right now. We can drive down to Buxton and I'll show you where Tyson and I used to go. Maybe we can come back this summer and do it for real. We'll get up early one morning and I'll take you for breakfast at Sam and Omie's and then head down there. It's a long drive from here. Maybe we'll see some ponies."

They took a walk along the beach and headed back up to the house. Stacie had left for work and Shelly was stretched out in the hammock on the porch, asleep, with a paperback book across her chest, the empty martini glass on the table beside her.

The Sound Side was packed with vacationers that evening, but the food was worth the wait. Chelsea looked around the rustic little place, charming with its weathered wood and polished old bar. A large sailboat model hung from the center of the ceiling. A mounted tuna hung over the bar. Each table was covered with white paper and lit with hurricane lamps. Fishing nets hung from the walls, attached with colorful buoys, shells, and boat paddles. Waiters and waitresses clad in T-shirts and white aprons scurried around with baskets of hush puppies and bottles of cold beers for the boisterous customers. Shelly, Kyle, and Chelsea were finishing a delicious dinner of savory crab cakes, slaw, and baked potatoes when Tyson joined them, bestowing a piece of key lime pie on the table with three spoons, and wiping his hands on his apron. Kyle embraced him warmly and introduced him to Chelsea and his mother.

Tyson was of average height and wiry, his arms well muscled and tanned as were all the locals, Chelsea had observed. He had a mop of dark, curly hair that probably never saw a comb, and deep-set green eyes that crinkled when he smiled, which was most of the time. They complimented him on the crab cakes, which he confessed were his favorite, too. He hoped they would stick around for the music later, when he and Stacie would be finished in the kitchen and could sit with them and visit. Stacie appeared moments later and introduced Shelly to her realtor friends. Then the four of them found another table where they could talk.

"Alone at last," Kyle said, reaching across the table for Chelsea's hands as Tyson walked by and discreetly set two beers on their table.

"Looks like we're going to stay buzzed here," Chelsea said, tipping the cold bottle to her lips.

Kyle nodded. "This is definitely different," he said, taking a swig off his beer. He looked toward the door and a large grin spread across his face, tanned from the afternoon on the beach. Chelsea followed his gaze and her heart sank as three beautiful girls walked toward their table, smiling just as enthusiastically at him.

"Oh, God, here comes the harem I was expecting," Chelsea thought as the girls headed their way. One was tall and blonde, sophisticated-looking and tanned, and wearing jeans and a tube top with a thin cardigan over it. The next one was shorter and curvier, with bouncy brown hair pulled back in a ponytail, and wearing a tight pink hoodie with lots of silver jewelry. The third was another blonde with a stunning white smile and dark eyebrows, wearing a light blue tank top with a navy sweater tied around her shoulders, and pearls at her earlobes. They could easily have been members of the U.S.A. soccer team or an elite group of models, and they definitely attracted stares from the male customers they passed.

"Oh my God," Kyle mumbled and stood up as they reached the table. They squealed and took turns hugging him and kissing his cheek. He turned and reached for Chelsea's hand and pulled her into the awkward mix. "Uh, girls…this is my girlfriend, Chelsea Davenport. Chelsea, this is Alex, and Lilia, and Kate," he introduced them as Chelsea's head swam. "We all worked together here last summer," he explained, looking back and forth at them all as they looked at each other. "Are you guys on Spring Break, too?"

"Yeah," said Lilia, the brunette, nodding and continuing to grin at him. "Wow, you look so good," she gushed at him.

Kyle looked at Chelsea. "You go to school at Mary Washington, right?"

"That's right," said Kate, the blonde with a whiter-than-white smile. "So, are you coming back to work here this summer?" she asked, hopefully.

"No," he said without hesitation. "Are you all?"

"That's why we came in tonight. We wanted to talk to Stacie to see if she still needs us. It's too bad you won't be back. You won't be *jail bait* anymore, if I remember right," Alex laughed.

"Uh, no, I guess not," he said, abashed.

"Where are you going to school in the fall?" she asked.

"University of Virginia," he smiled and they nodded.

"You, too, Chelsea?" asked Kate.

"No, I'll be at the School of the Arts," she said, demurely.

"Way to go, Chelsea," said Lilia, winking at her. "You did real good! It was nice to meet you," she smiled and they all agreed. Then they said goodbye, and went to the bar, looking for Stacie.

It was almost time for the music to start, and the band was tuning up on the little stage. Kyle turned back to her and sat in the seat beside her, circling his arm around her shoulders, nuzzling her cheek.

She sighed, "I knew this would happen eventually," she laughed, trying to breathe normally.

"That's as bad as it will ever get," he said, humoring her.

"Ever? Don't you know it's just starting?" She sighed, and imagined him on campus in Charlottesville, turning every girl's head, oblivious to most of it. But how long would that last? It wasn't like he was in a bubble. Someone would break him down. She shook her head to clear the image and saw him looking into her eyes. She felt the burn he was giving off, just for her.

"You don't get it, do you? It's just you. You're the one for me," he murmured, pulling her close and kissing her lightly on the lips. "I don't know how I'm gonna do college without you."

She laughed softly, imagining the same scene for herself, walking around campus and no men looking her way at all. It wasn't that kind of place. "I don't think you'll have to worry too much about me, where I'll be, and all."

He laughed gently into her hair. "Thank God for that," he said.

Sunday was even warmer and they had a chance to lie on the beach in their bathing suits after Kyle drove her around in the Audi with the top down, to give her a tour of the beach. They had planned to cook for the cooks on their night off, so Kyle and Shelly made their spaghetti and meatballs for Stacie and Tyson. After dinner, they put on sweatshirts and went to the beach for a bonfire as the sun set behind pink clouds. Tyson opened another bottle of merlot for the ladies and commented on the evening. "Red sky at night, sailor's delight."

"It'll be another beautiful day tomorrow," Stacie said, accepting a plastic cup of wine from him, her hair blowing loosely in the breeze. Chelsea was enthralled with her and watched the easy way they interacted and looked at each other. "You guys brought us good weather. You can stay as long as you want," she laughed. With her blue eyes twinkling, she raised her glass to them. Shelly raised hers, while Kyle and Chelsea raised their Coke-filled cups. Kyle stood by the fire and poked it to life with a stick as Tyson threw on another piece of driftwood he and Kyle had collected earlier in the day. The breeze and the soft roar of the ocean lulled Chelsea into a peaceful mood, and she snuggled into Kyle as he sat down beside her. Shelly smiled at them, and Chelsea realized she'd forgotten to be on her guard around his mother. Stacie was definitely having a positive effect.

Shelly sighed. "I'm so glad we came," she said, smiling at Kyle. "I know you two would have liked to have gone to Myrtle Beach with your friends, but it's nice having you here. When you go off to school, I don't know how much I'll see you."

Chelsea felt Kyle stiffen a bit, but he did not reply and instead stared into the fire.

"Have you heard from your friends down there?" asked Stacie.

"Abby and I have texted each other. They're having fun. Everyone is sunburned." She left out the part about them all being hung over.

SECRETS

"Nobody's gotten locked up yet?" Tyson asked, laughing.

"Not that I've heard," Chelsea laughed with him, then realized that the others were quiet. There would always be palpable discomfort whenever the topic of Spring Break came up, she realized.

The conversation shifted to Kyle's birthday, and Shelly seemed to be walking on eggshells. She had never had an eighteen-year-old, or even "the last one to leave home." Suddenly, Chelsea's heart went out to her. All of Shelly's waters were unfamiliar, she realized. How scary it would be to find yourself suddenly alone, when three years ago you had a family of four. And everything you did with your last remaining child would color his opinion of you forever.

The restaurant was still on its winter schedule and was only open Wednesdays through Saturdays until Summer began officially on Memorial Day. They would have dinner at home and open gifts on Tuesday night. Stacie and Shelly promised to make Kyle's favorite chocolate cake.

Chelsea watched the fire crackle and pop, and little orange sparks flashed as Kyle rubbed her shoulders. Stacie poured another cup of wine for Shelly and asked her about the tax audit. Shelly said she was glad it was over. It had dragged on and on, and the process had been both tedious and painful. It had taken all of her time, combined with settling Stuart's estate.

"Why did it take so *long*?" asked Stacie, taking a sip from her cup.

"Well, they went all the way back to 1993," said Shelly. "I didn't know it, but things were going on even back then."

Kyle was still looking into the fire and rubbing Chelsea's shoulders. "That was when I was two years old," he said. His hands went still. "What was he doing then?"

Shelly's eyes cast about. "Oh, honey, he was price-gouging his clients even then, when the company was Davis-Davenport Builders," she said, shaking her head.

He looked at Chelsea and then back to his mother. "You mean, this stuff was going on when he was working with Tom?"

He looked at Chelsea, and then at Shelly, who nodded.

"He was cheating Tom?" he said, his voice suddenly loud.

"No, not my dad. He told my dad about the money, but my dad didn't want it," Chelsea said, then instantly regretted speaking.

"You *knew about this*? I never knew this. That's why they dissolved their partnership, wasn't it? I thought they just didn't get along." His face clouded over and he looked at Chelsea with an expression of betrayal she didn't want to see. "How did *you* know?" he demanded.

She shook her head a little. "Uh, I guess I heard my parents talking about it." She looked at Shelly warily. Stacie looked troubled as well. Tyson looked at the fire and drank his beer.

"Honey, I didn't know until later on, either," Shelly said. "Tom talked to him and tried to get him to stop, but he didn't. Tom got fed up with him and washed his hands of the whole business."

"How did I not know this? Why didn't you tell me all this before?"

"What good does it do to know, Kyle? It only makes you think less of your father," Shelly said, helplessly.

He shook his head and cursed under his breath. Chelsea felt her face grow hot, felt his trust in her slip a little, even though she'd never intended to withhold anything from him. And then she felt a huge knot forming in her stomach when he looked at his mother and said, "What else haven't you told me? I'll be eighteen in a couple of days. I think I have a right to know." His blue eyes bored into Shelly's and she looked frightened. When he looked at Chelsea, she met his eyes momentarily, then glanced back at

Shelly, and then into the fire, knowing she had given it away. "What?" he cried, sharply at Chelsea. "What do you *know*?"

"I can't say it," she said quietly. "It's not my place to tell you."

Her face burned and she looked at Shelly, who sighed heavily and ran her fingers through her hair. Stacie shook her head and looked painfully at her sister and then at Kyle. "Oh, for Christ sake, Shelly! You haven't told him about Desiree?"

"What? Told me what, Mom?" he said loudly across the fire at her.

Shelly sighed again and shook her head. "Desiree…Desiree was pregnant and had an abortion during her senior year in high school," she said into the fire, and her voice drifted off.

He blinked hard and looked at her. He could not speak.

"It was right before Spring Break. She went with her friends to Florida…and stepped in front of that car."

Chelsea gasped at her wording of the incident, and Kyle looked back and forth between them. He looked at her. "You *knew*?"

"My sister told me. I didn't want to know," she said quickly.

He looked at Shelly again. "What are you saying? Suicide runs in the family?" he roared. He got to his feet and raked his hands through his hair. "God, Mom! I'm the only one you've got left! And…You've shut me out of everything! Sending me off to *Neverland* to run around the woods with the rich boys….and then sending me down here, to distract me!" He paced in front of the fire. Stacie looked up at him with tears in her eyes and Tyson remained glued to the fire.

"What are you *fucking thinking*? I could have been home, helping Dad, I don't know, being a *son*, maybe helping him get over Desiree instead of *drinking* himself to death over his grief and bad choices. What did you think you were doing with me? I'm all that's left of your family now. When were you planning to let me in? I've been alone all this time…trying to figure out what I want and how to live my life, and you've done nothing to help me! Maybe that was your plan. Well, that's some tough love, Mom. Some really tough love." He stalked away from them toward the beach as Shelly sat, white-faced and stricken by his words.

"It's true," she said, and Stacie reached out to hug her.

"I'm going to talk to him," Chelsea mumbled. She got to her feet and followed him out to the beach. She saw him pacing by the ocean and then standing still as she caught up to him. His arms were clasped over his head as cold waves washed over his bare feet. She rolled up her jeans and walked out to him, feeling the anger coming off him in hot waves. She touched his arm, having no idea what to say, and he turned away from her, making the knot in her stomach larger.

He turned back to her, dropped his hands, and looked at her sideways. "What else is there? What else don't I know?"

"That's it; I don't know anything else. Oh, Kyle, I'm so sorry."

"Well," he said gruffly, "that explains a whole lot." He looked out at the water. Only the angry foam was visible as it roiled onto the shore in front of them. He laughed. "No wonder they didn't want me anywhere near a *female*. And all this time I thought it was because they thought I was some kind of pervert. Who knew?"

He shoved his hands deep into his pockets. Her feet were getting numb as she stood with him in the frigid tide. She reached out again and put her arm around his waist, rubbed his back. "When did you find out about Desiree?" he asked, dully.

"When Charley was home at Thanksgiving. She told me…I wished she hadn't. I didn't know if you had been told. And then when you told me how they sat you down and warned you, I figured you didn't know. But it was never my place to tell you." She realized tears were sliding down her cheeks, but it seemed insensitive to wipe them. He was the one who was hurting.

"No, you're right. It *wasn't* your place." He pulled his hands out of his pockets and took her hand. "Let's get out of this cold water," he said roughly. He saw her tears in the moonlight and pulled her into his side. "Come here," he said a bit more gently and they walked closer to the dune where they'd been at the bonfire. Tyson stood by the fire, his denim shirttail flapping in the breeze, a beer bottle in his hand. He reminded her slightly of her father. Stacie and Shelly were gone.

Suddenly Kyle pulled her close into him and held her hard against him. "I don't want any more secrets between us," he said and kissed her passionately before she could answer. He reached inside her hooded shirt and placed his hand on her chest, sliding it to her shoulder and pulling her close to him by the neck. "I want you so bad," he said into her face as he wiped away her tears with his fingers.

"No," she managed to say.

"What's stopping us now? I'm done trying to humor my mother. Screw it."

"No, not like this. Not just because you're angry at her. This is not the way I want to remember my first time with you. There's no love in you right now."

He sighed and loosened his hold on her. "I'm sorry. You're right. I'm being an asshole. You're getting an eyeful of me tonight. I guess this is really me."

"No it's not you at all. It's like you said, you save your anger for the big stuff. Well, I'd say this is pretty big."

"Yes, it is. I wouldn't blame you if this turns you off. But I love you more than ever for standing here with me right now, calming me down."

She looked into his intense eyes and smiled a little. "My dad always says you should never let the sun go down on an argument when you love someone. You should go talk to your mom. I know she feels horrible about all this. I'm sure it's been hard for her, trying to figure out what to do. She's had a lot of hard stuff to deal with. Maybe she hasn't made all the right calls, but she did what she did to try and protect you from all the bad stuff. I did it, too…not telling you what I knew. It was because I love you and I didn't want to hurt you…And you're right; you're all she's got. Please go talk to her."

He hesitated and shook his head. "God, you're so good at this. I'm so, so sorry. Let's just start over. Okay?"

"Okay," she said. He took her head in his hands and kissed her tenderly. She sighed. "That's so much better. You're back."

They walked, arms around each other, back up to the dune where Tyson was still tending the fire. Kyle slapped his palm wordlessly and picked up the bag of trash Tyson had gathered, then walked across the boardwalk to the house. Chelsea stayed with Tyson and helped him kick sand onto the fire, until all that was left was smoke and ash.

• • •

Chelsea woke the next morning feeling as if she had slept for days, and at first, she had no idea where she was. Then the rich, nutty aroma of good coffee drifted into her consciousness and she remembered the night before. She sat up suddenly, stretched, and ran her hand through her hair. She smiled at the memory of walking back into the beach house with Tyson. There, Kyle and Shelly sat on the sofa, his mother ruffling his hair and hugging his large shoulders as Stacie bumped around nonchalantly in the kitchen, giving them space under her discreet, but watchful supervision. With that memory fresh in her mind, Chelsea slipped into the bathroom and brushed her teeth before padding into the kitchen where friendly voices were talking easily.

"Good morning, sunshine!" Stacie, in her pink plaid pajama bottoms and pink camisole top, grinned at her while sipping coffee. Hmm, tough as nails, Chelsea thought, and smiled back.

"Morning," she replied and went for the coffee pot. Shelly was beside Stacie at the counter, where they where they'd been looking at Kyle's project board and the small model of the deck he had built for Lily Jennings' family.

"Good morning, Chelsea. Did you sleep well?" Shelly asked, smiling at her, too.

"Like a rock," she said in a voice thick with sleep, glad her own blue striped pajamas were presentable.

Kyle appeared from the opposite side of the room in a T-shirt and boxers and groaned. "I can't believe you dragged that all the way down here," he said, referring to the board.

"Nonsense. I had to see this for myself. This is *impressive*," said Stacie, shoving him as he passed them on his way to Chelsea. "And look, there's Bono," she said, referring to one of the pictures on the board.

"Honey, put some clothes on," said Shelly, as she watched him pour his coffee and lean on the counter beside Chelsea, nuzzling her on the cheek.

"Mom, she has a brother. I'm sure she's seen a lot worse."

"Yeah, lighten up, Mom," said Stacie, clearly in their corner. Chelsea found herself grinning as Shelly giggled.

Kyle turned from them and murmured to her as he poured creamer into his coffee. "Thanks for what you did last night." He winked at her.

"So, what's the plan for the day?" Stacie asked energetically.

"I'm going to meet with Rob and Jeanna down at their real estate office around ten," said Shelly. "So I get first shower."

"I'm going for a run. Wanna come?" Kyle asked Chelsea.

She looked at him incredulously. "I don't *run*. But I may go on a nice long walk while you do that."

"Want some company?" asked Stacie.

"Sounds great," Chelsea replied.

They put on shorts and sweatshirts and walked, barefoot, over the boardwalk, pulling their hair back into ponytails in the morning breeze. Sandpipers skittered in and out of the tides in perfect synchrony up and over the uneven sand. This was unlike other beaches Chelsea had seen that were flat, wide, and white. She liked the wildness of it and the quiet. Few people were out and those who were chose to jog or shell hunt along the waters' edge. Chelsea knew a serious conversation was in the making, but she did not feel threatened.

"So, you haven't been here before?" Stacie asked her.

"No, but so far I love it. Your place is great, and the Sound Side is really cool."

"Thanks. I've really enjoyed it. You guys were so cute dancing out there on the deck the other night."

Chelsea laughed, remembering Kyle swooping her up in his arms when the singer belted out, "When a man loves a woman." He'd declared it was officially their song. "Yeah, that was fun. I didn't think I'd stand a chance against those girls from Mary Washington. They were a *little* intimidating!"

Stacie shook her head, "Girl, you have *nothing* to worry about. That boy has it *bad* for you!" She threw her head back and laughed her throaty laugh. "God, I've never seen him this happy in his *life*!"

Chelsea's eyebrows raised and she laughed. "Even after last night?"

"*Especially* after last night. That was the best thing that ever could have happened for Shelly and him. I guess it took you to set them straight. They had a really good talk."

"Well, I'm glad they're on track."

Stacie shook her head again, "Oh, Shelly's had such a hard time, but she's screwed it up so royally at the same time. I can't say I'm any shining example, but you should have seen them when she and Stu first got married. They had this storybook life, you know? They were both beautiful and well educated. They had two cute little kids and then it just spiraled into…what it is now. Stu got so greedy, and she didn't want to see it. She always thought she could make it right. Then when Desiree died, Stu started to drink more and shut her out. She didn't want Kyle to see them fall apart, so she sent him to boarding school and then…" her voice trailed off for a moment. "It wasn't her fault. She just couldn't fix it. But now at least *they* have a chance."

Chelsea tried to take it all in. "How does it get so messed up? I mean, when you think you love someone so much…"

Stacie smiled at her. "It's hard, even in the best relationships. Both people have to be on the same page…and if you're not, you'd better damn well find a way to get there. I certainly know that."

"Were you married?"

Stacie nodded. "I was. I wanted to have a bunch of kids, but he didn't want any. We just didn't make it. As it turns out, the life I'm living doesn't allow me much time for a family anyway. It's okay, actually. I love being Kyle's aunt, and I think I'm pretty good at it. With Tyson, it's just so easy. There aren't any expectations. We love each other and trust each other. But it's just us."

"How long have you two been together?"

"He's worked with me for about three years now, but this, our relationship, didn't really start until last summer, when he helped me with Kyle."

"Kyle told me you're tough as nails, but that doesn't seem to fit you at all."

"Oh, I was all over his ass last summer! I had to be. He was a mess. He was like a stone. Never talked, never smiled. Shelly was afraid he'd start drinking like Stu did, or go wild like Desiree. She couldn't handle it. So I told her to send him down here. He needed to get down and dirty. I put him to work like the common folk so he'd stop acting like a rich, spoiled brat."

"He was like that?"

"Oh, yeah. Tyson was good for him, too. He's kind of quiet, and they got into the surfing thing. Being a dishwasher was a pretty humbling experience for him, and it did him a world of good. He threw himself into working out and running on the beach every day, and it cleared his head. He was exhausted most of the time, but he turned out all right. And then he met you. Wow. I can finally lighten up and watch him enjoy himself!" She threw an arm around Chelsea's shoulders and squeezed her. "You saved him, Chelsea."

Chelsea swallowed a lump in her throat and couldn't speak. She was glad she had her sunglasses on. After a while, they turned around and headed back to the house. Stacie asked questions about Chelsea's family, fascinated by how they had moved in with Kitty and how Liz had taken over her care. She wanted to know about the house and all the generations of Davenports who'd lived there. She wanted to know about the Christmas tree business. She couldn't imagine living there in the winter and the snow and wondered how Shelly handled it by herself. It would be different when Kyle was gone. Chelsea urged her to come and visit. Stacie said she'd try to get there for Kyle's graduation.

He was getting out of the outdoor shower when they returned and he padded up the stairs with her, wrapped in a towel. Trying to control her breathing, she said casually, "Good run?"

"Uh-huh. Good walk?"

"It was great. Stacie and I are best friends now. I know *all* the poo on you."

"Hmm, I thought we said no more *secrets*," he said, winking at her, ramping up her heart another notch.

"Oh, it's nothing *you* don't know. Just, now *I* know, too," she said batting her eyes at him.

"You should check out that shower. It's amazing! Then I'm going to take you down to Buxton," he said, wrapping his free arm around her and wisely guarding his towel with the other hand.

• • •

They drove along the beach road with the top down in the Jeep, "Men at Work" blaring from the speakers. He took her to lunch at Sam and Omie's. In another time it would have been typical: a small, weathered old wooden building with old-fashioned beach shutters and a pitched roof. It reminded her of the Sound Side. The restaurant was nestled in the middle of an intersection known as "Whalebone Junction," just before the turn onto the road for Cape Hatteras National Seashore. It had been a hub of activity in times past, when anglers communed there in the mornings for breakfast and returned in the evening for beer and to swap stories. Pictures of beach scenes, sunsets and lighthouses, along with photos of fishermen and their catches, lined the walls, and the old floors creaked as folks tromped in and out, sliding back the rickety wooden chairs as dishes clinked in the background.

After finishing BLTs, they headed for Buxton and spent the day on the beach, watching surfers in wetsuits ride the moderate ocean swells. Kyle made her do dance moves on the sand, and he used her camera to take pictures of her leaping and posing. They went to his favorite surf shop and bought matching hemp bracelets, and he bought her a pair of small silver starfish earrings. "Beach stars," he said with a wink.

On the way back, he took her to another little place he'd learned about from Tyson, and they ate shrimp burgers for dinner. The grand finale, he said, was his favorite thing about Nags Head. They climbed Jockey's Ridge, enormous sand dunes in the middle of the island that divided the ocean from the Sound, and sat to wait for the sunset. If you stood up, you could see both bodies of water from a certain point, he showed her.

They sat, arms wrapped around their knees, and leaned into each other as they watched the sky progress from lavender to radiant magenta, and then to dark orange. He leaned over, kissed her temple, and murmured, "I've got the biggest crush on you."

Her heart thumped in her chest and she replied, coolly, "You are such a cheap date!"

"That's what I'm supposed to say. But it's the best kind, don't you think? Just simple, you know? Life should just be…easy. I like doing this stuff with you."

"I know. This is awesome, really. I'm just giving you a hard time. Thanks for bringing me here."

He was quiet for a moment, and rested his chin on his arm as he looked at her with his amazing blue eyes. His tan was back, and his windblown hair was lighter from the sun again, a look that made her heart pound a little harder than usual. She reached up and threaded her fingers through his surfer-like hair; she liked the softness of it.

"You have no idea what you did for me and my mom last night," he said, finally. "It's like we finally broke through the huge wall between us. Now I understand so much more about what she did and why she did it. I didn't know how unhappy my dad was after what happened to Desiree. God, I wish I could have stopped it."

"You probably couldn't have," she said, tentatively.

"I know. That's what Mom said, too. But she's sorry she kept me out of the loop." He looked at her seriously. "You know, she's thinking about coming down here if she can sell the house. The 'For Sale' sign is back in our yard. That means I have to start making my bed again," he said ruefully and she giggled.

"I wondered about that," she said, nodding. "That will be a good thing, right? She and Stacie seem to get along really well."

"Yeah, they do. And she hates being in the mountains all alone in that big house—especially in the winter. I mean, who's gonna shovel her driveway when I'm gone? Anyway, she's looking into real estate jobs here. Those people she went with today have a rental property business, so she might be able to work with them for a while if things work out."

"So…the plan is to move during the summer?"

He nodded. "I don't know if the house will sell, but yeah, that's what she hopes. I'll be able to help her move and all…" He looked away and she felt herself swallow a large lump in her throat. She took a deep breath. So, there would be no vacation rendezvous back home once college started. They would have to go back and forth on weekends. Her summer with him might even be cut short. "I didn't want to tell you about this, especially since it's my birthday tomorrow. What a bummer." His eyes were sad as he caressed the side of her face. They gazed at the horizon, which was the deep shade of blue it was just before nightfall. She kissed him tenderly and they held each other for a few minutes before they stood, brushed the sand off their jeans, and made their way down the large dune.

Chapter 16

RITES OF PASSAGE

Kyle's birthday was the warmest and balmiest day yet. A good omen, Shelly said, for his eighteenth year. They went to the grocery store, and when Stacie returned from her morning's work at the restaurant, she and Shelly set about baking the chocolate fudge birthday cake as they discussed the menu for the evening. Tyson came up after lunch and all of them went to the beach, where they played bocce ball and took walks. Kyle made Chelsea teach him how to do the dance lifts she did with Willie. Stacie and Shelly took pictures, applauding and cheering their efforts. He was certainly strong enough to lift her, but clumsy and uncoordinated about it. Laughing happily, she begged him to stop. Their boom box rocked with an eighties song, "Bad to the Bone," by George Thorogood and The Destroyers. Tyson and Kyle peeled off their shirts and threw the football at water's edge.

"Holy crap, Shelly! Look at your son. He is *one ripped dude*," said Stacie, sipping a wine cooler, as the three of them sat in beach chairs.

"Stacie, you're such a cougar," muttered Shelly. "And, you realize that's *my son* you're talking about…and Chelsea's boyfriend!"

"Chelsea isn't offended. *All* women are cougars," Stacie said, matter-of-factly. "You're one, too, but you think you're too good to admit it. There's nothing wrong with admiring beautiful men. It's not like I'm going to *do* him! He's my nephew, for God's sake. Guys say this kind of shit about us all the time. Why can't we have some fun, too? I just call it like I see it," Stacie said. She grinned at Chelsea, then said, "Ooh, honey, let me put more sunscreen on your back. You've done so well about not getting burned." Chelsea dutifully turned around to let Stacie protect her carefully cultivated Spring Break tan.

"Yeah, I should be more like that," Shelly said, giving in.

"It's very *freeing* in a way, when you just let yourself go," said Stacie. "There's something about this place, maybe it's the sea air, that changes you." She rubbed the lotion absently into Chelsea's skin and Chelsea closed her eyes, breathing deeply, feeling exactly what Stacie was talking about. She had never met anyone so open. She watched the men on the beach and let the image smolder into her memory.

Tyson made beer margaritas in the blender while Stacie prepped the steak fajitas they'd have for dinner with saffron rice and black beans. Shelly, Kyle, and Chelsea stood on the deck, sipping their drinks as Tyson went in to tend to round two. Kyle and Chelsea leaned against the railing, as Shelly looked out over the ocean. The wind had picked up and clouds moved in as they watched. They discussed Kyle's presents, a wetsuit from Shelly, hang-gliding lessons from Stacie and Tyson, and Journey concert tickets from Chelsea. He was stoked about the concert and Chelsea explained that Glen had bought tickets for Abby's birthday, which was in two weeks, so they could go together. "Glen got Abby's mom in on it. Abby's aunt, uncle, and cousins live in Raleigh, and they said we could all crash there after the concert in May. Don't tell Abby, though. It's supposed to be a surprise."

"Oh, right. Definitely not," said Kyle and stopped abruptly. She followed his gaze into the kitchen. Tyson's arms were around Stacie from behind, his hands cupped her breasts, and his mouth was at her ear. Kyle breathed in audibly and shifted his weight on the railing. Chelsea felt heat rise into her own cheeks, and she felt herself breathing in sharply as well. They turned simultaneously and walked toward Shelly, who was commenting on the sky.

"Looks like a storm's coming," Kyle said, and at that moment, thunder rumbled in the distance. Then Tyson was back with the pitcher. Kyle and Chelsea held out their glasses wordlessly, meeting each other's gazes briefly. Kyle seemed to make a point of not touching her, and was talking to Tyson about hang-gliding. They planned to go the next day if the weather held.

"If you can wait until about two-thirty, Stacie and I can come and watch on our break. Maybe this weather will have cleared out by then. Are you doing it too, Chelsea?" Tyson asked her.

"I'm game," she said bravely and Kyle smiled at her.

"That's my girl," he said, breaking down and pulling her close to him. The smell of fajitas drifted onto the deck, and they moved back inside, getting dishes and forks ready at the table, which had been set with blue and orange paper napkins, the colors of U.V.A.

After dinner and birthday cake, they cleaned up the kitchen in short order and moved to the living room to play cards. Chelsea's phone rang and she went into the kitchen to talk to her mother. She returned in a few moments and motioned to Kyle. She took his hand and they walked back out onto the deck. The wind had kicked up even more, and she pulled her hair to one side as he looked at her, concerned.

"What's wrong?" he asked.

"Kitty had another stroke today," she said through tears that were just starting to flow freely. He sighed and embraced her, murmuring how sorry he was. "She's in the hospital now and Mom and Dad are there."

"How bad is it? Do they know yet?"

"Mom said she can't talk, and she's having trouble moving her right arm," she said into the collar of his shirt as he kissed the top of her head.

"We can leave tomorrow if you want," he said immediately.

"No…Mom said not to come. She said it wouldn't do any good. I'll call her in the morning and see how she is. Maybe she'll come around quickly, like she did the first time."

"Is this just the second stroke she's had?" he asked, rubbing her back.

She nodded. "Maybe she'll be home when we get back on Friday."

"Look," he said. "We don't have to stay. We can go home any time you want. You just say the word. Mom can stay down here. She's got her car."

"Thank you…we'll see."

He rocked her back and forth. "I know you're scared." Rain started to spit at them, so they walked back inside, where Stacie was cranking up the blender again.

"Everything all right?" she said, seeing their expressions. Kyle filled her in. Tyson and Shelly came into the kitchen after hearing the news. Stacie and Shelly hugged Chelsea. They had the same conversation about leaving and decided to wait and see as Liz suggested. Then Kyle and Chelsea declined more drinks; he took her into the room where he stayed and they snuggled on the futon.

He stroked her hair and held her. They listened to the rain pattering against the windows. Lightning flashed occasionally as thunder rumbled closer. "It would be really different around your house without Kitty there," he said.

"I know. I thought about that, too. If she has to stay in the hospital a while, it will be so strange. You get used to a certain routine…and even though she doesn't talk a lot now, she's always *there*, you know? She's always had such a sweet personality, and it's just *there* all the time at home. My mom will probably be gone a lot, too, if that's the case, staying over at the hospital with her."

He continued to stroke her hair. "I'm sorry for her, and for your family. I hope she'll be okay and come back home soon," he said softly.

"This sure isn't the way I wanted your birthday to end. You should feel happy right now," she said, looking up at him.

"I am. I'm always happy when I'm with you. You're the best present I've gotten," he said wanly.

She smiled. "This has been a great week. Your family is really wonderful."

"Yeah, they are. I guess we're turning into something kind of solid. It's nice to have Tyson as part of it, too. I wasn't really expecting that, but he's right in there with Stacie. I've never had a brother, but I guess this is what it's like. I can't call him an *uncle!*"

"Hmm, you might be some day."

"Is that what Stacie told you?"

"No. She just said that they're in love and really comfortable with each other."

"That's *obvious*," he said, referring to what they had seen earlier, and they laughed.

"Did you know she wanted to have children?"

He nodded. "Yeah. She'd be a great mom if it ever worked out for her."

"They're good together."

"Kind of like us," he said, kissing her lightly on her lips again and again.

Tyson was at the door, clearing his throat discreetly. "Hey. Uh, Stacie rented *Twilight*," he said, rolling his eyes. "Do you guys want to watch it with us?"

"I thought the birthday boy gets to pick the flick. No *Fast and Furious*, or *Pineapple Express*?" Kyle laughed. Chelsea was the one to roll her eyes that time.

"Somehow, I think she thinks she's doing you a favor with this one, dude," Tyson said, laughing skeptically. "She said it's perfect for a rainy night, whatever that means."

"Okay, I can watch a chick flick if you can." He raised his eyebrows to see if she wanted to, and she nodded. They got up off the futon and joined the others in the den.

• • •

Friday was overcast and windy, and they hit the road for home early, hoping to be there between two and three. They were content to ride back quietly, thinking about how close they'd become, being together so much. They'd had so much fun, learning to hang-glide, then going back down to Buxton for Kyle to test out the wetsuit, surfing on Tyson's break the day before.

Toward the end, Shelly became talkative and seemed more relaxed than ever. She drove them around to some areas where she was looking at properties, which was a bit depressing for them, but she was into it. She had found some nice places, and Kyle was glad she would eventually be near Stacie. Chelsea found it hard to say goodbye to Stacie and hoped she'd make good on her promise to come to the mountains for their graduation.

They drove directly to the hospital and met Liz at the entrance to the rehab wing. Kitty was improving every day and was expected to go home the following week. They sat with her in the solarium. Chelsea held her hand, tiny and veined, and rubbed it and the engagement ring she wore—the only jewelry Chelsea had ever seen her wear. Kitty seemed in good spirits and smiled at them. Her speech hadn't returned; all she could say was "love." But that was all they needed to hear.

Liz hugged Kyle, wished him a happy birthday, and thanked him for taking Chelsea away for a well-needed break. "You two look wonderful.

And look at your tan," she said to Chelsea, touching her shoulder and then the starfish earrings delicately. "We *all* missed you, but *your dad* has been beside himself without you. And Kitty is so glad to see you. She wasn't this perky before you got here."

Later, Kyle took her home and carried her luggage upstairs. They sprawled across her small bed, exhausted from the trip and all the emotions. Liz was shaking them awake as the afternoon sun warmed them from her window. "Shelly called. She just got home and was checking to see that Kyle is okay."

Chelsea walked him to the Jeep. He kissed her sleepily and whispered, "I wish this didn't have to end."

School seemed unbearable after the break, and it was all they could do to concentrate on classwork and homework. Dance rehearsals were in full swing for *Giselle*, and Willie and Anthony's scenery was impressive in quality, and ethereal, as expected for the story. Talk at school was mostly about the prom. Abby, Meredith, and Chelsea planned a shopping trip to Blowing Rock to find perfect dresses. If that didn't pan out, they'd shop online as a last resort.

Liz was in a spin with wedding plans, especially after Kitty arrived back at home and needed more of her time than usual. Shelly gladly came to the rescue and took over some of the lists, helping Chelsea with the invitations and following up with the caterer and the florist. Everything seemed to be falling into place, and Shelly helped Liz relax and enjoy the process, a real role reversal for both of them.

Glen threw a surprise party for Abby on her eighteenth birthday at Café Portofino. She was thrilled with the Journey concert plans, amazed he'd been able to keep it all a secret. Chelsea was glad that the concert date was after her spring dance concert. She'd need to take class over the summer to be ready for U.N.C.S.A. in the fall, but essentially, the pressure would be gone in just a few short weeks.

Kyle spent his free time working out at a local gym and running every day. They went to Glen's baseball games, mostly to support Abby, who loathed baseball. Glen was ferocious about his baseball, even more so than skiing or football, and recruiters from Appalachian talked to him about being their first baseman next year.

The days ticked by slowly and Chelsea was glad, in contrast to the others' desire to be done with school. No one talked about Elle any more, and she remained under the radar at school. Shelly told them at the beach that Elle had been charged with a felony and was working at the food pantry a couple of times a week as community service, in addition to paying a large fine. She no longer looked at Kyle, under the threat of a restraining order that could be put in place at any time.

Charley came home for a visit to nail down remaining plans before the wedding, and Becky threw a bridal shower in her honor. Gifts for the new couple filled the sun porch, and more packages arrived after the invitations went out. Charley had picked up the dresses on her way home, and they were glad they'd all stayed the same size, so no alterations were needed. Chelsea and Charley had to drag Tom and Jay into the formal-wear shop to have their tux measurements taken. Jay and Lauren were still together, and it looked like the band would remain intact, at least through the reception.

The day of their senior prom turned out to be sunny and warm, despite a cold snap at the beginning of the week. The plan was for everyone to arrive at the Davenports' for pictures on the terrace, and then they'd go to Char for dinner before the dance. Chelsea and Abby got ready at Chelsea's house and Abby helped her with her hair. When Meredith and Tia arrived later, Abby did last-minute hair adjustments with them, too, before they met the guys downstairs. Liz fixed a spread of hors d'oeuvres for other parents who had arrived to take pictures.

Kyle arrived in his tux and a black tie, corsage in hand. Glen was with him, looking sharp in a deep blue tie to match Abby's strapless gown. Meredith and Anthony, matching in yellow, exchanged flowers, and Chelsea helped Mer with Anthony's boutonniere. Chelsea saw Kyle first, and her breath caught at the sight of him. He turned and saw Chelsea emerge onto the stone terrace in her narrow vintage ivory dress with tiny silver straps covered with iridescent and silver beads, hair swept back and curled. She wore tiny sparkling star earrings, in keeping with the star around her neck. His eyes popped when he saw her, and he smiled his slow smile at her and took her hand. The group of parents snapped photos and watched each couple connect and exchange flowers.

"Wow. You look...just...*delicious*," he said in her ear, so no one could hear. Tom winked at her and took their picture as Liz looked on. It would later be Chelsea's favorite shot of the night.

Willie was already there and said hello to her as well, then took her hands, and held her out from him. "*Baby*, you look *amazing*! No offense to *my* date," he said, inclining his head to Tia, beautiful in a pink and silver sparkly dress. "You are *seriously hot, girl!*" Kyle laughed at the conversation and Willie turned to include him. "Y'all look like y'all should be on top of a *wedding* cake!"

Kitty, just home from the hospital, clapped her hands and called them a rainbow as the girls, wearing an array of colors, stood together for pictures.

Later at the hotel, the Casablanca-themed prom was in full swing, and they made sure to dance with all the others' dates. Kyle finally got Chelsea back in his arms for Aerosmith's love song, "I Don't Want to Miss a Thing." He steered them over to a darker corner where they could be alone. When the song was over, he walked her toward the hotel veranda. The weather was still too cool to venture out; he wrapped his arms around her waist and they stood quietly for a minute or two. Then he looked down and sighed. She wondered what was up.

"My mom got a contract on our house yesterday," he said and met her eyes, pain showing in his own.

She gasped. "When? When will you be leaving? I mean, I'm glad for her and everything, but it's just…so *soon*."

"I know. She wants to stay until Charley's wedding and then we'll move."

"That's just five weeks," she breathed.

"I know."

"You'll be gone from me in five weeks…" She couldn't process it and stared at him, open-mouthed.

He nodded.

"I always thought you'd be here this summer. I just can't believe it." She placed the palm of her hand on his chest as if feeling to make sure he was still there. He touched her cheek with his fingertips and gently kissed her lips. "I'm not ready," she whispered.

"I know. I can't get my head around it, either. But, five weeks is a long time, really. We're going to have a lot of fun. And you can come to the beach whenever you want and stay with us. My mom would definitely be okay with that. It could be a good thing," he said, positively, searching her eyes for something of the same.

"And you can come back here and stay. My parents would be fine with it," she said. Her head was swimming, thinking of them burning up the road on those seven-hour trips. Her hand went to her head, and she shook it slightly as if trying to come to terms with it all.

Out of the corner of her eye, she saw someone walking toward them. Not now, she thought. When she looked up, she was shocked to see Elle McClarin standing in front of them in a bright coral strapless dress with sparkling chandelier earrings dangling from her ears. Chelsea clung to Kyle, wondering what this was all about. Aiden Caffey was standing nearby, watching them.

"Hey, guys," she said, cocking her head back, as if preparing for a rebuff. "Look, I know I'm the last person you want to see tonight, and I'm not going to make a scene, I promise. But I just wanted to tell you…I'm sorry for treating you like I did," she said directly to Chelsea. And then to Kyle, she said, "And I'm really sorry for what I did to you. It's unforgivable. I don't expect you to forgive me, but I know what I did was *really* wrong. I'm trying to get my act together…so I just wanted to say that I hope y'all are okay." They stared at her a moment and she gave a brief nod, cut her eyes away, and turned on her heel. Without waiting for a response, she went back to Aiden, who, after a wink to Kyle, escorted her out of the room.

They stood dumbfounded for a minute, then Kyle laughed and said, "Wow. That was weird. But I'm okay with it. Good for her."

Chelsea raised her eyebrows and nodded. "Sounds like one of those addiction therapy programs to me, like you see in the movies. That must have been the *making amends* part. I have to say, I'm impressed, though. I never expected her to speak to us again. I wonder what will happen to her."

"With a felony on her record, it's gonna be a totally different life for her. It's a good thing my mom didn't press the sexual assault charges. Then her life would've *really* been over."

Chelsea shivered at the thought. Abby, Glen, Meredith and Anthony were waving them over.

Kyle pulled her back before they walked over. "Look, I know what we talked about before is hard, but I promise you: I'll do whatever it takes to keep this relationship going with you, Chels," he said, his eyes burning into hers. "I can't lose you. Not now. It's gone way past that for me."

"Me too," she said, barely audible, spellbound in his gaze.

• • •

Willie and Chelsea *owned* the spring dance concert. An enormous crowd turned out at the new high school auditorium, partly due to the novelty of the venue, and partly because the seniors wanted to get a look at Anthony and Willie's incredible scenery for *Giselle*, in the second portion of the show. Brad and Sonya were delighted with the turnout and the audience's enthusiasm over the Studio One dancers' performance. Everyone knew that when Willie left, there would never be a group like this again. The ballet went well and got a standing ovation. Chelsea was especially moved by her contemporary dance, which was as emotionally charged as ever for her. Willie had yet another tear in his eye as she exited the stage.

It was bittersweet to finish dancing for the year. Although Chelsea was exhausted and glad the pressure was finally over, she knew she'd leave a part of herself with Sonya and Brad as she stepped into the new world of college and a dance program she knew very little about. She would miss seeing Willie every day, miss joining his hilarious conversations and listening to his contagious laughter, not to mention his heartfelt encouragement. Chelsea trusted him implicitly as a partner and would always be his biggest fan. They hugged each other and wept openly when the curtain went down.

Kyle's reaction touched her deeply. He met her backstage, took her in his arms, and murmured in her ear, "That was us, wasn't it?" And it was indeed what she had in mind all along.

Later in the lobby, Chelsea looked for her family and found them as Tom and Liz rolled Kitty, in her wheelchair, out of the auditorium. It meant the world to Chelsea that Kitty was home and had the strength to attend her final performance. Tom and Liz beamed at her, then caught her in a hug. Kitty touched her throat and looked troubled, as if searching for the words she wanted to say. Liz and Tom looked at one another as Kitty grabbed Chelsea's hand and repeatedly touched her throat.

"Are you sick, Mama?" Tom asked, a worried tone in his voice. Chelsea became nervous, herself. Kitty shook her head vigorously and tapped her own collarbone repeatedly as it dawned on Liz what she was trying to communicate.

"*Star!*" Liz exclaimed. Kitty nodded and smiled at Chelsea through eyes brimmed with tears. "Chelsea, your *star*," Liz explained, referring to her necklace. "Kitty means you're a *star*," she said. That started Chelsea's tears once again.

Nothing could have been more fun than the Journey concert in Raleigh over the Memorial Day weekend. Before the concert, Abby and Glen hadn't been big fans of the band. They were amazed at all the songs they knew but hadn't known were Journey songs. Kyle picked out a favorite song for Chelsea. As the band played, he wrapped his arms around her and sang "Open Arms" in her ear.

They crashed at Abby's relatives' house, girls upstairs, and guys on the pullout sofa in the basement. After breakfast at IHOP, they drove back home. Glen said it was like being on the first of many college road trips.

Reality set in rudely as they took their remaining finals, signed each other's yearbooks, and picked up their caps and gowns for graduation. Chelsea felt more unsettled than the others. Most of her friends would be heading to college with a friend or classmate, but no one else was going to the School of the Arts. She wondered who her roommate would be and whether they'd get along. She wondered about her ability—would she be a good dancer, or would she come home crying at Christmas with her tail between her legs? And how often would she see Kyle? With football, he'd have a busy autumn and not much time for her. He was quiet, too, probably having the same thoughts. He didn't know anyone going to U.V.A., had his own doubts about playing football, and wondered whether he'd be able to meet the challenge. It would be hard to leave their safe cocoon and emerge into the real world. They agreed that with their cell phones and Skype on their computers, they would make it work.

Graduation day arrived, and they marched boisterously into the gym to the requisite "Pomp and Circumstance." Kyle was behind Chelsea, and Glen a few feet back, followed by Anthony and Meredith. Chelsea's heart pounded with the music and excitement fueled by the crowd. She swallowed a lump in her throat and walked on. She wished Kyle had something funny to say, but when she turned to look at him, his eyes were glassed over and he had a faraway look. Then he saw her, winked, and gave her his lopsided smile. He took her hand for a moment as they stopped to wait for the lines to catch up. She scanned the crowd and found her family, easy to spot in the wheelchair section. Becky, Wayne, and her cousins pointed at her and waved. Her mom and Kitty were beside them. Her dad waved at her, too, and raised his camera to take her picture. She pulled Kyle into the shot and they waved as she saw the camera flash.

They had reservations at Casa Rustica for a late dinner celebration. Shelly and Stacie joined them. Tyson had remained behind to operate the restaurant, which was operating at full speed. Chelsea was suddenly overwhelmed by the large group. Kyle held her hand under the table, winking at her from time to time as she fought for composure. Four weeks, already gone…four whole weeks, rang repeatedly in her head. Stacie, sensing what she was feeling, smiled compassionately at her throughout dinner. Liz watched her too, over her red wine, and Chelsea felt her head swimming as she imagined Kyle and his mother packing up boxes and boxes of personal belongings they'd take to their new home not far from Stacie's house. It was much smaller, and she couldn't imagine what Shelly was going to do with all of their furniture. She imagined Kyle going to their friend Frank Maynard's house to say goodbye to his beloved chocolate lab, Bono. Suddenly, tears rolled down her cheeks. She wiped them away quickly, embarrassed, as her mother, Stacie, and Kyle shifted in their seats. Each attempted to come up with a way to humor her out of her misery.

"So, when are you coming to visit us, Chelsea?" Stacie asked, elegant in her black dress and hair in a loose twist, cajoling her with her most sincere smile.

Chelsea took a deep breath and shot a hopeful glance at her parents, who smiled sympathetically, while Kyle stroked her back with the palm of his hand. "Maybe in a couple of weeks, after they get settled in." To her relief, their waiter appeared at her elbow to clear away the dishes, and some of the attention shifted away from the sadness that showed in her red, hot face.

Shelly nodded, smiled, and confirmed the invitation she had given the night before. The adults took up the conversation and discussed details of the move. Then wedding preparations became the topic, and Chelsea was no longer the focus of attention. She and Kyle leaned into each other. "I'm *sorry*," she whispered in his ear. "I don't know why I'm losing it."

"It's okay," he said. "It's supposed to be a happy time, but for us…it's different," he said, his blue eyes sparkling at her. "We need to get out of here," he murmured. His mouth touched her face, and he looked at his mother, who seemed to anticipate his next move. He asked whether they could be excused from the table and everyone nodded. They thanked their parents for the nice dinner, and said they would meet back at home in a short while.

He put her into the Jeep and tucked her black dress in around her, giving her a quick kiss. They drove away from the restaurant with the top down, playing Guns and Roses and singing along to "Sweet Child O' Mine." They'd been invited to a party, but she knew he wasn't taking her there. She held her hair and grinned at him, thankful that he had saved her once again. He pulled into the school, and drove deep into the parking lot. They got out and walked barefoot onto the football field, which was dark and vacant, and sat together on his green blanket. They sat and watched the stars, quietly, as he stroked the back of her hand.

After a few minutes, he broke the silence. "One more week," he said softly, and looked over at her, his eyes deep and serious.

"I know," she breathed. "It's all I can think about. You have so much to do before you go."

"So do you, with the wedding next week. We'll find time. We'll just sneak out at night if we have to," he said. She shivered with the thought of a midnight rendezvous at the corner of her property, with Fella tagging along, no doubt. He ran his hand up under her hair and looked long into her eyes, making her head swim again. "This whole year with you has been so amazing. I don't think I would have made it if I hadn't met you. You helped me so much. You really know yourself."

"Me? You just rebuilt yourself. Right now, you know yourself better than anyone I can think of."

"No…it's just that you and your family are so full of love. Y'all are so… *solid*. How could *you not* get it, you know? It's taken me all year to work it all out—my whole life, I guess. I can't imagine being away from you now. I wish we could just…stay like this, forever," he said, pulling her close. He kissed her, and suddenly she felt wet, cold water splashing on her face and shoulder from the side.

"Damn!" he exclaimed, wiping water droplets from his face, jumping up and pulling her to her feet. He laughed and said, "I forgot about the sprinklers!"

Chapter 17

THE WEDDING

Bad rehearsal, good wedding. The Davenport-Jamieson rehearsal was living up to that axiom with alarming intensity. On the way to the church, the bottom fell out of the steely summer sky. Chelsea and Liz huddled under their umbrella and ran for the door, while Tom parked the car. As they entered the narthex of the little stone church, they heard an altercation underway. Charley, wild-eyed and livid, hissed at Jay, hopefully beyond the earshot of the others in the wedding party, who milled about at the front of the church.

"I'm not *believing* this! Oh, my God, you're such an *ass,*" she hissed at him, and smacked the side of his head with the palm of her right hand.

Chelsea's mouth dropped open and Liz intervened immediately. "Whoa! What's the problem? Honey, you're in a *church,*" she whispered to Charley. She placed her hand on Charley's arm and glared at Jay.

"Mom, I told him not to do this! Look at Lauren," she said, eyes blazing and gesturing sharply with her hand. Liz and Chelsea discreetly peeked into the sanctuary, where the string quartet was setting up in the choir loft. Lauren's eyes were decidedly puffy and red, as she held sheet music in her hand and conferred with Jason, who would sing with her during the rehearsal. Liz looked questioningly at them as Tom dripped in from the outside, shaking off his umbrella out the door. "He broke up with her last night," Charley hissed again, turning her intense eyes on Jay. "I'm going to talk to her. You are *dead meat*," she scorned him harshly, jabbed her finger at him, and stalked down the aisle.

"What the hell happened?" asked Tom, bemused, as he attempted to catch up. Liz shushed him with rolled eyes, disappointed with the irreverence she'd heard.

"*She* broke up with *me*. I didn't break up with her," said Jay, holding up his hands in self-defense.

"Well, why?" asked Chelsea suspiciously.

He looked around sheepishly. "She, uh, saw me with Jordan Buckman last night at a party."

"And just what were you two doing?" Liz asked, folding her arms as Tom glared at Jay through narrowed eyes.

He shrugged, "I, uh, kissed her."

Tom twisted his mouth and scrutinized Jay for a moment. "You're an idiot," he said, matter-of-factly. "You do know that, don't you?"

"Lord, Jay!" Liz whispered, forgetting her own standards. "How stupid are you trying to be? And now, of all times."

Father Michael appeared at the doorway, glasses and white Bible in hand, eyebrows raised. He looked at them from face to face, assessing the commotion. "Are you folks all right out here?" he asked earnestly.

"I think we are…for now. But this character may need your most fervent prayers," Tom told him, drolly, inclining his head toward Jay.

Father Michael looked deeply into Jay's face with an almost amused expression; nonetheless, Chelsea wanted to squirm. "That can be arranged.

THE WEDDING

It's always the way I tend to start these things. I'll throw in a special word for you…it couldn't hurt," he said to Jay and then laughed a deep and hearty laugh, surprising for his size since he met Chelsea at eye level. He slapped Jay on the shoulder, and they all went to join the others.

The rest of the rehearsal went off as planned, thanks in part to Father Michael's fervent prayer, and periodic dour looks from Charley. Lauren conducted herself like the professional she was, and sang "The Prayer" beautifully with Jason, accompanied by the string quartet. Chelsea had chill bumps throughout the song as their voices resonated beautifully in the small sanctuary.

The rain stopped during the rehearsal, and the party met with all the relatives and other guests for the rehearsal dinner at a charming small inn nearby. Kyle and Shelly were there, and Kyle sat beside Chelsea during the meal. Jay sat beside Lauren, hardly remorseful, but things seemed to be civil at least. Butterflies assaulted Chelsea's stomach from time to time as she waited for the time to make her maid-of-honor toast. She watched Charley, who'd relaxed, thanks to Steve, who seemed to keep a running commentary going that kept her laughing. He'd always been a calming influence on her, something the whole family loved about him, along with his easy smile and gentle but continuous energy. He was perfect for her. Who else in the world would be able to keep up with Charley? The thought made Chelsea smile. Kyle watched her, then commented on how fabulous she looked in his favorite crimson dress.

Waiters appeared, cleared the dishes away, and replaced them with bubbly-filled champagne flutes. She felt another wave of nerves overtake her. She concentrated as Father Michael explained that champagne had been invented by priests, and someone else commented that it tasted like swallowing stars. She took a deep breath and realized it was time for her to begin her toast. After looking at Kyle for last-minute encouragement, she stood and tapped her glass with her fork. Family and guests turned pleasantly toward her, expecting something wonderful and charming to flow from her lips.

She looked around and laughed quietly as Charley winked at her and raised her own glass just a bit. "Hi. I'm Chelsea, the little sister. You know, the one who gets all the hand-me-downs." There was a little laughter. "The car was hers, and those dents are *all hers*, by the way." There was louder laughter, especially from those who had ridden with Charley in the past. "And the clothes, too, except this is actually *my* dress…"

"Mm-*hmm!*" said Steve's brother from a table behind her, to more laughter.

She blushed a little and continued, "When Charley was about four years old, before I was born, her favorite movie was *The Little Mermaid*. She liked pretending she was Ariel, marrying the prince. She had the costume, and sang the little song all the time. Her swimming teacher thought her name really *was Ariel*. My mother was once paged to the front of Harris Teeter—'*Will Ariel's mother come to the front of the store?*'" More laughter. "My sister has always been a hopeless romantic, which isn't a bad thing. It makes me happy, because now, she really *has* found her prince. And he's great. I think she's going to keep him; I don't imagine he'll *ever* be a hand-me-down. I'm glad to be getting another brother," she said, winking at Jay. She raised her glass to Charley and Steve and they smiled at her. "So here's to Charley and Steve. May your life be full of rainbows!" People clapped and Charley wiped a tear from under each eye.

As Chelsea sat, relieved and happy, her father stood and tapped his own glass. He looked down, composed himself for a moment, then smiled. "Well, *Ariel!* You said you wanted to marry *me* when you were that age," he said, smiling at Charley in that way fathers smile at their daughters who are about to be married. "I hated to disappoint you. You obviously didn't get what was going on with me and your gorgeous mother! I didn't want to hurt your feelings, so I let you slide. I figured in time you'd forget about

THE WEDDING

me and find your own prince. And you did. You found the perfect man. I trust him completely to love and cherish you, to protect you, and to stand by you through the good times and the bad. You'll have all of that, trust me. So, good for you, Charley. Your mom and I couldn't be happier for you both. This is a blessing for all of us. Steve, welcome to the family," he said, raising his glass. "Bring her around when you can."

Despite the previous night's rain, the wedding day was lovely. A balmy breeze blew the mountain laurel, azaleas, and rhododendron blossoms that appeared just for the occasion. The ceremony was elegant and serene. Charley was a beautiful bride in her ivory strapless gown with the sweetheart bodice, asymmetrical and unexpected in design, with champagne lace and beading as accents. Her hair was twisted at the sides and swept up under her mother's veil. She was calm and happy, having made amends with Jay. In turn, he made amends with Lauren, who sang beautifully with Jason in another moving performance of "The Prayer." The bridesmaids were lovely in their lavender tea-length strapless dresses with similar, twisted heart-shaped bodices. Chelsea, Emma, and Bri carried pale pink peonies down the aisle as clear afternoon sunlight flickered through the hand-blown glass panes of the church windows, each accented with laurel blossoms and white candles. Chelsea came down the aisle last, and handed pink roses to Kitty and Liz's mother. Steve, his father, brother, and Jay wore black tuxedos with lavender vests and ties. Father Michael, splendid in white vestments, seemed beside himself with joy, and he conducted the ceremony with the proper balance of humor and reverence, delivering a touching homily. There wasn't a dry eye in the church.

Back at the house, the yard had been transformed into an ethereal fairyland of tiny paper lanterns and a white tent for dining. There was also a dance floor, complete with DJ booth for dancing after dinner. Jay and Lauren's band played several songs as guests arrived and greeted the newlyweds. Kitty was elegant in a silver-printed silk jacket and pants. Holding her pink rose in her lap like a treasure, she clasped her hands from time to time and sent her special smile Chelsea's way. Her mother was exceptionally gorgeous in a muted plum flowing silk dress and diamond jewelry she seldom wore. It was obvious that her father couldn't keep his eyes off her.

Kyle, accompanied by his sharply dressed mother, was stunning in his gray suit and her favorite black and silver tie. His eyes went directly to hers, a perfect déjà-vu from ten months earlier in the same spot. Chelsea felt as lightning-struck as she had the first time. Would this rocked-to-the-core feeling ever leave her? Because she felt the same way anytime he caught her off-guard. She tried to catch her breath. The butterflies in her stomach were ten times greater than what she'd felt the night before when she stood to deliver her toast.

Then it hit her. *One more day.* Her heart flip-flopped as he took her in his arms and caressed the side of her cheek with his lips, the familiar shape and feel for which she longed. His mother had tactfully wandered over to the Jamiesons, striking up a conversation. And then, there was no one else in the world but the two of them. Her eyes closed and she breathed in the scent of him, different today. He wore cologne, peppery and outdoorsy, but not overdone. He did the same to her and commented on her perfume as well, softly, in her ear, his breath sweet on her face. Suddenly, she was conscious of the situation and wished it was already dark, so no one would notice them, as was surely happening at that moment. She opened her eyes, breathed deeply, and looked around. Her mother looked at them with an almost melancholy expression and turned her eyes away. Chelsea was hit with a feeling of panic, and she touched his chest in response. He noticed it with a shiver and flashing eyes. Then, he took her hand and they joined the rest of the group.

They sat with her family and Shelly at a table under the tent, where the conversation was entertaining. It seemed that everyone was poised, trying to get a word in about the ceremony, as well as Charley and Steve's honeymoon trip to Italy. Chelsea was grateful for the distraction as she and Kyle exchanged wanton glances and ate steadily beside each other at the table. She made herself focus on the conversation, even though she did not care. She felt somewhat ashamed, being the maid of honor, but Charley and Steve were not the couple she was obsessed with at the moment.

Then finally, the DJ started the dance music, which gave them the excuse they needed to entwine themselves on the dance floor as the sunset bled into the evening sky. Kyle held her hand and pulled her close into his hips as they danced the slow dances everyone anticipated for the newlyweds. He spoke into her ear and looked into her eyes passionately, as never before, both of them knowing it was their last opportunity for this for a long time to come.

Her hands were in his hair as he breathed into her ear, "I'm so crazy in love with you." Her heart pounded as she pressed herself into him in response. She listened to his breathing as they continued to dance close, even when the music picked up. Holding hands and stealing glances at each other, they wandered out into the yard, wondering how to get through the next twenty-four hours respectably. "Would anybody notice if we sneaked off to your room?" he murmured excitedly into her ear, his hands caressing her shoulders and face. "Or hell, the barn?"

"Just look at my dad. His radar is up for sure. And your mom is all over it," she whispered. Her lips brushed his face and she placed her hand at the small of his back, under his jacket. She glanced around at the crowd on the terrace.

"I'd pay big money for a crack at the honeymoon suite with you tonight," he said, tempting her beyond belief. "They're watching us like hawks," he laughed quietly. "You'd think there would be some place, some way," he moaned in her ear.

"And here comes my *brother*," she said, as the air left her sails.

"Mom requests your presence at the bouquet tossing," said Jay, apologetically, as he approached them reluctantly. "Sorry..." he said as they sauntered his way. She looked at Kyle and felt her face flame. Her body was on fire for him, with every inch of her being. Their hands moved together sensually as they tried to walk nonchalantly through the crowd on the terrace. She watched his eyes study her curves hungrily as Charley poised herself to throw the bouquet of peonies over her shoulder. Suddenly, everyone was crying out and applauding because Lauren had caught the bouquet. She thought to peek at Jay, who looked like a deer caught in the headlights. He shot a vengeful look at Charley, who sneered good-naturedly at him. The shiny blue garter sailed into the air next and seemed to be aimed right at Jay. The throng peeled into laughter when he caught it in his hand. And then Kyle took Chelsea's hand again and led her to the front porch. They sat in the porch swing, listening to the music... "Oh, you-oo-oo-oo send me."

"God, every song I hear will remind me of you," he said, stroking her hand. He pushed the swing slowly back and forth with his foot, rhythmically, as they sat silently, her head nestled into his shoulder, and her hand on his stomach. Each reviewed their ten months together and imagined the future apart from each other. His lips touched her forehead, her face, her mouth, as their kisses locked them together.

It was solidly dark, with no moon at all, as the newlyweds prepared to leave their party. Guests threw birdseed to send them on their way in Steve's BMW, decorated with cans and shaving cream proclaiming *Just Married,* and *Had To,* in the rear window.

Reluctantly, Chelsea and Kyle rose from the swing and headed back to join the others. Tom wrapped his arm around her shoulders and handed her a net package of birdseed, tied with lavender ribbon. Shelly took Kyle's arm, as he and Chelsea sent furtive glances to each other, frantically, their intimate moments dissolving in front of them. Why couldn't they have what the others had? Surely they were more in love at this moment than anyone here. Surely, sadly, this could have easily been *their* wedding.

Then Monday came and he was gone. Devastated, she became a stone. It could not have been worse. On Wednesday morning, she padded downstairs in her favorite pajamas—a pale blue tank top and plaid shorts, expecting to find coffee and breakfast with Kitty and her mother, as Tom was usually at work at that hour. Instead, the scene was far from what she anticipated. There was her father, sitting in Kitty's chair, his head wrapped in Liz's arms, and both of them weeping silently. She knew in that instant: Kitty was gone. Gone from them all, forever, silently and peacefully, in her sleep, the kindest way imaginable. It hit her like an unexpected rogue wave. She had never thought about this, even in the times when Kitty suffered her strokes and spent time in the hospital and in rehabilitation. After all, Kitty would prevail forever, the family glue, the matriarch, the inspiration for all of them. And she was just….gone.

The days passed, empty and devoid of feeling, as relatives and friends came and went, dropping off food; some they would never eat, and some they wanted more and more of. Father Michael was there, commanding her attention, comforting them with his kind words, prayers, and love. Her mother planned the funeral service with help from Becky and Daisy Frazier. Jay stayed with them at home for a few days. Charley and Steve were still in Italy, and Charley was beside herself with conflict. Chelsea spoke to Kyle on the phone and he cried with her. He told her about their move-in, and that Shelly had taken a bad spill on the stairs and broken her ankle. She went by ambulance to the hospital in Nags Head, where orthopedic surgeons were able to repair the broken place in her ankle, but she was in extreme pain and needed lots of help. He was in the midst of unpacking, and Stacie and Tyson were helping as much as they could. Hopefully, his grandmother would come to help out too. He would try to get there for the funeral. She didn't count on it. She was a stone.

The funeral was, as people said, "lovely," and the little mountain church overflowed with friends and family, but Chelsea was numb to it all, like her father and mother. They were all stones. She had no idea who came to pay respects. No wonder people had those little white books for people to sign in. Then you could see later who was there, who you missed in your grief. As they sat in the parlor of the funeral home, Chelsea endured the never-ending line of well-wishers who hugged her identically, and murmured the same inane remarks."She's in a better place now…She lived such a full and wonderful life…I loved her tremendously…"

He was not there to hold her hand and sit with her silently as she had done years before with him. Her heart burned with betrayal, although she knew his reasons for not being there. It had to be hard in a new place, in a new house, with a debilitated mother who needed him at every beck and call. Still, it wasn't fair. She waited like a corpse herself, waited for her parents to summon her to the car with them. They took all the flowers home. She despised the smell of them. She never wanted to see another Peace Lily in her life. It would always remind her of death, finality, the most unpleasant of unpleasant memories. In the Tahoe on the way home, she struggled to hear Kitty's voice…the sound she remembered from when they could have unencumbered conversations. "A lady always carries her tissue," Kitty said, and Chelsea always had one tucked into the back pocket of her jeans. Jeans…an article of clothing Kitty Davenport had never owned or worn. "Those are *dungarees*," she'd said. "You know why? Because that's what you did in them, shoveled *dung* out of the barn."

They always laughed at her old-fashioned notions, but deep inside, Chelsea held her platitudes with the utmost respect. "Yes, ma'am, never 'yeah,'" Kitty corrected her on more than one occasion. She was never down with the current slang, or the casual toss of profanity.

Chelsea sat in the Tahoe, a variety of sickeningly sweet flora stuffed around her and her black dress. Was it the one she'd worn at graduation? She didn't know. She didn't care. She just wanted to get to her violet bedroom. She knew she would never slide the rug away from the grate again to hear the conversations from below. She would never care again what was said. Nothing mattered anymore. She was just a stone.

"Honey?" Liz called her out of her dismal thoughts as they pulled into the drive of Kitty's house, parked under Kitty's portico. She was surrounded by Kitty's flowers and Kitty's memories, and it was just too much. She couldn't talk. She didn't care. She looked at her mother blankly as Liz gave up and got out, taking two Peace Lilies from the car with her, and slowly made her way up the stairs. Tom stood on the other side of the car as Chelsea sat there in her funk. He moved potted plants to the stoop under Kitty's portico, glancing here and there at Chelsea, trying to think of something to say.

"Hey," he said, finally, extending a hand to her. "Come on, sweet pea. I could use a hand here," he said softly, his eyes red-rimmed and defeated, like hers. She made a move to extricate herself from the mums in baskets around her. Most of them were pink, Kitty's favorite color. Chelsea mechanically handed two of them to her father. He placed them on Kitty's ramp. Tears slid down her cheeks and she wiped them away, distractedly. When Tom held his hand out to her, she stonily climbed out of the Tahoe, feeling a hundred years old. They hugged and she cried some more. She saw him wipe tears off his own cheeks as he arranged the flowers onto the stoop. She could tell he didn't like them either. The smell of them was repulsive and she had to turn away. She heard the vague growling of an engine, a crunch of tires on gravel, and "Z.Z. Top." Then her father's eyes flashed over her head and a slow smile started beneath his mustache. He released her, patted her shoulder, and walked quickly inside the house as she turned around. The silver Audi came to a stop at the end of the drive and the music stopped. She watched Kyle get out of the sleek little car and run a hand through his windblown hair. He saw her and set his jaw, then reached inside the car to take out a long-stemmed pale pink rose. He walked toward her, trying to smile, but failing.

Her heart pounded, taking in what she thought she saw. Certainly, she was asleep and this was just a tragic dream she would wake from, weeping again. And then, he was there, embracing her, his arm around her back, his warm body fitting into hers as if he had never left her.

"There was a wreck on the bridge just when I was leaving. I thought I'd never get here," he breathed into her ear and kissed her temple. They walked, supporting each other, to the porch swing; then they collapsed into each other, and he held her hand, wordlessly.

Chapter 18

SIX YEARS LATER

She stood in the dimly lit wine section of the grocery store, not surprised that so many people were finishing their holiday food shopping two nights before Christmas. She listened to the Christmas carols in the background, and browsed absently through the Chardonnays. She sighed vacantly, feeling the old ache filling her heart again, and reminded herself to stay busy. It had been good to have a glass of wine with Abby earlier and listen to her chatter about her great job at the Mast Farm Inn, Glen's work on the police force in town, and him preparing to coach baseball at App in the Spring. She talked of wanting babies, and redecorating their cozy house in a shady neighborhood in Boone. Chelsea shared her news as well, and Abby was encouraging, hoping she would make the right choice.

And here she was, picking out a nice bottle of wine for her parents, who at this moment, were working the Christmas tree lot. She wasn't expected until the following evening, and it would be fun to surprise them. She'd had next to no time at home with them since she joined the Carolina Ballet two years ago. She smiled, and imagined her father dissolving into happy tears at the sight of her, like he always did. It's special being the favorite, she thought, smugly, and probably unrealistically, but then again she was prone to indulging herself in fantasies. That had saved her when she'd gone off to college years ago.

She became vaguely aware of a man beside her in the wine section. Smelling his coffee colored leather jacket reminded her of Kyle. She closed her eyes. Everything reminded her of him now. They'd made it work for the first three years, but it had fallen apart when she had met Conner. Kyle had backed off then, which had infuriated her. She didn't hear from him for weeks at a time. Abby and Glen had tried to bring their destinies full circle by forcing Kyle to escort her in their wedding two years ago. It had been awkward, at least for the first five minutes, and then it was like they had never been apart. But the cruel reality was that she danced every weekend in Raleigh, or somewhere in the world, and he worked for an architectural firm in Alexandria, Virginia. They were rarely able to see each other. She forced herself to keep busy and surrounded herself with people, losing herself in their lives. She even did charity work when she could find the time. But from time to time, she just closed her eyes and imagined that they were together, that she would see his eyes burning into hers—that would carry her along, through one more day.

She was in the Australian wine section when she sighed again. A green bottle of Sauvignon Blanc on the top shelf caught her eye and she reached for it, noticing the silvery starfish emblem on the label. She ran her fingertips over it. Anything with stars always captured her attention, made her aware of the sparkling silver star she still wore at her throat. As she gazed at the bottle, she realized the man beside her had said something to her. "Shopping the labels?"

She gasped and looked up into his intense blue eyes, the color of swimming pools on a hot summer day. He spoke again, "The love of my life shops the labels."

As Kyle smiled down at her, she felt the blood leave her face. There was a crash and she realized she'd dropped the bottle of wine on the floor. They both jumped a little and she floundered, confused, looking at him again as if he were an apparition.

"What are you doing here?" she whispered, shakily. She watched that radiant smile build across his rugged face as he reached out to her.

A store employee was there to clean up the mess. She was humiliated. She looked at the friendly-looking man and apologized. "It's all right, ma'am. It happens," he said, jovially, as Kyle moved her backwards toward a corner so the clean-up could begin.

She struggled for composure and her mouth felt oddly dry. "That was a twelve-dollar bottle of wine," she mumbled, distracted. Kyle grinned at her.

"What are *you* doing here?" he laughed gently. "You're not supposed to get here until tomorrow night," he said. Then he steadied her, his hand at her elbow; the feel of his touch nearly sending her through the roof.

She shook her head. "How do you know that?" she asked, more confused.

"I saw your parents today," he said.

"What?"

"Yeah," he said, putting down the basket. "I did a little tree shopping earlier."

"You're taking a tree home to D.C. tied to the top of your Audi?" she laughed, incredulously.

"Not exactly," he said cryptically.

"So, what are you really doing here? You…you don't live here anymore."

"I was here on business, actually. I'll tell you about it later. What are you doing now?"

"Well, I was just going to go home and hang out at the house until Mom and Dad are done at the lot. It's kind of nice to be there alone, you know, before it gets wild and everybody is there…"

"Are Charley and Steve coming?"

"They'll be in on Christmas Day, with little Kitty," she said, smiling. "You should see her. She's precious! She looks just like Steve with those chocolate M & M eyes and black hair...except it's curly, like Charley's."

"How old is she now?" he asked.

"She's four. And she talks constantly," she said and they laughed, knowing Kitty got that from Charley's side.

"I saw Jay today at the store with your parents. I guess you *will* have a full house, with Thomas running around, trying to keep up with Kitty."

She smiled. "Yes, and they won't be going anywhere. Lauren's baby is due on the twenty-seventh."

"Well...look...would you have dinner with me tonight?" he asked shyly. Her heart flip-flopped. She felt as if she were being pulled back into another time with him. Her head reeled as she looked at him, so handsome in the soft black turtleneck sweater she had given him the previous Christmas, and the soft leather jacket she had touched when he had steadied her moments ago. He wore dark jeans and expensive hiking boots.

"Yes," she breathed without hesitation.

He smiled at her again, picked up the shopping basket, took down another starfish bottle of wine, and added it to his things as they headed to the checkout counter. Outside, in the dark, it had begun to snow lightly, and she walked with him to his car, expecting to see the silver convertible, wondering how people tied trees to the tops of them. He stopped in front of the white Range Rover, which she recognized as his mother's. A very small tree was tied on its roof. He answered her questioning look. "I came from Kitty Hawk today. Mom and I swapped cars. Where are you parked?"

She gestured to the right. "Over there," she said and he broke into a huge grin.

"You still have the *Subaru*?"

"Yes. Remember? I'm a starving dancer. I work lunches at the deli. It still drives okay."

"How many miles are on that thing? You're probably just getting it broken in," he commented, opening the tailgate of the Range Rover and setting his bags inside. "I'll drive. Do you have a bag you'd like to bring along? We might get snowed in. You might want your toothbrush," he said suggestively and she felt the blood rush back to her face as fat white flakes of snow swirled around her head, making her even dizzier than she already was.

"Where are we going?" she asked suspiciously.

He grinned again. "It's a surprise." He retrieved her bag after she opened the passenger door of her car. She fiddled nervously with the pale green scarf at her neck and watched him stow the bag behind her seat. Then he waved her into the front seat of his car. He installed himself in the driver's seat, started the engine, and pushed the button on his iPod as she buckled her seatbelt. Then the music, "Sweet Emotion," by Aerosmith, started. She settled comfortably into the Range Rover's automatically heated seat, which felt pleasant underneath her. He pulled out of the parking lot and looked over at her, his lopsided smile beginning. "Tell you what…you just relax, sit back, and close your eyes. I'll tell you when to open them."

She obeyed him immediately. She felt him reach for her hand, caress her fingers, and touch the ring he had given her on her twenty-first birthday. The stone in the white gold setting was the palest aquamarine, "to match your eyes," he'd said, and she rarely took it off. She tried to imagine where he was taking her. He had groceries, so he must have rented a cabin somewhere. Perhaps it was a Mast Farm cabin and Abby was in on it, although she hadn't given anything away while they were together earlier. He told her about meeting Glen for a beer, earlier, and her curiosity continued. It was too ironic! Were Abby and Glen setting them up again? He laughed and told her he was glad he'd turned down Glen's invitation to go skiing that night. He had no idea he would run into her. The song changed and she let the words take over…let them play into her fantasy…

She realized he was humming along with the song, and she remembered it from their senior prom. She remembered how they'd danced together as that song played, so young, so full of hope. "I Don't Want To Miss A Thing," had always been her favorite song.

They were weaving around bends and turns, and she had no idea where they were. The song was over and the music ended as she realized they had turned into a bumpy road and he had slowed down considerably. One more turn and the car crunched to a stop. She felt him turn toward her and speak softly, "You can open your eyes now."

She opened her eyes and stared in disbelief. They were at the cabin his father had built, unchanged from the way she remembered it. She gasped and stared at him. "You rented it?"

He smiled sheepishly and said, "No, I *bought* it."

Her hand was at her mouth and she shook her head. "How?"

"I've kept up with Jim and Peggy. I told them that if they ever wanted to sell it, I wanted first right of refusal. Jim had to have knee surgery a while back, and they called me in the fall. He couldn't get around up here anymore, and it was a hassle renting it out, so they sold it to me!"

"But how?" she still didn't understand.

"My mom started a trust fund for me when she sold it to them in the first place. After she sold my dad's truck, the other house, and most of her furniture, she invested all of the money, and actually did really well with it. The idea was to give me money to start my own company someday, or buy into someone's business. Frank Maynard thought of it, actually, since I didn't get to go into my dad's business like he wanted," he said. His voice trailed off as they sat in the car and looked at the cabin, lit with the motion lights the car had set off.

SIX YEARS LATER

"But, what about the business?" she asked, tentatively.

He smiled a little. "There's money for that, too. It's one of the things she did right, or so she says," he laughed. "Want to go inside?"

He got the groceries, which she took as he hoisted their bags out of the car. It was snowing harder, and they tromped up the stairs and knocked a small amount of snow from their boots. He unlocked the door and went inside, flipping on lights. She followed, shook the snow from her hair, and blew warmth into her hands as he went to the gas logs and started them up, then adjusted the thermostat. After looking around, she realized he'd been there recently. Nothing looked different, really. It appeared much the same as she remembered from high school.

"When did this happen?" she asked, still amazed.

"I moved in at Thanksgiving. My mom sold them the place 'as is,' and they pretty much left it that way, except for personal things. There really wasn't much to do. She and Stacie and Tyson came up here and helped."

She noticed it immediately. "They changed the couch," she said. It reminded her of the soft, cushy, nubby cream-colored one in her parents' house. It even had the same type of pillows.

"No, actually I replaced it myself."

She nodded, understanding why he'd never want that couch. Then she felt hurt. "You moved in at Thanksgiving and didn't tell me? I wasn't here, but, still?"

He shrugged. "Surprise! Do you want some tea to warm you up?" he asked, shrugging off his jacket and reaching for her coat, as well.

She shook her head. "No, thanks. Red wine works just as well."

"That's my girl," he murmured. He hung their coats on pegs by the front door and set the grocery bags down on the kitchen counter. He turned to her suddenly and pulled her close to him. "Sorry, I haven't given you a proper hello," he said, melting away any awkwardness that remained between them. She felt his cool hand slide from her jaw into her hair and kissed him passionately. He let her go, took a bottle of Pinot Noir from the bag, uncorked it easily, then poured a glass for each of them. "You look great," he said, looking at the gray flannel slacks and the V-neck top she wore, the same color as the wine they were drinking. Her heeled boots made her taller, and she liked being closer to eye level with him.

"Thanks," she said, practicing the smoldering look on him that he was so good at giving her. They were themselves with each other again, and he looked at the star at her throat, pleased that she still wore it.

"Do you normally dress like this when you come home?" he asked. His eyes sparkled as he kissed the side of her face tenderly. He was always like this with her, never lewd or rough. It made her feel cherished, and she loved it.

She thought about his question, not ready to share the details yet. "I like to put my best foot forward from time to time," she said, and pressed her mouth gently into the side of his neck. She felt him respond, and he tightened his arm around her waist. He set his wine glass on the counter.

"Would you mind helping me with dinner?" When she nodded, he slid a container of grape tomatoes and two baking potatoes toward her. "If you'll wash these, I'll start on the steaks," he said. "Oh, do you still eat red meat?" he asked.

"I do when I feel like splurging. It's been a while," she said. She did her job quickly and opened the bag of spring mix, placing half of it with the tomatoes in the salad bowl he'd provided. Then she turned, watching him pour some of the wine over the filets and other ingredients. As she watched his tanned arms catch the light as he worked, she thought how sensual he was. Everything he did was sensual to her, she thought as she moved her hand to the belt loop in the back of his jeans, felt the small of his back, and rested her face on his shoulder. She breathed in the peppery, clean-clothes scent of him, and kissed his shoulder.

"Hmm, are you trying to distract me?" he asked, his lopsided smile starting.

"Hmm," she laughed gently. "Is it working?"

"Mmm-hmm," he said. She gave up and slipped the palm of her hand under his sweater, pressing it against the flat plane of his stomach. He smiled but continued working, jabbing the potatoes with a long fork. Heady memories from after high school, of making love with him, crowded her thoughts, and she didn't bother to try to clear her head. Instead, she closed her eyes and felt him turn to her, then kiss her as his hands ran through her hair. Her hands moved up and down his back, and she felt his skin prickle under her touch. He had lost some of his bulk from his college football days, but he felt taut and toned as if he still worked out. "You're really not into this dinner, are you?" he laughed softly into her ear.

"It can wait," she said as she pressed her lips into his neck. "You're getting goosebumps," she murmured, her hands moving over his chest now.

"Goosebumps—and so much more," he replied. He chuckled, pulled his head away, and held her slightly away from him. And suddenly, he was Kyle from high school again, looking at her soberly, keeping her at arm's length from him. She was confused. What was going on?

"You know, I should go out there and get that Christmas tree off the car before it gets any more snow on it...and get out the snow shovel. Why don't you take a look around and enjoy your wine? We need to talk, too," he said seriously. Her heart plummeted like a rock. He popped the potatoes into the microwave and hit a button, took his parka from a peg by the door, and was outside before she knew it.

She took a deep breath. *We need to talk* is never good, she thought. Taking her wine glass, she pushed her hair back nervously and wandered into the living room. She stopped to peek into the dark bedroom. Just moments ago, she'd imagined a trail of their clothes would soon litter the floor. On the bedside table, she thought she made out the picture of them from the prom, he in his tux and she in the vintage ivory dress, holding hands on the terrace. Was he breaking up with her? What else could it mean? *You think you can date a guy like Kyle Davis? He can have any girl he wants and he picks you?* The old, stinging words came back to haunt her like they sometimes did when she lost confidence in herself. How had she missed this? Maybe he was seeing someone else and decided to bring her here to tell her about it, thus saving her the embarrassment of having a scene in her parents' house. Maybe it was the attractive brunette, Emily, from college she'd seen him holding hands with. "I'll fight you for him," Emily had kidded Chelsea, after he'd told her they were just good friends and that Emily knew where his heart lay. Maybe she lived in D.C. now and he had given up trying to be true to her across all this impossible distance.

She took another deep breath, shivered, and walked over to the fire. Suddenly, she wanted to throw up. She heard him knock snow off the tree, then stand it up against the porch. He'd come in at any minute. There in front of the mantle, she sipped her wine and tried to collect herself. She'd do anything to prevent him from seeing her this way. She willed herself not to cry…and then she saw it. There, in the center of the mantle, stood the ceramic angel her mother had made six Christmases ago. Surely he wouldn't place her angel in such a prominent spot if he intended to dump her. And then tears streamed down her cheeks. As she heard him bumping around outside, she remembered the toolshed was just outside on the porch, a few feet from where she stood.

She wiped the tears off her face and breathed heavily until she heard him coming in from the cold.

"Wow, it's really coming down now!" he said from the porch. He removed his gloves, shook the snow off his parka, and raked it out of his hair, leaving it in wet spikes.

She set her mouth into a pleasant smile and watched as he took his glass of wine and joined her in front of the fire. He looked at the angel and said, "You saw?" She nodded and he said softly, "and it made you cry?" She realized she'd done a poor job of hiding her feelings. Then he took her hand and led her to the sofa. They sat down together and looked out the window in front of them as the snow fell in large, chunky flakes. He glanced at her and said, "This is the Christmas card window." In response to her questioning look, he added, "Your family isn't the only one steeped in traditions. When it snows here, you wake up in the morning and look out this window and it looks just like a Christmas card," he said wistfully.

"So, I'm going to wake up here in the morning?" she asked softly.

"I hope so. Only if you want to," he said. "I'll take you home if you want me to. We can get your car in the morning." He sounded disappointed, but hopeful, which only added to her confusion.

She smiled and they turned toward each other on the couch.

"It's like we never really miss a beat," she said, and tried to project the positive feelings she'd had when they kissed in the kitchen, the same place she'd told him she loved him the first time, and he'd returned the declaration.

He smiled and took her hand. "I know, even when Conner was in the picture, it's always just been us."

She shook her head. "It never was what you thought with him."

"I know that now. Leave it to you to find the only straight guy on campus. The guy adored you, Chels," he said, the old pain returning to his eyes.

"Well, you didn't do anything about it. I'm still mad at you for leaving me hanging like you did."

"I had to know. I had to see if you would fall for him. And yes, I did do something about it. I prayed every day that you'd break his heart," he said, poignantly, and his eyes reached deep into hers.

Her heart skipped a beat and she swallowed. "Well, it worked. How many hearts did *you* break?" she asked him softly.

He shrugged slightly and looked at her again. "I was just trying not to break *yours*," he whispered. She stopped breathing for a moment. And then he asked, "Are you happy?"

She gasped and touched his lips with her fingertips, felt their soft familiarity as he kissed her fingers. "What are you asking me? Are you breaking my heart now?" she whispered, hardly able to speak.

He looked at her, bewildered by the question. "No," he said quickly. "I hope not. I just meant, in your life, in your job, are you happy? Have you gotten what you wanted? We spent all that energy going after our dreams, and look where we are; not together. Was it worth it?"

Relief rushed through her. "You're not dumping me?"

His slow smile was sympathetic and he reached for her face tenderly. "Is that what you've been thinking? That's why you were crying? How could you even think that? I love you so much. We've been through so much. No, I'm not dumping you. I just want to know if you're happy with the way things turned out."

She sighed. "I thought it was what I wanted. I certainly worked my butt off to get where I am, but I don't know. Ballet is fine, but contemporary dance is my first love. And I'll never get to choreograph as long as I stay there. It's where I could get a job, but it just feels like something *big* is missing. Even if I were a principal like Willie is with Ailey Two in New York, I'd never get to see my family, or come home, or…see you." She looked at him and decided to tell him. "I came into town early for a job interview."

His eyebrows shot up. "That explains why you look like a million bucks. *I'd* hire you. What's the job?"

"Sonya and Brad hooked me up with a position at Appalachian on the dance faculty. A woman is retiring in May, so they suggested me for the job. They saw me dance once. So I sent them an application and came up here and visited a few weeks ago when I could sneak away. We had lunch with the people today and they offered me the job. I'd have a chance to work with Sonya and Brad again, and get back into modern again. I could teach and choreograph again. I could be home again. I never knew I missed all of these things so much."

His slow smile became huge across his face. "It's perfect. You said yes, right?"

She hesitated. "I haven't committed yet. It's farther away from you, but I don't get to see you anyway. Maybe we could be together more this way." She gestured around the cabin. "But now that you have this, maybe I should take it. I'd get to see my family more…"

He smiled and rubbed his hands slowly back and forth. "Okay, it's my turn," he said, pushing himself up off the sofa and running a hand through his hair. "I told you I was here on business. I'm thinking about making a job change myself."

"But you love your job. Aren't you happy?"

"Oh, it's a great job. I'm the youngest one there and it's great experience. I'm just…really lonely. I can't stand being without you anymore," he said, then looked into her eyes with the familiar smolder she needed to see. He sat close to her again and took her hands in his. "Did you know that someone bought the Green Park Inn in Blowing Rock?" She nodded and he continued. "The new owners want to renovate it, to bring it back to its rightful historic state. Frank Maynard won the bid for the restoration, and he's going to need some help. So he called me to ask if I would come to work for him. I love to do historic renovation, so I said yes. I start with him in February…and now I have a place to live. And you could be here, with me," he said, meeting her wide eyes with his sparkling blue ones. "Don't you see? It's all falling into place. God's hand is *all in this*."

Chills went up and down her spine as her head spun. She swallowed, unable to comment. He leaned his head in, close to hers.

"Chelsea…I knew I loved you from the first time I saw you in that white dress on Kitty's terrace, the day of the engagement party. You took my breath away…the way you still do every time we're together. You've *always* been the one for me. I love you with every ounce of my being, with all of my heart and soul. I want to be with you till the end of *time*. Will you marry me?" he breathed, searching her eyes, and holding her hands in his.

"Yes," came her excited whisper. Then she said it again and pulled him closer. "Yes, yes!"

He kissed the tears away from her face, and then kissed her lips and neck and held her, rocking her back and forth.

"That's why you went to see my parents today?" she asked, amazed. He nodded, and reached into his pocket. He held a small burgundy velvet box in his hand.

"My next stop after seeing them was supposed to be the jewelry store in Boone to pick up your ring. But when I asked your dad for permission to marry you, he told me to sit tight and came out of the bedroom with this." He opened the box and Chelsea gasped.

"It's Kitty's ring," she murmured. The sparkling rose-cut diamond was set in white gold, inside an ornate crown setting, with tiny diamonds spilling down each shoulder, typical of the Edwardian period. He took it from the box and slid it delicately on her finger. She knew it would fit perfectly, from a time long ago when Kitty had let her try it on.

"Your dad said Kitty left this for you in her will, and he and your mom wanted me to be the one to give it to you. He knew I'd come to him eventually," he said and laughed quietly. "He said to tell you he was getting damn tired of waiting, too."

"Ohhh, that is *so* my dad!" she said, laughing too. She put her arms around his neck, kissing him passionately again. Then she looked at the ring again. "Wow. Kyle, this isn't just Kitty's ring. It's also my great, great,

great Aunt Annette Davenport's ring."

His mouth fell open in surprise. "You mean the famous, glass-cutting Davenport family stone?"

She nodded. "The very same. I can't believe this ring is on my finger… and I'm yours forever," she said to him in wonder.

He pulled her up from the sofa and led her to the Christmas card window. "Well, there's only one thing left to do, in that case."

She slipped the ring off her finger, and he watched as she etched the letter "C" into the lower corner of the most prominent pane of glass in their home.

The End

Other Books by Mary Flinn...

SECOND TIME'S A CHARM

"Forgiveness is easy. Trust is harder."

"Mary Flinn is the female equivalent of author Nicholas Sparks. Her characters are as real as sunburn after a long day at the beach. Hot days and hotter nights make *Second Time's a Charm* an excellent sultry romance that will stay with readers long after the sun goes down. The second book in a series, this story is a movie waiting to happen."

— **Laura Wharton, author of**
The Pirate's Bastard and Leaving Lukens

THREE GIFTS

"There is a Celtic saying that heaven and earth are only three feet apart, but in the thin places, the distance is even smaller."

"Throughout *Three Gifts*, you will be rooting for Chelsea and Kyle, young marrieds so appealing, yet real that you'll wish you could clone them. They settle in the mountains, near Boone, North Carolina, and when they are faced with tragedies, they handle them with courage and grace. Even those oh-so-human doubts and fears that threaten occasionally to swamp them are banished through humor and the abiding love that sustains them. This is a journey of hope, faith, and love that you'll want to share with them."

> — Nancy Gotter Gates, author of the *Tommi Poag* and *Emma Daniel* mysteries, and women's fiction *Sand Castles* and *Life Studies*

A Forever Man

"There are friends and there are lovers; sometimes the line between is thinly drawn."

"Just when I thought I would never see Kyle and Chelsea Davis again, Mary Flinn brings them back in *A Forever Man*; they returned like old friends you feel comfortable with no matter how much time has passed, only this time with eight-year-old twin boys, and a new set of life-complications to work through. In this novel, Flinn provides a deft look at marriage when potential infidelity threatens it. *A Forever Man* is Flinn's masterpiece to date, and no reader will be disappointed."

> — Tyler R. Tichelaar, Ph.D., and author of *Spirit of the North: a paranormal romance*

And Her Stand-Alone Novels,
apart from the Kyle and Chelsea series:

The Nest

"Are things really meant to be, or are we just sitting around waiting for butterflies?"

"Mary Flinn realistically captures the ideals of an empty nest filled with rekindling passions of soon-to-retire Cherie and her rock-and-roll-loving husband Dave—then flips it all over when Hope, the jilted daughter, returns to the nest to heal her broken heart. Between her mother's comical hot flashes that only women of a certain age could appreciate, the loss of her laid-back father's sales job, and the good news-bad news of other family members' lives, can Hope find the courage to spread her wings and leave the nest again? Flinn's deft handling of story-telling through both Cherie and Hope's voices will send readers on a tremendously satisfying and wild flight back to *The Nest*."

— **Laura S. Wharton, author of the award-winning novels** *Leaving Lukens*, *The Pirate's Bastard*, **and others**

Breaking Out

"A harrowing incident involving her talented teenage son helps dermatologist Susannah realize she has kept herself from moving forward after the death of her beloved husband, Stan. At times humorous, at other times poignant, *Breaking Out* is an eloquent exploration of how difficult life can be following the unexpected death of a loved one. With a wealth of detail, including the complexities of family relationships, Mary Flinn creates a heartwarming story about the curious way two people can connect through grief and break out into a new life together."

— **Jane Tesh, author of the** *Madeline Maclin Mysteries* **and** *The Grace Street Series*

Author Biography: Mary Flinn

A native of North Carolina, award-winning author Mary Flinn long ago fell in love with her state's mountains and its coast, creating the backdrops for her series of novels, *The One, Second Time's a Charm, Three Gifts, A Forever Man, The Nest,* and *Breaking Out*. With degrees from both the University of North Carolina at Greensboro and East Carolina University, Flinn has retired from her first career as a speech pathologist in the NC public schools that began in 1981. Writing a novel had always been a dream for Flinn, who began crafting the pages of *The One*, when her younger daughter left for college at Appalachian State University in 2009.

The characters in this book have continued to call to her, wanting more of their story told, which bred the next three books in the series.

Flinn has recently been the recipient of the Reader Views Literary Awards 2012 Reviewers' Choice honorable mention in the romance category for *A Forever Man*. First Place Award for Romance Novel in the Reader Views 2011 Literary Book Awards, as well as the Pacific Book Review Best Romance Novel of 2011 went to *Three Gifts*. *Second Time's a Charm*, also released in 2011, won an Honorable Mention in the Reader Views Reviewers' Choice Awards.

Mary Flinn lives in Summerfield, North Carolina with her husband. They have two adult daughters.